P9-CCE-346

The Wolf's Pack

Forge Books by Richard Parry

NATHAN BLAYLOCK ADVENTURES
The Winter Wolf
The Wolf's Cub
The Wolf's Pack

The Wolf's Pack

Richard Parry

A TOM DOHERTY ASSOCIATES BOOK

NEW YORK

This is a work of fiction. All the characters and events por-
trayed in this novel are either fictitious or are used fictitiously.

THE WOLF'S PACK

Copyright © 1998 by Richard Parry

This book is printed on acid-free paper.

A Forge Book
Published by Tom Doherty Associates, Inc.
175 Fifth Avenue
New York, NY 10010

Forge® is a registered trademark of Tom Doherty Associates,
Inc.

Library of Congress Cataloging-in-Publication Data

Parry, Richard.
     The wolf's pack / Richard Parry.—1st ed.
          p.   cm.
     "A Tom Doherty Associates book."
     ISBN 0-312-86020-X (acid-free paper)
       1. Earp, Wyatt, 1848–1929—Alaska—Fiction.   I. Title.
PS3566.A764W65   1998
813'.54—dc21   98-23448
                                                              CIP

First Edition: November 1998

Printed in the United States of America

0 9 8 7 6 5 4 3 2 1

This book is dedicated to
the people of Fairbanks
past and present,
whose energy and imagination perpetuate the frontier spirit of this town
with a golden heart.

★ ★ ACKNOWLEDGMENTS ★ ★

I am deeply indebted to Tom Doherty, publisher of Tor/Forge, for making this series possible.

My agent, David Smith of DHS Literary, Inc., is far more than a literary agent: besides promoting my work, he is also that rarest of finds—a friend.

My editor, Doug Grad, continues to patiently shape my scribbling into something with order. His perception and attention to detail always keep me on track.

Many thanks to Sharon Coulter and Sarah Kavorkian Adkins for their enthusiastic support.

The scholarly work of Terrence Cole's *Crooked Past*, published by the University of Alaska Press, provided an invaluable resource on E. T. Barnette. Any reader interested in more detail concerning Barnette is encouraged to read Dr. Cole's book.

Last but far from the least, my thanks to my lovely wife, Kathie, for her patience, encouragement, and constant support.

★ ★ AUTHOR'S NOTE ★ ★

The wild series of events that led to the founding of the town of Fairbanks on a silty bank of the Chena River would tax even the most creative writer's imagination. Tall tales and truth stand shoulder to shoulder. Neither one of these willingly gives way to the other, and time has shown that the distinction between the two is sometimes the finest of lines.

All the events surrounding the discovery of gold, the ensuing stampede, the flood, and the fire are historically correct. The time line has been compressed when necessary to help the story. E. T. Barnette and Judge Wickersham were real people and, as such, played a vital—if not shining—part in all that followed. I have tried to portray their actions correctly with what is known fact and consistently with their characters whenever fiction fills the gaps of history.

There is no documentation that Wyatt Earp ever did visit Fairbanks, yet there is no evidence that he did not, either. However, monumental villains like Captain Barnette demand an equally prodigious adversary.

Nathan Blaylock, Doc, and Jim Riley are, of course, fictional characters; but in many ways, they represent an amalgam of those early gold seekers who struggled and suffered for that elusive yellow metal that even today exerts a wide allure. This is their story, but it is also the story of the thousands of pioneers that built Fairbanks. It is my hope that the reader will enjoy the story for what it is—a work of historical fiction—but also gain an appreciation and affection for a town in Alaska that is still a work in progress.

The Wolf's Pack

★ ★ **PROLOGUE** ★ ★

Tonopah, Nevada, 1902. A rim of orange light outlined the single hill that stood sullenly between the birth of a new day and the back window of the saloon. One of a dozen that catered to the needs of men killing themselves in search of gold, the Northern ranked as one of the better establishments, with gilt wallpaper, the new brass electric lamps, and a long, polished mahogany bar.

But, the Northern was empty, closed on this Sunday morning as were all the bars, shuttered by order of the town council. Blue laws came and went as fast as faro dealers in this boomtown, so the Northern simply waited for the next set of rules allowing it to open again on Sundays. Yet the bar wore its imposed rest period with an air of melancholy. A single bulb burned over the middle of the bar. Its paltry illumination failed to reach the far corners of the room.

A restless tapping came from the darkness near the back window, and a red eye winked and glowed in the gloom. The eye was the glowing tip of a cigar that wreathed its user in a cloud of smoke that appeared milky in the predawn light. A lone figure sat at a back table. His hands shuffled a deck of cards with the automatic precision of one long familiar with their use, cutting and spreading the pasteboards with fingers that worked without regard for a mind that was miles elsewhere.

Hidden amid the scattered and thrown-together shacks of this sprawling mining town, a rooster recognized the signs of daybreak and crowed. Encouraged by this signal, a ray of light pierced the sooty window to lance across the felt-covered table.

The hands ceased shuffling as the sunbeam cut across them. The man carefully set the worn deck down on the table-top and turned his hands over to inspect them. The harsh light illuminated the scars and wrinkles of a lifetime of use. The right index finger scraped at a brown age spot on the back of the left hand with no success. The sign of aging remained. As if admitting defeat, the man sighed deeply. Tipping back in his chair until its acute angle seemed to defy gravity, the smoker puffed more furiously and stretched his long legs beneath the table.

Wyatt Berry Stapp Earp was feeling his age. At fifty-four, the legendary gunfighter and lawman, survivor of a dozen battles, was feeling old and useless. Only in the hours of predawn dark-ness did this sour reflection plague him. It was then that the ghosts visited him.

Doc Holliday and Earp's brothers, Morgan and Warren, would appear to stand silently just outside his screen of cigar smoke. Never to speak, just to stand and listen. They were there to help him, he knew, tried and trusted friends, steady and comforting in death as they had been in life.

What bothered him most was they remained young while he was aging.

"You see that, Morg?" he asked, displaying his spotted hand to the smoke. "Look at these age spots! I'm beginning to look like Old Man Clanton, Ike's father, just before the old coot got drygulched by those *vaqueros.*"

Wyatt chuckled. "You fellows wouldn't tell me I look wrecked, even if I do, would you? Because you're my friends, I guess. It's a funny thing. None of those I killed ever come to visit. Not the McLaurys, not Frank Stilwell, not even Curly Bill—none of them. They'd tell me I'm turning into an old man even if you wouldn't." He reached up to extract the glow-ing cigar from his mouth, turning it over in his hand to in-spect its burning tip. "Yup, burning out like this weed, boys. While you stay young and light-footed like a mountain mus-tang. Like we all were once. . . ."

He blew on the smoking brand until the tip glowed a cheery red. The light gave him heart. He waved the rejuvenated cigar in the air before popping it back into the corner of his mouth. A feral grin turned the corners of his mouth, and the light reflected in his cold, pale eyes.

"No," he said flatly. "There's still life in this old dog. I've still got the fire in my belly, just like this smoke, even though my limbs get stiff at times. All I need is a little puff to get me going. I thought I'd like the quiet life, but it's driving me crazy. I need something to crank me up, like these newfangled motorcars. Why, look at Virge! Gold makes his eyes shine like silver dollars—that's his starting wind. He's mucking away in his mines like a crazed gopher, and he's older than me. But mining isn't enough for me. I need something more."

Wyatt looked up at the window. The dawn light was stronger now, strong enough to see the tabletop clearly. Outside the rooster was going crazy, filling the cool morning air with his frenzied shrieks. Earp parted his broadcloth coat and drew his pistol from its holster. The worn leather released the revolver with the smoothness of a hot knife cutting butter. Not a creak sounded from the leather. The gun sprang into Wyatt's hand as if it were a living, breathing extension of his being.

Wyatt turned the Colt over to inspect its polished sides. The gun's blueing was worn from the revolver's edges, exposing a dark steel rubbed smooth by years of use. The polished grips fit every contour of his hand. He spun the cylinder, listening with satisfaction to the clicks of its well-oiled pawls.

I'm not getting older, he thought. I'm becoming polished—just like this Colt .45. Just getting broken in. But the stiffness of his right hip begged to differ with him.

He slipped the gun back in its holster and rose to walk to the back of his saloon. A rush of cool morning air hit him as he opened the door and stared out into the shimmering dawn. The mountain was still there, ringed in crimson like a lump of shapeless dough on fire. Dotted sparsely with mesquite brush, it was a poor cousin to its spruce-covered brothers Wyatt so enjoyed in Alaska.

Alaska! I loved that place. Ah, but that's the place for younger men, he mused. If I were ten years younger—make that five years, he corrected himself—and Sadie didn't hate the cold so much, we'd still be there.

Screaming back at him from the top of a stick fence, the raucous cries of the rooster hurt his ears. The long-tailed Rhode Island Red strutted along the edge, swishing its tail and flipping its cockscomb with every screech it emitted.

Wyatt scowled at the disturbing bird. At twenty yards away, its noise still hurt his ears. "I thought I told you last week to bother someone else," he spoke to the bird. "Like the Savoy Bar or the Comstock, my competition. You fool bird, crowing all day long and half the night. It's too much! Beat it!"

The rooster responded with another series of ear-piercing cackles and haughtily swished its luxuriant tail at the gun-fighter.

"Okay, don't say I didn't warn you," Earp sniffed.

With a lightning sweep of his right arm, as well-oiled as his revolver, Wyatt drew his Colt. The weapon flew into a two-handed grip in a blur of gunmetal gray. In that split second, he matched the annoying cock with the flat blade of his front sight and pressed the finely honed trigger. The pistol responded with a satisfying kick into his clasped hands and a shattering explosion.

The rooster's tail vanished in a cloud of scattered feathers. The bird took one look at his denuded rear end, cut his crow short, and dove for cover. A satisfying silence returned to the morning.

Wyatt holstered his smoking gun with no visible effort. He watched the feathers settle gently in the still air. "Yup," he said with a smile. "I'm just getting broken in. . . ."

ONE

Dawson, the Northwest Territories, 1902. The winter of 1902 found the fledgling towns in Alaska and the Yukon tensely coiled like springs in a leghold trap—ready to snap at the slightest rumor of a new gold strike. The Great Stampede of '98 to the Klondike was finished. The lure of the golden sands of Nome had faded as well. Thousands of gold seekers suffered sullenly through the worst winter on record as they struggled to stay alive and waited for news of the next El Dorado. A new strike, a fabulous new find, that was the hope of these desperate men who fought to keep from freezing. That was their *only* hope.

The freewheeling days of the stampede were over. Gone were the days when a man might become a millionaire from the lucky fall of his pickax yet lose it that night with the turn of a card. Now cartels and giant mining consortiums controlled the goldfields where once luck and hard labor might line a man's poke with the shining metal that drove them all to madness. Few men worked for themselves anymore. The big companies saw to that, squeezing the small fry until they sold their claims and then forcing them to work for the organization to keep from starving. Giant gold dredges and dragline buckets ate the earth where individuals once scrabbled for the precious ore.

But these men were beaten, not broken, and so they lingered, biding their time and squirreling away a grubstake for the next stampede. Tempered by hardships, these miners had hauled a year's worth of supplies over the frozen White Pass, survived Horsetail Rapids, and chopped frozen bread with a hand ax while they thawed the icy muck in search of riches. The weak had died or crawled away long ago. Those who remained were in for good. The lure of gold had seeped into every fiber of their stringy muscle like the dirt that coated their threadbare clothing.

All who waited with the gold madness glinting in their eyes prayed for another chance. Silently they swore this time would be different. No more fabulous poker stakes, hundred-dollar cigars, or pouring gold dust on the heads of the dance hall girls. This time would be different. . . .

Even the most hardened cynic knew more gold lay hidden in this terrible country. But where? Was it deep in the frozen Interior, locked behind the razor-edged mountains that sullenly watched them? Or was it farther to the north in the countless riverbeds that washed the great plains of the Tanana and the Yukon Flats? More and more word came down of "lost creeks" with fabulous wealth below the Forty Mile.

So a hair trigger held the springs, and the slightest whisper of gold released a wild rush. Throughout the winter men had bolted on more than one worthless rumor only to return exhausted, sick, and disappointed. Now the mood of the men in Dawson had turned as sour as the pickled cabbage they ate to prevent scurvy.

Inside the Palace Saloon an edgy crowd gathered around a poker table where a one-armed man with a battered beaver fedora chewed on his cigar and squinted at the cards in his only hand. Despite his terrible scars and threadbare clothing, traces of gentility and breeding surrounded the player like the last vestiges of silver plate on a worn utensil. His bearing contrasted sharply with the barbarous nature of the card player opposite him. Although youthful, he affected the look of a *pistolero* with black vest and heavily tooled leather gunbelt to match. Even his dark wool mackinaw added to his sinister appearance.

"Hell, I knows you's cheating, Doc," the pimply-faced youth seated across from the player grunted. He spit a splintered toothpick onto the sleeve of his one-armed opponent. "Ain't nobody gits such good hands without cheating. Nobody."

The other two card players in the game shifted nervously in their chairs and cast anxious glances at the lad and the man in the hat.

The player shifted his cigar between his teeth and sighed. "Now where would I be hiding my extra cards, Billy? Up my other sleeve?" He nodded his head to the empty coat sleeve tucked inside his jacket pocket.

The crowd broke into loud guffaws and open laughter, but a glare from the youth silenced their mirth. Billy Wilson was known to have a mean streak and a short temper. Since his arrival in Dawson two months ago, rumor had it, he'd killed two Chinamen in the opium parlor across the line, and a whore in the White Castle District bore a broken nose as testament to his violent nature. The youth fostered this image by insisting on being called "Billy the Kid" or "Kid," after that infamous killer of the Lincoln County Range Wars. This Kid was no miner; he was a predator.

"Leave it be, Billy," the third player pleaded. He was a thin, pasty-faced store clerk who worked at the dry-goods store, hoping to scrape together enough for a grubstake for the next rush. "Doc's not cheating. You just had a string of bad luck."

"I've never known Doc Hennison to cheat," the fourth player added before he broke into a string of rachitic coughs. Working for the mining companies had filled his lungs with dust and sapped him of the vitality needed to work a strike on his own.

"Shut up!" the Kid snapped. "I say he's cheating, and I got a pair of kings." He laid his cards face up on the battered wood. "So this pot belongs to me." Wilson stretched both hands to encircle the pile of gold nuggets and leather pokes of dust.

"Ah, ah," Doc cautioned. He raised his chin slightly while his eyebrows arched closer to the ugly scar that crossed his forehead like a weary lightning bolt. "That's not your pot, William. It's mine. I don't need to cheat to beat you. All I have to do is use my brain. I've got three of a kind, and that beats your pair of kings." He spread the three queens face up on the gouged tabletop while a twitch of his head flicked the burning ash from his cigar onto the Kid's right hand.

"Why, you son of a bitch!" Wilson growled as he jumped to his feet. He slapped at the glowing coal that clung stubbornly to the back of his hand. His chair tipped backward to crash to the sodden sawdust floor with a muffled thump. "Your brain ain't gonna do you much good dished all over this saloon."

Muffled footsteps, falling chairs, and warnings filled the saloon as the crowd scattered to a wider circle. Missed shots killed more slow observers than antagonists, and that fact was widely known. Watching a gunfight was one cheap source of entertainment, but being shot by mistake was something else. In a flash, an empty void opened behind Doc except for one spectator standing in the shadows.

The Kid drew his coat back to expose a brace of pistols resting in tooled leather holsters with the butts facing forward. He stepped into an exaggerated stance and smirked down at the seated one-armed man. Wilson seemed to be toying with his next victim like a weasel with a cornered hare.

"Wearing your guns backwards, William?" Doc teased. "Planning on shooting the fellow behind you, are you? Or did your mama dress you funny this morning?" Nothing about the doctor's demeanor had changed with this threat to his life, although a careful observer would notice his teeth clamping deeper grooves into his cheroot. "Last person I knew who wore his pistols that way was Wild Bill Hickok, and for all his care he still got killed by a no-account. Mark my words, *William*: bad things happen to men with their guns on the wrong way."

"Only bad is gonna happen to you, you one-armed cripple."

"Ah, yes," Hennison continued. "I fit the description of your prey, don't I? Whores, Chinamen, and cripples, right?"

"You got any last words to say? 'Cause I'm tired of talking to you."

"Would it make any difference if I told you I'm unarmed?" Doc asked.

"You'd be lying, 'cause I know you carry a holdout gun." The Kid grinned nastily.

"What if I said I was sorry? Would that do?"

"Maybe. . . ." Wilson hesitated, sensing some trick. Doc never apologized.

Hennison shrugged his one shoulder and winced at the pain that he had lived with since his encounter with a Federal cannonball almost forty years earlier. That single shot had changed his life forever. With his right arm went his cause, his profession as a respected surgeon, and the one love of his life. Since then each sunrise brought only continued bitterness, which he hid with careful sarcasm. Life or death, he cared little for either, so threats from petty gunmen like the Kid carried no dread for Doc Hennison.

"Well, I'm not apologizing for being smarter than you, you little toad."

"Then I'm going to shoot you," Wilson stated matter-of-factly. "Plain and simple."

"I think not," a voice from the shadows spoke.

Wilson squinted past Hennison at the lone figure standing in the smoke-filled gloom. The man moved slowly from the shadows into the yellow circle cast by the oil lamps. He was taller than the Kid by a good head, broad-shouldered, and lean despite the bulk of his beaver parka. His mukluks scarcely made a sound on the beer-sodden sawdust floor, and he seemed to glide out of the gloom like some silent wraith. What unnerved the Kid most was the color of this stranger's eyes: they were pale and cold as glacier ice.

"This ain't none of your business, mister," Wilson grunted.

"I'm afraid it is. I can't let you kill Doc. He owes me money," the tall stranger replied.

Hennison snorted at that comment.

The Kid sized up this new threat. The stranger appeared to be wearing only one pistol, from the bulge beneath his parka, but its barrel appeared to be long. Wilson had heard of these long-barreled specials, best for long-range shoot-outs, but slower to draw. The U.S. marshal in Wrangell, Frank Canton, had been wearing one when Wilson passed through that town. But it was those piercing eyes that bothered him most. They bore right through him.

Secretly, the Kid wished he hadn't issued this challenge in front of so many. Now his reputation was on the line. A thin trickle of sweat ran down his back, although the potbellied stove in the far corner of the saloon did little more than keep the liquor and beer from freezing at this end of the bar.

"My fight is with Doc here, not you, mister," Wilson growled.

"Doc's my friend, so I'd suggest you drop the whole thing. But it's your call," the stranger replied. For emphasis, he opened his parka to clear the lengthy pistol at his hip. The grips of the .45 were polished by wear and void of notches.

A warning bell sounded in the back of Kid Wilson's anxious mind. Who was this man? Obviously not a miner or storekeeper. "What's your name?" he demanded.

"Blaylock."

A murmur arose from the crowd. They knew that name. Kid Wilson did, too. But this man was supposed to be dead.

"Nathan Blaylock?" The Kid's voice jumped a notch in spite of himself. "I heard of you. Heard you were good with a gun."

"He's good, Kid," an anonymous voice piped from the safety of the shadows. "Real good."

"Well, I've never heard of you," Nathan replied.

Kid Wilson's fingers twitched ever so slightly. Shooting unarmed Chinese was one thing; facing this cold-eyed craftsman was something entirely different. The Kid decided to bluff.

"People say you use a two-handed grip when you draw. Is that 'cause you're shaking so bad?"

His taunt brought no response except a feral grin that made Blaylock look even more like the arctic wolf that the Indians believed him to be.

"One-handed draw *always* beats a two-handed one," the Kid pressed. "That's what counts. You ought to know that, Blaylock."

"Only thing that counts is hitting what you aim at," Nathan added flatly.

At that moment the doors to the saloon burst open, and two men crashed inside in a cloud of swirling snow. The leading man lurched through the darkness, caught his boot in the leg of a chair, and tumbled over a table to smash against the gilded wallpaper in a jumble of chairs and woolen parka. His worn and scuffed gum-soled miner's boots dangled in front of him while he struggled to catch his breath. His partner skidded across the sawdust into his back.

All eyes turned on these two, except Blaylock's. Was this news of the next El Dorado? Even the Kid lost his concentration. Instantly recovering from his dangerous lapse, he looked back to see that Nathan Blaylock's eyes had never lost their unnerving lock on him.

The man on the floor gulped for air, found his voice, and spoke first in chopped phrases: "Just caught the bastard that started the last stampede! The false one! The fool came back into town to buy up all the woolen socks. Conley spotted him. Now we got him, and we're going to lynch the rat."

A short man named Olsen grabbed the collar of the fallen man and hoisted him to his feet. "Was that the one about gold on the Tanana River? Near Bates Rapids?" he cried.

"That's the one," the messenger replied, his head bobbing like a cork. "Near that rock creek they call the Chena. Close to Barnette's damn trading post."

"Goddamn his lying hide. I'll help pull the rope!" Olsen shouted. "My pard, Jimmy the Swede, froze to death on that fiasco, and I lost three toes to frostbite."

"Wait!" someone yelled. "What about the Mounties? They'll stop us for sure."

"No, they won't," the messenger's partner replied. "The whole detachment is downriver looking for those trappers that started a war with the Han Indians in Moosehide. They're chasing them toward Eagle. Won't be back until morning at the earliest. Only Mountie in town is Constable Tanner, and he's flat on his back with the flux. He's too weak to even lift his little finger. We're the only law in town, boys!"

A whoop filled the saloon.

"I say we hang him, straight out!" Olsen raised his fist in defiance. "Four good men died when they fell into the Yukon's overflow on that wild goose chase, and that man's responsible!"

A chorus of approving shouts followed. The showdown between Kid Wilson and Doc was forgotten as the crowd became a mob and surged out the saloon's doors into the night. As the doors slammed shut, a brittle silence expanded into the void. The acrid stench of stale cigar smoke, sweat, rancid beer, and sawdust settled back around the three antagonists to wait patiently. This saloon had seen a hundred years of human tragedy packed inside its gaudy walls—all in the space of a few years. Another shoot-out meant little. The silence solidified until Kid Wilson sighed and glanced at the door.

"Guess I'll let you go, Doc," Wilson said. "I don't want to miss a hanging." He backed carefully away from the table, moving in the direction of the closed doors.

Doc sniffed pretentiously. "Does that mean you don't want to kill me, William? Why, I'm disappointed at your fickle nature. One minute you want to shoot me, and now you'd rather see some poor sod get strung up. I'm hurt; truly I am."

"Leave it be, Doc," a fourth voice protested. "He's calling it off. Ain't you got the good sense to lay off?"

Without thinking, Kid Wilson's head snapped to the right, where he saw a grizzled face watching him from behind a post. Chiseled like weathered granite and sprouting a week's growth of gray stubble, the face smiled benignly and winked at the Kid. But the twin black eyes of a sawed-off shotgun peered from beneath his fur coat. Wilson cursed himself for not seeing the man before; but half-hidden by the pillar, he blended into the smoke and haze that perpetually filled the saloon. The shotgun barrel waggled in the direction of the door.

"Best go watch the hanging, Kid."

Doc Hennison watched his other protector with wry amusement. "Why, Riley, do I owe you money, too?" he smirked.

"Forget Doc's sour mouth and that pot as well, Kid," Jim Riley advised. "And leave while you got yer whole skin. You can't win. It ain't nothing personal. Doc sasses everyone. Don't take it to heart. It sure ain't worth spilling blood over."

"I do take it personal," Wilson hissed. "No broken-down bag of bones can talk to me that way."

Riley shrugged. "Well," he drawled, "it's your call. If Nat were to miss you—and I don't much think that he will—this here scattergun sure won't. I'd hate to ventilate that fancy vest you're wearing, seeing as how it's such a fine article of clothing."

"This ain't over, not by a long shot," Wilson advised as he backed toward the doors. "I won't forget the three of you."

With that last threat hanging in the air, Kid Wilson ducked out the saloon's front door. The hinges creaked and the portals slammed shut with a crack that portended dire things to follow. Neither Riley nor Blaylock moved, other than to keep watching the entrance. Doc shook his head and poured himself a drink from the half-empty bottle of rye on the table. Reaching inside his coat, he extracted a brown-colored flask and proceeded to carefully measure an equal amount of its contents into the chipped tumbler. Its ingredients seeped into the whiskey, turning it a dark mahogany. Hennison held his colored flask up for inspection.

"Getting low," he said to no one in particular. "I'd better brew up another batch before I drink up all my starter." He returned the flask to the safety of his inside pocket, then tilted the tumbler to his lips. His lids half-shuttered his eyes as the drink cut a burning track down the back of his throat. Blinking away the tears, he noticed his two friends still watching the door.

"Don't worry about William. He won't come charging back with his six-guns blazing. He's not the type. No stomach for a face-to-face encounter with any real threat. Backshooting is his specialty."

"You ought to be grateful he is yellow, you jackass!" Riley

27

exploded. "He'd have cut you down before Nathan and I could stop him if he'd made his move when he should have!"

Hennison struggled to look contrite. "Why did you, then?"

"Because I'd hate to have you kilt for cheating when you wasn't, Doc. That's why," Riley grumbled.

"But I was cheating." Doc smiled. Without taking his eyes off Riley, he slipped another queen from the folded cuff of his empty right sleeve. "Being shy one arm has some advantage."

Nathan Blaylock walked over to the seated man and rested his hand on Doc's back. "We stopped him because you're our partner, Doc, for good or bad. That's why."

A look of genuine gratitude flickered across Hennison's face before he quashed it with a Cheshire cat smile. "Damn, Nathan, I wish you hadn't said that. Now you'll want me to buy you breakfast at the Pioneer Bakery."

"Don't you think your life's worth more than a plate of cold bacon and beans, Doc?" Nathan asked sadly. Increasingly Doc's actions were turning more self-destructive.

"No, I don't," Hennison replied matter-of-factly. He took a long swallow to fill the embarrassed silence.

Riley jabbed his shotgun into the pile of winnings atop the table, sending the nuggets clanking into the whiskey bottle. "Hell, it's the least you can do, and I think you can afford to buy us a dozen of them one-dollar-apiece eggs that arrived yesterday on the mail sled. Now git up and let's skedaddle before young Wilson screws up his courage and comes back."

The three stepped outside into the blackness of the early arctic morning. The struggling sunrise was hours away, still caught behind the knife-edged peaks that surrounded Dawson like a hostile army. This early in the spring, sunlight was still scarce, lasting only a few hours while the beleaguered sun stumbled across the horizon. Ahead, a procession of torch-lights flowed down the street like glittering nuggets in a dark streambed.

Doc paused under the lamplight of the saloon to peer at his pocket watch. "Damn, it's five in the morning. Where did the night go?" he said.

"You gambled it away, you damned fool," Riley replied.

Nathan was studying the mob ahead. "The Pioneer Bakery is on the other side of that necktie party. We'll have to work our way past them unless you want to go up the backstreet."

"Hell, no. I don't want a detour," Hennison answered testily. "Those side streets are knee-deep in snow and muck and—"

Before he could finish his sentence, a flash of light erupted from the alley. Nathan drove his shoulder into his astonished friend with such force that the two of them went sprawling headlong into the snow littering the street. The corner post supporting the saloon's lamp exploded in a shower of splinters as a bullet smacked into the wood, followed closely by the crack of a pistol's report. A cloud of gunsmoke appeared in the air, marking the site of the flash, and Riley unloaded both barrels of his shotgun at the incriminating haze.

Ears still ringing from the shotgun blast, Nathan was on his feet and racing close behind Riley into the darkness. A shadow darted behind a freight wagon, exposing itself for an instant. Blaylock snapped off a shot with his pistol just as the would-be assassin vanished. Nathan heard the heavy bullet smack into the iron rim of the wagon's wheel and ricochet into the night with an angry whine. The young man grunted in disgust as he listened to their attacker's footsteps racing away.

"Missed him by a mile," Nathan swore.

"Lookey here." Riley probed a reddened patch of snow with his smoking barrels. "I think I winged the polecat. He'll think twice about bushwhacking us again with my double-aught shot tickling his ass." The grizzled gunfighter studied the tiny spot and frowned. "But he ain't hit bad from the looks of it. Jus' a scratch. Too bad."

Nathan holstered his Colt. "Well," he said with a sense of fatalism. "I got a feeling we'll be seeing Billy Wilson again. Best we watch our backs."

Riley shrugged. "Hell, that ain't nothing new. . . ."

★ ★ TWO ★ ★

A dozen flickering torches cast frightful shadows over the frightened face of the man in the wagon bed. Stout ropes bound his arms to his sides. A noose encircled his neck so tightly that the squat figure was forced to stretch his neck and stand on tiptoe just to breathe. Despite the icy dawn, sweat and tears poured from the terror-stricken man to cut rivulets down his grimy cheeks. His straight black hair, closely cropped Eskimo style, flew straight out as he shook his head violently to deny the charges hurled at him by the surrounding mob.

"Looks like the boys is planning to lynch an Eskimo," Riley commented to his friends.

The three stopped a few paces to the rear of the mass of angry miners that surrounded the man on the wagon and plugged the main street. Doc Hennison ran his hand over his own neck. Having once been the "guest" at a necktie party, he recalled the bite of the noose and shivered. Instinctively he edged away from the crowd, but more spectators pushed the three men closer to the front.

Nathan watched the scene with disgust. Madness contorted the faces of men he knew. Grocers, the blacksmith, and even the German watchmaker were there, wide-eyed and mad-looking, with spittle foaming from their mouths as they screamed for blood. What drove men to this insanity? he wondered. Come Sunday, these good men would all be in church, singing and acting pious. Yet now bloodlust ruled all their thoughts.

Nathan watched his friend, Jim Riley, spit and shuffle his feet uncomfortably. Blaylock knew they could just as easily be standing in that wagon bed. Between Riley and him, more than a dozen men lay in graves. Certainly, we have much to answer for to our Maker, Nathan thought, but every man we killed had a gun in his hand.

Riley read his thoughts. "Hell of a thing watching good folks go plumb nuts over stringing an Eskimo up. You'd think they'd caught Jack the Ripper instead of some poor sod."

"Well, we're not lily pure ourselves, Jim," Nathan whispered. "You and I probably killed more men than this entire mob." His heart warmed when his friend gave him the answer he wanted to hear.

"None o' them we laid low had their hands tied behind their backs, Nat. They was shooting at us in earnest. And we didn't hide behind half the goddamned town doing it, neither. And . . . well, hell, that's our work. We're shootists. That's jus' what we are. We ain't no damned greengrocer nor lace merchant. Nothin' of the sort." He stopped to reconsider when Doc's fidgeting caught his eye. "Course, that don't hold for Doc, here. He's more a *poisoner* than anything else. If anyone ought to swing, my vote would be for Doc."

"Quiet, you damned fool!" Hennison hissed. "Don't give these folks any ideas. Once they get their blood to boil . . ." He paused to nod solicitously to a man who was eyeing them. The fellow's brow wrinkled in thought as he tried to recall some grievence he had against Doc, but the idea passed and he moved on.

"Just remember, my friend," Doc sputtered. "That hanging rope is reusable."

Riley grinned lopsidedly. He loved needling Hennison. "Funny thing," he muttered. "I don't never recall no Eskimos caring one hoot for gold. They ain't got no use for it."

"So?" Doc responded.

"So, why would one start a stampede?"

Nathan squinted through the glare and smoke from the

pitch-soaked torches. The sweating face of the condemned man, swirling in and out of the fumes, looked familiar. He knew that man! The shock hit him like a fist.

"That's no Eskimo!" he cried. "That's Jujiro Wada!"

"Wada, the Jap?" Riley started. He crinkled his eyes in concentration. "Damnation, so it is. My eyes is gitting dim-sighted, or I'd have spotted him before. But it's him for sure. It ain't no Eskimo."

Hennison craned his neck for a better look. "Who's Wada?"

"He's a Japanese cook who works for E. T. Barnette at his trading post on the Chena River," Nathan said. His back tightened as he recalled Captain Barnette's attempts to kill Riley and him.

"Do you think Captain Barnette's still trying to do us in?" he asked Riley. "It's been over a year since our run-in. Maybe he's forgotten all about us?"

Riley snickered. "Not hardly. He may think *we* forgot about his past as a thief. But I doubt *he's* overlooked the fact you was humping his wife. A man like the captain don't take kindly to messing with his stock."

"Jeez, Riley, you make his wife sound like a cow in his herd," Doc rebuked the old fighter. Riley had a way of comparing everything in terms of cattle and ranches.

"That's the way Barnette looks at her," Riley replied flatly. "A part of his herd."

A chorus of shouts from the mob turned their attention back to the unfortunate Japanese cook. He had climbed up the side of the wagon to add more slack to his noose and now swayed precariously on the narrow wooden boards. Any minute his footing would slip or the crowd would pull the tongue of the wagon, jerking it from beneath his quivering legs.

Nathan hung his head, then shook it slowly from side to side. At the same time, he opened his beaver parka and drew his pistol. Deftly he ejected the spent cartridge and reloaded.

Riley kneaded his grizzled beard with his grubby hand. "I hope you ain't planning what I think you is?" he asked.

Nathan smiled lopsidedly. "Wada saved my life once, Jim. When I was trapped in Barnette's stockade. I owe him. I can't stand by while he gets lynched."

The old gunman shrugged stoically. Looking about at the more than a hundred enraged prospectors, he snapped the breech of his shotgun open and checked his charges. His left hand fished inside the pocket of his tattered coat for two more shotgun shells, which he crammed between his fingers for rapid reloading. "Guess you'll be needing someone to watch yer back."

Hennison's eyes nearly bugged out of his head at what he was hearing. "Are you two mad?" he stammered. "There's only the *two* of you!"

Nathan winked at his friend. "Yeah, Doc, but there's only *one* mob—"

The sharp report of a pistol shot overrode the cries of the crowd and forced them to turn in the direction of the crack. Holding his pistol high in the air, Nathan plowed steadily through the crowd with Jim backing along behind him. Faced with this unexpected event, the stunned mob parted for them until they reached the wagon. Quickly Blaylock sprang onto the wagon bed and pushed the would-be hangman off. Riley clambered onto the wagon seat, where all could get a good look at the barrels of his shotgun.

"What the hell are you doing, Blaylock?" a voice from the crowd yelled. "We're going to hang this bastard, so don't try to stop us!"

Nathan jerked the end of the rope out of the grocer's hand just as Wada collapsed onto his knees in the wagon bed. The frightened cook propped himself up and laid his head against Nathan's legs like a whipped puppy.

"I . . . I do nothing, Nathan. Nothing! Why they hang me?"

"Maybe they et yer cooking," Riley replied offhandedly.

A few chuckles erupted from the front row.

"Is that true?" Nathan shouted. "You going to hang Wada

here because he's a lousy cook?" His voice sounded half-hearted and amused, but there was no mistaking the hardness in his eyes or the steady grip on his Colt.

"Get down, Blaylock, or we'll rush you. You can't shoot us all," a reedy voice snarled behind Nathan's back.

Without turning, Nathan replied, "That's true, Cameron; I can't shoot you all. But you made the mistake of opening your mouth, so I know where you are, and I sure as hell can put a bullet through your head before anyone could stop me. And that goes for you, Tom Price, and you as well, Lem Granger. So what's it to be?"

A hush descended over the mob. Hanging a man within the protection of a faceless attack was one thing. Being shot as an individual was something else. Nathan pressed his point while he had their attention.

"But I don't want to shoot anyone. I just want to hear why you think Wada ought to be hanged. He helped me once, and I'd like to make sure he deserves this rope. I owe him that much. So, give me one good answer, and I'll be on my way."

"He started a false stampede that caused the death of three good men, Blaylock. That's what," Cameron replied, careful to keep his head behind the man in front of him.

Wada shook his head vehemently. "I just buy socks, Nathan. Just socks."

Riley shook his head in disbelief, but his shotgun stayed trained on the mob. "You'd hang a man for buying socks? God-damn! I'm glad I ain't bought no new long johns this year. No telling what you people would do to me." A few more laughs escaped, just what Riley hoped for. The bloodthirsty mood of the mob was weakening.

"He's lying, Blaylock," Olsen, the man from the saloon, piped up. "He brought word that the digs around Tanana were paying over five dollars a pan. Ask him!"

"Yeah," Cameron countered. "Then, he was stupid enough to come back and try to buy out all the woolen socks in town to sell to the stampeders when they got to the creeks."

Riley lowered his shotgun and leaned on it. "That do sound stupid," he snorted.

"I only buy socks, Nathan," Wada babbled. "Hope to make profit from miners. The captain send me with message of gold strike."

Nathan holstered his pistol and walked slowly over to Wada and placed his arm around the petrified man. "Did you hear that, boys?" He raised his voice. "The captain sent him. E. T. Barnette."

A ripple of angry shouts rolled over the upturned faces.

"Look," Nathan continued. "Wada, here, planned on making money selling you miners new socks when your old ones wore out at the digs. If there weren't any gold strike, he'd lose his money because none of you'd be mining. He must have believed what Barnette told him, too."

"That's right!" a voice shouted. "The Jap got bamboozled like the rest of us."

Nathan nodded. "Now, he's stuck with the largest collection of socks this side of White Pass, boys. You should feel sorry for him, not try to hang him. Barnette's the man you ought to talk to. Sounds like he's the one that started the rumor."

Cameron stepped forward. His red beard and wisps of stray hair jutting from beneath his woodchopper's hat gave him a fiery appearance in the glow of the torchlights. "It ain't the first time Barnette's done that, neither, Nathan!" he shouted while shaking his fist. "He sent another rumor early this winter."

"Why would he do that?" Nathan egged the man on, already knowing the answer.

"Because he's built himself a trading post right in the middle of nowheres. It's over a hundred miles from Circle and twice that distance to here. With no mining going on nearby, he ain't got no trade. He's sitting on his pile of beans and flour with no customers. If he can start a stampede, his fortune is made."

Blaylock smiled inwardly at the image painted by Cameron's words. He could picture Captain Barnette pacing

Richard Parry

back and forth—a virtual prisoner inside his very own stockade, thick black mustache bristling as he fretted about, snarling at his cowering wife and his motley supporters.

Barnette's original plan was to establish a trading post at Tanana Crossing, the halfway point between the seaport of Valdez and the goldfields around Dawson and the Forty Mile area. Stubborn and domineering, the captain's plan was to sail up the Tanana River in the *Lavelle Young,* a sternwheeler, to the crossing and dominate supplies on an All-American Route to the goldfields.

But the river had its own ideas. Dropping to levels too shallow for even the shoal-bottomed riverboat, Barnette was forced to off-load on the banks of a rocky stream that the Indians of the Tanana called the Chena. Stuck in the middle of the wilderness, the inventive Barnette fostered one false rumor after another of fabulous gold strikes near his trading post in hopes of attracting miners. The few weary veterans of the Klondike who trekked to the Chena returned with tales of no gold and many hardships.

"Yeah, that's the captain, all right!" Tom Price shouted. "When I was fool enough to fall for his line and hike to the Tanana, he wouldn't give me any credit. I had to borrow money to pay for my flour from my pards. And the price was damn dear. I'll tell you that!"

Nathan lifted the noose from Wada's neck and cut the ropes that bound his arms. The grateful Wada fell to his knees and sought to clasp his arms around the legs of his savior, but Nathan jumped back. Already the mob was dissolving into groups engaged in heated discussions of how Capt. E. T. Barnette had vexed them with his high-handed ways. Secretly, Nathan half-wished the captain were here, and he flushed in embarrassment when Riley read his thoughts.

"Sad the captain ain't around to step up and be the guest of honor. It's a shame to waste a perfectly good lynching party," he grunted. "And he'd be my vote, first and last."

Nathan shook his head. "I'm partly to fault for his hard feelings. Maybe we've misjudged him."

"No, we ain't, boy!" Riley warned him. "He'll hear of this, sure as shooting, and he'll chalk it up on his list of grievances against you—his *long* list. And the captain ain't one to turn the other cheek. No, sir. As long as old E. T. Barnette draws a breath, he'll make trouble for us. Mark my words . . . big trouble."

⋆ ⋆ THREE ⋆ ⋆

Frank Cleary smashed another mosquito into a bloody pulp with the back of his hand. Since July, the smaller version of these terrors had tormented every living animal in the Tanana Valley, with the brother-in-law of Capt. E. T. Barnette being no exception. Caribou, crazed by swarms of the pests, would stampede off cliffs or dive into the icy rivers and drown in their mad rush to escape the biting insects. One veteran prospector wryly remarked that the grizzly might rule the Interior, but even the great bear paid his pint of blood to the mosquitoes.

To Cleary's amazement, mosquito attacks began in the early spring with snow still covering the ground. Then the larger ones, lumbering along like drunken dragonflies, emerged from spruce bark and piles of leaves even before the spring melt. Those bugs were easy to avoid, Cleary recalled. Slow and readily spotted, they droned about indecisively, making them easy to swat before they bit you.

About June came the middle-sized mosquitoes, faster and more voracious. But July brought the worst. With these small ones, it was a duel, plain and simple. One-on-one. Either you killed the pest or he bit you. There was no in-between. And these smaller ones were fast.

Cleary watched another mosquito dive for the exposed patch of skin by his wrist. An instant after the insect landed, Frank squashed him as well, but an itch told him that the pest had already drawn blood. For protection, he'd tried covering his face with wood ashes and mud like the Indians, but with little success. In the end, he and the others at the trading post stoically resigned themselves to being covered with itching welts.

Shrugging off an attack on his cheek, Cleary continued his patrol around the rough walls that enclosed the captain's stockade. With his brother-in-law away, Cleary was in charge, a task he took very seriously, given the explosive temper of the captain and Barnette's tight-fisted grip on his trade goods. Cleary still smarted from the tongue-lashing he had received after resupplying two prospectors on credit. Felix Pedro and his partner, Frank Gilmore, might never find that "lost creek" they claimed to stumble upon back in '98, E. T. swore, so Cleary's loan was as good as forfeit as far as the captain was concerned. The two men wandered the creeks in the foothills for the next four years without success.

Cleary shifted his bolt-action Springfield in the crook of his arm and scanned the wide clearing that surrounded the stockade for a good hundred yards. Behind him the clearing ran headlong into the brooding strands of black spruce that lined the banks of the Chena River. Those trees seemed forever cloaked in shadow even in the midst of the summer sun. To the north, the field ran to the banks of the tea-colored river. Spruce stumps, cut waist-high, dotted the opening like disordered grave markers, adding to the chill that hung over the fortification. To Cleary, the stockade seemed built in the center of some vast cemetery. He shivered even though the day was warm.

The captain had warned Cleary to expect Indian attacks, but none came. Only the lurid tales of murdered prospectors who stumbled onto secret Athabascan burial sites or aroused the jealous wrath of a Native husband filtered inside the walls, brought by prospectors or trappers who passed through.

All in all the Natives were friendly, trading furs for iron pots, blankets, and steel knives. Cleary never sold them whiskey or the modern smokeless powder rifles he kept locked in the storehouse. If an attack did come, he had no wish to be killed by his own guns. With his handful of defenders, Cleary rea-

soned he stood a better chance fighting Indians who still carried smooth-bore trade muskets left over from the Hudson Bay
company's defunct outposts such as Fort Yukon.

Those trade furs saved the captain's own skin. With no gold
to show his backers in Seattle, E. T. Barnette relied on those
furs to show some profit. That's where he was now, Cleary reckoned, somewhere along the three thousand miles that separated Seattle from this lonely outpost. Knowing Barnette, he
figured the captain was at Saint Michael on the mouth of the
vast Yukon River, building another sternwheeler and loading
fresh supplies for a second attempt at reaching Tanana Crossing. With luck he might make it this time before the river
dropped as the creeks froze with the coming of fall. Squinting
into the blazing sun, Cleary found it hard to believe that on this
day, the twenty-eighth of July, autumn was only another month
away.

A shadow crossed his own, and the jittery man jumped
back. His rifle swept across the field. Nothing stirred from the
tree line down to the river except for the restless water that
continued its journey toward the silt-laden Tanana. A faint
breeze riffled the birch leaves on the opposite bank and stirred
the horsetail grass, but that was all. The silhouette returned,
forcing Cleary to shade his eyes as he searched the painfully
blue sky.

Overhead, a bald eagle soared in expanding arcs, searching
the Chena for the first run of king salmon that had struggled
all the way from the Arctic Ocean simply to spawn and die in
the dark heart of this endlessly green expanse. It was the bird's
shadow that Cleary saw.

He shuddered as he wondered if he was destined to die on
some lonely bank in this wilderness, gasping and struggling
for life like the salmon. He longed for the wide, grassy plains
of his home in Montana and the clean mountains that always
seemed within grasp. In Montana you could ride a horse all
day. In Alaska you were lucky if you could lead your horse for
an hour without him going lame on the flinty chert or founder-
ing in knee-deep muck.

Here in Alaska the mountains were either too close or too far. When you wanted to reach them it took weeks of slogging through dense forest and endless swamp; and when you didn't want to encounter them at all, you couldn't avoid the crags. Then, they barred your path, blocking whatever easy way you hoped would bypass them with their knife-sharp peaks and narrow passes. Ice and snow waited along their trails to smother the unwary crossing during most of the year while torrents of rain and mudslides filled the fleeting summer.

Cleary wished his sister had married someone in Montana—and stayed there. Then he might be back home, fishing for the cutthroat trout or the rainbows that hid in the quiet pools of Meadow Creek. The Montanan loved to fish, a passion that the Interior sneered at. Oh, the greyling with their irridescent sail-like back fins took his makeshift flies all right, but they were small and never kept well. You had to eat them at once or throw them away, they spoiled so fast. Only the king salmon and the chum tasted good smoked or dried on racks in the sun like the Athabascans did. The first run of the kings was just starting. Soon all the villages along the Tanana and the Yukon would glitter with the split carcasses of the fish draped over drying racks.

But these exhausted salmon never bit on a hook. Battered and gouged by their horrendous passage from the sea, spawning was all that filled their minds. Swimming constantly upstream against the force of the rivers, those who arrived had avoided bears, foxes, and eagles and been bashed by sweepers and rocks. And their wounded bodies showed every encounter. Great swaths of raw, exposed flesh glared from once-sleek sides, and many sported a rotting or missing eye.

They never ate. To Cleary, they seemed half-dead. He marveled at their commitment, laying their precious eggs at the cost of their own lives so that their species might survive. Snaring them in a net was the only way to catch them. A net or a willow salmon weir in their direct path was the only thing that could stop them. You used their drive and determination to trap and destroy them. Then they would pile one after the

41

other into your snare, refusing to believe that their instinct could lead them astray. You could catch hundreds of fish, but to Cleary it seemed unjust. If the starving Indians wanted to harvest the salmon that way, Cleary could understand, but he longed to feel the fight of a fish on the end of his line.

He chuckled halfheartedly to himself as he resumed his patrol. His brother-in-law, the captain, was a lot like those salmon, driven by the all-consuming will to succeed. Barnette's drive had raised him from a deathbed more than once to press onward up the Tanana. And what had it got them? Now Cleary and his few men were marooned on the banks of this river just like the salmon, and the captain with his sister were lost as well, swallowed up in this vast emptiness. Barnette's ambition had lured them to this uncertain fate, and Cleary wondered if E. T.'s instincts would doom them just as the salmon's had.

Well, things could be worse. Cleary tried to look on the bright side. The stockade was done. The trading post with its high sides dominated the fort, spreading out from the center of the compound like a half-opened book. The log shacks of the men and the cook's shed surrounded the store. Barnette's house was the next largest log cabin after the trading post. With the buildings completed, Cleary hoped the coming winter would be more comfortable than the last one.

A flicker of movement upriver caught his eye. Something was moving toward the camp. Cleary worked the bolt of his rifle and chambered a round. One could never be too careful.

A patch of sunlight ignited a splash of crimson where he'd spotted the movement, but only for an instant before it vanished. Cleary strained to see what it was. To his amazement, it looked like a swatch of red flannel bobbing along the trail.

Spellbound, Cleary watched the scarlet cloth wend in and out of the shadows as it worked its way around the strands of spruce and clumps of silver birch that dotted the riverbank. A man was approaching, a white man. Probably another disappointed gold seeker, tired, half-starving, and with nothing in his pants pockets to show for his labors but holes, Cleary thought.

But something about the figure seemed familiar, something about the slouch of the thin figure or the dragging walk. The man looked as worn out as his tattered jacket and patched trousers. A wide-brimmed slouch hat covered the back of the visitor's head, and a thick turtle-necked sweater fended off the mosquitoes that followed him in a faithful swarm. Even the red wool jacket was faded and threadbare.

As he approached, Frank Cleary got a better look at the visitor's face. The man's eyes were set in a perpetual squint, and his mouth drew upward in a fixed grimace beneath a bushy black mustache. He gave the impression of staring into the sun or being in ceaseless anguish.

Cleary recognized him at once.

It was the tired little prospector Felix Pedro, whose line of credit had caused Cleary such grief and whose "lost creek" made him the laughingstock of his peers. Pedro waved as he picked his way over a pile of fallen spruce logs driven onto the cut bank by last winter's ice floes and tangled during breakup.

What was Pedro doing back so soon? His "loan" of a grubstake should have lasted him for a good six months more. Had he lost it to floods, or had his cache been plundered by a bear? Cleary bit his lip. Extending the man's credit was not possible. The captain had seen to that. Silently he watched the worn prospector climb the rise and approach the gate of the stockade. Cleary made his decision: the least he could do was offer the man a hot meal and a glass of whiskey. The poor man deserved that much hospitality. Besides, Cleary hoped Barnette would never miss a few potatoes or an ounce of liquor. He waved Pedro inside the gate.

Felix Pedro stopped just inside the opening and leaned against the rough spruce barricade. It was as if his legs had not yet realized his journey was over and struggled to press on. He removed his hat and wiped the sweat from his face with his ratty sleeve. As Cleary approached him, he was shocked by the little man's appearance. Felix Pedro looked more worn and frail than on their last visit, something Cleary had not thought possible.

"Felix, my friend, I didn't expect to see you so soon," Cleary said, greeting the prospector. "Can I buy you a drink?"

Pedro shook his head and fought to catch his breath. Years of digging coal on his hands and knees in the mines of Italy had robbed him of his youth. Arriving in America in 1881, his twenty-three-year-old lungs carried the black dust of those years of dirty work. He'd vowed then to work for himself. All he knew was the darkness of mining, but he swore to spend what was left of his precious health as his own boss—in search of that elusive yellow metal instead of coal. That quest had carried him to the Far North and forced him to be frugal with both his money and his efforts. He neither drank nor gambled, devoting all his energy to prospecting. In that regard he struggled tirelessly. Now, at forty-four, he sensed he had few years left.

"No whiskey, just water," he replied.

Cleary propped his rifle against the wall and handed Pedro a dipper of water from the water cask beside the entrance. Happily he noted that water was not on the captain's inventory list.

Pedro drank slowly, then wiped his mouth on his sleeve before handing the dipper back. The water appeared to revive him, and he straightened his back and looked carefully about. Ben Atwater, a giant who boasted of being the strongest man in the world, was wrestling with a crate of tinned peas that belonged in the storehouse, and Jim Eagle, an old Indian fighter, was walking his post as guard of the south side of the stockade. Both men were well beyond earshot.

Noting Pedro's apprehension, Frank spoke. "Ah, Captain Barnette's not here, Felix. He's downriver building another boat. One he hopes will be shallow enough to get across Bates Rapids so he can make it to Tanacross this time."

Pedro looked at the few patches of yellow leaves in the scattered birch. Some of the trees were turning even though it was only the end of July. On his trip to the trading post, Pedro had seen early formations of geese driving their wedge south in the evening. It would be an early winter.

"He better hurry," he said in his halting English. "Winter coming."

Cleary nodded. He'd noticed the geese, too. But he hoped they were early birds. If the captain arrived with another load of supplies only to get stuck a hundred miles from Tanana Crossing again, there would be hell to pay. Worse, they would be ruined. Bankrupt. Isolated from buyers with tons of worthless supplies piled on the banks of a river strewn with rocks.

He forced those thoughts from his mind. "Come on, Felix. Let me buy you a meal. Eagle shot a young caribou two days ago, and it's been simmering all day. Wada's baked some fresh bread, too. The Jap's been staying close to the kitchen since he nearly got hanged in Dawson."

Pedro's stomach groaned audibly. He nodded eagerly. "But bring me a plate out here," he ordered. "I got something important to tell you. Just you." He glanced at the others. *"Just you,"* he emphasized.

Cleary smiled. Pedro had reason to be cautious. Feelings were touchy among the men who stumbled about these drainages, and Pedro's lost creek had got him into trouble. Last fall, the little man found color in the branches of the Salcha River and announced he'd rediscovered his missing strike. A rush ensued—with disastrous results. Nothing turned up in spite of a hundred holes being dug. Men cursed Pedro, calling him a witch among other things.

"Sure, Felix," Cleary said. "I'll fetch a plate for each of us and we can sit outside. What the hell. Even though we got sun round-the-clock, it won't last forever."

When Cleary returned with two heaping plates of caribou stew and thick slabs of Wada's bread, he found the little man sitting with his back against a stump and gazing back in the direction from which he'd come. To Cleary's surprise, Pedro didn't snatch the plate from his hands as expected. Instead, he pointed to a rounded hill far to the east.

"I think I name that Pedro Dome after myself," the prospector said. "What you think about that, Frank?"

"Sure, Felix," Cleary agreed as he handed the platter to Pedro and sat down beside him. "Call it what you like. It's got no name I know of. Pedro Dome sounds nice. Why not? You got as much right to call it after yourself as anyone. You've walked over it more than any white man I know. Pedro Dome it is."

Pedro picked up the slab of bread and turned it over in his hand. Still, his eyes remained fixed on his mountain. "You remember the trouble I got in over Ninety-eight Creek, Frank?" Pedro asked.

Cleary nodded. Pedro had named that branch on the Salcha after his lost creek of 1898. But it wasn't the bonanza they all hoped for.

Pedro looked at the bread for the first time and replaced it carefully on the edge of his tin plate. "I don't want no more trouble like that, again. You understand, Frank?"

"I do. I surely do." He blamed Captain Barnette for some of that. Barnette had been salting creeks and spreading rumors in a desperate attempt to create a market for his marooned goods. Cleary wondered where it would stop. Barnette might go too far one day, he feared. Part of the man's past was a blank, and that worried Cleary. To hide his concern, Cleary took a bite of his own bread and stuffed a hunk of caribou meat in after it.

"That's why it's important to keep this a secret," Pedro continued. He slid his right hand out of his pocket and turned it palm outward.

The clinking sound that action produced drew Frank Cleary's attention from his thoughts of the captain. He choked on his mouthful of food while his eyes bulged from their sockets at the sight of the miner's hand.

Nestled in Pedro's palm were a dozen gold nuggets the size of hens' eggs. . . .

★ ★ FOUR ★ ★

E. T. Barnette drove his fist into the sack of flour so hard the seam split and its white contents poured onto the decking. His crew watched in alarm as their captain stomped about, swearing and gnashing his teeth while his feet ground the flour into the cracks of the rough-hewn planks of the *Isabelle*.

"Ruined! Goddamned ruined. That's what I am! Ruined!" Barnette screamed as he struck the helpless sack again.

Meehan, his chief engineer, grimaced at this loss of control and turned away to look awkwardly at the deckhands who clustered around the grounded prow of the steamer. What a shame, Meehan thought. They'd not even got as far as the captain's trading post on the Chena River. And Barnette had built this boat especially to go so much farther. The *Isabelle* was supposed to reach Tanana Crossing, the place Barnette had failed to reach over a year ago, and here it was run aground over four miles below the captain's trading post.

Meehan sighed. To come all the way yet still be nowhere close to their destination was heartbreaking, but losing control in front of the men didn't help. He glanced anxiously at Mrs. Barnette, the ship's namesake, as she held a handkerchief to her mouth and backed away from her husband. Meehan had no doubt the captain would punch her if the fancy struck him, a fact Isabelle Barnette's defensive actions seemed to confirm.

The engineer continued to watch Barnette venting his anger on the flour sack while he studied their options. The *Isabelle* was hard aground, no question of that. Despite being designed with a shallow draft and perfectly flat bottom, the boat was firmly wedged on a bar near the middle of the Tanana. Meehan hated to see the vessel in such straits. He had assembled her in Saint Michael at the Northern Commercial Company shipyard with all the loving care of a concerned mother. The little sternwheeler had faithfully performed her duty, driving them against the swift current of the Yukon to the mouth of the Tanana and then up the Tanana itself. But she would never make it the four hundred miles from the mouth of that river to Tanana Crossing, where Barnette dreamed of placing his store. Never in a million years.

The crafty Tanana River had outsmarted Barnette, again. This first week in September, the river was lower than he'd ever seen her. Barnette should have heeded the warnings from the Athabascans they encountered along the river. They pointed to the smoke and haze that obscured the distant mountains and shook their heads when the captain asked them about the river ahead. Both Meehan and the captain had missed their point. The smoke meant forest fires, and forest fires meant the land was dry, suffering from lack of rain. And no rain meant no runoff from the myriad of nameless creeks and tributaries that fed the Tanana. Furthermore, the early cold choked all snowmelt from the glaciers and mountain passes. None of the water that carried the powdered stone, turning the river the color of spoiled milk, ever reached the wilting river.

Meehan winced as the captain issued another string of invectives. There was nothing left to do but unload the *Isabelle* and pack her goods the four miles up the Chena to the captain's post. There would be no Barnette's Trading Post built at Tanacross this year.

"What damned good is *two shiploads* of goods here on the Chena!" Barnette ranted. "I'm ruined. My creditors will call in their notes, and I'll have nothing to show for it."

Meehan cautiously ventured a suggestion. "You could sell this boatload to George Belt and his partner Hendricks. They have that little trading post over there."

The engineer pointed to smoke rising from a low log cabin

across the river. Belt and Hendricks's store was another thorn in the captain's side. Small as it was, it still represented competition for what few miners straggled about. Barnette cared little that Belt and Hendricks had come first, building their log shack on the far bank of the Tanana almost opposite the mouth of the Chena. Hanging on by their fingernails, his rivals supplied goods to the Indians and to the army while the Signal Corps struggled to string a telegraph line across the Interior. Worse still, those two had been trading up and down the river for years and had developed a solid reputation with the prospectors.

Barnette's shoulders sagged, his anger spent on the flour sack. Paying his men extra to pack his goods over the swampy trail to his outpost would double his cost. Meehan's idea had merit. "Sure, send a boat over to them. Invite them aboard for a parley."

An hour later, Belt and Hendricks clambered aboard the stricken *Isabelle*. Like so many partners, the two men were wildly dissimilar. George Belt was short while Nathan Hendricks was tall. Where one wore his hair closely cropped, the other sprouted a bushy beard and a nest of wiry locks drawn back by a leather ribbon. Bush talked constantly while Hendricks glared about with his stony face set in silence.

Immediately after the two men set foot aboard the *Isabelle*, Meehan regretted his suggestion. Barnette's temper mixed with the others' obvious glee at the captain's distress could lead to no bartering other than the trading of blows.

"Stuck, eh?" Belt chortled as he peered over the side at the keel of the sternwheeler embedded in the gray silt. "I could have told you so. Could've saved you the trouble. No one's ever going to get past Bates Rapids lest they got wings and can fly. Your idea of getting upriver to Tanacross is pure foolishness."

Hendricks grunted and nodded in agreement. He shed his wool mackinaw on the railing and turned to lift a crate of tinned beef, judging its value, before moving on to prod a sack of rice. His actions gave Meehan the impression of a ghoul stripping the dead on a battlefield. Hendricks's greasy hair and vest, stippled with a year's worth of dinner scraps, brought that comparison readily to mind. As did the black gap in his crooked smile where two rotted teeth had fallen out.

"It can be done, Belt," Barnette countered. "And I'll prove it. I'll be sitting in my store on the Crossing while you two will be scraping the moss off your front door. Wait and see."

Belt spit a stream of tobacco juice on the planking inches from Barnette's boots. "Ain't never gonna happen! And John Jerome Healy ain't never gonna build no road from Valdez all the way to Eagle, neither. That's a fact. Even if you got set up on Tanacross, you'd be as bad off as you are here. Maybe worse."

Barnette glowered at the tobacco stain on his deck. His boat was named after his wife, and Belt's action affronted him. Keeping his eyes fixed on Belt, he bent over and wiped away the stain with the sleeve of Hendricks's coat. "I think the road will be built," he said.

"Well, if it does or if it doesn't, won't get your goods off this mud bar," Belt crowed. "You're stuck solid. So I guess you'd like to sell, or else you'd never have asked us aboard."

"I'm considering it."

Belt grew even craftier, and his partner doubled his efforts to assess the cargo. "Well, seeing as how you ain't got no buyers crowding about the boat, my partner and me are your only hope," he said slowly. "What's your cargo?"

"The usual," Barnette answered. "Rice, flour, beans, tinned beef—"

"Got any mining tools?" Belt interrupted.

"Picks, shovels, the makings of riffles for sluice boxes. But we also have a hundred blankets and ten dozen rubber boots."

"Hang the boots," Belt snapped. "Mercury, man! Have you got any mercury?"

A warning sounded in Barnette's head. This close to winter, food and clothing should be the main concern of anyone in his right mind—not mercury! Mercury, that poisonous, shiny quicksilver, was used to separate gold. Mixed with low-grade gold ore it formed an amalgam with the gold. After heating, the mercury vaporized, leaving pure gold. Why was Belt asking about mercury? Unless . . .

"Well, yes, I do have a crate with ten flasks of mercury on board," the captain replied cautiously. "Why do you ask?"

Hendricks stumbled over his feet, nearly falling overboard, in his hurry to return from the stern of the *Isabelle*. A worried look covered his face. "Don't . . . tell . . . !" he croaked to his partner.

Meehan watched this banter with amazement. It was the first time he'd ever heard Hendricks speak, and the man's voice was high-pitched and reedy like a young girl's, totally out of keeping with the size of the trader. And E. T. Barnette and George Belt were circling each other like fighting cocks, ready to draw blood. The engineer almost laughed, the scene was so comical, until he realized both men were armed.

Belt's hand sliced through the air with a chopping motion that cut off Hendricks in midsentence. But the action and Belt's face told Barnette all he needed to know.

Belt pressed on. "I'm prepared to do you a favor, Barnette. Your goods are next to worthless here, but I'll buy the whole lot from you. Lock, stock, and barrel. Hendricks and me will probably lose our shirts doing so, but I feel sorry for you, Barnette. You've had more than your share of hard luck on this river. What do you say?"

"Everything?"

"Yup. On account of my good nature. I'll even take the mercury. It's no good to you, and it's damned heavy for the space it takes up. Why, even taking that crate of it off might help float this tub of yours."

"Tub?"

"Ah, the *Isabelle* is named after Mrs. *Isabelle* Barnette, the captain's wife," Meehan pointed out. He was quick to notice the florid change in his skipper's complexion, a change that George Belt inexplicably had missed.

"Whatever." Belt shrugged.

Captain Barnette seemed to have lost his voice.

"Ten cents on the dollar, Barnette," Belt pressed. "A more than generous offer."

"Ten cents." The words were little more than a whisper.

"No need to thank me, Barnette." Belt turned to wink at his hulking partner.

That was a mistake.

In turning, Belt missed seeing the fist that caught him behind his right ear. The blow drove him to his knees and knocked his beaver hat into the river, where the swift current swept it out of sight. Instantly Barnette was on top of the stunned Belt, hammering at his head and face with both hands. Hendricks reached for the revolver stuck inside his waistband only to find his arms pinned to his sides by Meehan and two deckhands. The three men lifted the struggling Hendricks and threw him overboard. The giant landed with a loud splash and vanished beneath the milky surface. A second later, he breached like a sounding whale, sputtering and swearing in his squeaky voice, just as his partner joined him in the icy waters. The swift current carried the two, cursing and shaking their fists, to the far bank where their settlement lay.

"Not for a hundred and ten cents on the dollar!" Barnette shouted. "I'd rather burn my cargo than sell one stick of it to you two grave robbers!"

He ripped open his jacket and snatched his own revolver from its holster. "I'll kill those sons of bitches!" he swore as he thumbed back the hammer and took aim at the bobbing heads of his rivals.

Only Meehan's hasty action stopped Barnette. He grabbed the captain's gun with both hands, forcing it up, just as it fired. The bullet clipped the top of the wooden pole in the center of the foredeck while its sound ricocheted off the rocky cut bank behind them. The engineer continued his grip on the pistol until the murderous look of his skipper evaporated.

Only then did the two men see a small boat approaching them from the mouth of the Chena. Frank Cleary was trying his best to work the oars and wave his hands at the same time. Finally, he gave up and stood in the rocking craft while the current carried it swirling toward the grounded sternwheeler. His voice was lost in the low rumble of the Tanana even though he cupped his hands as he shouted to the *Isabelle.*

"What is it, Frank?" Barnette bellowed back.

"Gold! Gold! E. T., they struck gold!" Cleary cried.

Barnette and his entire crew rushed to help Cleary aboard. His skiff was forgotten and drifted away as Barnette's brother-in-law was manhandled onto the maindeck.

"What's this about gold, Frank?" Barnette questioned. "This isn't one of those rumors, is it?"

"Hell, no, E. T.," Cleary laughed. "This time it's for real." To emphasize his point he thrust a handful of gleaming nuggets into the captain's hands. "Already the word has spread to Dawson, Eagle, and Circle. A surefire stampede is on. We've got sixty miners camped around the trading post already, clamoring to buy a grubstake."

"Sweet Jesus!" Barnette exclaimed. "And I'm right in the middle of it!"

FIVE

Tonopah, Nevada. The faintest sound of a footfall caught Wyatt's ears as he bent over his writing desk. As he was not one for writing, the letter he was working on was especially difficult. Strange, he mused, that fingers so nimble at dealing faro or poker would balk at the simple task of scribbling a few lines on a scrap of paper. But he knew the reason. It was the heart that balked at this effort. The fingers only followed his heart's lead.

This was his fifth attempt to write to his son, born out of wedlock to his second and common-law wife, Mattie Blaylock. Probably my best-kept secret, he thought grimly. Every damned nickel-plated gunman can recite my shoot-out at the O.K. Corral by heart, but less than five people on this earth know Nathan Blaylock is my son.

And it'll stay that way, he vowed, as long as I can help it. He leaned back and stretched his long legs beneath the table while his ears kept tuned to the soft footsteps that stealthily approached. His right hand tapped his pen impatiently on the wooden surface. Best leave Nathan free and clear of my past, he reasoned. Wyatt's paternal pride bristled at an unpleasant thought. Wouldn't want those two-bit backshooters trying to make a name for themselves by killing my boy. The lad had a right to a life of his own—free and clear of the shadow of his father. This is one case where the sins of the father won't be camping on the doorsteps of the son, he promised himself.

But it hurt. When he sat in church and looked at the other men with their sons or watched them working together, that pang of regret always returned. It was the only thing he regretted about his past, and yet what could he have done differently? After Tombstone, he was on the run—and on a mission of vengeance. Sleeping in the saddle, hiding out, and always hunting for those who had killed his brother Morgan and crippled Virgil.

He and Doc Holliday had killed them all. Sherm McMasters and Turkey Creek Jack Johnson had helped, but the pool of blood kept spreading, refusing to stop. Others kept stepping forward to replace those they had killed. Fortune hunters, glory seekers, friends of the Clantons, the list seemed endless. Later they killed his brother Warren. The wisest thing he could do was keep his boy hidden.

He hoped Nathan understood and wouldn't think Wyatt was ashamed of him in some way. Far from that. Nathan was a son to make a father proud enough to burst the buttons on his waistcoat. Wyatt chuckled to himself. Maybe he grew up so well *because* I didn't get my hands on him, he thought wryly.

But what do you say to a son that you never knew existed? Mattie had seen to that. But her vengeful plan had backfired and brought the two men together in that fateful meeting on the sands of Nome. Well, Wyatt resolved, I can sure as hell write to him and let him know he's always on my mind.

A floorboard creaked under a soft step, almost catlike. He was being stalked.

Without the slightest sign of increased alertness, Wyatt puffed deeply on his cigar, surrounding himself with a cloud of smoke. Within this smoke screen, he bent over the papers and coughed. While his body shielded the desk, his hands shuffled the order of the papers. Then, he leaned back and continued his writing.

Josie refused to even talk about Nathan. His very existence stood as a glaring reminder of the two babies she had lost, of her failed promise to Wyatt that she would give him a family. She still grieved for the little boy they had lost in San Francisco, and Wyatt understood her feelings. He hoped to bring her around and to show her that Nathan could never threaten the love he held for her. But she was stubborn as a mule—and willful. It would take time. And gentle handling, like breaking a high-strung mustang. He would have to go slowly.

A perfumed hand caught his ear. "Got you, Wyatt Earp!" Josie cried triumphantly. "I snuck up on you, and you never even suspected," she laughed. "You better watch out; I might not have been friendly."

He twisted in his chair and drew her into his arms. She was wearing that Japanese silk dressing gown that he liked so much, the one from San Francisco with the pale blue flowers. He drew her close to him and buried his face in her hair, and Josie responded by wrapping her arms around his neck. Yet, out of the corner of her eye, she carefully studied the materials on his desk without seeming to.

"I've never known you not to be friendly to me, Sadie."

She tousled his hair playfully, pausing instinctively to study a patch of gray hair in her fingers. "I could be *more* friendly if you'd put away these papers and come to bed," she purred. She released her hold and twisted in his lap. "What have you here?" she asked, her eyes wide with feigned innocence.

"Oh, a letter from Frank Canton."

"Frank Canton, the U.S. marshal that we met in Alaska?" she asked while her fingers darted for the papers on his desktop.

Wyatt caught her hand and kissed her palm. "Uh-huh."

"What on earth would Mr. Canton want, Wyatt? He didn't ask you to go back to Alaska to help him, did he?" Her fingers wriggled, attempting to free themselves from his grasp and reach their objective, but he held on.

"No, Sadie, he didn't. In fact, he's not in Alaska anymore. He's in Oklahoma."

Josie's face bent into a frown. "Wasn't that the marshal you told me was really an outlaw?"

"Yup. I knew him as Joe Horner. He was wanted for bank robbery in Oklahoma."

Josie stopped her struggling and looked Wyatt straight in the eye. "And he went back to Oklahoma? Why on earth would he do that?"

Wyatt smiled. "He got himself pardoned by the governor, sweetheart. He writes to say he got snowblind in '98 and so he left Alaska. Retired, I gather, and returned to Oklahoma to ask for a pardon."

"Isn't that nice. I'm happy for him. He was very kind to us when we went north."

Wyatt picked Canton's crumpled letter from his desk and handed it to his wife. When she turned it over in her hand and returned it to him, he adjusted his spectacles and started to read. In another year Josie would need glasses, too, he realized.

"He used his record as a marshal to show he'd gone straight. Apparently, the governor of Oklahoma believed him and gave him a full pardon. He wrote to thank me for not giving him away when we met and says if I ever need a favor, just ask."

"And do you need a favor, Wyatt?" Josie asked sharply. "Are you planning something?"

"Well," he drawled, "I was wondering if he could help me find a younger woman—"

He never finished his sentence before her elbow dug into his ribs, making him grunt. "Sharp little elbow for someone as soft as you, Sadie," he groaned.

"Just another of a woman's secret weapons," she said smugly. "We're not to be underestimated."

"I see."

"No, you don't, mister. You're up to something, and don't think I don't know what it is. What are you hiding under that plain piece of paper?"

"Nothing." He blanched.

"Wyatt Earp, I wasn't born yesterday. I can tell when you're up to something. Your ears turn red. You're writing to that . . . that boy, Nathan. The one who *claims* to be your son." Her hand swept away the empty sheet of foolscap to pounce on his letter beneath. She held it up as if it were poisoned and squinted her eyes.

" 'Dear son,' " she read. " 'Where do I begin . . .' " She stopped to cast a mocking glance at him. "Is that all you wrote?"

He hung his head. "It's hard trying to catch up twenty years of neglect. I . . . I don't know where to begin, what to say."

"Well, I'll make it easy for you, Wyatt. Don't say anything." She crumpled the letter into a tight ball. "He's not your son, and you have no need to write to him."

"Sadie," he pleaded. "You know that's not true. He's the spitting image of me. You saw him yourself."

With that she jumped from his lap. "Not the spitting image," she protested. "He's taller, and . . . and I think his feet are bigger, too."

"Sadie—"

"Wyatt, what does that prove? When I was in San Francisco, I ran into a woman who could have been my twin sister. But she wasn't! Some people look like others, but that doesn't make them kin!"

Wyatt watched her pace about, hands on hips, arguing her point. There were tears in her eyes, something he hated to see.

"Look at you and Virgil. You're so tall and handsome, and he looks like a . . . an old walrus with lumbago. You are both brothers, yet you look totally different."

"Don't tell Allie what you think about Virge," he cautioned.

"Don't try to distract me," she sobbed. She looked down at the letter balled in her fist. "I want you to let me tear up this letter, Wyatt. Please!"

He shrugged. "Okay, Sadie. It's not much good all crumpled up like this. You can have it."

Josie's fingers tore the letter apart. She cast the scraps into the stove by the wall. Then she rewarded his cooperation with a kiss that lingered on his lips. Her tongue flicked lightly across his lips, a promise of rewards to come when he followed her into the bedroom. She twisted adroitly to free herself from his grasp and scampered away, leaving him smiling up at her.

"Give me ten minutes to arrange myself, Wyatt," she teased. "Then, come to bed. I'll be waiting for you."

Josie danced away, swishing her gown for his benefit. Wyatt was such a dear, she mused, but no match for her theatrical skills. She repressed a momentary pang of remorse for using tears on him. But it was for his own good, she reminded herself. He wasn't going to come around without the tears. They were necessary. Too bad there was only one member of the audience, she thought. This was one of my better performances.

Wyatt watched his wife prance away. He sighed deeply. Josie was something, indeed. He shook his head in amazement. How could women crank up those tears on a moment's notice? he wondered. It's something a man would never understand.

He glanced at the bedroom door after she closed it. When he judged it safe, he carefully reached into the middle of his sheaf of writing paper and withdrew his finished letter to Nathan. He licked the envelope and began his return address with "William Stapp," using part of his middle name. If it fell into the wrong hands, no one would be the wiser. But his son, Nathan, would know it was from him.

He slipped the letter into his boot, making a mental note to post it first thing in the morning. With luck, Nathan would receive it within a month.

★ ★ SIX ★ ★

Nathan Blaylock shed his pack in one fluid motion and flopped onto his back in the fresh snow. Bundled in a thick beaver parka, he grinned up at his friend. Jim Riley merely squatted on his haunches with his back resting against a spruce trunk. Too many years of squatting around a campfire on endless cattle drives had ingrained in Riley that position to the level of a reflex. Being in Alaska made little difference. His legs still thought of themselves as belonging to a cowman and acted accordingly.

Nathan stuffed a handful of snow into his mouth and rolled onto his side to gaze at the miles of rolling hills and ravines that stretched beneath them. From their vantage point on this windswept bluff over the upper reaches of the Tanana River they could see as far as the curve of the earth allowed. Behind them, the blending of the Alaska Mountain Range, flowing south and east into the softer curves of the Chugach Mountains, presented them with a picture of soft purples and violet hues to tax any artist's palette. Before them, the braided course of the river headed north, peeking at times from beneath the mantle of white that blanketed the riverbed.

"I was freezing to death as a penniless, broke-down cowpuncher when I first met you, boy," Riley grumbled good-naturedly. "And look how far I've come since then. I'm still broke, and I'm still freezing."

"But look how far you have come, Jim." Nathan drew himself into a crouch and waved his arm at the vast expanse that lay before them. "We've made it to the top of the world. How many can make that claim? Here the air is fresh and free. We're free! Free to come and go as we please—"

Riley's snowball cut him off in midsentence. "You've been reading too many of them trashy dime novels," the older man scolded. "Stick to the classics, I always say. Dickens, Shakespeare, them guys. They got a real feel for life. All that back stabbing in dark castle halls and poison drinks. Yessiree, them writers knew their fellowmen."

Blaylock smiled inwardly. Four years ago, his friend could neither read nor write his name, never having the opportunity to learn in almost fifty years of hard life, one spent on the run or in hiding because of his prowess with a pistol in Arizona. Nathan had taught him in exchange for his teaching Nathan an equally useful skill—handling a revolver. The result produced a mix greater than the sum of its parts: the young man became deadly with a gun, and old Jim Riley became literary. A literary critic, Nathan corrected his thoughts.

"No. Dickens is too depressing for me, Jim. I need something lighter."

Riley frowned. "Then, go back to reading the labels on them bean cans if you like. But the Immortal Bard throws a straight loop when he writes about the dark side of people. You ought to know that. You've seen enough to know better."

Riley's comment on can labels reminded Nathan of his friend's voracious appetite when it came to reading. Riley, like a man starving for words, had read anything printed at first, learning as he went. From cans he had pressed on until now he studied the classics. Secretly the two men relished the improvements each had wrought on the other. Those changes, mixed with their adventures in Alaska, and a dozen gunfights had forged a bond between them stronger than blood ties could ever do.

Nathan munched thoughtfully on some more snow. Jim was right, he reminded himself. He *had* seen more than enough to sour him, but somehow he couldn't find it in his heart to turn bitter. Whenever his thoughts turned in that direction, someone came along to reaffirm his faith in at least *some* of the human race. And when the press of the towns grew too much for him, he'd head out for the open wilderness to clear his head and cleanse his soul in the unsullied air. Lately he'd been spending more time away from his fellowman. It was over three months since the two of them strode down a man-made street.

"I guess you're right, Jim," Nathan said. "That's why I love it out here so much. No dog catchers or bill collectors to complicate my life."

"Don't ya mean no fillies to complicate yer life?"

"That's a sore subject, my friend. Besides, you've made more out of that than there was."

"Oh, no, I ain't. You never saw how serious that gal in Dawson was. That's what tripped you up. That and the velvet a-growing on yer antlers."

"I don't want to talk about it, Jim." Nathan focused on the azure sky overhead. Not a single cloud sullied the sheet of blue.

"Well, we ought to," Riley insisted. "Don't want to be making the same mistake twice. Besides, we nearly had to shoot her two brothers because of yer misunderstanding."

"So what did I do wrong?" Nathan asked in exasperation. "I thought she liked me."

"She did. A whole lot."

"Yeah. She even baked me cookies."

Riley snorted. "Baking someone cookies ain't no clear signal that a woman wants a man to jump on her—leastways not until after they's got hitched."

"How was I to know that, Jim? She never said anything about getting married."

"It was ignorance on yer part, son, not stupidity. You never realized the difference between a sporting gal the likes of which live in them cribs in the Whitecastle District and that sweet little thing who worked in the bakery. And I blame myself for that gap in yer education, seeing as how I never introduced you to none of the night-working ones."

Nathan shook his head. The girl had come after him like a

fox making a beeline to a crippled ptarmigan. "Well, how do you tell the difference?"

Riley scratched his grizzled beard. "It ain't easy," he said slowly. In fact, he was unsure himself. "Skin 'em down to their skivvies and soak 'em in the river and you can't tell Snake Hips Alice from the parson's sister. Fully dressed, it's nigh impossible."

"That's no help. Give me something I can use, Jim. Something specific."

Riley realized he was treading on thin ice. His experience with "decent" women, other than his mother, was nonexistent. Struggling, he hit on a solution. "Watches," he said proudly. "Watches."

"Watches?"

"Yup. If you encounter a woman on the street with one of them little watches pinned to her dress, she's probably a sporting lady."

The young man looked all the more confused. "Well, I sure don't understand."

"If she's wearing a watch, it's to time you, son. That way she can make sure you don't overstay yer hour. She don't want to git shortchanged. Don't you see?"

Nathan shook his head. "I don't know about that." He turned onto his side and studied the frozen river snaking through its cuts in the mountains. Dark puddles of overflow spread across the icy surface at random intervals. "Well, I won't see any woman out here, Jim. Not this far from a settlement. No women, no one at all, not even an Indian—unless she's lost."

A slight movement caught Riley's eye, and he shifted his head to follow a string of caribou wending their way in single file across the scoured gravel of the riverbed and up the slope of the next hill. What spooked them? he wondered. Most likely they had spotted a pack of wolves. He looked beyond the caribou.

Suddenly the old man stiffened. "Well, I'll be damned," he

swore. "Look down there. Do you see what them men are doing down there? Raising crosses?" His mittened hand pointed back at the pass.

Nathan shaded his eyes from the glare. "Stringing tele-graph wire," he said. The words cut through his heart like a sharp knife, and his stomach knotted into a ball. They were no longer alone. His wilderness was invaded. Men were stringing wire for a telegraph down there, and with that wire would come roads and wagons and all the things he had come this far into the Interior to escape.

Slowly Nathan rose to his knees and adjusted the bindings of his snowshoes. "Well, Jim," he said with resignation. "We'd best go down there and see what they're up to. Maybe they got something to trade for fresh meat."

"I could use some real tobacco," Riley said. "This alder bark don't cut it for smoking."

With that, Blaylock hefted his pack and slung the string of ptarmigan they'd shot over his shoulder and started down. Half-sliding, half-falling, the men worked their way down the slope. Loose scree and icy overhangs made the descent treach-erous and time-consuming. At times they slid down the rock face, dropping from handhold to handhold, praying all the while the slim brush would hold them back from death so they would not fall.

Two hours passed before the tired men trod into the camp. Men struggled about in their heavy clothing, raising poles, un-rolling huge bales of wire from dog teams, and stringing it onto the posts. No one took much notice of them, so they wan-dered through the camp, peering into the open tents until a man approached them.

"What do you want?" he barked at them. The sight of both men clothed from head to toe in furs like Natives, except for Riley, who still wore his battered Stetson lashed tightly about his ears with a wool scarf, clearly upset the man.

Riley turned to Nathan and gave him a disgusted look. "Army," he said flatly.

"You're damn right there, old-timer!" the man bellowed.

"And I'm Sergeant Muller. And I asked you nice and politely what the hell you two want? This is an army base, and you're trespassing."

"I guess that's as polite as a three-striper can get," Riley replied. He shook his head sadly. "We can't be trespassing, Sergeant, 'cause we own all this land."

"Own it?" Muller looked confused. "How can you own it? It's wilderness—"

"We wondered if you need fresh meat," Nathan interrupted. He lifted the string of birds and dropped them at the sergeant's feet.

Before the sergeant could comment, a voice behind him asked, "What's the problem, Sergeant?"

Muller spun on his heel and answered, "Nothing, sir. Just two trappers looking for a free handout. I'll shivvy them on their way, with the lieutenant's permission."

"We ain't asking for no charity," Riley snapped. "We thought you might like some meat that ain't spent four years living in a can in Santiago, Cuba."

"Thank you, Sergeant; I'll look after these men." The lieutenant approached with a wry smile on his face. He moved with the easy grace of an athlete, and the wolverine ruff of his parka combined with his manner to make him seem taller than he was. Windburn marks across his cheeks only served to accentuate his chiseled features. His nose was large and straight, leading from his deepset eyes down to his full lips. On a street in San Francisco Nathan might have figured him for a dandy, but the cut of his parka and the way his lanyard was looped around his mittens signaled that this man was no stranger to the Arctic.

He stripped off a thick sealskin mitten and extended his hand. "My name's Lt. William Mitchell, but most civilians call me Billy Mitchell." He glanced at the string of birds. "And you're right about our canned beef. We could use some fresh meat. My men are good at stringing wire, but they can't hunt. Unfortunately, I'm too busy to shoot game myself."

"Nathan Blaylock and Jim Riley," Nathan responded as he

shook the man's hand. The grip was firm, consistent with Nathan's impression of the rest of the man. This Mitchell was a doer, he realized. If he was assigned to string a telegraph wire, it would get strung.

"Good-looking birds," Mitchell remarked. "I see you shot each in the head. That's good. I hate spitting out a load of birdshot from my arctic chicken." He stopped to eye them closely. "That also tells me you two are damn good shots."

"Pretty damned good," Riley admitted. "Some of them birds was taken with the same bullet."

"Lawmen?"

Nathan shook his head. "No, just trappers. What are you doing here, Lieutenant? There's no settlement between here and Rampart for your telegraph. You don't plan on stringing wire all the way to Rampart, do you?"

Riley chuckled. "And if you're stringing to Dawson, you're carrying yer compass too close to yer pistol. It swung the wrong way. Dawson and Eagle are east—off to yer right."

Billy Mitchell smiled. "You boys are wrong on all accounts. This is part of WAMCATS."

"What in tarnation is a 'WAMCATS'?" Riley asked.

"The Washington–Alaska Military Cable and Telegraph Service. It's being built by the Army Signal Corps. The plan is to link Alaska with Seattle by an underwater cable. The line already runs from Fort Liscum in Valdez to Fort Egbert."

"In Eagle," Nathan said. "We know about that. But what are you doing here?"

Mitchell looked at them with a twinkle in his eye. "How long since you boys been into a town?" he asked.

"Three, four months. Why?"

"A lot's been happening in those three months. We're stringing this line all the way to Nome."

"Nome?" Riley stammered. "There ain't no way you can get to Nome from here, not unless you got help from eagles and mountain goats, Lieutenant. Them mountains is blocking yer way."

Mitchell smiled. "It can be done, and it will. I surveyed a route last year."

"And where might that be?" Riley stopped snickering and asked.

"We've already come down a branch of the Forty Mile, and from here we're heading along the Goodpasture River to the Tanana. I'll connect at Fort Gibbon where the Tanana runs into the Yukon. Then it's down the Yukon to Fort Saint Michael. From there it's an easy run to Nome. Oh, and on the way along the Tanana we'll have a station at the Chena and Fairbanks."

"Fairbanks?" Riley snorted. "Now I know you've got a touch of snow blindness, Billy. There ain't no such place as Fairbanks."

"There most certainly is, my friend. Eight or nine hundred people, mostly miners, living about five miles in on the Chena, and it's growing daily."

Nathan looked puzzled. "We know about that army post at the mouth of the Chena, near Belt and Hendricks's place, but there's nothing up the Chena except a trading post run by Captain Barnette. He was planning to move it to Tanana Crossing when the river got deep. I suspect he's there by now."

Mitchell shook his head, smiling at the confusion his words brought. "Luckily for him he didn't move. His trading post is sitting right in the middle of a gold strike. Some say it's as big as Nome or the Klondike ever were. Anyway, Barnette's got himself a town. He practically owns it, and he named it Fairbanks after some senator from the Midwest. So what do you think of that?"

Shocked, all Nathan could do was hand his string of ptarmigan over to the puzzled lieutenant and walk away in stunned silence.

Later that evening, Jim Riley flung his well-picked drumstick into the darkness, wiped his hands on his parka, and sat back to light his pipe. With his back resting against an overturned sled, he tamped the precious tobacco into the chipped bowl and thrust a burning brand from the fire into his pipe. He drew on the pipe until a cloud of gray smoke surrounded his head. Then he closed his eyes and emitted a contented sigh.

"I surely thank you, Lieutenant, for this trade. Alder and birch bark don't make no proper smoking material." He blew a giant cloud up at the twinkling stars. " 'While the fates permit, live happily . . . ,' " he quoted.

Billy Mitchell stopped chewing on the last of his ptarmigan and cast an astonished glance at the careworn smoker. "Seneca, isn't it?" he asked in astonishment.

"Yup," Riley grunted with his pipe stem firmly clamped between his teeth. "The old Roman hisself. Do I surprise you, Billy? Seeing as how this old coot heard about the classics."

"Frankly, yes. The last thing I expected you to quote was Seneca, Mr. Riley. But it's a pleasant surprise, I'll admit."

Nathan looked through the blaze of the campfire he shared with the two other men. "You'd be amazed at what Jim reads, Lieutenant. Whenever we have the chance he reads a book."

Mitchell smiled. "Nothing better than to study during these long winter nights. I've spent my time studying lighter-than-air vehicles, especially last winter when I was surveying the line."

"Flying things?" Riley asked. "Like kites?"

"No, vessels that are powered, not just gliders. A true flying machine."

Riley guffawed. "Something with a wood-fired boiler? Ain't no way something the weight of a solid heifer could stay in the air, let alone get off the ground."

Mitchell nodded sagely. "It will happen, my friend. Mark my words. Someday, we'll fly over these mountains and all around this territory."

"Not in yer wildest dreams."

"Do you really think so?" Nathan asked.

"I do," Mitchell replied. "I've studied the engineering part of flying, and it can be done. It's only a matter of time. Look at all the changes taking place in Alaska in the last few years."

Nathan swept his hand at the telegraph wire that ran overhead to disappear into the night. Its malignant gleam glared back down at him. In an instant he realized how the Plains Indians must have felt as the tracks of the Iron Horse divided the open spaces. "All this came from gold, Billy. Gold drives men mad. I've seen it in Dawson and in Nome. But I don't think gold will empower men to fly. That metal tends to tie men to the ground that holds it."

Mitchell looked closely at the young man. These two puzzled him. They failed to fit into the neat categories he had constructed for those he met in this wilderness. "What you say about gold is true, Nathan," he said slowly as a troubled expression crossed his face. "I've been sorely disappointed by the effect of gold on men I considered reasonable. Too many lives have been lost searching for gold, and I'm afraid I've contributed to that waste without intending to."

"How so, Billy?" Riley queried between long puffs.

"Well, I told you about the route I've surveyed for the WAMCATS. It's acceptable for a telegraph wire, but the way down the Goodpasture is not a safe route to travel to the goldfields around Fairbanks."

Nathan agreed. "To much overflow on the Goodpasture. Parts of it never freeze solid like the Yukon or most of the Tanana. We've run into that on the Goodpasture, and it was terrible. Almost froze to death after our sled ran through a stretch of water covering the ice."

Mitchell hung his head and stared into the coals. "Some fools even called my survey line the Goodpasture Trail, can you believe it? It's no trail at all."

Suddenly Nathan understood. "Oh, somebody looked at the map and saw your telegraph line was a hundred miles shorter than taking the old trail down the Yukon to Circle City and then down the Tanana."

"Yes," Mitchell replied sadly. "I told them it was no trail. Even wrote to the commissioner in Eagle, and the soldiers at Fort Egbert turned those they could back. I went so far as to send a dispatch to the paper in Dawson, but it did no good."

Riley puffed contentedly. He'd heard it all before. "Bet

they accused you of trying to keep them from taking the fastest trail. Probably said you wanted to keep the gold for yourself, eh?"

"Yes. And the damned traders on the Forty Mile River encouraged them to take the Goodpasture. *Encouraged them!* Can you believe that!"

"Sure." Riley settled his hat lower over his ears. "The greedy pigs got to sell them cheechakos their grubstake instead of them buying it in Circle. Why, Billy, I'm astonished at you. Did you expect better of your fellowman?"

"Many lost their lives or suffered horribly from frostbite. The lucky ones were the ones that turned back. All they lost was their supplies and their mules."

That last remark struck a resonant note with Riley. With the exception of his friend Nathan, Jim Riley felt that animals belonged above humans in all things. "It's a damned shame when a hardworking mule loses his life on account of the foolishness of his master."

"And they're blaming me," Mitchell sighed. "I hope I'm not remembered for my trail costing the lives of all those stampeders."

"Well." Riley rose, stretched his limbs, and patted the distraught officer on the arm. "I wouldn't lose no sleep over it. Look at all the hundreds of miners that vanished crossing the Valdez Glacier, swallowed up in them crevasses and holes. I recall Abercrombie blazed that trail, and ain't no one blames him for them fools that got themselves kilt. In manners of gold rushing, one man's misfortune is another's gain. Those that make out because some poor sod went under never complain. They all figure that's so much more paystreak for them to play with. Gold they ain't gotta share. For all you know, the live ones are secretly thanking you for reducing their competition." With that Riley wandered off into the night, snaking a trail of smoke behind him.

Shortly afterward, Mitchell said good night, leaving Nathan alone by the campfire. The fire had burned down to a bed of coals. The youth glanced back at the canvas-walled tent the lieutenant had provided for them.

Using the broad side of his ax, Nathan scooped a pile of coals and layered them into two shallow pits he'd dug in the gravel riverbed where the camp lay. Then he spread the caribou robes he and Jim used instead of wool blankets over the coals after covering those embers with a few inches of dirt. When he was satisfied their beds would be warm for the night, Nathan returned to his pack by the smoldering campfire.

Reaching into his pack, he carefully removed an oilskin packet and unwrapped it. Inside was a folded piece of paper, worn smooth and tattered at the edges by repeated handling. Nathan fingered the paper with reverence, as if it were some priceless artifact. Unfolding it, he found the feeble coals too poor a source of light. He toyed with the idea of adding more wood, but then the coal oil lamp inside the army tent caught his eye.

Nathan lit the lamp after cautiously looking about and sat down to read the letter for the hundredth time. He knew the words by heart, but they still managed to raise a lump in his throat and roil his insides with a mixture of pride and longing whenever he read them. His eyes lingered over the writing, studying the script.

He could recite the letter with his eyes closed, but holding the paper and seeing the actual words gave him as much pleasure as the sentiments they expressed.

Tonopah, Nevada
1902

Dear Son,

Well, Sadie and I are in Nevada now, following the silver rush. I'm doing a little prospecting with Virgil, but you might term that recreational since it's mostly work and little profit. The real money is in entertaining the miners, as usual. I've opened another saloon, called the Northern. I named it that to remind me of the Dexter I had in Nome. Nome was as good a burg to me as any I've been in. I'll always have a warm place in my heart for that place, as that's where we met. If I were twenty years younger and Sadie didn't hate the cold so, I'd still be there.

I hear you've been getting good use out of my pistol, and from all reports, you're doing me proud. I ran into Frank Canton when he came to San Francisco on his marshal's business, and he told me you have built a name for yourself. A good name. I almost burst the buttons off my waistcoat when he said that. Frank was a bit curious at my interest in you, but he is a good friend and did his best to provide me with all the details of your adventures. Of course, I can't let on you are my son. That would only place you in grave danger from all my enemies, something you do not deserve. I suspect Frank knows who you are, but he never let on and neither did I.

Sadie is still as stubborn as ever in refusing to admit you are my son. I guess the fact she never had a child like she hoped still weighs heavily on her, and having a full-grown man like you pop up is still too much for her to accept. She's got a good heart, though, and I'm still working on her. I think she'll come around.

Well, I'll close by telling you I'm mighty proud of you. The best advice I can give you is follow your heart and keep your Colt clean and handy. The world is full of two-legged snakes, even in Alaska.

> Affectionately, your father,
> Wyatt Earp

The words blurred before Nathan's eyes, and he refolded the letter and held it in his hand until his vision cleared. Must be the smoke from the lamp, he lied to himself, but he was glad

Jim was still out. A grown man wasn't supposed to cry, Nathan reminded himself—leastways not over a letter.

Rewrapping the only thing he had from his father except for the Colt .45 at his side, Nathan slipped the oilskin packet safely back inside his pack. Jim was probably down at the other end of the camp, sampling some medicinal whiskey with the senior enlisted men. Riley had a nose like a grizzly where hard liquor was involved. "Don't wait up for me," he'd say if Nathan went looking for him.

Well, Nathan thought, I can't begrudge him a drink. It's been several months since he tasted anything other than tea or coffee, and we even ran out of those two weeks ago. The young man chuckled to himself. If Jim had found any whiskey, he'd have his snout into it like a hog in clover. He'd be gone until sunup. Best get some sleep. It wouldn't do to have both partners bleary-eyed, Nathan realized.

Unnoticed by the young man, a pair of eyes watched him from beneath the partly closed flap of another tent. Sergeant Muller smiled craftily and his eyes glinted in the reflected light of Nathan's lamp. "What have you got there, me boyo?" he muttered. "Something worth a lot, I'd wager. Look at the way the lad holds that paper—like it was made of gold, he thought. Blind me if that isn't some sort of map. I'd stake my stripes on that being a map to a gold mine, he reasoned. No one wanders around this God-cursed country with its frozen muck without a damned good purpose.

Muller knew these two were more than they seemed. Even now, the older one was tight-lipped in spite of all the whiskey Muller and his men used to loosen his tongue. It had to be gold. These men had found a bonanza, and all this trapper shit was just a diversion.

Muller fingered the edge of his bowie knife. The razor-sharp edge drew blood from his slight pressure. The sergeant smiled grimly. When Blaylock went to sleep, he would pay him a visit and appropriate his treasure map. In the morning? Who

Richard Parry

would know anything about a missing map? And if the young
fool was unlucky enough to wake up and struggle? Well, what
was one more dead stampeder to this frightful land? . . .

Nathan rolled into his bed, drawing the thick caribou hide
over his head, and turned with his back to the smoldering embers. He was bone weary, but his mind refused to allow him
sleep. Reading that letter, as he did most nights, always raised
a longing in him that he knew could never be cured. He pondered what might have been and how his fate was linked to a
gunfight in a dusty alley in Tombstone—one that took place
before he was born. Twenty-seven seconds was all it took, he'd
read. Less than half a minute. But three men's lives had ended,
and many more would feel the lingering effect. The ripple continues to widen, he thought, and my life is rocked along with
the rest. That fight robbed him of his childhood.

Nathan scowled. "No regrets," that's what Wyatt would say.
"Play the cards life deals you. It's not the hand alone. It's what
you do with it that matters. Play your strongest cards and bluff
when you have to," he'd say. "And don't sit in if you can't handle the losses."

The young man grinned. God, he thought, maybe I should
consider myself lucky Wyatt *didn't* raise me. He would have
whipped the hide off my backside for some of the tricks I
pulled. I should count myself lucky. I've got the best of both
worlds, now, with Jim and Doc and this letter from my father.
He closed his eyes and fell fast asleep.

A soft footfall crunched on the gravel outside the tent. Instantly Nathan was awake. All his senses came to full alert. His
fingers moved imperceptibly to contact the worn handle of his
revolver. With no external evidence, all his muscles tightened
like coiled springs, ready to react at a split second's notice.
Nathan trained his ears and eyes in the darkness. By the silence of the camp and the burned-down campfires he esti-
mated it was well past midnight. What he could see of the
inside of the tent glowed softly with that eerie predawn light
that shone more as a sensation than as actual illumination.

74

The sound repeated. A carefully placed footstep. Riley coming back from his night revelry, Nathan imagined. Drunk and embarrassed and doing his best not to wake me. Nathan relaxed. He rolled over to greet his friend.

"No use trying to be quiet, Jim," he sighed. "You're making as much noise as a moose wearing snowshoes."

A flash of light, soft and silvery, darted for his throat! Only instinct saved Nathan. He jerked to one side just as the heavy blade sank into the caribou hide by his neck. Even then, the knife sliced across his left cheek, laying it open to the cheek-bone.

Nathan clamped his hand around the fist that held the knife, pinning it down and burying the weapon to the hilt in his spruce mattress. At the same time, his fingers gripped his revolver.

But Sergeant Muller was a skilled fighter. With his knife hand checked, he brought his entire weight to bear on his victim. His knee drove into Nathan's chest while his other hand grappled with the young man's pistol. Muller outweighed Nathan by a good seventy pounds, but all of young Blaylock was muscle.

Nathan felt his breath being crushed out of his lungs by the sergeant's weight, and the man's stinking breath filled his nostrils. Straining every fiber of his being, Nathan lifted the sergeant off his body until he could free his legs. With a swift kick, Nathan drove his knee into the man's midsection.

Muller's eyes bulged in the dim light and he grunted in pain as the blow stunned him, but he held on in desperation. His easy quarry had turned the tables and now hunted him. All this time, their death struggle took place within earshot of the sleeping troopers. Blissfully unaware, they lay in the warmth of their cots while these two men fought for their lives.

Slowly, ever so slowly, Nathan's strength forced Muller back. Inch by inch the burly man was lifted off his victim until Nathan had enough room. Now desperation filled Muller's sweating face.

With lightning quickness, Muller broke free of Nathan's

grip, aided by the grease and sweat that covered his wrists. He launched an all-out attack on his prone opponent, knife held high for the killing blow. A sardonic snigger escaped from his lips as he sensed the kill.

But Nathan bunched his knees together and drove them into the rushing man just as he grasped Muller's knife hand and jerked forward. Uttering an astonished cry, Muller flew over Nathan to land on his back, shattering the oil lamp with his fall.

The noise awoke the camp. Now sleepy voices filled the night with alarms. Muller, his entire body slick with coal oil, realized he had to finish this fight quickly. He would make up the story that he had gone to pay a friendly visit to the lad and the trapper had gone mad and attacked him. Self-defense, they would call it. The army would close the books quickly on this with no fuss.

Lurching to his feet again, Muller rushed at Nathan. Slippery with the fuel, the young man would have no secure grip to stop him, he realized. Nathan realized that as well. All he could do was twist to one side to avoid the slashing steel that drove at him.

Muller's knife missed its prey by less than an inch. In doing so it struck the flinty gravel that Nathan had heaped over the coals beneath his robe, scattering a spray of dirt and coals into the air. A glowing ember erupted.

The oil-soaked clothing of Sergeant Muller burst into flames. The astonished man jumped to his feet just as a ball of fire engulfed him, and for that terrible instant Nathan recognized his assailant. Staggering and shrieking, Muller crashed into the side of the tent, igniting the canvas of the roof. Fire spread to everything as the spruce pitch of the branches caught and crackled into flames. Instantly the tent was a roaring inferno.

Nathan barely had time to roll from the tent as his robe ignited. Tumbling through the snow, he smothered the flames, and he was left with only his clothing singed. He rose shakily to his feet to watch the fireball that was Sergeant Muller dashing in the darkness like a Roman candle gone out of control.

The screams stopped. Muller ceased his frantic evasions and crumpled to his knees. His comrades rushed to give aid, but they were too late. The intensity of the blazing sergeant kept the others at bay, and the horror of this scene paralyzed them. At best, all they could do was throw handfuls of snow at the stricken man. With one last agonized groan, Muller fell forward on his face, a smoldering pile.

Mitchell arrived from his tent on the far side of the camp. "For God's sake, use your coats!" he ordered. "Extinguish the fire!"

His orders broke the trance and galvanized his men. The troopers jumped into action and beat out the flames with blankets and coats. But no movement came from the smoking body. One of the men approached the body and rolled it onto its back with his shovel. He knelt down and studied the remains. Then he stood up.

"He's dead, sir," he said to Lieutenant Mitchell.

The lieutenant studied the charred remains. The burned features were unrecognizable. "Who is it?" he asked.

"Sergeant Muller," Nathan answered.

Mitchell walked over to where the young man now squatted in the snow with smoke still rising from his smoldering caribou robe. He looked down at Nathan, studying his singed hair and smudged face. Blaylock's angry and defiant look told him more than he wanted to know. "What happened here?" he asked Nathan.

Nathan simply shook his head.

Whatever it was, Mitchell realized, Muller had started it. The man was a thief and a bully, a bad apple in his company, where every man needed to be true as brass to best this unforgiving wilderness. He'd had his suspicions about Sergeant Muller for some time, but no proof.

Mitchell turned to look at the dead body. "Cover the body with a blanket, men," he ordered. "We'll bury Sergeant Muller in the morning. There was a terrible accident."

Nathan rose to his feet. He gazed at the body and then at

his tent. Nothing remained but blackened piles of ash. Everything was destroyed. His stomach knotted in despair. *His father's letter had burned.* One of two possessions he prized more than anything else he owned, burned to cinders. Gone! Only his pistol survived. He shivered in the freezing air, but not from the cold. Was this an omen? he wondered. Nathan turned to look up at the sky. The night looked darker than he had ever remembered. And he felt alone.

"Yes," he sighed. "A terrible accident. . . ."

★ ★ SEVEN ★ ★

"Sweet Jesus!" Jim Riley swore softly to himself. "What in heaven's name happened here?"

Standing on a rise and looking across the Tanana River to the mouth of the Chena River, he and Nathan had expected to find the old trading post of Belt and Hendricks. Instead, they were standing on the abandoned remains of the store. But it was what they saw across the river that amazed them.

Where moose once browsed on the willows along the flood plain of the Chena and ducks paddled in the shallow slough, a whole town now existed. The rolling fields of alder and brush were hacked into disordered lots like the remnants of a recent battlefield, and scattered shacks and log cabins rose from the silty marsh. Anchoring this boomtown to the banks of the river was a huge log building that housed the new trading post of Messrs. Belt and Hendricks—no longer simple traders—now entrepreneurs and land speculators in the stampede for gold in the valley.

Nathan shook his head sadly and pointed to the thick, black smoke belching from the stacks of two sternwheeled boats tied up at a makeshift jetty. "That's what we've been smelling all day. Smoke from the riverboats. I thought there was a forest fire."

He squatted on the rise to watch myriad tiny figures streaking up and down the pier and the muddy street, unloading cargo like a troop of army ants in high gear. Plumes of smoke rose from a dozen cabins to mingle in the air with that from the paddlewheelers amid shouts and curses from all sectors of this jumbled outpost. After weeks in the solitude of spruce forests and the rocky ledges of the Alaska Range and the wide, frozen tundra that filled the gap between the giant oxbow of the Tanana River, this frenetic activity jarred his senses.

Riley voiced his friend's thoughts. "Sort of reminds you of a lunatic asylum, don't it? All them people down there trespassing in our wilderness. I got half a mind to go down there and shoot 'em all, except I ain't got enough bullets to do the task."

Nathan nudged his pal good-naturedly. "It's not our wilderness, Jim. Leastways, not anymore. Besides, more would just come."

Riley spit in response.

"Look on the bright side, Jim." Nathan searched for something positive to make out of this drastic change to the land. "Maybe Doc's down there. We haven't seen him since we left Dawson."

Riley spit again. "That ain't no bright side," he snorted. "I ain't missed that smarmy scoundrel since we parted ways. Not one instant."

Nathan sighed. While he could find good in both of his adopted mentors, it was no secret that neither cared much for the other. The only thing they had in common was Nathan. "Smarmy? That's a pretty fancy word, Jim. Where'd you find it?"

"In the dictionary," the gunfighter answered proudly. "It's a grand one, ain't it? Come to think of it, it's too grand for that snake oil drummer."

Riley scrounged about for a patch of clean snow that still survived the spring thaw. He found what he was looking for in the shadow of a clump of sedges and scooped up a handful. Munching on it thoughtfully, he rubbed the rest of the snow across the back of his neck. "There must be half of Dawson down there. One thing for sure."

"What's that?"

"We ain't alone out here no more. Guess we're being civilized, again, whether we like it or not. Damn! I thought I'd get used to it by now, but I ain't. It's a shock every time it happens."

Nathan rose slowly to his feet. "I guess," he said.

"Yup," Riley continued his homespun analogy. "It's always a shock. Jus' like sitting down on the frozen seat of an outhouse. . . ."

The two men climbed down the bank toward the river crossing, laughing as they went.

If he expected to slip into the boomtown of Chena unnoticed, Nathan was sorely mistaken. The two men had just passed the muddy furrow that passed for the main street and were busy slogging their way up the silt-churned road when a voice called out to them.

"Nathan! Nathan Blaylock? Is that you? And Riley?"

The two men stopped with their legs straddling a deep rut to look ahead in the direction of the sound. Standing on the porch of their newly created store was George Belt, the shorter of the pair of Belt and Hendricks. While his hair was unchanged, he now wore a tweed suit with the legs tucked into a pair of mud-encrusted rubber miner's boots and a black cravat knotted around a celluloid wing collar at his neck. Behind him rose an enormous log building, almost two stories high, of carelessly peeled spruce logs, sporting a shiny roof of corrugated tin, and crowned with a painted sign that proclaimed: BELT AND HENDRICKS TRADE. Through two glass windows the men could see long counters stacked with goods while packed shelves covered the wall to the height of the ceiling.

"It's us," Riley replied. "But is that you, George? What are you all duded up for? Did yer partner Hendricks die or something?"

"Hell, no. He's alive and kicking. We own this town, and I'm now dressing as befits my elevated status," Belt answered. "Come on in. You two are just the men I've been looking for. I'll buy you both a drink." Belt pivoted grandly on his gum boots and entered his establishment.

"Looks like a little piggy wearing a tuxedo," Riley remarked

Richard Parry

under his breath to Nathan. "He's gone daft like the rest of this asylum. Elevated status, my ass! In my book, that boy's still a pinchpenny who waters his whiskey. Don't he know we ain't forgot what he looked like when his long johns had as many holes as old Bill Doolin after he got shotgunned in Lawson, Oklahoma?"

Nathan gave his friend a wary look, only to smile when Riley corrected himself.

"I know, I know, I got to dust off my table manners now that we're back in civilization," Riley grunted. "I'll be sweet. But that's about it. I ain't kissing his butt for no watered glass of red-eye."

The activity inside astonished Nathan. Men were snatching picks and gold pans from piles as if they were precious gems and scurrying around the store collecting everything necessary for their grubstake. Harried clerks tallied the purchases and carried bundles outside as an unending stream of miners filed through the store.

Blaylock and Riley elbowed their way to the far corner of the bar where Belt was wiping three tumblers on his coattail. The proprietor clinked the edge of each glass with his bottle as he poured each man a dollop of liquor. Riley's eyebrows arched at Belt's generosity.

"I want you to kill someone for me," Belt whispered.

Riley downed his drink while Nathan studied the shopkeeper carefully. "Come right to the point, don't you, Belt?" the old gunman sniffed.

Belt's eyes darted from one wooden face to another as he struggled with the awkward silence that followed. The stony faces gave him little comfort. He decided to sweeten the pot. "And other things, too. I can keep you busy. Full-time work."

Riley glanced about at the bustling store. "Want us to kill everyone in town, George?" he countered sarcastically.

"No, no," the little man protested. "Just one. The rest is running off lot jumpers. It's a full time job; believe me."

"What's a lot jumper?" Nathan asked. His drink was still untouched, a fact not unnoticed by either Belt or Riley. The

82

storekeeper retrieved Nathan's drink and started to pour it back into his bottle, but Riley snatched the glass from his hand and drank it with a Cheshire grin.

"Squatters, that's who. Hendricks and I have staked this whole town. We own the biggest and best parcels, and now stampeders are jumping onto our lots. Why, if we don't drive them off, they put up a shack in a day and claim it's theirs. There's been gunplay!" He poured himself another drink only to find Riley's glass held under his nose.

"We're partners," Riley explained. "But I do the drinking for *both* of us when it suits the occasion." He waggled his glass until it was refilled.

"And robbery, too!"

"They caught you with yer finger on the scale, did they?" Riley chuckled.

Belt shook his head vigorously. "Not me. Miners' pokes and grubstakes are being snatched in broad daylight. We're trying hard to make this a decent town. There are plans of building a railroad, we've already got the telegraph, and the riverboats—"

"You mentioned a killing," Nathan interrupted. It didn't take a banker's mind to realize that a stable town with commerce so close to the goldfields would only boost the value of these traders' lands. "Who are you talking about?"

Belt glanced about nervously, then placed his lips near Nathan's ear. "E. T. Barnette," he whispered.

"Barnette!" Riley snapped. "That polecat. Ain't nobody lynched him yet?"

"Not hardly. He's growing more prosperous by the minute. All because of his damned luck. When his boat was stuck with his near-worthless goods, I offered to buy them off him—and for a fair price. And do you know what he did?" Belt's face glowed with righteous indignation.

"I'll wager he didn't kiss you," Riley countered. The three glasses of whiskey simmered inside his gut and loosened his general dislike for these captains of commerce who plagued him, changing and civilizing his world no matter how far he fled. Now they were at it again, even extending into the swamps and creeks of the Tanana Valley.

"He threw Hendricks and me overboard!"

"So you want him killed for giving you a bath?" Nathan chuckled. Riley's insolent attitude was infectious.

"Look. This is business," Belt protested in exasperation. "Barnette will ruin us. He plans on strangling Chena town until his Fairbanks is the only place left. He's got hired guns working for him, so I need them, too."

"Sounds like the Lincoln County range wars all over again," Riley said. He squinted through the pall of smoke that hung in the air at the smudged windows. Spruce-covered hills back from the river waited with stoic patience to be cut down for cabins and firewood. Bald patches of clearcut land glared back from the hillside like raw scalp from a bad haircut. Suddenly the gunman felt old beyond his years.

"He's got to be stopped, and I want you two to—"

Suddenly Belt stiffened like a man in apoplexy. His words cut off in midsentence while his face snapped into a wooden smile. Nathan turned to look at what had frightened the storekeeper. Another man stood in the doorway, glancing about with impatience. While he was merely average in height, his air of authority coupled with the thick beaver coat he wore exuded an impression of power. A dark bristle mustache cloaked his upper lip and spilled over to droop along the corners of his lip, giving his mouth a stern scowl. He stood with his deep-set eyes darting about and his chin set at an imperious angle.

"Judge Wickersham!" Belt exclaimed. He rushed to greet his visitor with outstretched hands. "What a pleasant surprise!"

"So that's why Belt is all duded up," Riley spoke out of the side of his mouth to Nathan. "He was expecting this legal hebull. Imagine that, a judge here in this swamp settlement. Now I know civilization has struck."

George Belt shook the judge's hand vigorously with both of his, but Wickersham showed little enthusiasm in returning the clasp. His sharp eyes settled on the two men Belt was talking to, and he pushed past the trader to approach them.

Nathan noted with concern that the crowd parted for the judge. "Sort of like Moses and the Red Sea," he quipped to Riley.

The lubricated old gunman snorted just as Wickersham reached them.

"Do you find something amusing about me?" the judge asked sternly.

Riley shook his head, but the silly grin widened as he looked down at this man. Beneath his fur coat Wickersham wore a white, starched wing collar like Belt's with a somber cravat. Despite the judge's meticulous dress, the omnipresent mud from the streets coated his boots and speckled his trousers. The word *popinjay* kept running through the gunman's thoughts, and that prevented him from keeping a straight face.

Belt hastened to defuse the situation. "Ah, Judge Wickersham, may I present Nathan Blaylock and Jim Riley. Ah, acquaintances of mine. Boys, this is Judge James Wickersham of the U.S. District Court. One of the three judges appointed to Alaska."

"I thought the courts were in Juneau, Nome, and Eagle?" Nathan asked. He recalled the corrupt Judge Alfred Noyes, who had teamed with McKenzie to form the Spoilers, who ran roughshod over Nome until federal marshals arrested McKenzie. That experience left Nathan with little love for these political appointees.

"I'm moving the court," Wickersham announced. "I am the law here, now."

Riley wiped his nose on the back of his hand. "Last fellow I heard say that was Pat Garrett, and he got hisself shot to death taking a piss."

"Ah . . . ah." Belt issued a strangled plea.

Wickersham drew himself up to his full height. "I was personally appointed to this post by President McKinley himself. I am the U.S. district judge for this region. That makes me the most powerful person here."

"McKinley got hisself shot, too, Yer Honor," Riley persisted.

Richard Parry

"No offense intended, but ain't Teddy the president now?"

"Yes," the judge replied slowly. "And I'm still the district judge. What do you two men do? You don't look like miners to me. In fact, you have the look of gunmen."

"We know which end of the tube the bullet comes out of, if that's what you mean," Riley answered.

"There's no room for hired killers in my district."

Nathan stepped in front of his prickly partner. "Excuse my friend, Your Honor; he's forgotten his manners. We've been trapping for most of the year; and being that long in the wilderness, he forgets he belongs to the human race. And we do mine for gold at times. We had a claim once in Dawson back in '98. If the opportunity presents itself, we might stake a claim here as well—assuming there's no law against doing so."

Wickersham studied the pale eyes that stared unblinking at him. The man's face looked disturbingly familiar, but he couldn't place him. "I accept your apology, er, what was it? Babcock?"

"Blaylock."

"Quite so. Blaylock." The young man had not risen to the bait as the judge had expected. He made a mental note to watch these two. Clearly, this Blaylock was the more dangerous of the two.

"Ah, what can I do to help you, Judge?" Belt found his tongue.

Wickersham turned toward the owner but kept his eyes fixed on Nathan as he spoke. "I came to notify you, Mr. Belt, that I have reached a decision as to where to place my court."

Belt looked as if he might faint. "Here? In Chena?" he asked hopefully.

"Sorry, I've decided against Chena City. I shall locate the court in Fairbanks."

"Fairbanks!" Belt croaked. "Please, no!"

"I'm afraid so. If you and Mr. Hendricks had laid out a proper town plot like Fairbanks has and not laid claim to all the land yourself, my decision might have been different. As it is,

86

this town is a mess without proper streets and without a proper city plan."

"Barnette staked land, too!" Belt protested.

"Only three hundred fifty square feet by the river, not the entire quarter section you two grabbed. There's no suitable land to build here, lest one buys it from you."

"The free land Barnette gave you to build your courthouse didn't color your decision, did it?" Belt shouted. His voice had grown high-pitched and shrill, and he was standing on his tip-toes to make his point. "Or the *free* land he gave your brother! Or the fact he named his stinking town Fairbanks after your po-litical patron, the senator of Indiana!?"

"My decision is final. If you would be so kind as to inform the other members of your committee, I would appreciate it," Wickersham added formally. He spun on his heel and marched out.

Belt watched the door slam shut, and his shoulders sagged. After a moment of silence, he swung around to face the two men. "All the more reason for Barnette to have some sort of ac-cident," he snarled. "Without him, Fairbanks will dry up and blow away. Wickersham will have to move his district court here after all. I can't wait to see that swell come crawling back on his hands and knees." Buoyed by that mental image, the trader regained his composure. Instantly his mind set to calculating how cheaply he could get by with eliminating his rival. "One thousand, apiece," he decided out loud.

Riley looked at Nathan, who said nothing, but Belt misin-terpreted their silence.

"Two thousand each."

Nathan shook his head. "I don't think so," he said slowly. Already the young man realized there was no good side to this fight. Both sides were bad.

"Ten thousand, tops. That's my final offer. Barnette's not the damned president of the United States, you know. He's just a two-bit storekeeper for Christ's sake!"

"Like you, George?" Nathan replied. "No, we're not interested. Thank you for your generous offer, but Jim and I plan on trying our luck at the digs—like I told the judge. We're sort of retired from 'regulating.' "

With that Nathan took hold of his partner's sleeve and guided him through the throng and out the door, leaving the astonished Belt with his mouth still hanging open.

Riley sucked in a lungful of cold spring air and wiped the smoke from his eyes. He shrugged philosophically. "We could've used the ten thousand for a grubstake," he said flatly. "And it ain't like Barnette is our friend or nothin'. Why, when we show up in his burg, I'd be surprised if he don't run us off or try to shoot us himself."

Nathan picked up his pack and searched inside for the few coins he had. "We're not assassins, Jim. If Barnette forces a fight—well, that'd be something else, but you never taught me to be a bushwhacker."

Riley pursed his lips. "Yer right, pard. I'm glad you remember all them high-and-mighty principles. I sometimes forget when my old bones get to complaining about the cold. Ten thousand to kill a skunk would buy me a lot of nice rocking chairs."

"What would you do in a rocking chair, Jim?" Nathan chided his friend.

"Well, I could find a good-looking nurse to rock me . . . and speaking of pretty gals, look what's coming this way. That sweet young thing is prettier than a newborn heifer." Riley gestured with his head in the direction of the river.

Coming toward them was a vision of sunshine. A young woman threaded her way along the packed boardwalk, walking carefully to avoid the loose boards and piles of mud that covered the springy planks. A plain straw hat rode atop a mass of golden curls that hung about her ears and rolled down the back of her neck. The spring sunlight made her hair glow like spun gold, and her topaz eyes sparkled with joy at this pleasant day. The dark print dress she wore was prim and proper but did little to hide her narrow waist and the curves that threatened to burst free from the confines of the fabric. Beneath her left arm she carried a parcel wrapped in brown paper and tied with a length of twine. A tiny gold watch, pinned to her bodice, was the only jewelry she wore.

"And she's wearing one of them watch pins fer timing the fellas!" Riley exclaimed. He jabbed his elbow into Nathan's ribs excitedly. "Remember our discussion on the trail? She's got to be one of them sporting ladies."

Instantly Nathan straightened up. He removed his fur hat and patted at the mass of unruly hair on his head, but his efforts only attracted more static, causing his dark strands to splay on end like an angry grizzly. As an afterthought he swiped his coat sleeve across his dirty face.

"It's a fine day, ma'am," he said with a half-bow as the woman approached.

She returned his greeting with a dazzling smile that dashed what little courage Nathan had mustered. But her smile turned to a look of puzzlement when he stood there tongue-tied.

"Yes, it is," she said when the silence grew more embarrassing. "May I help you?"

Only a sharp nudge from Riley loosened Nathan's tongue. "Ah, ah . . ."

"Yes?" She cocked her head to study Nathan with an amused smile.

"Well," he stammered as he looked hard at the toes of his mukluks. He kept his eyes averted lest her beauty rob him of his courage. "Well, we were wondering how much you charge?"

The blow from her parcel caught him completely by surprise.

Riley scurried to help his friend up from the street where the impact had knocked him. A dazed Nathan rubbed the welt on his cheek and felt blood. The corner of the package had split open the knife scar from Sergeant Muller's attack. From his position in a soggy rut in the road Nathan watched the back of the woman as she strode angrily away. He cast a puzzled look at his friend.

"Maybe I got that part about the watch backwards," Riley said tentatively.

"But you said—"

Riley helped his befuddled friend up. "I know what I said! But, you ought to know better than to trust my advice where women is concerned. What the hell do I know about women? I've spent all my life sleeping in a saddle or hiding out from posses," he added defensively.

"I guess your idea about the watch is wrong. She didn't act like a sporting woman," Nathan said.

"She ain't no sporting woman, you young fool!" A grizzled miner laughed down at them. "Can't you tell the difference? She's the librarian in Fairbanks." He ducked into a saloon, still laughing, before the two could react.

"Oh, Lord," Riley moaned. "Now you've gone and done it! You insulted the prettiest gal in this whole valley and fixed it so's I can't get no books from the town library."

★ ★ EIGHT ★ ★

While the sudden appearance of a town at the mouth of the Chena shocked the two wanderers, the even greater change on that shadow-laden bank seven miles up the same river astounded them. Barnette's Trading Post was as they last remembered, with few added embellishments. But spreading out from that stockade over the knoll was a town of at least five hundred. Three streets, little more than rut-scoured, muddy tracts and studded with unpulled stumps, ran parallel to the river and embraced Barnette's stockade.

A two-story square frame building, sporting the name "Fairbanks Hotel," rose from the east side of the trading post. It was half-finished, its windows still being cut. On its right, lined up shoulder-to-shoulder, were four saloons, the Tanana, the Lacey, the Eagle, and the Senate, each proudly proclaiming its name in painted letters across its flat storefront. To the left, sod-roofed log cabins followed the curve of the river to end with a tin-covered warehouse with a single freight door. N.C. CO. was painted in red letters above the entrance.

Nathan and Riley strolled along the bank in a daze while men bustled about them, carrying rolls of canvas and skidding logs to the sawmill that filled the once-quiet air with the whine of its sawblade and belched smoke into the air. Those fumes mingled with the soot rising from the funnel of the *Isabelle* tied alongside. The boomtown's construction had erased every sign of vegetation from the riverbank, creating a stark moonscape of mud and reworked silt. Resting along this mire, gangplanks and boarding ladders poked into the air, and deep ditches ran from the river to drain the hovels.

Nathan paused to step around a refuse pile of sheet metal and wire cable. His eyes drifted along the roads where canvas tents and log shacks sprawled away from the river to bump into the dark strands of yet-uncleared forests.

"Maybe we should kill Barnette after all," he said half-heartedly. "Look what he's done to this place. It looks like one giant garbage dump. But I'm afraid it wouldn't do any good. The damage is done."

"Twern't him alone," Riley added. "It's the yellow metal madness for sure. Look over yonder." He gestured with his head at the low-lying hills across the river that surrounded the Chena with gentle folds like a carelessly tossed blanket.

Where spruce and birch forests once battled for supremacy on the hillsides a stark vision greeted them. Vast swatches of tree stumps stood like mute headstones amid trees and branches scattered like jackstraws. Shacks and sluice boxes covered the opened ground, and a hundred plumes of smoke rose into the blue sky until a perpetual haze filled the valley. As far as the eye could see, the process repeated itself.

"It's the gold all right," Riley continued. "They're thawing the ground for their placer mines just like in Dawson. Can't dig until the ground is soft. You remember them mines, don't you, Nat?" The old gunman shivered. Nothing in all his years on the open plain could prepare him for the suffocating confines of mining. He hated it more than anything he could recall. Worse, he feared it.

"How could I forget?" Nathan breathed. The cold, dark, twisting tunnels, dripping slime and dirt and sucking at his boots as he churned the floor into quicksand, still haunted him in his dreams. It was madness indeed that drove men underground for the yellow metal, but it was a madness born of desperation and poverty and greed. Gold dust and nuggets gave a man a false sense of immortality and power that could drive back the terrors of the mine. With the yellow metal, a man could achieve instant status. With gold he could be some-thing—someone. Nathan straightened his shoulders and shook his head to clear those thoughts. Greed had driven him belowground once, and he feared it might do so again.

Riley read his thoughts. "Gold fever and all its craziness wrecked many a poor boy's life and it looks about to ruin this spot on earth."

In more of a daze, the two men trod down the rutted path along the river's edge, passing an angled sign that proclaimed the road as FIRST AVENUE. They paused to gaze at the Northern Commercial Company's new building before walking past Bar-nette's stockade.

Riley elbowed his friend in the ribs. "Maybe we ought to drop in and pay our respects to the captain and his lady," he joshed, adding a lecherous wink. "As I recall, she was kind of sweet on you, Nat. Couldn't keep her hands off you, now that I think of it."

Nathan bristled. "Yeah, and neither could the captain, for that reason. But he wanted to string us up. You ought to recall that, too."

Riley nodded good-naturedly to two teamsters as they strug-gled through the main gate with a roll of tar paper. "Serves you right for humping his wife. He had every right to hang you," he chuckled.

"I was younger then," Nathan protested. "I've grown older and wiser. I'd do things differently now."

"Oh, yeah? Older by a year or two! What would you do dif-ferently?"

"I sure as hell wouldn't get caught," Nathan replied seri-ously.

Riley burst into a fit of laughter and dragged his friend into the Lacey saloon, two doors down from the banging and sawing of the budding Fairbanks Hotel. If he expected to be greeted by miners delirious with gold fever, he found himself sorely mistaken. A dozen glum faces turned to study the new arrivals. Their sour looks matched the dark bands of dirt and grime streaking their faces. Three men turned back to the bar to stare sullenly into their half-finished beers. Only the bartender looked pleased at their visit.

"By God!" a voice bellowed from a dark corner. "It's Nat and Jim. Now our luck will change! Let me buy you a drink, boys."

Nathan turned just in time to catch a solid slap on his back from Doc Hennison while Riley dodged the arm meant for him by turning with his back to the bar.

"Doc, I might have suspected you'd be here. How'd you get here? Last we saw of you was that night they tried to hang Wada the Jap in Dawson."

"You vanished like a scalded polecat," Riley muttered, fending off Hennison's advances. "We could've used an extra hand with that mob."

"I'm allergic to lynch mobs, as you two well know," Hennison sniffed. "I thought it wise to take my leave before those upstanding citizens decided to look for someone else to string up. Besides, you two were doing just fine. I see they didn't hang either of you, and I know Wada escaped because he's working for Barnette."

With the mention of the captain's name a collective groan issued from the miners. Nathan watched the negative impact Barnette's name had on these men out of the corner of his eye. Riley, too, noted the effect.

Only Doc raised his voice as he pointed to his friends. "Like I said," he shouted, "things are on the upturn now that my pards are here!"

"I sure hope so." A giant man at the far corner came to life. He wore a dusty mackinaw with the sleeves cut off above the elbow tucked into tin pants and a shapeless black fedora. "They can't get much worse. The diggings here are terrible, wicked hard."

"Ya, wicked hard," the man to his right elbow agreed. His voice carried a thick Swedish accent. "And the captain makes it harder."

Doc's head bobbed in agreement. "This town is cinched up by Barnette tighter than a belt on a starving man. He controls everything—lock, stock, and barrel."

The giant drifted over to the three, drawn by Doc's promise of luck exuding from the two tired gunmen. "The worst digs I ever saw. There's isn't a creek producing paystreak that Barnette's not already got staked. The lucky bastard rushed out and laid claim to the best as soon as Felix Pedro make his strike. The rest of us are forced to set drift mines."

"Well, Dawson was the same way," Nathan answered. He accepted a foamy mug of beer from the bartender.

The giant shook his head, causing the edges of his fedora to flap like tired wings. "Worse. Much worse than Dawson. I worked a claim in the Klondike and this is much harder. Here the gold veins run a hundred feet underground. You spend all your time chopping wood and tending a fire just to thaw out the frozen muck. You can thaw six, maybe ten inches of muck a day—twelve on a good day. And then, after you've moiled your way down to bedrock, chances are you'll find a cold hole with no color."

Riley looked around in amazement. "You mean to tell me all this frenzy is for naught? There's no gold?"

"No, not for naught, friend," the big man responded. "There's gold here, maybe more than was ever dug in the Klondike, but it's the devil's luck if you can find it. And the devil to pay to get it out."

"He means all this takes time and money," Doc interpreted. "Time and money. Their time and their money to buy supplies from Barnette." He hung his head over the bar. "That leaves nothing for recreational card games. Meaning, nothing for me."

More miners joined the discussion. The big man continued his list of grievances. "Barnette is hauling one to two boatloads of supplies a week on his cursed *Isabelle,* yet he says he's short of supplies. What's more, he won't sell flour or beans by themselves. You have to buy his damned tins of pickled beets or rotted bully beef. Four cans for each five-pound sack of flour."

"Why don't you buy your goods from Chena?" Nathan asked. "It's only seven miles downriver."

"Young fellow," a gray-haired miner spoke up. "Belt and Hendricks are just as bad. Besides, they won't sell to us from Fairbanks. 'Buy your grub where you built your cabin' is the saying in Chena. They want us to fail so their town gets the railroad and Fairbanks dries up."

The big man, whose name was Iverson, shook his head sadly. "That might just happen. The river's so low the boats are running aground before they get here. Only the *Isabelle* can make the trip, and not all the time at that."

A low rumbling cut further discussion short. It rose steadily, coming down the street until the noise poured into the entrance of the saloon with the arrival of a dozen flushed and angry faces. These men shoved their way into the bar and stood there with ax handles and wooden clubs in their hands. Nathan noticed that many of the men wore revolvers strapped to their sides or carried lever-action .30-30s. Their faces were flushed and dripped sweat even in the cold room. A strong smell of alcohol, liberally imbibed for liquid courage, filled the crowded space.

"Are you coming, boys?" a voice in the crowd beckoned. "We're headed to Barnette's." The speaker shook a stout length of rope already fashioned into a hangman's noose. "If he won't sell us flour without his damned spoiled tins, we'll make him swing for it. Then, we'll take what we want! What about you, Iverson? Are you with us?"

Without waiting for an answer, the mob swept out the door and headed in the direction of Barnette's stockade.

Nathan arched his eyebrow as he looked at Riley. The gunman was calmly finishing his beer while Doc had ducked behind the bar for protection. Blaylock swept the mob with a practiced eye. While emotions ran high in the mob, Nathan knew it would take more than whiskey, hard words, and a few barrel staves to best E. T. Barnette, let alone pry supplies from his grasping fingers. None of the men looked able to shoot straight. These were miners and tradesmen, not hard cases that would buckle down with the first whiff of gunsmoke.

An alarm sounded in the back of Nathan's mind. Barnette *had* hard cases in his pay. And they wouldn't hesitate to shoot. If these men stormed the stockade, it would be a bloodbath.

"Maybe we ought to go along, Jim?" Nathan suggested. "Just to see that the captain plays fair. What do you say?"

"Damn! There you go again," Riley complained. He preferred to look longingly at the last of his beer instead of at this rabble of citizenry. Clearly, none of them could hit the side of a barn, even from inside. Still, lesser men than these had cleared the plains of the worst outlaws the West had seen, many of whom had been Riley's friends. It rankled the old expert that men of his trade had been overwhelmed by sheer numbers of these liquored buffoons rather than bested by skill and cunning. "I say leave them to their just desserts," he grumbled. "These fools are growed men, and that entitles them to get their dang heads shot off if they're stupid enough. Besides, we ain't no gol-derned referees. They's just as liable to shoot us by mistake rather than Barnette's boys if we ain't behind sensible cover."

"You're right, Jim, of course," Nathan said soothingly. "All the same, I think I'll poke along just to see if the old captain has grown a new set of horns since our last encounter. But you stay here and keep Doc company." He opened his parka and tightened his gunbelt before following the crowd.

Riley sighed. He hadn't lived this long by being bold or foolish. Old and bold never went together when describing a man whose occupation involved throwing lead. But Riley could never abandon his friend. Each owed the other his life a hundred times over. And something in the gunman had changed. Before he'd met Nathan, he would not have wasted a spit over that entire mob. But now he would defend the whole passel to help his partner. He must be getting soft in the head as well as old, the gunfighter allowed. With another sigh, Jim Riley cinched his own belt and followed his friend.

Riley caught up with Nathan standing at the back of the mob watching the events unfold. Clustering around the closed gates of the stockade, the protesters were yelling and waving lighted torches at the wall of sharpened spruce stakes. Atop the barrier, ten men, each with a lever-action Winchester, glared down at the miners.

To Riley's chagrin, a grizzled miner with a full beard and fuzzy white hair was standing out from the crowd to harangue the guards. Seemingly fearless, the old man spewed invectives and shook his fists at his adversaries with total disregard for their weapons. Adding to Riley's unease, he noted the white-haired man's words were having an effect. Several had trained their rifles on the old man with grim determination, and more than one guard's face carried the look of someone about to exterminate a pest.

Riley stopped at Nathan's side and commented on the red shirt the bearded man wore, "They ain't gonna shoot Santa Claus, are they?"

"I hope not," Nathan replied. "He's not armed."

"Not with no gun, but his tongue is sure having an effect. Who is that jasper, anyway? He don't look like no dirt miner to me."

"Haven't you met old Ezra, yet? You must be new in town." A man in the crowd turned to answer Riley's question. "He's Ezra Hayes, and you're right, friend; he's no miner. He's the editor of the *Fairbanks Daily Times.*"

Nathan studied the man in disbelief. "This place has a newspaper!?"

"Three of them," came the reply. "The *Fairbanks News* and the *Tanana Miner* are the other two. Of course, those two are in Barnette's back pocket. But not old Ezra. He hates the captain like poison and says so every chance he gets in his editorials."

"Seems like a sensible man," Riley smirked. The gunman's words were cut short when he saw Nathan pushing his way to the front of the mob. "Whoa there, Nat! Where do you think you're going? The safe place is back here."

Nathan called over his shoulder, "It would be a shame to lose someone who agrees with us! Especially an editor of the newspaper!" The young man worked his way forward until he came to stand beside the red-faced editor. Only then did he realize what fueled the old man's courage. A strong whiff of whiskey confirmed why the speaker's face was so red. He was seriously drunk.

"Better put old Ezra to bed, sonny!" one of the guards shouted down at Nathan. "He looks like he's got a real toot on, and he's liable to get himself accidentally shot."

A chorus of jeers rolled down from the wall. Which only aggravated Ezra. He jerked his arm away from Nathan and staggered forward in a widely placed stance.

"Go ahead and shoot, you low-down rascals. I'm unarmed, and that's the way you like it best, isn't it," Hayes challenged while his fists battered the air. He turned his back to them. "Try my back. You scum are skilled at backshooting, I hear. Try mine."

"Don't tempt us, old man!" a voice snarled.

"Mr. Hayes," Nathan spoke softly as he attempted to reason with the editor, "this isn't wise. Step back, please."

To his amazement, Hayes slyly winked at him. The move was so quick and unexpected from a man Nathan assumed was staggering drunk that it caught him completely off guard. At first he thought his eyes had deceived him. But Hayes repeated the wink, again so subtly that only Nathan was the wiser. Certainly none of those on top of the barricade noticed.

"Easy, lad," the editor whispered. "I'm not that drunk. In vino veritas!" He lurched to one side. " 'Shoot upon this old gray head,' " he quoted. "Have no fear. Judge Wickersham will set you free. After all, that political crony wouldn't want the captain to take away his new jail or kick him out of his cozy room in the trading post." Hayes spit on the ground in disgust.

"Why are you doing this?" Nathan whispered back.

Ezra Hayes swiveled his head just enough to reply. His words slipped from the corner of his crooked smile with all the skill of a consummate ventriloquist. "Because it's the truth.

Barnette needs to be exposed. And what better forum than this. Half these men can't read, and the other half are too busy mining, but they all have ears! Besides," the old man added, "it's damn good advertising. It might sell more papers."

"Don't be so sure they won't shoot," Nathan warned. The hairs on the back of his neck tingled as he saw a familiar figure dressed in black leathers edging his way along the parapet. A wide-brimmed black hat covered the man's face in shadow until he tipped it up to reveal a weasel face. Their eyes met and locked on one another while the man smiled savagely.

Billy Wilson was in town.

"Stand aside, Blaylock!" Wilson commanded. "I'm going to put a bullet in this old coot. His jawing hurts my ears."

"You missed us that night in Dawson," Nathan snarled. "That was a big mistake, Billy." While he talked, he edged in front of Hayes, shielding him with his body.

As Jim Riley desperately fought his way through the tightly packed throng his blood chilled when he caught sight of Billy Wilson. That killer held a Winchester while both their rifles still rested back in the Lacey saloon. The gunfighter rued this careless lapse. Getting old and foolish, he cursed. But then, how was he to know that Nathan would become the point man for these dirt pushers? You ought to have known, you fool, he scolded himself. How long had he ridden with Nathan not to realize he loved lost causes? Frantically Riley searched about in the milling mass of men for another rifle, something to even the odds. None were within grasp, and the excited crowd was packed so tightly that he was unable to move toward those that held rifles. His friend was isolated. His foot stumbled against something, producing a clinking sound, and he looked down to see a half-empty bottle of *Doctor Hennison's Wonder Elixir* buried in the mud. Nathan had no chance against Billy Wilson and that long gun, unless . . .

Nathan, too, realized his precarious position. While the others who held rifles and worked for Barnette were mainly hired hands, Wilson was not. He was a cold-blooded killer. His addition to this equation raised the stakes considerably. Laborers and teamsters with rifles might not shoot, but Wilson would.

With icy precision, Nathan weighed his options. A good ten feet separated the editor and him from the safety of the crowd. Wilson would pick them off before they could cover the distance. Besides, Nathan preferred not to be shot in the back. To either side, the ground was cleared for the entire length of First Avenue. The churned mud offered no cover. A pile of lumber was stacked, half-submerged, in the slime too far to his left to be of value. The closest cover was in front.

The last thing Wilson will expect is for me to move toward him. He smiled inwardly when he looked back at the grinning Wilson. Overconfidence will get you killed Billy, he mused. *You haven't cocked the hammer of your Winchester, yet.*

Nathan's left heel slid backward until it made contact with Ezra Hayes's boot toe. He ground his heel into the man's shoe, hoping the pain would hold his attention. A grunt of pain rewarded Nathan's efforts, and Hayes stopped his haranguing.

"Listen, carefully," Nathan spoke. He held his voice low, but his words and tone carried the impact of a .45 bullet. "Get ready to jump forward. When I move, you move with me. Quick as you can. . . ."

Now all he needed was a diversion.

A flaming object like a shooting star shot high into the blue sky from the body of the mob. Sailing across the gap that separated those men from the stockade in a burning arc that caught everyone's attention, the fiery trail rose to its apogee, paused in the glittering sunlight for an instant before crashing into the side of the wooden barrier. A burst of flame spread across the spruce poles.

In that instant, Nathan sprang forward and clamped a steely grip on Wilson's right hand, fusing fingers and rifle together. He jerked viciously, and the astonished Wilson lurched over the parapet behind his rifle.

A split second was all it took Nathan to complete his move. When Barnette's distracted guards looked back from the fire now burning part of their cover, they saw their leader, Billy

Wilson, now a human shield, struggling with his own rifle held clamped across his neck in a choke hold. Directly behind him crouched Nathan, his pistol thrust into the side of Wilson's head. Behind them, Ezra Hayes pressed into the flat of Blaylock's back. No one could shoot without hitting Billy Wilson.

For a long minute, neither side moved. The shocked guards gawked at their helpless leader, the side of the stockade burned merrily, and the miners stood in stunned silence. Then E. T. Barnette's fur cap rose above the barricade. He glanced quickly at the fire destroying his wall before casting a long look at the captive Wilson. Barnette's eyes fastened on Nathan, and a glimmer of recognition lit his face. He grunted, more in annoyance than in alarm, as one would at a mosquito bite rather than at a charging bear.

"Blaylock," he snapped. "Is this your work? Are you burning down my store?"

"Call off your hired guns, Captain," Nathan answered. "Settle this dispute peacefully."

Barnette contemplated the offer. His head bobbed in agreement. "Okay. I can't fight these miners and the fire at the same time. What do they want?"

"Fair prices and freedom to choose!" Hayes suddenly sobered and jumped upright. "No more forcing them to buy rotten cans with their flour and rice."

Barnette shrugged. "I was only trying to distribute my goods evenly so that every miner could have an even grubstake. But, I guess, if you boys are grown-up enough to want to lynch me, you're grown-up enough to plan ahead for the winter. Okay, I'll cut the price of flour in half. You can buy as much as you want—without buying any canned goods." His voice hardened. "This store is a business, not a charity. It won't be my fault if I'm sold out of flour by the end of the week. You asked for it! Now help my boys put out that goddamned fire you started, and I'll open the gates."

A wild cheer went up from the crowd. Rifles clattered to the dirt, and the men rushed down to the edge of the river to form a bucket brigade. In minutes, streams of water-laden buckets flowed up from the bank to splash against the fire.

Barnette watched as the flames vanished in a swirl of smoke. He cocked his head to receive a message from one of his men. The report was as he hoped. Two-thirds of his precious flour bags were safely hidden. As the gates swung open, E. T. Barnette nodded in satisfaction. He would triple the price again when the rivers froze. . . .

NINE

"The man's a liar and a thief!" Ezra Hayes pounded the palm of his hand with his fist for emphasis. "He runs this town like some . . . some medieval fiefdom. But we bested him this time, by God, thanks to these two strangers."

The crowd of miners packed the small office of the *Daily Times* just off Third Avenue, fighting for room next to the antiquated printing press and rows of type that overflowed into the space. Save for a potbellied woodstove in the back and an apple crate that served as a cramped desk, the press was the sole furnishing. Faded pictures of Abraham Lincoln and George Washington were all that covered the wall. A gallon of coffee bubbling in a dented pot on top of the stove added its nutty fragrance to the mix of sweaty bodies and cigar smoke.

Nathan, Doc, and Jim Riley stood, back-to-back for self-protection from the backslaps of their admirers, and sipped the thick brew from equally battered cups. Hayes had insisted on a party at his newspaper office, and Doc joined the celebration as soon as he discovered the flaming bomb that turned the tables was his very own and highly flammable elixir for everything.

"What made you think of using Doc's snake oil?" Ezra asked Riley.

"Well, I've had experience with Doc's brew before," Riley added modestly. His fingers drummed nervously on the sides of his tin cup. A lifetime of being on the run left him ill-prepared for such adulation.

"You two are just what we need to go against Barnette,"

Hayes urged. "None of us can handle a gun. But, by God, you can!" He slapped Nathan's shoulder for emphasis. "I never saw anyone move as fast as you did, son. You got your pistol out quicker than greased lightning!"

The young man smiled sheepishly. Such praise seemed undeserved. What he had done was foolish, and only luck and Riley's quick thinking had saved him.

His old friend reminded him of that fact. He leaned over, and with a cold, fixed smile on his unshaven face he whispered to Nathan. "Don't never do nothing so stupid as that again. You forgot everything I taught you."

Nathan grimaced in agreement. "Got my ass stuck in a bear trap, didn't I?"

The door pushed open until its knob clattered against a box of type, and two miners elbowed their way into the room. "We've been swindled by Barnette, again!" one shouted.

An immediate silence descended on the room. Heads swiveled toward the newcomers like noses sniffing a scent while Hayes pushed to their side.

"What do you mean, swindled?" the editor asked.

Feet shuffled nervously in the silence.

"Barnette's sold out of flour already!" the one man cried. His response drew an immediate chorus of groans. Flour was the basic staple of each stampeder's Spartan diet, the one ingredient necessary for the sourdough that they lived on. Without flour, they could not mine.

"Half his shelves were already empty when we got inside," the man explained. "Gone. Empty. And he says he doesn't expect another shipment until freeze-up. We're finished."

Hayes waved his fist in the air. "The skunk! He stashed the rest! I just know it. We ought to go back there and tear down his stockade, stick by stick, until we find the rest of his stores."

"Hold on!" Nathan shouted over the noise. He had little faith his luck would hold twice on the same day. "Barnette will expect that. He's probably cached his food where we'll never find it."

The door to the office opened, again. To the amazement

of everyone, the object of their distaste, Capt. E. T. Barnette himself, stepped inside flanked by Billy Wilson and Ben Atwater, the muscular employee who claimed to be the world's strongest man. Barnette strode in with the cocky self-assurance of the victor that he was, adding a touch of swagger to his walk while his fur cap sat at a rakish angle on his head. He paused to survey the group, then headed directly toward Ezra Hayes. A path opened through the miners as though a leper walked among them. Atwater followed with an embarrassed look, but Wilson glared at the surrounding faces like a rattlesnake mesmerizing a covey of quail.

"Gentlemen." Barnette touched his hat. "I hope I'm not interrupting anything, but I came to inform you that my flour stocks are depleted." He paused to savor this moment, wiping the back of his hand across his full mustache. "As I predicted," he added.

"We already know that," Hayes responded. "And my next edition will accuse you of deliberately hiding your goods."

Barnette's eyebrows shot upward in mock surprise, but Nathan noted a twitch by the corner of his left eye that betrayed his hatred for this newsman. "I thought as much, old man," he said. "That's one reason I came down to this rag you call a newspaper. Let me remind you: printing that story without proof would be most unwise. The judge takes a dim view of libelous editorials."

"Obviously, neither of you have read the Bill of Rights!" Hayes snapped. "This is still a territory of the United States, in case you've forgotten, and freedom of the press is a guaranteed right."

"Nothin's guaranteed except what the capt'n says it is!" Wilson snapped. His public humiliation still smarted, prompting him to be all the more vicious and unpredictable.

"Suit yourself," Barnette answered. He turned to leave, sauntering to the door, where he paused. "Oh, here's a piece of news for your rag. I've named the two cross streets Lacey and Cushman after friends of Judge Wickersham, and that building at the corner of Third and Cushman that is progressing so well is to be the new jail. Judge Wickersham has appointed his brother, Edgar, deputy U.S. marshal."

A collective groan filled the office.

Barnette savored the moment before letting his other bombshell fall. "And I've sold my trading post to the Northern Commercial Company. You'll have to deal with them from now on, and I doubt you'll find them as soft as I was in the credit department."

Hayes hooted derisively. "I never realized you had so droll a wit, Captain. I hope this sale means you'll be taking the lovely Mrs. Barnette south to more civilized climes?"

Barnette lips widened into a serpentine smile. "Not really, Ezra. But I do need something to occupy my time. Luckily, I've been appointed the new postmaster."

With that last barb, the captain slammed the door and strode back to his stockade, leaving the men in the *Daily Times* office staring at each other in stunned silence.

"That does it, then," someone groaned. "We might as well pack it in. Ain't no way we can fight the judge, the captain, and the marshal all at the same time."

Nathan sought out the speaker. "Why can't you keep on mining in spite of what Barnette said?" he asked.

"Because, mister, we ain't got the wherewithall, that's why. We ain't got the money to buy the captain's overpriced grub for the length of time it takes to dig to bedrock. The pay dirt in this damned valley is deeper than anything we ever saw around Dawson. It's over a hundred feet down in most places. It takes a man and his partner weeks to thaw out the frozen muck just to get to the color. We got to have supplies during that time, rope, kerosene to start green spruce fires, nails, and most of all food. We got to eat. And until we hit the gold, we got no way of paying for those things. Especially without Barnette giving us credit."

Ezra Hayes placed his hand on Nathan's shoulder. "He's right. Half the men here are just sitting around, staring down at their unfinished shafts, for want of supplies, and the other half will run out of the necessities before they can reach the gold. Johanssen here has about another week's worth of lamp oil. Without that he's done. Kurt there has run out of rope to tie up his trusses. Each man you see here needs something to keep on going. Barnette sees that his supplies only go to those working on his claims or to his friends, and he's the only store. It's a hopeless situation."

Nathan thought for a moment. An idea formed in his head. He looked at the grim faces surrounding him before asking, "What if everyone worked together and pooled their supplies? Surely, there ought to be enough then to keep some of the mines open."

Hayes chuckled at this man's naïveté. "Gold miners don't work that way, son. They work in twos and threes, keeping their finds secret. Better ask a miner to share his wife than share his stores or his gold. It's just not done."

Nathan persisted. "It can be! I bet most of you worked for the big mining concerns around Dawson after they took over. You can work together."

Most shook their heads. Working for the big companies was something akin to selling one's soul to the Devil. Those that had did so only long enough to scrape together a grub-stake. They loved being independent. The rest lived from hand to mouth on a daily basis, wandering the creeks with their gold pans, ever in search of that elusive creek where the water had done their work for them and nuggets the size of their fists waited to be picked from the icy stream. They showed their distaste for Nathan's idea by shaking their heads, muttering, and turning away from him. Slowly, they shuffled toward the door.

"Wait!" Riley's voice stopped them. "It can be done. Cow-men ain't that different from gold miners."

"What have you been drinking, mister?" Johanssen questioned. "We don't ride no horses! We dig holes. Deep holes under the ground."

"And you're both proud, ornery cusses and independent as hell," the gunman countered.

"Ya. So?"

"So the small cattle owners along the Panhandle had the same problem you jaspers have. They had a few head of cattle with no market. They banded together, added their beeves into a big herd, and drove it to the railheads up north in Kansas. Ain't a single one of them could've got through by his-self, not with the rivers, rustlers, and the redskins. But together they did. A single rancher would have lost his scalp and all his stock."

Johanssen wrinkled his face as he pondered the concept. The others stopped their exodus.

"You miners are just the same. Barnette can chew you up for breakfast, one at a time. Work together and you got him beat. Share yer rope and yer lamp oil and whatever else you need. If you don't you're done for."

Hayes wrapped his arms around both Riley and Nathan in a bear hug and added his support. "Why not, boys? What have you got to lose?"

"We lose our gold, that's what!" someone complained. "I don't want this Swede taking *my* gold."

"It ain't nobody's if it don't never get dug up!" Riley protested. "And it's all going to stay undiscovered until Gabriel blows his horn unless you men can mine."

"How would we do this sharing?" the same skeptic asked. "Whose claim gets worked and whose don't?"

Blaylock thought for a moment. "Draw lots, I guess. Pick four or five claims to all work on together. Make it fair or else it won't work. Divide into groups and work the claims that got picked, and everyone shares their stores and shares whatever gold you find. If the mines pan out, keep working them. If one doesn't, pick another one. At least you'll be able to work this fall and through the winter."

"Let's do it, boys!" Hayes urged. "Barnette can't keep this valley locked up forever. If we stick together, we can break his stranglehold."

"We need a leader. Will you lead us?" Johanssen asked Nathan.

Nathan looked at his friend. All they had wanted was to

pass through Fairbanks to buy supplies. And to satisfy his curiosity. Now he felt the town drawing him into its problems with the relentlessness of the muskeg that surrounded the sloughs.

He knew how much Riley hated digging, how every fiber of his being cried out for a limitless horizon and a big sky over his head. Years ago, a mudslide following a flash flood on a cattle drive had entombed Jim Riley and his horse in an *arroyo* for three days. Buried up to his neck, the young puncher almost went mad before they found him. He never forgot that, never got over the fear of being buried alive. When Nathan, Doc, and Riley worked their claim in Dawson, Riley could scarcely put in a hour's work in the dark shaft. Nathan remembered him coming to the surface dripping with sweat even in the dead of winter. Each minute without the sky for reference was a living hell for his friend.

Nathan looked at Riley. Both men knew this miners' cooperative would fail without a strong leader. But it was too much to ask of his friend. He opened his mouth to refuse.

"Hell, yes, he'll help you," Riley beat him to the punch. "Nat and I'll see you muckers ain't outgunned by Barnette and his regulators. That's one thing we're good at for damned sure. Editor Hayes ought to be in charge of all the paperwork, the divvying up and such. I ain't no decent hand at writing. We wouldn't want none of you fellows getting riled on account you can't read my script." He shrugged offhandedly. "And who knows? We might even strike it rich for once."

The cramped office shook with the cheers of those inside. Runners carried the news to the other miners until the shop was packed and a crowd spilled out onto the darkening street. Lamps were lit while Hayes tallied their resources. Like the parable of the loaves and the fishes, food and supplies multiplied in miraculous fashion. Hard-case miners produced gear hidden for emergencies.

By the first sign of morning, the miners' cooperative had settled on grouping the hundreds of miners on the eight most promising creeks. They would work in shifts, sharing profits and losses until they struck it rich, went bust, or broke Barnette's stranglehold on them. With mixed feelings of gloom and elation, the men shuffled out into the new day to filter back to their shacks. Only the two gunfighters and Ezra Hayes remained.

Nathan pushed back from the littered desk and rubbed his tired eyes. Ezra Hayes snored quietly with his head resting on his typesetting desk. Riley slept as well, curled beside the dying stove with a doormat pulled over him for want of a blanket. Their gear was still by the river, everything they owned save for their weapons. Nathan checked the long-barreled Colt he carried. Now, more than ever, he realized, he and Riley would eat and sleep with pistols by their sides. The captain was not one to forget or forgive.

The young man shuffled outside, taking great care to step over his friend without waking him. Nathan filled his lungs with cold air and rubbed the back of his stiff neck while he waited for the air to clear his head. With persistent kneading the cramp in his neck subsided.

Already this new town called Fairbanks was awakening. Scattered roosters crowed, and random lights appeared in the rows of tents and shacks stretching to the black shadows of the spruce forest. A few people walked the streets. Nathan's practiced eye scanned these for possible threats and saw none—an Athabascan coming to trade furs, several women, and a stevedore sitting on the riverbank.

A light touch on his back spun him around. His hand automatically went to his pistol, but what he saw stopped him from drawing. Where had she come from? he wondered.

"I wanted to thank you for saving my Uncle Ezra yesterday," she said in a soft voice. The girl blinked at him with her topaz eyes wide and fearful, reminding him of a startled doe, uncertain whether to stand or flee. But her resolve held her fast.

Before Nathan could respond, she rose on tiptoe and

kissed him on his unshaven cheek. Then she darted away, vanishing through a cleft between the newspaper office and the saloon next door.

Nathan stood there with his skin tingling from the kiss and the smell of her perfume still playing with his mind. With his thoughts so startled, all he could focus on were her eyes and the gold watch pinned to her coat.

It was the girl he had insulted in Chena town. . . .

★ ★ TEN ★ ★

Tonopah, Nevada. The square-set man lumbered through the door of the Northern Saloon, all but filling the opening with his broad expanse. He paused momentarily to rasp a pound of congealed mud from his boots on the bootscraper just inside the door. A broad-brimmed hat shaded his face, but his blue eyes beneath the straight rim darted about with a quickness that belied his bulk. A dark mustache drooped heavily from the corners of his mouth. Everything about the man cried of solidity. A polished lawman's shield, pinned to his dusty coat, added to that image.

The peace officer's eye caught sight of a card game at a back table, and the man strode directly to the game. The crowd parted for him like brush before a buffalo.

Standing over the table, the lawman looked down at the players and scowled. The game stopped under the scrutiny of this moving mountain, and three of the four players fidgeted nervously. But the fourth casually removed his cigar, looked up at this visitor, and winked.

"Well, hello, Virgil," Wyatt greeted his brother. "What brings you to Tonopah? Your own town of Goldfield getting too tame?"

Virgil shook his head. "Hell, no. Goldfield's still keeping me busy. I came to pick up a prisoner from the jail here and take him back." The older Earp glanced about for an empty chair. He spied one and dragged it over to the table before turning it around. Then he slouched onto the chair, resting his right arm on the straight back. Either by instinct or by intent, Virgil positioned himself so he covered Wyatt's back while his own back faced the wall.

Wyatt glanced fleetingly at his brother's left arm, hanging uselessly at his side, crippled by a shotgun blast that followed closely on the heels of that fateful gunfight at the O.K. Corral in Tombstone. Ambushed in the night from a darkened alley. Wyatt's eyes narrowed, and he drew slowly on his cigar as he recalled that night, Virgil lurching into the Oriental Saloon, pale and shaken, with blood pouring down his blasted coat sleeve.

That was Curly Bill Brocius's work. And maybe the rifle shot that shattered Morgan's spine while he bent over that pool table. It was night, too, when they shot Morgan. Vermin worked best in the dark.

Funny thing, Wyatt thought. I'll never forget the look on Morgan's face when he died in my arms, but I can't recall how Curly Bill looked when I cut him in two with both barrels of my shotgun. Nor any of the others' faces.

Virgil broke his train of thought. "It wouldn't be bribing a peace officer if you were to offer me a cigar, Wyatt," he grunted. "Or are you getting as cheap as your wife?"

"Damn, Virge, you're beginning to sound more like Allie by the day. I know she and Sadie don't get along; but, I swear, next thing she'll turn you against me." Wyatt handed his brother a cigar.

"Well." Virgil pursed his lips and rolled the cigar between his fingers. "It's no secret there's no love lost between those gals. Allie still blames Josie for what happened to Mattie, but I know poor Mattie was round the bend by the time you met Josephine. Don't pay Allie no mind. She was eating a pickle when I first saw her, and that vinegary nature just stayed with her. She's never lost one drop of it in all these years."

"How's your gold mine?" Wyatt changed the subject.

Virgil accepted a light from the player to his left and puffed thoughtfully before answering. "A little here, a little there. Shaking the gold fever is a hard thing, Wyatt. So, I keep on digging. It keeps me busy—that and this deputy sheriff job. But I may quit the sheriff's job if I have to drive that newfangled auto car one more time. I tell you, the damned thing liked to shook my bones out of my skin. It lost a wheel an hour out of Goldfield, and the contraption makes so much noise a buffalo herd could run over you and you'd never hear them coming."

Wyatt smiled sadly. "No need to worry about the buffalo. We killed them off, and I did my share. I'm not proud of that bit of progress."

Virgil waved his one hand in the air. Of all the brothers, only Wyatt had a melancholy streak, and the older brother knew it. "No sense fretting on it, Wyatt. Someone else would have just shot your share, and you would have starved to death instead of working as a buffalo skinner. Besides, you might never have met Bat Masterson otherwise."

Virgil's cigar went out, so he paused while Wyatt relit it. "Say, I hear Bat's writing for some newspaper back east. Doing sports or such. Having a hard time convincing them eastern dudes that he's half-human and not just some murdering son of a bitch from the Wild West."

"That's hard to do," Wyatt replied. His thoughts lingered on the men he'd killed. Why would his mind refuse to dredge up their death masks? "Hard to do," he repeated, "when we're a little bit of both."

Wyatt pushed his cards to the center of the table along with his stack of poker chips and stood slowly. "Boys, this deck has gone cold on me. Divvy up my winnings among yourselves. I'm dropping out to have lunch with my brother."

None of the other players complained about this generous move. A new dealer sat in, and the game resumed as the two men walked toward the door. Only a thin man with a pock-marked face who leaned against the far corner of the bar watched them leave. While he kept his head low, the brim of his hat failed to hide the sharp interest his eyes held for the Earp brothers. Not even the bartender noticed the way the man nervously licked his lips and repeatedly ran one finger over the rim of his warming glass of beer.

Twenty minutes later, Wyatt watched his plate of steak and fried potatoes cool into a congealed mass of thickening gravy and grease. He raised his coffee cup to his lips and swallowed. At least the coffee was still warm, he noted. Virgil was always the slowest one in the family.

Wyatt was just about to ask the waiter to take the food back when his brother entered the dining room of the Delmonico Restaurant. The older Earp removed his hat and wiped the sweat from his forehead on his coat sleeve.

"Sit down, Brother, and eat your lunch before it gets cold. I thought you said you'd only be five minutes, so I went ahead and ordered for both of us. I see now that was a mistake."

"Would you believe it, Wyatt?" Virgil sank heavily into a chair opposite his brother and tucked a checkered napkin into his celluloid collar. He shook his head disgustedly. "The sheriff here released that jasper I was supposed to transport this morning. Let him go on bail. Here I drove that backfiring rattlebone all the way over and for nothing. The man's long gone."

"And the sheriff didn't call you on the telephone?"

Virgil shook his head as he forked a fist-sized slab of steak into his mouth. He mumbled something incoherent. Two deliberate chews and Virgil swallowed the mouthful. Wyatt watched his brother's neck, half-expecting it to swell like a rat snake swallowing a chicken egg. But the wad of food passed without notice while Virgil shoveled a forkful of potato right behind it. Virgil is the slowest of the family, except when it comes to eating, Wyatt corrected himself.

Virgil paused to wave his fork at his brother. "Telephone? No, Wyatt, I don't use that newfangled gadget. I can't get the hang of standing there like some fool touched with sunstroke and talking into an empty box. Reminds me of setting in front of a *saguaro* cactus and bellowing down the hole made by a pygmy owl. I half-expect the owl to stick his head out and nip my tongue. Besides, my right ear is gone deaf after all my shooting. What with my bum left arm and my bad right ear, I can't juggle the earpiece too well." He stopped chewing to ask thoughtfully, "Say, are you paying for this or am I?"

Wyatt chuckled. "It's on me, Virge. I don't suspect the good citizens are paying law officers top dollar these days."

"Hell, no. Two dollars a day for this special assignment. And that's a treat." Virgil squinted at the prices on the menu card that lay on the corner of the table. "This fare would bust me."

"My treat, Virgil. I don't get to see you much, and James stays in California."

Virgil looked glumly at his brother. "I know. Our family has shrunk considerably since Warren was *murdered.*" He emphasized the last word even though the jury in Globe had acquited the killer on the grounds of self-defense. "Johnny Boyet knew Warren wasn't carrying a pistol when he shot him. Those cattlemen paid to have Warren killed, and they bought off the jury, too."

Wyatt sipped his coffee as he watched Virgil's face grow florid with the painful recollection. "It seems like only yesterday," Wyatt said slowly. "But it's been almost four years."

Virgil stopped chewing. "Well, we got justice for Warren even if the jury couldn't, Wyatt. I doubt they'll ever find Johnny Boyet's body. We hid him where even the buzzards couldn't find him."

Wyatt sipped his coffee and said nothing. He could still remember how Boyet had pleaded with them for his life, had offered them money and even promised to turn state's evidence against his employers. At least I gave him a fair chance, Wyatt mused. I gave him a chance to draw. That was more than he gave Warren. What Boyet said about the men that hired him was rubbish. Those men controlled the town of Globe and would never be convicted. Boyet did draw after Wyatt holstered his pistol. Even then, his bullet missed. Rushed his shot and didn't aim, Wyatt thought. He could remember Boyet's shot clipping the side of his hat like an angry hornet while Wyatt focused on the front sight of his Colt and pressed the trigger. Another explosion, another cloud of smoke, and another score settled.

And, Johnny Boyet's face became a darkened, faded shadow in his mind—like the others.

"We made a mistake, Wyatt," Virgil interrupted his thoughts. "We should have called Boyet out and shot him down in the street—like the old days," Virgil rasped. "Where everyone could see him get his medicine. They could see what a coward he was."

"No." Wyatt shook his head. "Look what those old days got us, Virge. Nothing but heartache. The O.K. Corral marked us as gunfighters and brought us nothing but grief. It didn't stop there, and the fight created more problems than it solved. Look what followed: Morg backshot, you bushwhacked. And it's not over yet. Even though Ike Clanton is dead, the repercussions continue. If I've learned one thing, it's that rats like Clanton have no shortage of friends. The world is full of rats like him. Sneaky rats."

"Are you saying we should just give up and let them buffalo us, Wyatt? Is that what my one ear is hearing? Because I don't want to hear that."

"No, I'm saying the rules have changed. Shoot-outs in the streets are a losing proposition—as foolish a move as drawing to an inside straight. If you win, you still lose because the fight focuses all the attention on you. All the bleeding hearts come forth to tell how the scum you just gunned down was good to his mother or sang in the choir or never kicked a dog in his short life. The 'decent citizens' back away from you even though you did them a favor. And the rat's friends or those that hired him in the first place just wait for you in some dark alley."

"And—?"

"So do your cleaning in quiet." Wyatt spread his hands across the checkered tablecloth.

"Become a bushwhacker?" Virgil choked out the words. This conversation had stopped his eating.

"Not at all. Tombstone and our ride for vengeance won't play nowadays. Too much has changed. The quiet way we cleaned up Johnny Boyet will. I've learned another thing as well. Other than the mean drunk who goes for his gun out of pure orneriness, most of these desperadoes have some power-ful men behind them. Especially where control of a town or even a state is at stake. Do you think Ike Clanton or Curly Bill had the brains to organize more than a handful of rowdies?"

"No."

"Precisely my point. We killed those three in Tombstone and a dozen more after they shot you and Morg, but the prob-lem continued. Special interests wanted us out of the way in Tombstone, and they got just that. They also ran off John Clum and Luke Short. Now those men own all the gambling and sa-loons there."

Wyatt paused to sip his coffee. He needed that action to calm himself and collect his thoughts. Living with this theory day and night caused him to overreact when he spoke about it. Virgil resumed his eating, but more slowly this time, as if he were chewing and digesting each piece of Wyatt's explanation.

"It's not just in Tombstone, Virgil. Those same types of in-terests caused Warren's death in Globe. And I ran smack dab into the same corruption in Nome. Alexander McKenzie and Judge Noyes tied up all the richest claims through Noyes's cor-rupt court. They grabbed Lucky Baldwin's bar and tried to take mine. Money and power, they go hand in hand. I kept think-ing, How can this be happening here in Nome, thousands of miles away? It can't be happening. But it was happening.

"So, I solved my problem in private—in the bush and on deserted strips of the beach—with no witnesses who'd go to the papers. Use their own tactics against them and they don't know where to strike back. Stand up to them directly and they throw the entire weight of their operation against you. Call them out and a crooked judge will issue a warrant for your ar-rest. But strike back in secret and they don't know where to turn. With nothing but shadows to hit, they're powerless.

"I tried it in Nome, and it worked, Brother. It worked just fine. They all think I'm retired or over the hill or washed up or a big blowhard or whatever suits them. That suits me just fine, because I've come out ahead each time."

Virgil looked at his brother strangely. "You aren't planning on running for Congress, are you, Wyatt? That sounded like a campaign speech if I ever heard one."

Wyatt grinned fiercely like the gray wolf he had become. "Now, that would really be stupid." He collected his thoughts. When he was young and rash, he would have rushed in head-on, but now he was learning to do something different. He hoped Nathan would remember those same words of advice he had just given Virgil. Somehow, Wyatt feared the young man would charge in recklessly just as he would have done thirty years ago.

Wyatt looked down at Virgil's empty plate. "Remember, Virge, I said I'm buying lunch."

"In that case, Brother, I think I'll have some of that fresh-baked apple pie. I'll need all my strength to wrestle that auto car back to Goldfield."

The sound of a backfiring motorcar ricocheted around the foothills like rhythmic rifle fire before rolling away to be lost among the juniper and creosote brush that speckled the valley. Down below, the car followed the wagon ruts like a blind man feeling his way along a ledge. A telltale plume of smoke and dust dragged doggedly behind the rattling Ford. With little light left in the day, Virgil Earp was pushing his motorcar as fast as he felt was prudent.

That task took all his concentration, for the beast seemed predisposed to roll over rocks and head directly for ditches. Silently Virgil longed for a solid horse instead of this mechanical runaway, a flesh-and-blood horse whose mind would guide its feet onto the straight and narrow instead of into a hole. Never knew this road had so damned many rocks, he thought as his head snapped back with a bone-jarring lurch to the left, but I've run over every one.

With his mind focused on the pitfalls ahead, Virgil failed to see the sun glint off a rifle barrel on the hill to his right. The low-hanging sun helped to hide that side of the road by blinding any glance along the rim of those rocks. Blissfully ignorant, the deputy sheriff bounced along.

Two hundred yards above the road, the scar-faced man from the Northern Saloon cleaned the glass lense of the telescopic sight on his bolt-action Mauser rifle. The man knew the rifle's long-range accuracy well from bitter firsthand experience. Too many of his army buddies in Cuba had died at the hands of Spanish marksmen and this efficient 7mm cartridge during the last war. The pockmarked man remembered the days of frustration dueling with Spanish riflemen with his less-efficient .30-40 Krag; and so when he returned home, he carried with him one of those rifles that had made his life a living hell. Since then, he had used his Mauser three times on his fellow Americans—always for pay and always with fatal results for his target.

The assassin adjusted his crosshairs for the distance and waited for the motorcar to reach the switchback that allowed the road to descend to the flat of the valley. Wagon trains and stagecoaches had used this route for nearly forty years, but the iron rims of the heavy ore wagons, hauling silver ore to the smelters, had cut permanent grooves into the rock face. To attempt a shortcut past the loop courted disaster from a broken wheel or from tipping over on the steep grade. With no cause for alarm, Virgil would have no reason not to follow the route.

The switchback was important since the road turned to run directly toward the killer's position. The motorcar would travel in a straight line approaching his rifle for a quarter of a mile. There would be no need to lead his target. Virgil would be driving directly toward him like an unsuspecting antelope walking to water.

Five hundred dollars for this one, the killer thought. And two thousand dollars for Wyatt. Obviously, the man who had paid him considered Wyatt Earp worth more than his crippled brother. The killer smirked. A lot of money to kill two long-in-the-tooth old has-beens, he thought. Both men were twice his age. He'd heard about their gunfight in Tombstone, but he was unimpressed. The man in the motorcar was well past his prime, fat and lazy, and his brother, the notorious Wyatt, needed glasses to read. First drill this old fool, then Wyatt before the

news of his brother reached him and he became cautious—
that was the killer's plan. He'd picked this route the minute he
first saw it when he rode into town. Neither of his two victims
suspected that Virgil's coming to Tonopah was part of the plan.
A setup. This would be easy . . . easy.

He should have asked for more, he realized. "Killer" Jim
Miller got at least eight hundred dollars for bushwhacking
lowly dirt farmers and a lot more for someone important. After
these two, he would have five notches to his credit as a hired assassin. When he got to ten or twelve like Jim Miller, he could
command a higher price.

Funny thing, though, the man recalled. The person who
had hired him let slip that he had offered the job to "Killer"
Miller—and Miller had refused. That puzzled him. Was Miller
afraid of these has-beens? Did their reputation still scare him?
He wondered.

A bead of sweat separated itself from the hairs of his eyebrow and slid into his right eye. He cursed as his sight picture
momentarily vanished into a cloud of haze. He blinked and
wiped the sweat with his sleeve. When this was over, he would
treat himself to a cold beer. That would taste real fine, he
thought. A beer at the Northern Saloon. He would enjoy the
irony of drinking that icy beer in Wyatt's own saloon. He might
even buy Wyatt a beer as well. That would be rich, drinking a
beer with his next victim, knowing he had already killed the
man's brother.

He squinted into the telescopic sight. These Germans knew
how to make a fine rifle sight, he admitted. But his warm feeling vanished in an instant.

The motorcar had vanished.

Panic roiled the assassin's stomach. Had his target seen
him? He cursed himself for not rubbing lampblack on his barrel. The bluing had worn thin in places on the barrel, and it reflected light if he was not careful.

Calming his shaken nerves, the man reasoned that the sun
at his back would hide any reflection from his rifle. Anyone
below him would be blinded by the glare. Still, he shouldn't get

sloppy, he reminded himself. He vowed to darken his gun before he went after Wyatt. Even in the gloom, a stray beam of light might give him away.

Mechanically he opened the rifle bolt and checked the magazine. Four brass cartridges, stacked atop one another, glinted back wickedly at him. Another cartridge slid back halfway from the rifle's breech, gripped tightly in the claw extractor of the rifle bolt. He slammed the bolt shut, listening to the satisfying crisp click of the closing.

Where was that motorcar? One minute it was chugging along down the road, and the next it had disappeared. It was just passing behind that jumble of boulders when the sweat distracted him. It should have reappeared on the other side. Where was it?

Had the old fool fallen asleep and run the thing off the road and into the *arroyo* below? If he'd broken his scrawny neck, all the better. Dead was dead. Accident or not.

The pockmarked killer cocked his ear and listened. There, he heard it, the clattering of the car's motor. The sound rattled upward from behind the boulders. It was still there. But why hadn't it come out?

The killer rose slowly to his feet to get a better view. From its sounds, the motorcar was still running behind the rocks. Did the old goat stop to take a piss? he wondered. Maybe the car had broken down? He craned his neck, seeking to spy over the top of the rocks.

A sound like something punching a sack of grain reached his ears.

He remembered that sound, but this time it was louder than he recalled. But the noise was all too familiar to him. It brought back the steaming swamps of Cuba with its stiffling humidity and beaches clicking with the movement of hundreds of land crabs. Crabs that would tear the flesh off a wounded man before he could even die. The sound came from a bullet striking flesh.

The killer looked down at the hole that had unexpectedly appeared in the center of his chest. He could fit his fist into the opening. Bright red blood stained the front of his shirt. A split second later the crack of a rifle reverberated around the rocks of his hiding place.

The would-be assassin's face frowned in confusion as his legs gave way and he fell heavily onto his back. The last thing he saw was the blazing sun he had expected to hide behind.

A deathly quiet returned to the valley, save only for the persistent chugging of the gas engine. Then gravel crunched beneath two sets of boots and a pair of shadows fell across the fallen man.

"Lord, that old .50-cal. Sharps sure makes a hell of a hole in a man," Virgil said as he sucked air between his teeth.

Wyatt shifted the heavy rifle in his arms before opening the smoking breech and removing the long brass casing. "Well," he said with finality. "I could knock down a buff at a thousand yards once. I was hoping I wouldn't miss."

Virgil gave his brother a strange look. "I'm glad you didn't tell me that before. . . . What kind of rifle is that he was carrying, Wyatt? I never saw one like that before."

"One of those Spanish Mausers brought back from Cuba, I presume." The toe of his boot eased the rifle out of the dead man's stiffening grasp, causing it to clatter against the rocks. He winked at his brother. "It makes an impressive hole, too, Virgil."

Virgil straightened up from rifling the assassin's pockets. "Twenty-five hundred dollars, Wyatt, and not a lick of any other papers on him. Do you suppose all that money was for shooting me?"

"Us, Virge. It's for both of us. Twenty-four hundred and ninety-nine dollars for me and one dollar for you. . . ."

Virgil stared at the money. There was more here than he made in a year as deputy sheriff. He shrugged. "Maybe he won it playing cards? Maybe today? The bills look crisp and brand-new."

Wyatt shouldered the long-barreled Sharps and turned away. His theory was proving itself true, once again. Times had definitely changed. No one would call him out or face him in a gunfight like the old days. Backshooting and bushwhacking were the order of the day. And he would deal with them like this killer—quietly, without publicity.

The coyotes and buzzards would clean up this trash. There would be nothing to link either Virgil or him to this shooting. And that was just the way he wanted it.

Looking back at his brother, Wyatt replied, "I don't think he won that money at gambling, Virge. This definitely was *not* his lucky day."

★ ★ ELEVEN ★ ★

Spring slipped into the mature green of summer to the accompanying sounds of hammers and saws ringing throughout
the bowl of the Tanana Valley. More men poured over the
White Mountain passes from Circle and Dawson and Eagle
while the town of Rampart emptied itself into whatever would
float and paddle up the Yukon to this new El Dorado.

But the verdant slopes suffered from these invasions. Once-
clear streams now ran muddy, choked with the silt of a hundred sluice boxes, and the clacking sound of the rocker boxes
sounded as long as the alpine glow of the arctic summer provided light. Unique engineering feats forced the restless water
to run where nature never intended it to in order to satisfy the
demand for the hungry sluice boxes. These planked and enclosed channels could be seen zigzagging across the gullies
and valleys like bolts of lightning turned to wood.

Smoke boiled skyward in a thousand sooty tendrils from
fires that thawed the stubborn overburden while vast swaths of
forest disappeared with the constant search for firewood. The
hillside grew to resemble a deranged checkerboard of fresh-
sawed stumps and fallen trees, scattered like a giant's jackstraws
as men struggled to keep their fires lit.

Giant patches of frozen ground, permafrost, blanketed the
land in this site just below the Arctic Circle where the ice had
held the ground prisoner since the last ice age. Now the fires
broke that grip and turned the ground into spongy muck that
fostered more dysentery and more mosquitoes.

Fairbanks changed as well. Over five hundred homes clustered around Barnette's Trading Post, including the new court-house, registrar's cabin, and seven prosperous saloons. The town boasted of two tin shops, three sawmills, a hospital, four doctors, four lawyers, and two bathhouses.

Thanks to the actions of Judge Wickersham the seat of the regional government now rested firmly on land "donated" by E. T. Barnette. The sawmills and repair shops ran round-the-clock while bathhouses sat vacant until Friday nights. Then the line would extend around the block as men spiffed themselves up for the trip down the road to the rows of cribs and shacks in the red-light district.

But little gold was found. The land gripped its secrets tightly in its frozen fingers.

By summer's end, the word that Fairbanks was a bust reached back to the other towns. The rush dried to a trickle, producing a "six-man stampede" over an entire month. By autumn, the stampede stopped.

Adding to the town's woes was the drop in the fickle Chena River. Falling to levels so shallow that even the *Isabelle* struggled, the essential artery of supply vanished, leaving the town cut off. All this time, Captain Barnette fumed and fussed and spread more rumors in hopes of fueling the dying rush. And all this time Nathan and his cooperatives worked the creeks with feverish desperation.

Jim Riley paused from chopping wood to sink his ax into the head of a stump. He straightened his aching back and wiped the sweat from his face with his tattered sleeve. A cloud of mosquitoes circled his head, preparing another attack. One dove for his lips. Riley clamped his jaws and swallowed the bug. He turned to the clattering steam engine puffing merrily by his side and spit on its glowing side. He grunted in satisfaction as his saliva vaporized on contact with the cherry red cast-iron firebox after emitting a loud crackle.

"Ain't you never gonna get full, you goddamned heartless piece of scrap metal?" he swore at the machine.

In response the six-horsepower engine chugged on, pumping live steam to the five throbbing hoses that snaked over the rim of the mine shaft to disappear into the darkness. Billowing clouds of vapor rose from the depths to the accompanying clangs of men driving the steam points far below ground.

With his fear of tunnels, Riley had opted to keep the steam engine fueled, hunt, fish, and pick berries in return for a reprieve from working underground. As long as he kept the engine fed with wood it would pump live steam to iron rods that the men below would hammer into the frozen ground. In turn, the steam would thaw another six to eight feet of permafrost into icy slush and rock. With faltering coal oil lamps the men would peruse the muck for the glint of gold before pressing on. Then the process would start all over again.

Belowground, Nathan Blaylock, stripped to the waist like his four fellow workers, struggled to pound his iron steam point into the unyielding ground in a six-by-six-foot tunnel while his friend fed wood to the burner above. The two men worked with Jesse Noble, owner of this miserable piece of land, which he called Discovery Claim, on Cleary Creek. The fact that the stream bore the name of Barnette's brother-in-law did little to make them love the place. Leery about hiring a pair of gunfighters, Noble soon recognized them as two of his best workers, and their presence removed all fear of claim jumpers.

Riley cast another log into the firebox, picking up a splinter. He teased it free with his teeth before returning to his chopping.

"I'm ruining my delicate hands," he spoke to himself. "Look at my nails. All broke. This ain't no way for a *pistolero*'s hands to look. Especially not an educated *pistolero* like me. I don't recall Wesley Hardin ever having no hands like these," he grumbled.

Riley paused to reflect. "On the other hand, Hardin's dead, and I ain't. And so's old Dynamite Dick Clifton, and Flat Nose George Curry."

"Flat Nose Curry?" A sodden face appeared above the timbers bracketing the entrance to the mine. Jesse Noble rose amid the squealing of the rusting cables to the hoist. Slime covered his face and clothing, sparing only his eyes and mouth, so that he looked like a black-faced minstrel singer. "Who's this 'Flat Nose' fellow?"

Riley stopped his loading, glad for someone to talk to. "Flat Nose George Curry? He was a desperado I knew. Use to ride with Harvy Logan and the Sundance Kid. I heard he got killed three years ago near Castle Gate, Utah. We used to break horses together in our quieter days."

"How'd he get that name, Flat Nose?"

"Got hisself kicked in the snoot by a horse. Mashed his nose all to hell."

"Too bad." Noble collapsed on a stump and rinsed his mouth with water from a bucket. He emptied the rest of the dipper over his head. The rivulets cut streaks in his dirty mask, exposing startling patches of white skin.

"That ain't the worst of what happened to poor old George. Whenever I gets to feeling sorry for myself, you know, working up here like some slave, I gets to thinking about how poor George Curry met his end. Then my lot don't seem half so bad."

Noble wiped his face with the tail of his shirt, succeeding only in smearing his stripes into gray pools. "What happened to him?"

"Well." Riley sat on his pile of wood across from Noble. "He held up a train at Wilcox Siding in Wyoming, and the posse finally caught him in Utah. When they got finished with George, they kilt him and skinned him to boot."

"Skinned him?" Noble gasped, his eyes wide in fright.

"Yup." Riley nodded. "Turned his chest into a batch of wallets and moccasins. So, I figure chopping wood and feeding this infernal steam contraption, as I am, is still a damn sight better than being a pocketbook for some swell or wrapping about some smelly foot."

Noble stared at Riley in disbelief. "Is that story true?" he asked.

Before the gunman could answer, a low rumbling reached their ears. The ground shook. Both men staggered to their feet and struggled to remain upright.

"Earthquake!" Noble cried.

"Get them men up outta that shaft!" Riley shouted as he lurched for the shutoff valves that fed the live steam to the steam points. A line whipping around under pressure might cut an unwary miner in two or, if the line burst, cook him in seconds.

Already the alarm bell, nothing more than a string leading from the depths of the mine to a brass bell mounted on the poles bracing the entrance, jumped to life as someone in the mine jerked the string frantically. The clanging brought men racing from the corners of the creek, many still clutching their gold pans.

Riley threw the lever to start the wire drums to the lift. The engine emitted a sickening groan and stopped. The earthquake had bent the arms to the engine's flywheel.

"Damned thing's busted!" he swore. "We got to winch them up by hand. Give us a hand here! Help me haul them up!" he called to the others.

In seconds, a dozen helpers, fighting the heavy drums, inched the cable tighter with each turn until the tops of the miners' heads emerged from the clouds of steam and dirt billowing up from the shaft.

Riley's heart stopped. Nathan was not with the rescued men.

Gently they lifted three shaken men to the ground, where they lay coughing and dazed. One man was scarcely breathing, and another retched incessantly.

"Where's my pard?" Riley screamed at the most conscious of the three. "Did you see him? Did you see Nat?" He twisted the man's filthy shirt into a knot and lifted him into the air.

The man, a Scot named Menzes, blinked upward at Riley and shook his head. "No, man," he sputtered. "He was farthest in the tunnel when it went. My God, that quake hit us at the worst moment. The steam from the points had thawed the roof, turning it to melt. We were just about to call up for more timber to shore up the roof when it hit. The whole bloody roof came down on us! I had to pull Simon over there out by his legs. He was trapped in the muck." Menzes dropped his head into his hands. "I never saw young Nat." His voice broke as he fought back his tears. "The lamps went out and it was dark as pitch. I'm sorry, Jim. I never saw him."

"Losing the lamps saved our lives," the other man mumbled. "That quake broke open a pocket of swamp gas."

"Methane gas!" Noble shouted. "Douse those fires! It'll blow us all to kingdom come."

"We got to go back down there to find Nathan!" Riley pleaded. "Got to get him out!"

"It's no use, Jim," Noble said. "If the cave-in didn't bury him, he'll be dead from the methane gas by now."

"Not if he's in a pocket of good air," someone in the crowd volunteered. "Swamp gas is heavier than air. It sinks to the bottom and fills up the low spots. If Nathan was working near the top of the cut, he might still be alive."

Jesse Noble shot a hard look at the speaker. One death in his mine was bad enough. "I'm not allowing anyone to go back down there. One spark will blow up the mine. Two or three more dead men won't bring Nat back, and it might ruin all we've worked this hard for."

A chorus of agreeing voices backed his logic. After all, men were killed in mining accidents every day. Just last week two men blew themselves up through careless handling of their dynamite. But as he turned to face Riley, he found the gunman's revolver pointing at the center of his forehead. While Riley's face was white as a sheet and his lips trembled, there was no mistaking the resolve in his eyes.

"I'm going down there to look for my partner," he snarled. "And I'll put a bullet through the first man that tries to stop me."

"Best leave it be. You can't shoot us all, Jim!" another miner cried. "We have to stop you for your own good, man."

"The hell I can't shoot you all. I've killed more men than you muckers combined with my eyes closed and still had time to fart," he warned them. "Now, just give me that rope and stand back before I gits to proving my point!"

Noble stepped back. "You can't use any lamps, Jim. You know that?"

"I know that!" Riley snapped as he snatched the coil of rope from an outstretched hand. "I ain't deef! Jus' you keep a tight hold on the other end of this rope, and when you feel me tug three times, you pull like yer lives depended on it. 'Cause they do! If one of you drops yer end, I'll come back and find him and kill him and half the town he growed up in. That's a promise!"

A dozen pairs of hands caught hold of the end handed to them. Without another word, Riley gritted his teeth and slipped over the rim to vanish into the soggy gloom.

Jim Riley felt his heart pounding as if it would burst from his chest as he lowered himself into the darkness. Hand over hand he descended, trying to control the wild direction of his thoughts. The edges of the shaft closed about him as the light from above grew dimmer. He glanced up at the shrinking square of light from the opening for reference. Immediately he knew this was a mistake. His throat seized, and his heart almost stopped when he saw the tiny patch glowing so far overhead.

Suddenly he was trapped again. His body froze as the weight of wet clay and mud entombed him to the neck. Once again, he felt his horse shuddering and quivering between his legs as it struggled for air, felt the life leak out from the animal's sides as mud filled its nostrils and choked it to death. Trapped, helpless, and paralyzed with fear, he hung on the rope while his mind replayed every minute detail his accident had burned into his memory over thirty years ago.

A handful of dirt struck his face, falling from the damaged sides of the shaft and hitting his left eye. The icy, wet mud startled him. How could something fall on his head if he were buried? Riley blinked and shook his head to clear his vision. All he could see in the sparse illumination were his hands clenched around the rope inches from his face.

He wasn't buried in a mudslide, he realized. He was in a mine shaft, and his only friend needed his help. Summoning all his will, Riley's mind pushed his past nightmare back into memory.

"Jus' focus on yer hands," he ordered himself. "Nothin' else. Hand over hand, we're going down this rope. Don't look at nothin' else. Don't think of nothin' else. Just keep looking at them fingers."

His words, ringing against his ears in the silence like peals of thunder, gave him courage. Gritting his teeth, Riley forced his fingers to function. After a dozen handholds, even his limited sight vanished as the tunnel turned to pitch-blackness. Still, he continued his descent.

After what seemed like a thousand years, his feet touched bottom. He tried to stand, but the slime shifted, and he fell heavily onto his back, wrenching his grip free of the safety rope. Tumbling and sliding along the corridor, he crashed to a stop against a hard edge. With a grunt of pain, Riley rolled onto his knees. His hands felt about him. The object that had stopped him was a splintered support beam, twisted and shattered by the cave-in.

A whiff of foul-smelling gas caused him to retch, and his head spun. Methane gas!, he realized. While his lungs cried out for air, Riley groped frantically about to orient himself. His fingers rasped against the sagging roof of the passage, and he pressed his face to the dripping ceiling. His nose sought a pocket of unsullied air trapped near the roof. His mind swam and his knees buckled as he shuffled along the tunnel, arms flailing like those of a blind man, until he thought his lungs would burst. Then, just when he had abandoned hope, he sniffed clean air.

Riley gulped what air he could. His need for air now temporarily filled, he suddenly realized his safety line was lost. Minutes passed while he searched for the line amid the rubble of broken rock, ice, water, and shattered beams. Although he could not see them, Riley realized his fingers were rubbed raw and his nails were splintered and bleeding.

One finger hooked a cord. He snatched at it and pulled. The cable rose from the mud and snapped taut under his efforts. It was the safety line, he realized, and it was still intact. He giggled with joy.

But his happiness was short-lived. Riley realized that he had lost all orientation. Which way led deeper into the tunnel? If he chose the wrong direction, he would lose precious time and find himself back underneath the shaft to the surface. All his efforts would be for naught.

"Well, I ain't going back up without Nat," he spoke aloud. "Either two of us is coming out or it ain't going to be none."

An idea bloomed in his jumbled thoughts. Carefully he squatted down until his right hand touched the floor of the narrow passage. His left hand maintained a desperate grip on the safety rope. He felt about, analyzing what his cut hand felt. He was standing in freezing water, filled with chunks of ice and mud over a foot deep. The sound of the water slowly moving reached his ears in the thundering silence.

"Now, when I got dumped on my arse underneath the vertical shaft I was standing in less than a foot of muck," he reasoned out loud. "Right here it's over a foot deep. They must've dug their tunnel deeper, looking for the seam. That means the water's running into the far end of the mine—away from the entrance. Damn!" He smiled. "All that reading pays off. Good thing for both of us I'm an educated man!"

He felt, again. The water was flowing to his right. Hang on, Nathan, he prayed silently. I'm a-coming. Jus' hang on. Riley gulped another lungful of air before ducking his head. Cautiously he dropped to his hands and knees and edged his way to the right, deeper into the darkness.

Aboveground, Jesse Noble wiped his sweating hands on his coveralls and stared about helplessly. Swede, next to him, stared fixedly at the scratched face of his watch crystal. The old timepiece was a gift from his father in the old country and his pride and joy. It had seen Swede through his passage to America, his sailing around the Horn, and kept time faithfully while he searched for gold. Now it timed the lives of two men. Each tick of the second hand drove another nail into those men's coffins.

Swede looked up. "It's been twenty minutes, Jesse," he whispered. "Too long down there, I think. They both gonna be dead, for damn sure."

"Shut up, Swede!" Noble snapped.

"You don't be afraid of being shot, Jesse," Swede reasoned. "Riley can't shoot you if he's dead."

"I'm not afraid, I tell you, goddamn it! We're holding this rope because I gave my word, that's why. We're holding this rope until the snow falls if that's what it takes."

"You're crazy," another man muttered. "This whole damned valley is gone nuts." He dropped his section of the rope and backed away from the line.

"Get back on that line, Jensen!" Noble ordered. "You ain't slacking off now."

"I'm going," Jensen answered defiantly. "What we're doing is plain crazy. I don't want no part of it, not no more. I'm pulling up stakes and leaving."

"Get back on that line, or I'll shoot you myself!"

"You ain't got no gun, Noble."

"I got my fists!" With that Noble dropped his hold on the line and launched himself at the departing Jensen. His right fist caught the startled man on the side of his head, knocking him down and sending his hat sailing into a cranberry bush.

Jensen scrambled to his knees and drove his own fist into Noble's stomach. Both men crashed to the ground in a cloud of flailing fists and feet. Mud and moss flew from their boots, and dirt coated them as they rolled about.

"Fight fair," Swede implored. "No biting or eye gouging."

Those still holding the safety line released their hold, one by one, and gravitated to the two fighting men. A brawl was more interesting than holding a rope that would never be needed. Clearly, both Riley and Blaylock were goners. Not a single man there could ever remember anyone surviving more than ten minutes in a shaft filled with methane.

Swede tried to break the fight up, but the others stopped him. Careful examination revealed that neither Noble nor Jensen really knew how to fight. Both men were miners, plain and simple, used to fighting the ground rather than other men. Their wild roundhouse punches mostly missed their marks, as did their kicks. But it made for a good show.

"Let 'um fight and get it out of their system," one man suggested. "There won't be no damage to speak of, and they need to get it out of their craws."

Jensen and Noble's combat carried them downhill into the creek, and their spectators eagerly followed. With water added to the event, not a single man remained to hold the line. Everyone crowded around the thrashing fighters, egging them on and placing bets. Friday night was still days off, and midweek entertainment was a welcomed event. Besides, this was free, something even the poorest could enjoy. More than a few of those watching had no money left at all. For them Friday night in town was an unattainable dream.

No one noticed the three tugs on the unattended line.

"Who's the winner?" Swede asked as both exhausted men ceased their fighting and flopped onto the creek bank.

Jensen struggled to his knees, only to slide back into the silty water. He dipped his face into the stream to wash the mud from his face. His left eye was swollen shut, and a goose egg protruded from the angle of his jaw. Noble's nose was bleeding, sending twin streams of blood through the mud that covered his beard. A corner of his ear was missing.

"Jensen, I'd say," a white-haired prospector from the next creek judged. "He don't look as beat-up as Jesse."

"But look at Jesse's ear," Swede urged. "It's been bit. That disqualifies Jensen."

Jensen sat back on his haunches, chest heaving, as he studied the damage to Noble's ear. "I didn't bite him," he protested.

Noble clapped his hand to his injured ear, then studied the bloodstains on that hand like a fortune-teller perusing tea leaves. He shook his head. "Must have been a rock that cut me. Jensen didn't bite me," he gasped. "Not that I recall."

"Thank you," his opponent said.

Swede stuck his broad face close to the two panting men. "Maybe you be friends again now. Yes?"

Noble nodded. "Sure. I forgot what we were fighting about."

Swede turned to look uphill at the lifeline that had started the quarrel. His eyes started from his head. "It's gone!" he gasped. "By God, the rope is gone!"

The startled miners rushed back to where they had stood. Only a shallow track in the mud marked where they had dropped the rope.

"It must have slipped down the shaft," Noble said in disbelief as he staggered to their sides. "Good God, they're both dead now. For sure." Grief-stricken, he slumped to the ground and buried his head in his hands. "Dead for sure," he repeated.

"Not by a damned sight!" a voice snarled from the opening. The statement boomed like the voice of Death himself as it echoed off the sides of the shaft. *"We ain't dead—no thanks to you, assholes!"*

The men rushed to the mouth of the pit to stare dumbfounded at Jim Riley clawing his way up the shaft. His bleeding fingers and splintered nails grasped the log shoring like an eagle's talons. Hanging from his back was an unconscious Nathan Blaylock, his hands clenched into fight fists and his wrists tied together with part of the useless safety line. Riley had looped Nathan's bound arms over his neck like a sling and climbed up the shaft with the full weight of his friend on his back.

A dozen hands reached into the shaft to pull the two men to safety. They gently removed Nathan from Riley and laid him out on a blanket. The lad coughed.

"He's still alive!" Noble shouted. "Quick, hitch up my horse and ride for the doctor. Help me carry him to my cabin."

"Of course he's still alive," Riley snapped. "I should've

known better than to trust you fools with the simple task of holding a length of rope. None of you could be trusted to hobble a blind mule with a broken leg!" He glared about at them. The whites of his eyes flashed at them in terrible contrast to the soot and silt that blackened his face. "Guess I got to kill off a whole bunch of towns," he growled threateningly.

"Holy Mother Mary!" the white-haired miner swore. "Look at this!" He had been helping wrap Nathan in a blanket, but now he simply stood and stared openmouthed at the young man's still-clenched fists.

Clutched tightly in both of Nathan's hands were a dozen gleaming gold nuggets.

★ ★ TWELVE ★ ★

Nathan awoke in a series of waves as his senses dragged him back to consciousness. From deep within a black pit, one with neither feeling nor sensations, a force pulled him steadily upward toward a distant light. At first, this light was nothing more than a notion, an impression of some feeble illumination high above his head. Yet, as he soared toward it, the light grew until it hurt his eyes. Stranger still, it moved from side to side.

Nathan's eyelids fluttered open. A coal lamp shone directly into his face, held by a hand that moved it about to inspect his condition. The light caused his head to feel as if it would explode, and he winced and turned his head toward the cooling shadows.

"By God, he is awake," a voice spoke the words. But the sounds struck Nathan's ears like thunderbolts. The voice was familiar.

Nathan squeezed his lids into narrowed slits while he struggled to focus on the face behind the annoying light. Instantly his body tensed.

He stared into the solid face of Capt. E. T. Barnette.

I'm dead now, Nathan thought. Somehow, I've fallen into the clutches of the captain. His fingers groped around for his pistol while his eyes kept themselves locked on Barnette's face like a sparrow mesmerized by a rattlesnake. How had this happened? Frantically his mind sought an answer while his fingers continued their search for his weapon. But it was futile. He was lying in a bed, naked except for the heavy blanket that covered him, and all his mind could remember was the mine shaft shaking as a thunderous rumble rose from the very bowels of the earth. If Barnette had him in his clutches, Jim must be dead, Nathan realized. And his pistol was gone.

Barnette seized the initiative. "Not so brave without your pistol, are you, boy?" he gloated. "You might say I've got you just where I want you now."

"You plan on shooting me, Captain?" The words rasped out of his parched throat, sounding like they originated from someone else. "Or are you going to try to hang me like you did before?"

Barnette's face reflected his toying with both ideas, but he shook his head. This young man represented a threat to his ruling Fairbanks—and always would as long as he drew a breath. But today Barnette was feeling expansive. Today was not the day, he realized, not with that deadly old gunman, Jim Riley, within earshot. Besides, Nathan was a hero of sorts.

"Shoot you? Not at all. I ought to kiss you, Blaylock. You've made me a very rich man!"

Nathan struggled to his elbows. The effort made his head spin, and a wave of nausea rocked his stomach. What was Barnette talking about? Expecting some trick, Nathan willed his head to clear as he peered closely at the beaming captain. "What do you mean?" he asked.

"Simple, boy. Don't you recall? You found gold on Discovery Creek—a hell of a lot of gold. They dragged you out of that hole with your fists wrapped around a fortune in nuggets."

"I . . . I don't remember."

Barnette leaned closer. "What you found lit a fire under the other miners. Noble and his crew were down that shaft the minute the wagon hauled you off. Every mother's son of them, except your partner, Riley. He's been here all the time, watching over you like a wet nurse instead of making a fortune like the rest. By God, I wish I had a man half as loyal as him! Anyway, you stumbled onto something. Pure gold. There's a vein down there two feet wide with no end in sight. Two other claims came in four days later. The whole valley is finally booming with an honest-to-God gold rush this time. The miners are hauling in over five thousand in dust and nuggets a day."

"Four days?" Nathan stammered. "How long have I been laid up?"

"The good part of a week."

"A week?" Nathan passed his hand before his eyes, testing his focus. Tales of methane gas robbing healthy men of their sight flooded his mind. His vision snapped into painful sharpness, and every hair and scuff on the back of his hand stood out in sharp contrast. He said a silent prayer that his eyesight was intact. Then what Barnette had said took hold. Jim was alive.

"You said you were a rich man?" Nathan questioned the captain. Every fiber in his body screamed for more rest, but he stubbornly pressed on.

"Yes, sir. You found that gold just when the *Isabelle* arrived on her last trip for the season. The rivers are dropping like rocks. No more boats this year. Fortunately for me she was packed to the gills with supplies . . . and she carried a special item. That and your discovery has made me the richest man in the Interior. You see, I own the mining rights to one of the finds. I'm making money without so much as an ounce of dirt getting under my fingernails." To make his point, he spread his soap-washed fingers before Nathan's face and turned them over slowly.

"What was the special item?" Nathan suppressed his disgust at this man's all too obvious self-interest.

Barnette rose and slapped his knee with one hand. "A safe!" he chuckled. "Would you believe it? The *Isabelle* brought me a heavy iron safe. The best thing I could possibly have asked for, don't you think?"

"I still don't understand?"

"With all that gold floating around, the miners need a safe place to store their newfound wealth. Hell, they don't even trust one another to share their grub, let alone their gold. No, my naïve young friend, only a great metal-banded, nine-hundred-pound iron safe would suit those suspicious fools. My safe!"

Nathan still struggled with the concept. Why would the miners give their gold to Barnette for safekeeping when they knew he cheated them at his trading post?

"You don't understand, do you? I've created a bank! The Fairbanks Banking and Safe Depositing Company. I plan on adding a vault next spring. Why, the fools are flocking— flocking, I tell you—to place their precious gold in my safe. I charge them, of course, and as president of the bank, I get two-thirds of all the bank's profits. The sweetest deal I could ever think of."

Nathan watched Barnette's face glow with excitement. Caution told him to keep his peace, but he rashly spoke out, wanting more than anything to puncture the balloon of this prancing montebank. "Aren't you afraid that Jim and I might tell the miners that you are a thief?" He spoke slowly and deliberately, watching the captain's face closely for a reaction. "That you spent time in jail for robbing a man?"

His words had their effect. Barnette blanched, and his eyes narrowed into thin slits from which his dark pupils flashed dangerously. "I wondered when you'd drag that out. The newspaper clipping you found on that dead man two years ago? Isabelle thought you might not remember, but I knew you would. Your kind never forgets those sort of things. But I served my time, Blaylock, and got a parole. I paid my debt. I'm entitled to a fresh start."

Nathan watched him silently. The gall of Barnette amazed him. Speaking earnestly and sincerely to him, the captain could have been a born-again Christian like those repentant sinners Nathan saw outside the missions in Circle and Dawson. His heart wanted to believe.

Barnette noted the effect of his words and pressed onward like a revivalist. "I was young then, Blaylock, just like you. I made a mistake, and I'm sorry for it. Haven't you ever made a mistake? Are you so perfect that you can cast the first stone?"

Nathan sank back in his bed. This discussion was more tiring than he had imagined. Barnette's words dredged up all the youth's own shortcomings and errors that he wished he could correct. The number of men he had killed flooded his thoughts. True, they were all bad, but some *might* have reformed. But now he'd never know. How can you give back a man's life? A bullet was too quick and final. He hung his head and spoke softly.

"I'm far from perfect, Captain. . . ."

"Then, you'll give me another chance?" Barnette's eyes filled with tears. "You won't say anything?"

Nathan nodded.

"Bless you, son!" Barnette made to pat the stricken Nathan but decided against it. His hand wavered in midair for a second before he thrust it back into his pocket. With a new spring in his step, the captain spun on his heels and stepped out of the room.

Nathan lay against his pillow with his eyes tightly closed. His head pounded, and every muscle in his back protested holding the weight of his spine upright. The room was still save for the ticking of a brass clock somewhere in the house.

"He ain't no more sorry for the things he done than a rattlesnake is for all the gophers he's et," Jim Riley's voice broke the silence. "Like that Shakespeare wrote: 'The gentleman's protesting too much.' "

Nathan's head jerked up to see his friend leaning against the door frame. With his battered Stetson mismatched with moosehide pants and low-slung pistol belt, Riley looked like a child who had dressed himself yet still needed help. But his grizzled gray beard and wind-seamed face suggested something entirely different. Nathan's heart soared. With Riley around, the lad knew the world would always have an island of straightforward sensibility.

"The man's a snake, and he'll always be a snake," Riley continued. "Ain't nothin' to git upset about. It's all the man's made of. He can't be nothin' different. You don't go off kicking an armadillo just 'cause he can't fly, do you?"

Nathan grinned widely and shook his head despite the pain it caused.

"No. So don't go feeling sorry for the captain 'cause he

can't walk straight." Riley watched his friend, reading his mind even further. Shrewdly he continued. "And don't be feeling sorry for them rats you shot, neither," he said sternly. " 'Cause you'd be dead now if you hadn't plugged them. It was either you or them, plain as day. And each one was face-to-face. Ain't no shame in that. You ain't no bushwhacker and never will be."

"But there's no pride in it, either, Jim. Is there?"

Riley rubbed the stubble on his chin with his callused knuckles and rubbed his chapped hands together. The friction of the dry skin sounded like rustling leaves in the stillness of the room. He focused carefully on his battered hands, pausing to pick at a flap of skin near his broken thumbnail. The hangnail came away in a strip of dry skin.

"Pride?" Riley pursed his lips and frowned. "I don't know. A man ought to take a certain *satisfaction* in the fact he's good at something. Being the best sets you apart from the rest. People respect that 'cause they recognize you got something they ain't got. Jesse James was the best at robbing trains, and people still sing ballads about him even though he weren't nothing more than a crook.

"You sure as hell ought to be happy that you wasn't the one that got kilt. But you ought to scratch that word *pride* out of your dictionary, just like the word *fair*. Both them words are like a worn-out lariat that won't hold a good loop. The dern thing won't go where you toss it, and the rope keeps tangling yer feet or yer mount and tripping you up. *Fair* and *pride* are just like that. When someone starts laying those words on you, better check yer pockets. 'Cause odds are good he's got his hand on yer wallet."

A soft rustling caused Riley to stop his sermon. He was thankful for the interruption, for he realized he was preaching. It was just that Nathan meant the world to him. While not his flesh and blood, Nathan was all the family the old gunfighter would ever have. If Riley could steer the lad away from some of the pitfalls he had stepped into, he could die a happy man.

The young woman with the topaz eyes was standing in the

doorway with a pitcher and towels in her arms. She smiled warmly at the older man.

"Morning, Miss Molly." Riley pinched the rim of his Stetson and folded it down in his version of tipping his hat. "I was just leaving. I'm glad you came. It shut my running mouth. Best way to shut up an old man's flapping gums is either with a boot or with a pretty gal." He almost blushed.

Molly Hayes curtsied while her smile widened. "I was enjoying what you said, Mr. Riley. I've never met anyone like you or Mr. Blaylock in Boston."

"Well, I suspect Boston has its share of dangerous men, miss." Riley grinned sheepishly. "But they can't be as handsome as the two of us."

Riley's quip did make Nathan blush, turning his face a bright crimson, and suddenly the young man was painfully aware that only a thin blanket separated his bare skin from this girl's fascinating eyes. He tried to shrink beneath the cover without appearing to do so. But the girl's quick eyes caught him, and a look of amusement flickered across her face.

Riley waggled a finger at Nathan as he backed toward the exit. "Remember what I said. Especially about the captain. While he was asking for your blessing, did he tell you he just swindled Johnny Long out of being elected mayor of this burg? Ain't no way E. T. Barnette will ever change. . . ." With that, Riley winked at his friend and bolted out of the room.

"What did he mean by that?" Nathan asked.

Molly Hayes looked directly at her charge. "Last week there was an election. Three, to be exact. The end result was Captain Barnette is now mayor of Fairbanks as well as postmaster, banker, and partners with the Northern Commercial Company." Exasperation crept into her voice. "We should rename this town Barnetteville."

"You sound like your uncle, Miss . . . er, Molly."

"Molly, call me Molly. 'Miss Molly' makes me feel so old." She paused and a frown knitted her eyebrows. She clutched the towels tightly to her breast. "I'm worried about Uncle Ezra. He's very upset about the elections. He's been printing terrible things about Captain Barnette. I'm afraid for his life. He told me that the captain has threatened him already if he doesn't stop."

Nathan sat up before he realized the blanket didn't follow his movement. Quickly he slid back to safety. "Your uncle is the only one who is printing the whole truth. He's got to continue. The *Fairbanks Miner* sure won't."

Molly snorted in derision. "The *Fairbanks Miner!* Judge Wickersham owns that newspaper! What would you expect of it?"

Nathan nodded in agreement. "Maybe Wickershamville would be a better name than Barnetteville?" he suggested.

The two of them laughed, and Nathan watched how her laughing face seemed to illuminate the whole room.

"Tell me about this election," he asked. "I've got a lot of catching up to do. Barnette said I was out for almost a week." Suddenly Nathan realized his face was clean-shaven and he didn't smell like he'd been untended for days. In fact, he smelled of lavender soap. When he was shot, Riley never washed him, preferring like a man to focus his attention on the bandage that dressed his wounds. He stiffened at the thought.

"Did . . . ?" He looked beneath his covers at his body. "Did you . . . ?"

"Yes."

"Damn."

"Don't feel so embarrassed, Mr. Blaylock," she replied tartly. "I do have younger brothers, you know. I've seen a naked man before. And you aren't so special." But secretly she admitted she was lying. Nathan Blaylock's naked body was nothing like her little brothers'. Even now the thought of him sent shivers down her spine.

Nathan gulped at her directness. "Ma'am, you shouldn't be talking like that."

"And why not?" Now she stepped closer, set down her towels, and placed her hands on her hips like a schoolteacher.

"Well, because . . ." His words trailed off.

Out of puckishness she teased him. Pointing to the pitcher,

she said, "And now I'm going to give you another bath. You need it."

He reacted like she expected, clutching his covers like his life depended on it. "No . . . thank you. I . . . I can do it myself."

She shook her head in disgust. "Why you men worry so about your modesty amazes me. You blush and get all red in the face around a girl until she lets you inside her bloomers, and then a team of fire horses couldn't keep a single stitch of clothing on you!"

Nathan gasped. She'd read a dark corner of his mind—and beat him to the punch. He was wondering about what she would be like in his arms just when she spoke. This girl had turned the tables on him. Now he was the defensive person.

"Where did you learn to talk like that?" he stammered.

"I'm not blind. Every day I walk to the bakery or along the river front. I pass the 'Row' where all those fancy women, as you call them, work. The townsfolk are building a fence to protect sensitive eyes like mine, but the fence has lots of gaps." She bit her lip as she calculated what those women made per hour. "They must be making a small fortune for the length of the lines outside some of their cribs. I doubt much money goes into furnishings."

Nathan could hardly believe his ears. "You . . . you went inside?"

She nodded, savoring his discomfort. "Once. Snake Hips Alice's. She was sitting outside. I believe she said she was taking a break. She was very nice, but most surprised a 'lady' would even talk to her."

"She's from Dawson," Nathan blurted out. Immediately he wished he had not disclosed that fact, for Molly looked at him sternly.

"So, you know her? She told me that men are a miserly sort and often refuse to pay for her favors." Molly tried to draw him out. "I hope you are not one of that kind, Mr. Blaylock."

"No, ma'am." Nathan had stumbled over his tongue once more. This girl had a way of making him sound like he was simpleminded. Befuddled, he corrected himself.

"No?" She raised her eyebrows. "What does that mean? No?"

Nathan recovered. "It means I met Alice in Dawson when I lived there. And, *no,* I never visited her, and *no,* I never paid her because I never used her . . . her services."

"Not your type, I suppose." Offhandedly she asked as she leaned against the wall, "Would you pay for my services, Mr. Blaylock?"

He'd had enough of this. Looking her straight in the eye, Nathan ignored her last question. "I knew Snake Hips Alice because we were neighbors. My wife was Chinese, and the good citizens of Dawson forced us to live in a shanty in the Whitecastle District with the whores and other riffraff."

His reply drove the wind from her sails with the force of a well-placed blow. Molly's face drained of color, and her eyes widened in shock.

"You're married?" Her voice sounded small and far away, like that of a child upon being told there was no Santa Claus.

Nathan looked down at his sheet as he knotted it tightly between his two fists. The raven-haired image of Wei-Li filled his mind. Her worldly serenity and strength stood in vivid contrast to this golden-haired girl, like a polished jade statue to a fluttering swallow. "She's dead. She died giving birth to my son."

Molly's mind whirled under this added piece of news. Here this young man she had scrubbed so clean while he was unconscious, this man with no blemishes save for the bullet scar in his side, this man for whom she had fashioned a past, present, and future, had a past of his own. A rare thing occurred: she was speechless.

Nathan saw the dismay his words caused, and he regretted his harsh utterance. "I haven't seen my son for several years now. He's being raised in Panama."

"By another woman?" Molly found her voice.

"Yes."

"My!" Molly blurted out. "No wonder you never visited Alice! You certainly don't want for female companionship. I suppose women throw themselves at you wherever you go, Mr.

Blaylock!" With that she whirled around and fled the room, slamming the door behind her.

Molly paused in the hall to press the back of her hand against her mouth. What had possessed her to act and speak like that? she wondered in dismay. She looked up to see her uncle watching her closely. Before he could speak, she ran to her room.

Ezra Hayes backed into Nathan's room still studying the door that Molly had nearly slammed off its flimsy hinges. He turned to shake his head at Nathan. Easing himself onto the corner of the bed, Hayes pulled at his ear in puzzlement. "Sometimes, I worry about that girl," he said slowly. "What did you do, try to jump on her the minute you regained consciousness?"

"I didn't do anything," Nathan protested.

Hayes watched the door closely over ink-smudged half-glasses. He was wearing a printer's rubber apron and a green half-shade, but more ink smeared his face and hands than covered the apron. He shrugged. "Maybe that explains it. She might have been expecting you to." He wiped his grimy hands on his vest and grinned benignly. "She nursed you like a mother with a newborn babe. For the whole week; can you imagine that?"

"I suspect she'd just as soon cut my heart out right now," Nathan replied.

"Yup. I think she likes you. Well, I didn't come here to figure out Molly's devious woman's mind. I thought I'd give you an update of what happened while you were catching up on your beauty sleep."

Nathan sat upright in bed. "Jim mentioned something about an election. Barnette the mayor now?"

"Three elections, can you believe it? In a town this size. First, the boys got together and elected Doc Medill, the dentist, mayor of Fairbanks. I guess they figured he was as impartial a man as could be found. Doc's so busy drilling teeth instead of drilling dirt, he hasn't yet filed a claim. He's probably the only one that hasn't."

Nathan smiled. The little dentist would make a fine mayor.

"But Judge Wickersham ruled that election invalid. Seems we need the *permission* of His Royal Highness to even have an election. My guess is that we caught Barnette and his boys off guard and left them no time to stuff the ballot box. So they went crying to the judge to void the results. Well, next time we got the judge's consent. But by that time the captain and his henchmen were ready for us. Every man who could crawl turned out to vote. It was damned close. Our man, Johnny Long, edged out the captain by six votes, and there was nothing Wickersham could do about that. It was fair and square." Hayes dropped his hands into his lap and shook his head in disgust. "But it was all for naught!"

"Why? What happened?"

"Barnette got his pals who were elected to the city council to vote him in as mayor at the first council meeting. Word has it he paid some handsome bribes to those sitting on the fence. So, E. T. Barnette is now mayor of this fair town, postmaster, partners with the Northern Commercial Company, and president of the only bank in town, with his fingers into a dozen lucrative mines to boot. It's a god-awful mess, son."

Nathan shrugged. "You never know. With all the enemies he's made, someone might just shoot him."

Hayes shook his head. "He's too big to just shoot now. He'd have to be assassinated, and there's little chance of that. Wherever he goes, he's surrounded by his hired goons, especially that Wilson. He's the worst of the lot. Last week he pistol-whipped Tim Sanders just for saying the captain was two-faced."

"And nothing came of that?"

"Oh, sure Wickersham's brother arrested Wilson, seeing as how he's deputy marshal, but the judge dismissed the charges. Said it was aggravated assault, or some such nonsense. All he did was give Wilson a five-dollar fine. Five dollars, and Sanders' head was nearly split in two by the Kid's pistol barrel."

Nathan recalled the reptilian look that filled Billy Wilson's face whenever he did harm. Perhaps Riley was right. Some people could never change. It went against their very nature, like trying to tame a rabid weasel. When he looked up, he saw Ezra's face creased with worry. "There's something else, Ezra. What is it?"

Hayes rubbed his hands up and down his apron, mindless of the printer's ink he was spreading. "I'm worried about my paper. The *Daily Times* is struggling what with all the rags that are sprouting up. If I go under, there won't be a single paper left to expose the captain's crookedness. But my competition is growing by the minute, and Barnette held up my last order for newsprint. He's deliberately helping the *Miner* and the *News*. He just bought out the *News* and his buddy Judge Wickersham runs the *Miner*. I've heard of the left hand washing the right, but Wickersham and Barnette are taking a bath together."

"You have to keep your paper going, Mr. Hayes," Nathan urged. "Without you, Barnette will have a free hand."

"Oh, don't fret. I'm a muckraker to the quick. I'll keep printing the truth as long as I've got the strength to set type. Couldn't stop if I tried. But I'm worried about Molly. Last night someone threw a rock through the front window, and it's not the first time something like that happened." Hayes stopped to look at Nathan. "She means the world to me. Her mother, my sister, sent her to me for safekeeping. If I should meet with a fatal accident—well, I've lived a full life, but Molly is just beginning. Promise me, Nathan that you'll look after her. See that no harm comes to her."

"I don't know, Ezra. I don't think she wants me anywhere near her."

"Nonsense, boy. She can't keep her eyes off you. She's smitten; I can tell."

Nathan gave the editor a hard look. "Somehow, I don't think you're any better a judge of women than I am, Ezra. I noticed you're not married."

"Never could find a woman who would tolerate my prickly nature. But I'm asking you as a favor. Will you watch over Molly? You'd be doing an old man the greatest service. And it will free my mind to concentrate on the captain and his schemes."

Before Nathan could answer, Jim Riley burst into the room, breathless and flushed. He tried to speak but was too winded for words. Nathan leapt from his bed and struggled into his pants while searching for his gun belt. His action made the room spin, but he clutched the bedpost for support. Even Ezra sprang to his feet with the arrival of Riley. Whatever flustered him must be of monumental importance. Usually, nothing short of a forest fire or an earthquake could prompt the laconic gunman to this level of emotion.

"Jim! What is it? What's the matter?" Nathan asked as his fingers cinched his gun belt tightly around his hips.

But Riley simply spun around the room, gesturing in all directions and gulping for air. Finally, he dropped to the bed and puffed out his cheeks. A figure appeared in the doorway, and Nathan almost drew his pistol. But it was Molly, hurrying to the sound of the commotion. She gave a small squeak upon seeing the dangerous look in Nathan's eyes and ran into the arms of her uncle.

Riley was on his feet again, this time grinning from ear to ear. He gulped air and tried to calm himself.

"What is it, Jim?" Nathan pressed. Riley's smile caused him to relax.

"I'm in love!"

"What?" Nathan fought back an urge to laugh. But the sincerity of his friend's declaration warned against levity.

"She's just beautiful," Riley continued, now that he'd recovered his speech. "Prettiest brown eyes you ever saw, and the sweetest disposition."

His last remark caused Nathan to look directly at Molly. Their eyes locked, and she blushed furiously. He dropped his gaze as if he'd been scalded.

"Do I know her, Mr. Riley?" Molly asked. *"Does Mr. Blaylock know her?* He appears to know every woman in the valley!" she added shrewishly.

"Her name is Susie," Riley sighed, "and I brought her along. She's outside."

Susie? Molly Hayes wondered that this girl had no last name. Was she from across the "Row"? She steeled herself, but her uncle was patting Riley on the back.

"Good for you, Jim," Ezra said. "Bring her on in. Don't keep her waiting outside. That's impolite."

"You're sure you won't mind?" Riley asked tentatively.

"No, sir." The editor disregarded a warning glance from his niece. "Your gal is welcome in my house. Bring her right inside. I want to meet her."

"I knew you'd understand," Riley sighed. He rushed away.

"What if she's one of those . . . those, you know, fancy women, Uncle Ezra?" Molly cautioned.

"She can't be," Nathan refuted her. "I'd know her if she were since I know all the easy women. You said so yourself."

Molly answered his jab by sticking out her tongue.

Ezra held up his hand. "No matter. Riley's friend is welcome in my house whatever she is."

A scuffling on the wooden floor announced the arrival of Jim Riley and his true love. Instantly Ezra Hayes regretted his cavalier remark. But Susie beamed at her newfound acceptance, showing her teeth and laying back her ears.

Susie was a mule.

THIRTEEN

Tonopah, Nevada. Wyatt reined in his horse, rose in the stirrups, and glanced back at the town. He sighed at the patent ugliness of these mining camps. Goldfield, Tonopah, and a hundred more all looked the same. Each one of those boomtowns appeared as if some thoughtless giant had cast a handful of shacks into whatever cleft in the land would hold them. Herded by the folds and the vagaries of topography, the hovels would clump together or string along like a drunken wagon train with no thought for civic planning. Only after the claims proved up would the churches, stores, and schools wedge themselves into the jumble. Even those proved poor anchors for a town whose mines dried up. Then the place would clear out as mysteriously as when it started, leaving alkali dust and tumbleweed to skirt around the open doors and vacant windows.

He preferred San Francisco. But that place was all sewn up. Grimly Wyatt smiled to himself. After his disasterous handling of the Fitzimmons–Sharkey fight, he was better off away from there. One more mistake in a string of many, he thought.

His horse remembered the place and swung her head to munch on the brush that grew in the protection of the old pine. She was a good mare, Wyatt admitted, but no Dick Nailer. He missed old Dick and the spirit that stallion had. Always ready to race. The scent of another horse would lay old Dick's ears flat and flare his nostrils. You had to rein him in, or he'd be off. A solid piece of horseflesh, Wyatt mused, one fitting for a daring man. Not like this tame mare who'd rather eat than race.

But Dick Nailer was gone. And so was the West he knew. Too tame. Motorcars and telephones had begun to cross the land where buffalo and badmen once grew unfettered. True, men still carried six-guns and robbed trains and banks, but now they seemed almost like a footnote rather than the main text. It was a new century, and *development* was the word rather than *discovery*.

Wyatt slipped from the saddle and adjusted his gun belt. Thinking like that will land me in the old folks home, he warned himself. Remember, I'm just getting broken in like my Colt.

His mare shied at a movement. A diamondback rattler slid off the rock where it had been sunning itself and moved sullenly into the brush. Still plenty of danger, Wyatt reminded himself. Snakebite or a fall from a horse breaking your back can strike without notice. One minute you're laughing and the next you're lying in a pine box with your hands crossed over your chest.

That image brought back the bodies of Billy Clanton and the two McLaurys propped up in their coffins for photographs and people to gawk at. Like store mannequins, not men.

He hoped he would never come to that end—propped up like a crate of spoiled apples and dusted with that powder the undertakers use. All that stuff ever did was make the body more ghastly, like some unnatural clay rather than cold flesh. And the crafty way those morticians pointed out the bullet holes for the onlookers. Depending on who paid for the preparations, the holes could be covered with a black patch of cloth or a wad of wax. But they never left any doubt as to where the lead had struck.

He never let them do that to Morgan or to Warren. In Globe a photographer even offered to pay for Warren's funeral expenses if he could get a picture of Wyatt's dead brother. Wyatt recalled throwing the man into an empty pine box and sticking his pistol in the man's face. Would he like his own picture as a dead man? Wyatt had asked. The price would be the same.

Why was he still living? Wyatt asked himself. Young Clanton and the McLaurys and Curly Bill and Johnny Ringo and all the rest—they'd had their chance to put a bullet in him. And they'd missed. With all the lead flying around at the O.K. Corral, only he was unscathed. Not a scratch even though he planted his feet like they were set in cement for the whole fight. Clanton and Tom McLaury were dancing about like ants on a hot griddle, but he kept put. So did Frank McLaury.

Good thing I shot him first, Wyatt thought, just as I planned. Frank was the deadliest one. He had a cool head, and he took his time in a fight.

There must be a reason why I'm still here. Something I've yet to do, he thought.

As he settled against the rock, his hand sought the crumpled piece of paper in his pocket. He smiled as he withdrew the letter from Nathan. If there is a reason for my still stomping about, it must have to do with my boy, he guessed. Adjusting his hat so that the brim shaded his eyes, Wyatt took out his glasses and opened the letter. The paper was spotted and torn as if it had made its passage from Alaska on the floor of a cattle barge. The ink had run in many places, but the writing was clear, with a bold hand.

Fairbanks, Alaska

Dear Father,

What a happy surprise to have this letter delivered to me. It made the rounds of the territory, going first to Rampart and then to Eagle before coming back downriver to Circle. Some miners who knew I was in Fairbanks and were heading that way finally brought it. I lost your first letter in a fire, and when this one arrived, my day was much brighter.

Jim and I are doing some mining on Discovery Creek outside of this town along with a bit of hunting for meat for the camps. Jim can't take working underground much, so we mostly hunt now. Fairbanks is booming with gold in almost every creek. But it's deep in the bedrock, making this place much harder to mine than Dawson. I never got to try my luck at Nome, but I heard the gold was right on the beach in the sand. Well, none of that here in the Tanana Valley. But hard work is making more than a few men into millionaires. So far the Swedes seem to have the best idea. They dig test holes looking for the gold vein. If they find one, they drill more holes until they've mapped out where it goes. Then they dig a shaft. It saves them wasting all summer thawing the overburden and digging down to find a dry hole as so often happens. Still, the Germans and the Irish refuse to adopt an idea they didn't think up, especially a Swedish one. So, they still prospect the old way—with mixed results.

Felix Pedro was the first to make a strike, but the real finds came in on Cleary, Ester, and Fairbanks Creeks. I had a hand in finding gold on Cleary Creek, I'm proud to say, but I was working as a hired hand. So, there's still no millionaires in the family. I don't know if it's worth it. Poor Felix is worn out with prospecting. He's still young at almost fifty, but his health is failing fast.

Still young at fifty! Wyatt straightened his shoulders. The boy had a remarkable grasp of the useful age of an active man. He wrote well, too. It must have been the teaching of those nuns in Denver, he judged. Well, that was one good thing Mattie did for their boy, putting him in that orphanage. Whether she intended it or not, the lad got a fine education, far better than one he would have got with either Mattie or him. And his partner, that Jim Riley. Wyatt had heard of him. Also, he'd made discreet inquiries about Riley after they'd met. Their all too brief encounter in Nome had impressed Wyatt that Riley was of the old school like himself. Riley was good with a gun, and people said he was honest. Wyatt was happy Nathan had a man like Riley to watch his back. It appeared the lad was collecting his own set of enemies. He adjusted his spectacles and read on.

It would be wonderful if you and Josie could come to Fairbanks, but I doubt that will happen anytime soon. Perhaps it's all for the better. One man here has a lock on the entire town. His name is E. T. Barnette, and he is the mayor, postmaster, and main banker. Unfortunately, he and I have bumped heads on more than one occasion. To make matters worse, the U.S. judge, Judge Wickersham, and Barnette appear to be working together.

The hairs prickled on the back of Wyatt's neck. The judge and the town's main businessman in cahoots. It sounded like Tombstone and Nome all over again. Judge Noyes and McKenzie working together to pick the bones of Nome clean, stealing the gold from all the productive mines through a holding company appointed by Noyes and run by McKenzie. He recalled Nome's crooked sheriff and McKenzie's Spoilers trying to force his friend Lucky Baldwin into selling his saloon for a pittance. Only Wyatt's intervention with a cash loan and his thinly veiled threat of using the coil of hemp in his hand to hang the next person to try something crooked kept Lucky from losing his shirt. Sheriff Vawter stood by and did nothing.

If Nathan faced a similar situation, he had problems indeed. Wyatt cursed himself for not bringing writing materials with him. He would have to remember to write back immediately. He made a mental note to warn his son to be very careful. More than ever, he wished Frank Canton was still U.S. marshal in Alaska. Canton would see justice done regardless of some back-pocket judge. Fidgeting because the distance made him helpless, Wyatt adjusted his glasses and read on.

I remembered what you told me about the crooked bosses you encountered in Nome, and I'm following your advice about watching my back and not giving them any excuse to use the law against me. Fairbanks sounds like the makings of another Nome.

Bless the boy for heeding his father's words of warning, Wyatt thought.

This town is growing by the minute. I suppose it is like what happened to Nome and Tombstone when you were there, but Dawson was full-grown when I got there, so watching a town balloon like this is new to me. You can't leave on a hunting trip for more than two days without finding the place has grown by double when you return. Work is presently under way to build not one but two bridges over the Chena River, one upriver of the other. The Cushman Street bridge will be the bigger of the two when it's finished. It will make it easier for the miners to cross the river to town. At present they have to use boats or the rope ferry. All the claims lie in the valley across the Chena from Fairbanks.

A fierce competition is under way between Fairbanks and the town of Chena City downriver where the Chena joins the Tanana. Chena has the advantage of being served by deeper water, and the town just got started on a railroad to link up with the goldfield in Ester and along the Chatanika River. But Judge Wickersham and Captain Barnette are doing all they can to ensure Fairbanks becomes the center of the Interior. The judge chose Fairbanks for his courthouse and ordered the sheriff's office and the claims registrar to locate there, too. Word has it that Barnette gave the judge several of the choicest lots. I suppose that helped him make up his mind.

Did I tell you I met a girl? Her uncle runs one of the papers and is the most vocal of the captain's critics. I think she likes me, but she sure is hard to read. One minute she'll like to bite my head off, and the next she's all smiles. Wei-Li was never like that, and her actions have got me stumped. Oh, Jim has a girl, too. A pretty mule named Susie that he bought for two hundred dollars. That price broke the two of us, but he was smitten, and animals are worth their weight in gold here. The town hasn't got more than a handful of horses and mules. What we'll do with Susie when the winter comes I don't know. I expect she'll be staying inside our cabin when the mercury drops to forty below zero.

Now Wyatt was really worried. He withdrew a cigar from his vest pocket and jammed it into his mouth while he assessed the situation. Mix a woman into any situation like Nathan described, and the brew got explosive. A female adding herself to the equation was worse than playing with the nitro that sweated off of old dynamite and just as incendiary. He knew from bitter experience. Didn't Josie make matters worse in Tombstone? She was Johnny Behan's girl when he first met her. And Behan treated her like dirt, Wyatt reminded himself. Wooing her away from that tinhorn was one of the easiest things he'd ever done. But the bad blood it created with Behan made the Clantons all the more bold. With Johnny carrying a grudge against Wyatt, Ike thought what law Tombstone had would look the other way on that fateful day in 1881. In fact, Behan tried to hinder Wyatt and his brothers by saying he had disarmed the McLaurys and Billy Clanton. That was either a downright lie or a foolish notion, Wyatt thought. But it might have got us killed if we'd believed Behan. As it was, neither of those gunmen were hampered by lack of shooting irons when the "ball opened" as Ike had once bragged.

Well, I'll close now. The next mail pouch is due to leave on the riverboat in one hour, and I want this letter to go out on it. With the river running low, you never know when the next boat might make it out. I hope you can write again. Using "William Stapp" is a good idea. Captain Barnette's the postmaster, and I wouldn't want him to know about us. I wouldn't put it past him to open my mail, but he's so busy raking in the gold and making deals that I don't think he even goes to the post office anymore. His assistant handles all the mail as far as I can figure. Just the same, it's better to be safe than sorry. Give my best wishes to Josie. I know she wants to pretend I don't exist, but I'd be proud to have her call me son. And she'd make a wonderful grandmother to my son, Jeremiah.

Love, Nathan.

Wyatt coughed and nearly swallowed his cigar. *Josie a grandmother!* No way in hell was she prepared for that! Now, he knew for certain that he'd have to proceed very slowly with breaking *that* news to her.

FOURTEEN

Fairbanks. Jim Riley slid from his saddle onto the soggy ground. Walking slowly around in front of his mule, he cast a weary look at the animal while he mopped his brow with the back of his sleeve. The day had been hotter than usual, and his ride in from Discovery Claim had taken longer than expected. Normally he and Susie, his mule, covered the distance in three hours, but not this day. Heavy rains for the last nine days had left his route a miasma of boot-sucking mud, crossed by numerous flooding creeks and plagued by clouds of mosquitoes waiting at every bend. Susie's fetlocks were laden with caked mud and her eyelids swollen from repeated insect attacks.

Funny thing, Riley noted. The rain usually cleared the air. A thousand fires, burning around-the-clock in that mad race to thaw the frozen muck, carpeted the valley with a constant amber smudge. Worse, lightning strikes across the Tanana had set the flats afire, adding to the smoke that filled the air. The sun, whenever it chose to appear, presented itself as a sullen orange ball that usually cast little warmth and even less cheer.

The old gunfighter rubbed his mule's muzzle affectionately. In theory, half of Susie belonged to Nathan, but in fact, she was all Riley's. Since her purchase, the two had been inseparable. The mule basked in the loving care Riley lavished upon her, and the animal's presence repaired a rent in the gunman's spirit that only a four-legged means of transportation could possibly do.

So the arrival of Susie carried multiple blessings for all concerned.

It seemed like Jim Riley was a centaur. Years of riding herd and crisscrossing the plains had fused a part of his soul to a saddle. Long hours of driving cattle and breaking horses had left on him an indelible stamp that marked him as a rider. He preferred to squat on his haunches rather than use a chair, he walked with a rolling gait like a seaman, and he slept better in a saddle than in a bed. Without a mount, according to Riley, a man was less than whole.

Yet Alaska was hostile to horses and mules, a bitter lesson learned by both Nathan and Riley on crossing Dead Horse Canyon. With little natural graze, the land extracted a terrible toll on all who trespassed. Dense brush that hid waiting grizzlies, steep-walled canyons, and scree so loose it skidded on contact—all made travel on four feet harder than passage on two.

Men tried every conceivable way of transportation. Once, on the route north from Tanana Crossing, the two travelers had encountered a pack train of goats. With a mix of sadness and amusement they watched the train wending its way into the distance and into history. Never again did they see another goat train.

Only dogs fared well in the Interior, thriving in harness by day while they listened at night to their wild cousins, the wolves, howling at the Northern Lights. But Riley regarded sled dogs as more work than their worth. And dogsleds were limited to use on snow. During the short summer, the rivers offered the fastest form of passage.

Riley let the reins drop as he walked to the edge of the bridge. The wooden planks extending from the riverbank onto the Wendell Street bridge looked as unstable as ever, so he tested them with his boot. The planks responded with their usual spongy sag. But the force of the river was dragging away several of the supporting beams. Driftwood freed from the embankments upriver sped past the pilings on their way to the

Tanana. Like battering rams, the fallen spruce trunks and up-rooted stumps crashed against the supports with increasing frequency. Whenever a log hit its support, the bridge shivered and groaned like a wounded animal.

Watching the river's mounting assault, Riley agreed his animal had good reason to balk at crossing the bridge ahead. Especially with the Chena swollen into a raging, foaming torrent beneath, anyone falling into that frothing wake would surely drown.

"Ain't the most solid structure in the world, is it?" Riley remarked. "Not like them aqueducts the Romans built." A new book from the town library about ancient Rome was Riley's current reading material. So Susie's ear was filled with passages from that book.

The mule looked thoughtfully at Riley.

"Cheap bastards spent half as much on this rickety catwalk as they did on the Cushman bridge," Riley complained. "I suppose the captain was behind that. Just like him to want a grand path straight to his bank. Like a damned Appian Way. He wouldn't want nothing to interfere with them miners bringing their sacks of gold directly to him. I tell you, Susie, once upon a time you'd worry about robbers getting into yer bank. That's where iron safes and vaults came into play. But there ain't no defense against a robber already owning the derned bank. Being inside like that, the crook has got all the advantages. We're better off hiding our money under a rock."

Susie twitched her ears and snorted.

Riley pushed his hat back on his head. "Well, yes. You're right there, girl. Banks ain't our major concern since we ain't got no money to speak of. Funny, but I find that fact sort of comforting. With no money, we ain't got to worry about it being in Barnette's Banking and Safe Depositing Company.

Riley looked past the bridge to where the overtaxed lumber mill spewed smoke. With the town growing daily, the mill worked around-the-clock to meet the need for boards and planks. Anchored along the shore, a log boom corralled a field of floating logs for the mill. His eyes followed a freshly cut log tearing free of the raft and surging downstream to batter the supports of the trestle before escaping underneath the Cushman Street bridge.

Riley pondered the possibility of using the stronger bridge downriver. Doing so would require backtracking to the fork in the road that bypassed the swampy section along the north bank of the river that some were sarcastically calling the Garden Islands. The shortcut was even worse. A treacherous slough wound its way among the tangles of willow and alder, and this, too, was swollen with the rains and the help of ambitious beaver dams. A wag with bitter experience in Nome had named the swamp Noyes Slough after the infamous Judge Noyes who had just been run out of Nome. It was a scandal that Judge Wickersham refused to open hearings into Noyes's disreputable mishandling of the law in that town. Ominously, Noyes Slough connected downriver with Deadman's Slough.

Riley cursed his lack of foresight in taking this road to the Wendell bridge. To retrace their footsteps now would take half the afternoon.

"Best we git on with it, old girl. That wreck ain't getting no stronger as we watch it, and it's too late in the day to backtrack. Besides, you don't want to mess with the mosquitoes back in the slough, do you?"

The baleful look on the mule's face suggested that she would. Only Riley's persistent pull on her reins convinced her to step onto the wobbling planks. Even then the animal shivered nervously and laid her ears back close to her neck.

Halfway across, Riley glanced down at a dugout canoe tethered to the supporting post directly beneath him. Larger boats like the sternwheelers were too tall to pass the Cushman bridge, and so they lay tied to the log siding below that bridge or moored to the supports of the trestle. But this canoe was small enough to pass freely between the two structures and so was tied to the Wendell bridge. Half-sunk already by the rains, the canoe faced added assault from a tangle of driftwood, brush, and sweepers trapped between the craft and the wooden pillars of the bridge.

As Riley watched, his mouth dropped in amazement. While the brush held the boat fast, a massive log sweeper, complete with gnarled roots and snapped-off limbs, rose from the swirling foam beneath the bridge and rammed the side of the canoe. Wood splintered as the log punched through the side of the boat. There it stayed, embedded in the sinking boat like a massive arrow. With the canoe filled with water and still sporting the tree from this fatal wound in its side, the craft's weight multiplied tenfold.

That sudden jerk, combined with the surge of the current, snapped the twelve-inch-diameter beam that supported the section of bridge upon which Riley and his mule now stood. With an ear-splitting shriek, the trestle lurched to the left before the planks bent like a corkscrew. Susie staggered toward the lower side just as Riley lost his footing and fell to his knees. With all four legs splayed apart for balance, the animal desperately fought for her balance, even as the bridge began to disintegrate.

The groaning and screeching of the tortured planks filled the air with noise that drowned whatever cries Riley made for help. Workers on the shore froze in their tracks at this sudden calamity. A few rushed to the town's side of the bridge only to have that section evaporate in their faces.

More onlookers gathered on both banks as the bridge continued its demise. Helplessly they watched the lone man and his mule struggling for their lives on the last remnant of the swaying bridge, isolated from shore and safety by a widening gap of churning water and tumbling flotsam.

Riley lost his footing as the boards beneath him dropped away. Sliding toward the water, he clutched Susie's reins in desperation. For an awful minute the man hung suspended in midair like a leaf while the mule pulled against his weight. Then, as if in slow motion, this last island of wood that once was a proud bridge slid sideways into the foaming torrent, dragging Riley and his mule with it.

Nathan stopped at the sound of the bridge's mangled cries.

Even as far as below the Cushman bridge, the snapping wood beams sounded like the screams of some tortured animal. The sounds cut through the drunken haze that surrounded Doc Hennison. He put away his pocket flask and staggered to the railing of the *Columbian,* the sternwheeler where he now plied his faro table. In another hour the ship would back downriver and shuttle to Circle, Rampart, and the newly founded town of Nenana at the junction of the Tanana with the Nenana River. Lucky miners with gold to spare would enjoy a good card game to fill the monotonous passage.

Nathan had come onboard to see his friend off. Doc's constant drinking and sulfurous nature ensured that no one else would. And the lad still hoped to persuade Hennison to seek help.

The bridge failure drew them both to the ship's rail. From the ship they could barely discern the frantic figure on the falling trestle.

"By God, I knew that rattletrap would collapse," Hennison slurred. "I could have built a better one myself, and that's the least favorable pronouncement I could issue against the idiot who constructed that bridge. It would serve him right if he went into the drink with his bridge." With that, Hennison raised his bottle and cheered at a blacksmith running past. "Here's to the fool engineer. May he go down with his bridge like an incompetent captain goes down with his ship."

The blacksmith, who was running away from the scene of disaster, skidded to a halt and shouted up at the two, "That's your friend Riley and his mule on that bridge, not the engineer!"

Instantly Nathan vaulted the upper railing of the steamer to drop to the riverbank below. He hit the ground running and was halfway to the dying Wendell bridge before Doc could gather his wits.

As he raced along the riverbank, Nathan was shocked to see the last remnants of the structure surging past on a wall of water. Riley, clutching his animal's mane, bobbed within the jackstrawed jumble of lumber and driftwood. As heavy timbers snapped and porpoised under the water's force, Riley's head dropped in and out of sight.

Then a deadly mishap compounded this growing disaster. The wreck of the bridge snagged the log boom that encircled the cut timber rafted alongside the sawmill. Planks and tar-soaked beams battered the linked logs until one stout pillar jammed itself between the chains and the rafted wood like a giant's pry bar. With the weight of the river's water levering against it, the chains connecting the raft snapped. Issuing a mournful groan, the entire supply for the lumber mill broke loose and headed downstream.

Nathan skidded to a halt. Scrambling down the mud, he plunged into the water, wading as far as he could while the current buckled his knees and the icy cold numbed his body.

Nathan forced his legs forward into the churning water. Riley would pass within reach if he could get out only a foot or more from shore. A plank struck him, spinning him around, and his senseless feet lost their grip on the slick mud. He foundered and went under. The opening in the water's surface closed overhead, blocking the sunlight that filtered through the water and trapping him beneath the flotsam. His lungs threatened to burst while his eyes searched frantically for an opening. His ears rang in alarm.

There a patch of blue opened where his hands punched through to the surface, tearing the skin on his knuckles on the rough fir siding. His head broke from the surface. While his lungs gasped air, Nathan spun about for his friend.

Riley was inches away. His eyes fixed on Nathan with his hands still locked on Susie's mane, Riley shouted for the youth to save himself. But his words were lost in the roaring of the tidal wave that swept him onward.

Nathan strained his arms to their limits. His effort was rewarded when his nails fastened on Riley's shirt. He clutched the fabric, braced his legs, and gritted his teeth. The weight of both his friend and the mule threatened to wrench his arms from their sockets, but he held on.

Riley stopped in the water. Hope flared in Nathan's mind. But, just then, a log sporting a remnant of chain struck his shoulder like an ax. Nathan's right arm went numb from the blow, and his grip loosened.

In a heartbeat, the current plucked Riley and the mule out of Nathan's grasp. Terror gripped his heart as his friend drifted past in a sea of splinters—only inches out of reach.

With a cry of anguish, Nathan made to follow his friend, but strong hands dragged him back to safety. Fighting their efforts, Nathan felt himself dragged onto the slippery shore. Even then, he kept his eyes fixed on his friend's head as it bobbed toward the Cushman bridge.

Doc Hennison raced to Nathan's side. He ducked his flailing arms. "Easy, Nat," he warned. "You'll only drown yourself. You can't reach Riley from here. Just pray he can catch hold of the Cushman bridge." With his one arm he helped the quivering youth to his feet.

A dozen voices shouted as the tiny heads of Riley and his animal stopped underneath the bridge. Nathan staggered back down the riverbank with Doc helping to support him.

Coming to a halt on the bank upstream of the bridge, what they saw stunned them.

The debris from the smaller bridge added to contents of the log boom had packed against the solidly built Cushman bridge. But this was no cause for rejoicing. The piled lumber now dammed the flow of the swollen river, diverting the river into Fairbanks. The frigid waters of the Chena now flooded the south bank of the river and coursed, unimpeded, along First Avenue. Already the saloons, the Hotel Columbia, and a dozen log houses were engulfed by swirling water and a sea of unpeeled logs. Worse, the river, boiling into its new course, now blocked any passage to the Cushman bridge.

A handful of grim-faced men passed the stunned Nathan. Two of them were carrying sticks of dynamite. Nathan clutched one of the miner's arms. It was his former boss, Jesse Noble.

"Where are you going with that dynamite?" Nathan demanded.

Noble turned his sympathetic gaze on the man who had made a fortune for him. In the short time Riley and this lad had worked for him, Noble had grown to like them. But, he knew what had to be done.

"We've got to blow the bridge, son," he said. "It's holding the logjam in place."

"You can't!" Nathan protested. "The blast will kill Jim!"

Noble jerked his head at the heads bobbing beneath the bridge. "The town's flooding, Nat. We've got to! The whole damned place will be underwater in two more hours. There's no time to waste." He paused to place his free hand on the youth's shoulder. "Riley's done for. No one can help him, bridge or no bridge. The logjam will crush him even if we don't dynamite the Cushman bridge." Noble raised the bundle of explosives high above his head. "I'm asking for volunteers to blow that bridge. I need two men with experience with dynamite!" he shouted.

Nathan pulled his arm down. "I'll do it. And I think I can save Riley in the bargain. If the jam on this side of the river is blown a minute or two before the charge below Riley, the jam will shift away from him. I think I can get a rope around him and pull him free."

"You're crazy, kid," someone muttered. "You'd have less than two minutes before the whole bridge broke loose. One mistake and you'd be trapped out there. Besides, Riley's probably crushed already."

"No, no, he's alive. I saw his head moving," Nathan pleaded. "And I owe him my life. I have to try."

Noble nodded slowly. "Okay, but I'll place another charge in the logjam at the bank. If your idea doesn't do the trick, I'll be forced to blow the jam behind you. You know that, don't you?"

"Yes. If I can't get Jim free and my charge doesn't work, you have my permission to blow this side of the pileup even though I'm still on the bridge."

"This is madness. Look; I still need another volunteer. Is there anyone as crazy as this kid?" Noble turned away from the determined look of this youth and searched the grim faces in the crowd. Nathan's desire to help a man they all thought dead already upped the ante and added to the danger considerably.

"I'll go." Doc Hennison stepped forward and held out his left hand for the dynamite. "I was bored today, anyway," he added offhandedly. "This might liven my day."

"Step back, Doc." Noble frowned. "You're drunk."

Hennison stood his ground. Raising his chin, he declared, "Drunk or sober, I'm volunteering. Besides, I do my best work when I'm under the spell of John Barleycorn."

"What do you know about dynamite, Doc?"

"More than you might expect," Hennison sniffed. He tapped his missing right arm. "I have an intimate experience with explosives, especially Yankee powder. In the late, great war of secession, explosives took my right arm. It would be only sporting to give it another chance at the rest of me—and only fitting if it completed its job. Besides, I put a tad of nitro in my elixir from time to time—just to give it a kick. Now, be a good soul and give me the dynamite, Noble. This is the only time in my life I plan on volunteering, so don't make it any more difficult for me."

Nathan placed his arm around Doc's frail body. Despite Hennison's and Riley's constant fighting, the young man knew it hid an affection for one another. "Thanks, Doc," he said.

"Careful, Nathan," Hennison whispered from the side of his mouth. "Don't let this scum see your true feelings. We wouldn't want to confuse their simple minds."

Nathan chuckled to himself while he looped a coil of rope over his shoulder and tied the bundle of dynamite sticks to the line. Doc would never change. He'd rather die than expose his tender side.

A loud rasping sound from the logjam ended their conversation and sent them running to help their friend. Even now, the rising water was shifting the pile, threatening to compress new driftwood into the mess or cause it to override the tightly packed barricade.

Reaching the bridge from above the jam took all their skill.

Nathan leapt from trunk to trunk while Doc followed along with equal deftness. Where the youth had two arms to save himself when a log tipped or rolled, Hennison had only one. But the doctor had stuck the bundle of explosives inside a deep pocket of his coat, which normally carried a bottle of his elixir, so his only arm was free to help him.

Slipping and skidding across the shifting dam took an eternity, but the two made it to the cheers of the watching townsfolk. Now they raced across the solid planks of the Cushman bridge to the middle of the span. Nathan held his breath as he peered over the railing into the jumble of logs and boards driven into the side of the crossing. His eyes searched among the wreckage for Riley. But for the magnitude of scale he could have been sighting a ptarmigan amid a thicket, except each tree trunk snarled below him weighed over a ton and he was looking for his friend rather than a bird. Adding to his anxiety was the constant motion of this deadly trap.

His heart missed a beat when he spotted Riley's worn Stetson floating amid the wreckage the instant a massive trunk, complete with tangled roots, rolled over and crushed the hat beneath the waves.

"I see him!" Doc shouted. "He's down here!" Frantically he jabbed his arm at a pile directly below him.

Nathan ran to his side. Riley's sodden head glared up at him from an unstable stockade of wood wedged against itself. By some miracle, the gunman and his mule floated inside a tiny space that an enormous log had formed as it speared the trestle supporting that section. More flotsam piled around their shoulders, but not enough to bury them, and the strength of the log fended off the crushing forces of the pileup.

But they would have to work fast. Even now, the force of the damming water was starting to splinter the trunk. The creaks and groans of the bending log spoke to the need for great urgency.

"Git the hell off this bridge!" Riley yelled up between coughing out mouthfuls of foul water. His one arm was wrapped around a limb while his other hand clamped one ear of the frightened animal and pressed her head and neck across the log in an effort to keep her head above water. "Save yourselves!" Riley choked.

Nathan ignored his friend. Dropping to his knees, he assessed the situation. Any minute the jam might shift and kill Riley, but the space that protected them only allowed enough room for their heads. He was unable to pull Riley to safety while he held onto his mule.

"Let go of that damned ass!" Doc shouted. "And we'll drop you a line and pull you up!"

Riley shook his head vehemently. "I'm not abandoning Susie."

"I always knew you were crazy," Doc railed. "By God, now I've got the proof I need. You'd lose your life over a dumb animal? That's plain insane."

"It's the dumb animals like her that need protecting," Riley sputtered. "It's not the slicksters like you. The world needs more of these beasts, but there ain't no shortage of fools to play cards." Susie struggled at the sound of his words, forcing him to tighten his grip on her ear.

Nathan looked about wildly. What was he to do? Even if the space were widened by some miracle, he and Doc would be unable to raise both Riley and his mule out of the water. Then he got an idea. Riley and his animal were caught in the outer rim of the ever-growing pileup. As the jam grew, it forced their part of the dam farther from the town's side, sliding it laterally along the resistance of the stout pilings of the Cushman bridge.

But that pushed it closer to the far side of the river. If Nathan could break loose the jam below Riley, he might stand a chance. If, that is, he could swim to the opposite bank without being ridden down by the surging tree trunks. If he could blow the lower part of the piled logs, below Riley, that part would break free and run downstream. The trees encircling his friend would run with those logs, separating into smaller clumps as they went. Riley and his mule could swim for the far shore. It would require luck and split-second timing. A hundred things could go wrong: the blast might shock them, the pileup might not separate as Nathan planned, or the logs might ride his friend onto the shallow riverbank with the wall of water, smashing him like an insignificant bug against a rock. Still, it was a chance, however slim, and Jim's only chance.

Nathan hung over the edge of the bridge until his face was as close to his friend's as possible and jabbed his finger to the south shore. "Jim, listen to me. I aim to crawl over that pile of driftwood beyond you. If I can blast the logs over there apart, it might free you enough to make it to the other side. What do you think?"

Riley grinned as best he could while the water slopped into his face. The struggle against both Susie and the undertow was taking its toll. His face was pale from the effort. "Give it yer best shot, Nat," he gasped. "I don't much relish what I'm doing right now. And I'm running out of steam."

"Once that blows, Jim, you swim like hell. When I see you and Susie reach the shore, Doc and I will race along the bridge and blow the other side." So focused was Nathan on his talk with Riley that he failed to notice Doc crouched by his side, listening intently. Hennison's eyes lighted as he comprehended the plan.

Riley nodded. But before Nathan could rise, Hennison climbed the railing and dropped onto the twisted nightmare of wood. With surprising agility, the one-armed man clambered over the giant jackstraws like a monkey. Nathan yelled after him, but Doc only waved back at the young man without turning around or breaking his stride. In two minutes, Hennison reached the spot. Riding the undulating logs with his legs wide set, he withdrew his bundle of dynamite from his frock coat and wedged the deadly parcel against the underside of the heaviest trunk.

Nathan's heart soared as he watched Doc rise to wave back at them. "He's got the charge placed!" Nathan relayed the news to Riley. "Come on, Doc!" he screamed, but he knew the thunder of the jam would overwhelm his words. "Light the fuse and get out of there!" Nathan found himself waving his arms like a windmill. It would work; he knew it in his heart as soon as he saw Doc straighten. The charge was exactly where he wanted it. It would free Riley; then he and Doc would place the next charge. They would all escape unscathed as they had countless times before, the town would be saved, and the three of them would each have a beer tonight to celebrate. . . .

An explosion drove Nathan onto his side, followed abruptly by an ear-splitting roar. The Cushman bridge buckled under his side and lifted him into the air while a hot wall of water and smoke broke over him. Like a cat, Nathan scrambled to his feet. He blinked away the water that blinded him. What had happened?

Worse than the slap of a bullet, the realization struck him. Someone had already blown the bridge behind him! Noble had not waited.

Already the section of bridge closest to town was breaking up, torn apart by the blast and the force of the damned water and logs. Rushing toward him like the hand of doom was a wall of water that buckled the bridge planks as it approached. In seconds, that wall would hit with the force of a steam engine. The bridge under him would disintegrate, throwing him alongside Riley to be pulverized by the massive wave as it roiled the forest of floating wood.

And there was nothing he could do. The premature dynamiting had reversed his plan. Even if Doc lit the fuse now, it would be in vain. His fuse was purposefully cut long enough to allow Doc to escape the blast. It would never explode that bundle of dynamite before the tidal wave swept over them all.

Tears welled in the youth's eyes. It would have worked, he knew. But now all was lost.

But Doc had witnessed what transpired. Standing on the logs, he could see the tidal wave of trees and water rushing toward them. He saw—and understood what had to be done. If he could blow the jam before the wave reached them, they still stood a chance. But that left no time for him to retreat before his charges exploded. He must not use the long wick.

Backing a few steps from the sticks of explosives, Doc shook his head at the irony he perceived. "I hope they don't think I did this to save that mule," he spoke out loud. But the roar of the water swallowed his words.

Slowly, with exaggerated decorum, Doc Hennison drew himself to his full height while he pulled his derringer from another inside pocket. He cast an offhanded salute at his friend Nathan, touching the side of his forehead briefly with the gun barrel, before taking careful aim at the firing cap wedged in the center of dynamite sticks. He paused for a split second. Then he squeezed the trigger.

A second blast rocked the afternoon.

★ ★ FIFTEEN ★ ★

Tonopah, Nevada. Wyatt looked up from the cards in his hand to study the man entering the saloon. Half-cloaked in shadow, the man's other side blazed with illuminated light from the noonday sun. The figure paused at the entrance to survey the long room. His eyes swept over the polished bar and down the length of sawdust-strewn floor to stop at the table where Wyatt sat with his brother and one other man. Glancing neither to the left nor to the right, he strode directly toward them.

The conversation in the Northern dropped to a low undertone of murmurs and nervous coughs as shielded eyes cast furtive looks at this intruder. Only the metallic clink of his spurs sounded above the low hum as he passed table after table without pausing.

Wyatt noted this progress without the faintest sign of emotion. But when this stranger reached the halfway mark, Wyatt's right boot tapped Virgil's foot. Virgil's eyes drifted slowly up to lock on the stranger, and his great walrus mustache twitched slightly at one corner. With a lengthy sigh his gaze returned to the pasteboards dwarfed in his beefy hands. The third man at the table also watched this arrival from the corner of his eye. None of the three men sat with his back to the open door.

The bartender paused in his polishing of beer glasses and calculated the distance from his right hand with its stained towel to the sawed-off shotgun clipped beneath the edge of the bar. Nothing about this newcomer looked reassuring. His soiled duster draped unbuttoned across a white shirt with string tie. Dark brown pin-striped pants tucked into knee-high boots covered his lower half.

What especially caught the bartender's attention was the heavy leather gun belt strapped around the man's waist. A single holster enclosed a long-barreled Colt .45 revolver that appeared welded to the man's right side. As the man walked, the gun moved as freely and as naturally as if it were a part of him. The weapon acted like an extension of the man's will, fused to his side from years of service.

The handle of the pistol, the holster, and the belt were free of even the smallest speck of dust, yet alkali powder covered the man's boots, hat, and duster until they looked almost white. Far more telling was the condition of the side arm. The revolver was oiled and brown-stained like a fine watch.

This was a man who made his living with his gun, the barkeep decided.

The newcomer stopped two paces from the table and looked down. "You're one damned hard man to find, Wyatt Earp," he said.

Wyatt smiled over his cards and pretended to ignore the remark. He was holding three queens, and he guessed his brother only had a pair of kings. He sucked his teeth as he figured the odds of the other player having a better hand. Six hundred dollars lay on the table, and he dearly wished to finish this hand. Still, this visitor had to be reckoned with. . . .

Virgil beat him to the punch. "By God, look what the cat dragged in!" the big man exclaimed as he jumped to his feet with a quickness that belied his bulk and shot out his hand. "Frank Leslie! I haven't seen you in a month of Sundays."

Buckskin Frank Leslie clamped Virgil's hand in his as the two struggled to mangle each other's hand in their grip. "That's 'cause you're too chicken-livered to venture up north to the cold of Alaska like your brother, Virge." Leslie cocked his head at the slouching Wyatt. "Although it looks to me like Wyatt's gone to seed a mite since he last passed through Wrangell. Both you Earp brothers aren't getting soft on me, are you?" Leslie extracted his bloodless fingers from Virgil's crushing grip and shook it to return the feeling. He wiggled his throbbing hand. "I guess that don't hold true for Virgil," he said begrudgingly.

Wyatt straightened his back and tightened his stomach muscles, making the slight bulge at his beltline vanish. "The good cooking of a loving woman can be more dangerous than many a shootist, I've discovered. Sadie's trying to fatten me up so no other gal will look at me," he laughed.

Frank Leslie placed both hands on his hips, showing off his still trim figure. "Not me, Wyatt. Whores and bad grub is keeping me fit."

Virgil guffawed while he tried to sneak a peek at Wyatt's hand. "Don't let Allie or Josie hear you talk so. They'll run you out of town."

Wyatt guarded his hand. "Frank, I assume you know Frank Canton since you both are U.S. marshals for Alaska."

"*Former* marshal," Canton corrected Wyatt. "I'm officially retired since my snow blindness." He rose to shake Leslie's hand. "How are you, Frank?"

"I'm fine. Say, I heard you got pardoned by the governor of Oklahoma. That's just grand. You deserved having your slate wiped clean. I never heard a single complaint about how you handled your part of the territory. We miss you up north a whole hell of a lot."

Canton raised his eyebrows. "Been so long since I used Joe Horner for a handle, I've got used to Frank Canton rather than my real name. I guess the governor figured my marshaling paid for my bank robbing days. Keeping the law in Alaska had to be stiffer than any jail sentence, he told me."

Leslie found an empty chair and drew it up. "Well, your governor never saw Yuma Territorial Prison, I'd wager. Alaska is bad enough, but it never got as hot as that damned hole."

Leslie looked around for the bartender and signaled for a cold beer. The relieved employee all but flew to his side with a foaming mug of his finest brew. Leslie emptied the glass and motioned for another. "Damn, this heat is getting to me. I'm out of practice at sweating since I moved to Alaska. Not much call there."

"We sweated there," Wyatt reminded him. "But it was cold sweat."

"You got pardoned, too, didn't you, Frank? Same as me?" Canton continued.

Leslie nodded. "Yeah. I did time in Yuma, and I deserved it. Killing a woman like I did was wrong, but I did my time, and I got pardoned just like you, Canton. The only difference was my pardon came before I took to marshaling instead of after like yours did."

"Well, are you two going to play or just gab like two old women?" Wyatt asked impatiently. The cards were burning his fingers. "If anything is getting cold around here it's this pot. You boys plan on playing, folding, or what?"

"A pair of kings," Virgil grunted as he laid down his hand. Wyatt's enthusiasm told him his two kings would not take the pot.

"I fold," Frank Canton followed suit. He looked carefully at Leslie. "Buckskin, how long since you been back west?"

"Must be . . . hell, almost five years, I guess. Working that far up north don't exactly make travel easy. Besides that, the work has kept me damned busy. Why?"

Canton wiped back the corners of his mustache. "It's changed, Buckskin. It's really changed," he sighed. "Almost nothing's the same as it was. Telephones sprouting up like tumbleweed. Why, banks and the railroads own just about all there is that's worth owning, and every damned pokey burg has more church socials on Sunday than you can shake a stick at."

"And automobile cars," Virgil added. "Don't hardly pay to own a horse anymore, Frank. The damned gasoline cars run you off the road."

Frank Leslie cast a confused look at Wyatt. "What are they saying, Wyatt?"

"Everything is too damned civilized, Buckskin," Wyatt answered.

"Hmm." Leslie scratched the back of his neck. "Sort of like Frisco without the salt air and fresh oysters?"

The three other men nodded.

"Well, that's a shame, fellows. I suspect I won't know how to act."

"Oklahoma is downright boring," Canton sniffed. "I do a little part-time as a lawman, and most is chasing loose dogs and running down stray husbands. It's damned humiliating. They won't even let me shoot the dogs, let alone the husbands. I'd give my eyeteeth for a good bank robbery—just one. But all the cash is transferred by train, nowadays. Robbing stages is a thing of the past, too. And a posse? Whoa! Why, if there was ever need for one, the air would be filled with the stink of motorcars, and all the telephones for a hundred miles around would be ringing off their hooks."

"Virge here is an expert with auto cars," Wyatt quipped.

"Wyatt's exaggerating a mite, boys," Virgil protested. "He tends to run a bit optimistic, as well. Sort of like that fella who got scalped by the Utes during their last fracas said after he survived the event."

"What did he say?" Canton took the bait.

Virgil grinned from ear to ear, causing his mustache to rise at both corners like the wings of a seagull. "Well, sir, he said he was grateful to them Utes for relieving him of any fear of going bald in the future."

Wyatt chuckled politely while the three other men broke into belly laughs. Virgil loved a good joke.

After the humor had run its course, a silence descended over the table. Frank Canton spread his fingers across the tabletop and studied the creases and scars of forty years of frontier life.

"Sort of makes a fellow feel useless," he said quietly. "All them modern contraptions have wiped out what skill the four of us built up over all these years."

Buckskin Frank Leslie cocked his head. "Maybe," he drawled, "but we sure raised some hell during our heyday, didn't we? There's never been another shoot-out to match the likes of the Earps and the Clantons, and I doubt there ever will."

"Thank God for that," Wyatt interjected. "Nothing good came out of that showdown."

"You're wrong there, Wyatt." Leslie waved his beer glass at his friend. "No matter what you think, your brothers and Doc Holliday standing up with you against Ike Clanton and his crew sent a message to two-bit gunmen everywhere that law officers are willing to face them—no matter what the risk or what it costs. And that message set a standard for the rest of us. One that still holds. It makes them think twice about taking to the outlaw trail, believe me. And that's more important, in my book, than all the fancy speeches and laws coming out of Washington or New York or San Francisco."

"Amen to that," Canton added.

"It cost my family a hell of a lot," Wyatt argued.

Canton shook his head. "Those rats would have bushwhacked Morgan and Virgil sometime or another. Your plugging three of them just helped even the odds, and probably helped keep you alive."

"Hell," Leslie snorted. "We evened the odds a *whole* lot more after we took to the trail to hunt down the rest of them cowboys. You missed it, Virge, but Wyatt was a real helldorado on four legs. I've never seen such grim determination. Wading into the middle of Iron Springs with bullets kicking up water all around him to cut Curly Bill Brocius down with his sawed-off scattergun. And Doc . . . he was a fighting fool."

Wyatt let a slight smile escape. "Not much clear-headed thinking was done during that ride. What there was you could carry around in a lady's handbag."

"But weren't we magnificent!" Leslie blurted out. "The Two Jacks—Texas Jack and Turkey Creek Johnson—you, me, and Doc. The world will never see another ride like that. We were the best." He pounded the heel of his glass on the table for emphasis.

Virgil looked around the table. Unlike him, the three other men were still lean and rawboned. Despite the obvious gray that dusted their hair and the creases lining all four faces, every man's eyes were clear and sparkling with an unwavering gaze. "We're still the best," he said suddenly. "Look at us. We may be worn a bit at the edges, but that just adds character. None of us are feeble. None of us got the shakes. The big difference is now we've gotten more experience than back then."

Wyatt looked in amazement at his brother. A fire burned in his brother's eyes that Wyatt had not seen for some time. "Maybe *smarter* is a better word, Virge."

"All right, smarter. But we still have the makings."

"He's right," Canton agreed. The enthusiasm now infected him. He was on his feet with his face shining. "Each one of us can shoot the eyes out of a gnat, and we still have the nerve. Why, we'd be the toughest posse you ever did see if we rode together. Just think of it, what a Class A posse we'd make."

Wyatt's grin widened until it seemed to touch each ear. "There's not an outlaw gang bad enough to need our services, gentlemen. Not since they shot up the Daltons in Coffeyville and Sundance and Cassidy went to Bolivia."

Leslie leaned over the table and whispered conspiratorially, "Well, then, *we* could rob banks. I'm sure we could do that better than these . . . these amateurs we've got to deal with."

Frank Canton almost choked on his drink. Only the wink Leslie gave him made him realize the man was joking.

Wyatt played along. "What would we call ourselves, Buckskin? Maybe, the 'Not So Wild Gang'? Or the 'Still Wild Bunch'? I don't want you calling us the Earp Gang. Sadie would tan my hide if I sullied our good name."

"Allie, too," Virgil added. "And she's a terror when she's got her dander up, in spite of her size."

"The Hole in the Pants Gang," Canton laughed.

Leslie waved his arm over all their heads. "Have you looked at the four of us? With our handlebar mustaches, we look enough alike to be brothers. Think about that. We could call ourselves the brothers something or another."

"Better make it something anonymous," Virgil counseled. "Something our wives won't recognize."

"The Smith Brothers," Wyatt suggested.

"The Smith Brothers it is." Canton seconded the notion. "If we ever decide to hit the outlaw trail, we call ourselves the Smith Brothers."

"To the Smith Brothers!" they all toasted.

"And God help those who cross our path," Virgil added.

The four men broke into laughter and clinked their glasses against Wyatt's coffee mug. He passed out cigars to all. In minutes, a garland of smoke wreathed their table as each man sat, tipped back in his chair, and dreamed of past glories.

After a time, Canton interrupted their thoughts. "I don't know about the Earps here, Buckskin, but I'd hold onto your marshal's job as long as you can. I find this being retired goddamned boring. In fact, I'm so bored that I could spit. It's so bad that for an instant I actually *liked* the idea of being one of the Smith Brothers."

Wyatt gave his friend a sharp look. "Frank, you could no more rob a bank than shoot down some widow woman while she prayed in church. None of us could. We've all carried a tin star far too long to break the law. Upholding the law is burned deeper into our hides than any branding iron could ever do."

"You mean the *right* law, don't you Wyatt?" Virgil corrected his brother. "All of us have seen too many bad rules and regulations pushed on us by crooked town bosses and their paid-off judges. Look what happened in Tombstone, and the same damned thing occurred in Nome."

Canton grunted in disgust. "I heard about the Spoilers in Nome. McKenzie and Judge Alfred Noyes—what a disgrace! I wanted to head up to Nome myself, but my hands were full with my own district. I was never so happy as when those marshals arrived from Frisco to arrest the both of them. Still, the other federal judge, Wickersham, refused to investigate Noyes's actions. It's enough to make you sick."

Wickersham! The name rang a warning bell in the back of Wyatt's mind. Wasn't that the name of the judge that Nathan had written about in his last letter? Wyatt closed his eyes and said a silent prayer that his son might be spared from dealing with any corrupt judge. Instead of feeling the guiding hand of Providence in answer to his imprecation, he felt a dark idea shimmer through his thoughts. To his surprise, this twisted idea appealed to him.

Slowly, Wyatt rose to his feet. He snubbed out his cigar on the brass ashtray beside him and raised his coffee cup. He fixed his friends with his iron gray eyes, and immediately all conversation stopped. He waited until he held the undivided attention of the others.

"To the Smith Brothers!" he toasted. "May they never sink so low as to break the law. *But—if the need should ever arise—may they ride in defense of justice!*"

★ ★ SIXTEEN ★ ★

Fairbanks. Nathan stood beside the mound of dirt representing the remains of his friend and companion, Doc Hennison, and bowed his head. No body was recovered from the icy waters of the Chena even though Nathan and Riley had searched both banks from the wreck of the bridge to the mouth of the Tanana. Nothing was found of Nathan's friend except his hip flask, battered and twisted and wedged into the crotch of a half-sunken tree, and a torn scrap of the jacket that Doc had been wearing.

Heartbroken, Nathan stared glumly at the pile of freshly turned soil. A dozen prayers that the nuns had driven into his resisting skull came to mind. Even his fingers wished for the comforting touch of rosary beads. It had been a lifetime since he last felt the need for formal prayer. He was like a madman, then. Now, he simply felt hollow.

Mostly, Nathan thanked Providence in an easy, disconnected way whenever the occasion arose. During a safe passage, while watching a shooting star cut across the Northern Lights, or after a gorgeous sunrise, he would speak mainly from his heart. But Doc's death called for something more.

At his feet the freshly turned soil along the riverbank looked bleak and barren compared to the surrounding green hills and the Chena River. Even the other graves in this new cemetery by the river's edge sported flowers or blades of grass. Pneumonia, mining accidents, and murder accounted for the occupants of this site, and now an unreformed gambler joined their ranks.

Nathan kneeled and placed his armful of wildflowers on top of the grave. Mostly fireweed, the mix contained a scattering of wild roses, sweet peas, and dark blue forget-me-nots. From deep within the swamp Jim Riley had fetched a single chocolate lily, so rare this late in the season and so poignant with its solitary brown color. It lay beside the other flowers like a broken heart.

Already over half the pink flowers of the fireweed were gone, turned to wispy, silvery fluff and scattered before the wind. Folklore pronounced that summer ended with the last blooming of the fireweed. These flowers warned of the coming of winter. It would be a cold and dark winter without Doc, Nathan thought.

The youth tried to speak, but the tightness in his throat stifled whatever he hoped to say. Instead, he looked imploringly to Riley.

Riley stepped forward and removed his battered Stetson. Strangely, the broad-brimmed cover looked out of place for the first time to its owner. Why the river chose to release his hat while it took Doc's life Riley could not imagine. He and his hat had crossed many a desert and many a mountain, and both bore the marks of their journeys. He twisted the hat in his hands as he collected his thoughts.

Riley, his mule, and even his hat had survived the catastrophe in the river to wash up on the far bank with Nathan, shaken and barked, but alive. Doc's unselfish act had saved them all.

Riley bowed his head and spoke.

"Dear Lord, we stand before the last remains of Doc Hennison. He had many first names, but he always answered to 'Doc.' " Riley shifted his feet while he struggled for the right words. In the end, his mind balked, so his thoughts poured directly from his heart, free of any gloss or sheen his mind might try to place upon them.

"I suspect old Doc is standing before you right now, Lord. He may strike you as a greasy, tinhorn so-and-so, but he's really better than he looks. Now, he ain't perfect, Lord. Far from it.

His life weren't the softest, and I figure that made him sour like he was. But his living was cut off before he had a chance to reform because he got killed saving us. Lord, if you was to see your way clear to let him in, Nathan and I would be mighty grateful. We owe him our lives. So, if you're the forgiving kind like my mama always taught me, you'll let him through them Pearly Gates and make a spot for him. One thing for certain: you sure won't have to worry about the place being dull with Doc around. Amen."

Riley settled his hat back in place, embarrassed by his show of emotion. "I guess that about says it, Nat," he said plainly.

Nathan unfolded his hands and smiled at his remaining friend. "A good prayer, Jim. No preacher could have done better."

Riley looked about at the scattering of graves. "Well, I don't see none of the occupants of these graves pulling up stakes and leaving because of Doc joining them. So, maybe he made it through them gates after all."

Nathan was about to agree when his back stiffened at what he saw. Standing at the edge of the cemetery clearing was Jesse Noble. Nathan cinched his pistol belt tight and walked directly toward the nervous man.

Noble kept his arms far from his sides while his unbuttoned jacket revealed he carried no visible weapon. "Don't shoot, Nathan," he pleaded. "I'm not armed."

"You'd better get one," Nathan hissed, "or I might just shoot you whether you're carrying or not."

Noble quailed at the vehemence of Nathan's words.

"I told you not to light your charge unless all else failed," Nathan continued. "You never gave us a chance. You blew the bridge from under our feet. You killed Doc as surely as if you put a bullet through his back."

Riley stepped beside his friend. "Better git yerself a gun, Jesse, and say a prayer 'cause I'm going to kill you if Nathan changes his mind," he said coldly. "What you did to them was worse than a skunk would do. It was pure murder."

"I . . . I didn't do it!"

"What do you mean?"

"I didn't light any charge," Noble stuttered. "I never even got time to place the dynamite I had."

Riley stepped closer and poked his face close to Noble's blinking eyes. His nose stopped an inch from the frightened miner's visage. "Then who in hell did? That damned bridge didn't just blow up all by itself."

"I don't know."

"Billy Wilson," a voice said. "It was Billy Wilson who blew up the Cushman bridge while you were still on it."

Nathan spun around to see Ezra Hayes striding toward them. "Billy Wilson?"

"Yes." Hayes nodded. "I saw him doing something on the bridge just after you and Doc headed across to where Riley was caught in the water. But I didn't pay much attention at first. I was dragging newsprint and type out of my flooded office when he rushed by me. I was trying to salvage what was left of my press, and the water was rising fast. Something made me look over to the bridge. There I saw Wilson placing a bundle underneath the supports of the bridge—right near this side. He climbed back up and took off running like a scared rabbit. Next thing I knew an explosion knocked me flat on my back. When I pulled myself out of the water and logs in the flooded street, the bridge was blown to smithereens."

"You're sure of this?" Nathan demanded. "No mistake about it? It was Wilson?"

"It was Wilson. No question in my mind. There's no mistaking his outfit—all dressed in black like some warlock. It was him all right. He blew up the bridge while you were still in the middle of the river. He's the one, not Noble, who killed Doc Hennison."

"Then he's as good as dead," Nathan proclaimed. "Where is he?"

Hayes jerked his head toward the bend in the river that marked the center of Fairbanks. "Hiding behind the captain's skirts, I'd imagine. He was strutting around like a banty rooster until he found out you and Riley were still alive. Someone told

Richard Parry

him about you two, and—I swear—he turned white as a sheet
and took off like a scalded dog in the direction of Barnette's
bank. I wouldn't be surprised to find him hiding in the captain's vault."

Nathan looked at Riley. "Guess we ought to pay the captain
a visit, don't you agree, Jim?"

"I'm coming along," Ezra Hayes spoke first, "and so is Jesse
here. You two might need proper witnesses, especially with the
judge and his brother in Barnette's back pocket."

Noble bobbed his head in consent. Without another word,
they started walking toward Barnette's bank. As the procession
moved, Ezra, acting like the town crier, announced their plans
and intentions as loudly as his failing voice could shout to anyone they happened to meet. By the time the four men had
moved along the river and cut down the sodden path that was
First Avenue, six other men had joined them. Most were
miners who carried grudges against Barnette, but two were
gamblers who liked Doc and had gambled with him on the
riverboats.

The party slogged through the knee-deep mud that once
was the main thoroughfare of town and clambered over logs,
branches, and planks that littered the route. Nathan had time
to examine the damage done to this part of town. Once the
center of Fairbanks, with saloons jammed shoulder to shoulder
with boardinghouses and stores, the street now carried the appearance of total disarray.

A score of log structures lay snatched from their founda-
tions and scattered randomly beside the street. Three or four
cabins had floated free with the force of the flood and come to
rest directly in the center of First Avenue. Those structures
constructed with sawed lumber from the new mill fared an
even worse fate. Slab siding lay stripped from still-dripping fa-
cades or splintered by the battering ram effects of the heavy
logs that charged down the street with the wall of water.

As if acting in collusion with Barnette, the debris blocking
the road made passage to his bank all but impossible. The mud
sucked at their boots; the displaced houses forced them to

190

clamber over piles of brush and tree limbs to bypass the build-ings only to find their route blocked by more obstacles.

At each juncture they met townsfolk struggling to salvage whatever they could. A woman was collecting tin washtubs that had floated away down the street in such good order as to shame a naval flotilla. Strung out alongside the tubs were hun-dreds of bars of soap, freed from their barrel and deposited high and dry atop the mud. Dozens of beer bottles and half-filled whiskey bottles liberated from the riverfront saloons lay upended in the silt. A scattering of chickens roosted on still-floating crates and cartons along the road while casting a wary eye on a sharp-shinned hawk that soared overhead. A solitary pig took advantage of the chaos to wallow in one new water hole after another.

Even though a day had passed since the flood, people still walked about in a trance, moving slowly like sleepwalkers as they salvaged their goods. Few had slept that night, and even fewer had seen a warm meal.

Whenever the group encountered someone struggling with a crate or heavy box, they stopped to help. Splintered doors were wrestled free of mud and back into their doorways, cast-iron stoves dug out of the mud, and wagons righted. All in all, it was punishing work. No one kept count of how many they helped, and few of those they aided could muster more than a feeble thanks or tired smile.

A good four hours passed before they stood at the steps of Captain Barnette's bank and safe-deposit company. By that time, their company was reduced to the original four. The ed-itor and Jesse Noble were exhausted and too muddied to be of much threat to the captain, but grim determination drove Nathan and his friend onward. Both men had taken extra pains to keep their firearms clean of the slime that coated everything else.

To their amazement, Barnette's bank appeared unscathed. A secondary logjam one hundred feet upstream of his building had diverted the river's water and flotsam past the bank and into the side of the Cushman bridge. The newly built Northern

Commercial Company's warehouse with its shiny tin roof sporting brightly painted red letters was also untouched by the deluge. To Nathan's chagrin, he realized that blowing the bridge and the log pile had saved the bank and the supply company that the captain partly owned. Once again, E. T. Barnette's luck had proved exceptional. This disaster had only served to increase his wealth.

The door of the bank opened, and E. T. Barnette stepped onto the front porch. Making no attempt to conceal his swagger, he walked to the edge of the raised platform, placed his hands on both hips, and looked down at the bedraggled party. The dark green riding coat with its buffed leather collar and the spotless polish on his knee-high boots contrasted sharply with the torn, mud-encrusted rags his visitors wore.

"Well, well, gentlemen, what can I do for you? Surely you don't wish to make a deposit, do you?"

"I'm looking for Billy Wilson, Captain," Nathan said, cutting directly to the point.

"*We're* looking for the Kid," Riley corrected him.

"And what would you want with *Mister* Wilson?"

"I saw him blow up the bridge when Nat and Doc—"

Nathan held up his hand, silencing Ezra Hayes. "We came to drill the polecat through his yellow gizzard," he snarled. "Now, tell him to come out, or we're coming inside to look for him."

"He ought to be easy to find," Riley snapped. "We'll jus' nose around until we sniff out his stench. Someone as rotten as the Kid must smell real rank."

"He's not here," Barnette lied flatly. "In fact, I haven't seen him for some time, nor do I expect to."

While the the men argued and the captain focused his attention on Nathan and Riley, Ezra Hayes slipped around the side of the bank, intent on scouting the alley behind the bank. Jesse Noble simply collapsed on the lower step of the bank, too played out to take more than a passing interest in anything now but sleep. Within minutes, Ezra returned from the scouting foray he had conducted. He ears perked up at Barnette's denial of Kid Wilson's whereabouts.

"Don't know where he is, eh? Well, how come his horse is tied up at the hitching post behind your bank, Captain? I don't suppose you agreed to feed and water it for him?"

Barnette's face flushed and the muscles of his jaw rippled as he clenched his teeth. He had warned that stupid Wilson to move his horse, and the Kid had said he did.

Barnette made a mental note to arrange for Wilson's removal from his employment as soon as his services were no longer absolutely necessary. Being mayor and with his bank flourishing, he was making money hand over fist. But all that depended on people trusting his bank enough to deposit their gold within its four walls. Wilson's bloodthirsty talents would soon be an embarrassment. Having Wilson around and his handful of regulators tarnished Barnette's image of respectability.

And that image was crucial at this time. Unbeknownst to anyone but one other person, Elbridge T. Barnette was hatching a plot to make himself a millionaire—many times over. Surrounded by bags of gold dust and satchels of gold nuggets, the captain with his scheming mind saw another avenue to self-enrichment.

Although he was already the wealthiest man in the interior of Alaska, Barnette's extravagance demanded more. Hidden from general knowledge, Barnette was investing heavily in Mexican estates and land speculation. He even threw money into breeding race horses in Kentucky. For all he made, his thirst for riches remained unchecked. Even the prospect of a railroad into Fairbanks, bringing cheaper supplies, and the exclusive contract his brother-in-law, Jim Hill, received from Judge Wickersham to be the sole supplier of electric power to the growing town were not enough. He wanted more.

The arrival of Jim Hill gave him the idea. He appointed Hill as another officer of his bank, bypassing R. C. Wood, Barnette's teller, whose honesty the miners trusted implicitly.

With the aid of the indebted Hill, the captain was busy stealing. Screened by a barricade of carefully juggled books, Barnette shipped portions of each gold deposit to banks outside for his own use. While the ledgers balanced to the pennyweight, what gold resided in the captain's secure deposit vaults was actually far less than it ought to be.

Unwittingly the miners locked the golden eggs from their geese inside a vault that already held the fox. Barnette wanted nothing to expose that truth. Therefore, his unblemished image was all-important.

His mind snapped back to the problem at hand. "Where Wilson ties his horse is no concern of mine."

Nathan stepped forward with his hand gripping the butt of his pistol. "It is to us. Step aside, Captain. I'm going inside to look around."

Before he reached the top step, another figure appeared in the doorway behind Barnette. Nathan stopped in midstride, shocked by what he saw. His mouth gaped open while his eyes blinked as if to wipe away what his mind refused to accept.

Behind the captain stood Molly Hayes.

"May we help you, Mr. Blaylock?" she asked.

Nathan swayed uncertainly with his right foot poised in the air. "Molly," he blurted out, "what are you doing here?"

"Yes!" The editor added his question. "Molly Hayes, what the devil are you doing in Barnette's bank?" Where Nathan acted confused, old Ezra exuded anger and indignation. "Has he laid a finger on you?" he steamed.

Molly flashed in anger. "I am here with Mrs. Barnette to organize a ladies' relief effort for the unfortunate victims of the flood!"

Compounding Nathan's confusion, Isabelle Barnette stepped out beside Molly. For an instant the youth feared the two ladies had been sharing their impressions of him. But the look on Isabelle Barnette's face told him otherwise.

"Good afternoon, Mr. Blaylock," she said with the same nod of her head that a duchess might give to her stable boy.

It was over a year since Nathan last saw the captain's wife.

In that year, she had undergone a world of change. Nathan could scarcely link that girl of his memories with the woman who stood before him.

A year ago, Isabelle Barnette, bored, frightened, and neglected by her husband, had slipped naked into an icy pool where Nathan bathed and made passionate love to him. Nathan could still recall the heat of her burning kisses cutting through the chill of the stream and the warmth of her skin as they lay in each other's arms on the moss-covered floor of the forest.

But this was a far different Isabelle. Gone was the lonely girl, and in her place stood a regal woman. Her demeanor and dress marked her as the preeminent lady of this booming town. That she might even notice him as he passed on the street now seemed inconceivable. Isabelle, it appeared, had relegated him to the dark recesses of her mind like some unacceptable dream.

Nathan shook his head, trying to reconcile the disparate images his own mind held. Before him stood a woman dressed demurely in a somber burgundy dress complete with high lace collar and one of those damned watches pinned to her bodice. Yet he had only to blink to recall the goose bumps covering her shivering breasts. These contradictory thoughts left him more shaken and speechless than might the impact of a bullet.

Worse still was his knowledge that Captain Barnette knew Nathan had slept with his wife and had tried to hang him for it. And would again if he got the chance.

Yet here they were standing around like deacons at a church social.

Instantly Molly's intuition honed in on Nathan's distress. His confusion and Isabelle's coldness told her all she needed to know. Despite all her efforts, her topaz-colored eyes widened and a scarlet flush appeared at the neckline of dress. She willed her voice to remain level and her face to fix into a mask equal to the one Isabelle wore.

"Well, my business is done here," Molly said as she smiled frostily at the Barnettes. Clamping her hands primly together, she turned her back on them and marched to stand in front of Nathan. "Will you escort me home, Mr. Blaylock?" she asked.

Before he could stammer any answer, Molly slipped her arm inside his so adroitly that it seemed as if he had offered her his arm and led the dazed young man away.

Barnette clasped his wife's elbow and jerked her back into his bank. The silence that followed lasted little more than a split second. The slamming of the bank's door made Ezra jump. When he recovered his wits he turned to look at the departing backs of Nathan and his niece.

"I guess this sortie is over," Jesse Noble said tiredly.

"And a lot of good it did us, too," the editor added. "Did I miss something? What just happened?" He sounded like a balloon deflating from a dozen puncture wounds.

Riley watched his friend struggling to keep up with the woman linked to his arm. "I think that boy's in more danger with yer niece than he would be facing Billy Wilson's gun," he drawled. He looked down at his filthy boots and spit a stream of tobacco juice on the left toe. The fluid ate away enough of the mud to expose the scuffed leather. He shook his head in bewilderment. "I swear! If women ever gits to favoring six-guns, we men ought to just roll over and play dead. They got some moves built into them that would shame a diamondback rattler when it comes to speed. Did you see how fast Molly caught the drift of what passed between Nat and Mrs. Barnette? Whew! I ain't never seen nothing strike that fast." He squinted after the departing couple. "I pity the lad," he murmured.

Molly marched Nathan the length of the wrecked First Avenue without a word and with little regard for the impediments caused by the flood. Holding her head high, she made a bee-line for what remained of her uncle's newspaper. Obediently Nathan wedged open the door that hung by only its upper hinges and followed her inside.

The printing press room was a mess. Mud and slime covered the floor, and sodden rolls of newsprint lay scattered about. What trays of type Ezra had saved were stacked crookedly on top of the press, tilting at a precarious angle that defied gravity.

Molly led Nathan by his hand past the debris to the back door that separated her living quarters from the press room. She opened the door and pulled him inside.

By some oddity, the floodwaters had scarcely wetted the floor of their apartments, sparing that corner of the house where the building was uprooted and tilted atop a series of tree stumps.

Molly slammed the door behind her, pressing her back against the wood as if to block Nathan's escape. The lock snapped shut as she twisted the key, but the sprung framework failed to hold the bolt.

"You slept with that woman!" Molly screamed as she accused him. "How could you do such a thing?"

Nathan's eyes darted about for avenues of rapid departure, but the hall had no windows and Molly guarded the only door. Truly this young lady had lost her mind, he deduced. But for what reason he could not imagine. Maybe it was the shock of the flood?

"How could you! After all I did, nursing you back to health after the mine accident. You . . . you blackguard!" Tears welled in her eyes, and her voice quivered with a mixture of rage and disappointment.

Nathan had no idea what to say, so he kept quiet. But Molly insisted on a response.

"Well, what have you to say for yourself, Nathan Blaylock?" she demanded.

"How did you know?" he blurted out. It was the wrong answer.

"*I knew it!*" she shrieked. "I just knew you did!" She rushed him, fists flailing against his chest.

Nathan caught her in his arms and pinned her hammering fists between their chests where they could do little damage. Lamely he offered an explanation. "It was before I met you, Molly," he said.

"That's no excuse!"

"It isn't?"

"No! You should have kept yourself for me," she countered.

"But, I didn't know you existed," he pleaded. "You can't expect me to wait for someone I never knew about."

"Yes I can, and you should have," she said with what appeared to her to be logic. Her eyes blazed up into his face through narrowed eyelids.

Nathan's mind reeled in confusion. To release Molly meant a renewed attack, yet holding her this close presented possibilities equally fraught with danger, especially the way her body squirmed against his. Without thinking, he bent down and kissed her pouting lips. Molly bit him.

"Ouch! Damn it, that hurt!" he cried. "Stop that. You had no call to bite me, Molly. You don't own me, and besides, Isabelle Barnette wasn't my first woman. You forget I was married, and I have a son."

"I've already forgiven your indiscretion with that China girl," she pouted. "You were too young to know your own mind, and she took advantage of you. But . . . Isabelle Barnette! You should have known better!"

Nathan stared bewildered at the wild thing in his arms. The heat from her body threatened to blister his skin, even through his wool shirt. He sucked at the blood that welled inside his mouth. Riley was right, he thought, when he said a man could never understand which way a woman would buck and that was why men limited their efforts to breaking horses rather than the females of their own species.

To Nathan's utter amazement, Molly twisted free and kissed him back. Her hands slipped out of his startled grip and clasped his head, smashing his mouth into hers. When he tried to break free, she hung on even more fiercely while her tongue licked his wounded lip.

"Can Mrs. Barnette kiss like that?" she demanded.

Nathan recalled the scratches on his back from his encounter with the wife of the present mayor, but he thought better of mentioning that. "Well, she sure didn't bite my lip off," he admitted.

That answer pleased Molly. She almost purred like a cat before she kissed him again. This time it was a long, lingering kiss, and her tongue darted into his mouth.

Nathan flinched. "Where did you learn that?" he asked in dismay.

"None of your business."

"But why were you so—"

He never finished his sentence. This time she smothered his lips with hers, and he kissed her back. She arched her back and pressed her body tightly against him.

"Did you enjoy making love to her?" Molly probed after she allowed Nathan to catch his breath.

This sensuous interrogation inserted between passionate kisses left Nathan completely flustered. He was used to dealing directly with the matter at hand where hot-blooded women were concerned, not confusing the issue with forays into past history. What he had done with other women ought not to be brought into present activities, he decided. It was a private matter best relegated to the past.

"I'm not going to tell you," he said firmly, preparing himself for another punch. "It's really none of your business."

Molly took that to be a yes, and she rose to the challenge.

The young lady backed away from him while her hands did something behind her back. The high-necked collar of her dress relaxed, and the taut fabric went slack. With a simple shrug of her shoulders, the dress fell to the floor in a soft rustle of calico.

Nathan gulped. Molly Hayes stepped toward him, naked as the day she was born. But there had been some major improvements in her body since birth, Nathan noticed. Standing in the diffuse light from the hallway, half her body lay cloaked by shadows that caressed her skin like a feathery cape. The rise and fall of her chest with her heavy breathing caused the highlights to play across her skin like wind rustling soft spring grass. Her taut stomach and long legs beckoned.

Richard Parry

For an instant Nathan regarded the flimsy door that separated them from the printing press. Surely her Uncle Ezra would be arriving soon. But Molly gave him no time to dwell on that fear. The space between them evaporated as she reached for him. Nathan shed his own mud-caked garments without thinking.

While her mouth smothered his, Molly drew Nathan into her bedroom, a small alcove separated from the hallway by a blanket hung across its entrance. In their excitement, the covering was ripped from its nails to hang limply from one corner. They tumbled onto Molly's small bed with arms and legs intertwined.

A rattle of the doorknob in the hallway caused Nathan to freeze. His eyes widened as he heard Ezra Hayes scraping around the far side of the door while he mumbled something about the flood. The door started to open. Nathan's right hand darted out to snatch their pile of clothing behind the hanging drape. From the corner of his eye Nathan saw Ezra Hayes's shadow fall across the floor where their clothes lay only an instant before. He held his breath as the curtain wafted from his action.

The editor peered into the hallway. All the while Molly's hands explored Nathan's body.

"Molly? Molly, are you there?" Ezra's voice echoed down the hall.

Nathan clenched his teeth and shut his eyes. Molly was blowing in his ear and giggling softly. The young man prayed the editor did not hear her sounds of pleasure. After a moment of silence, the door rasped shut, and he heard Hayes moving around. Molly watched Nathan's alarm with sly amusement. Then the footsteps shuffled off.

She reached down only to look up at him a second later with a frown. "Oh," she complained, "Uncle Ezra scared something away."

"Maybe this isn't a good idea," Nathan whispered. He kept his eyes fixed on the door. "Your uncle might come back."

"Oh, no," she sighed. "You're not getting off that easily.

I've got you, now, and I'm not finished with you. And after I'm done, you'll never again think about Isabelle Barnette or any other woman. You'll only think about me. . . ."

As she pulled him on top of her eager body, Nathan caught a glimpse of Molly's gold watch pinned to her rumpled dress. A thought struck him: maybe Riley's theory about those watches was closer to the truth than he realized.

★ ★ SEVENTEEN ★ ★

Tonopah, Nevada. The miner shifted the Winchester into the crook of his other arm and removed his floppy hat. After using the hat to mop the sweat from his forehead, he held it high to shade his eyes from the blazing sun. The tangled skein of the greasy beard covering his chest contrasted sharply with the beads of sweat sprouting over his shaved head. His shapeless trousers and dusty boots marked him as another miner disturbing the dry soil of this piece of Nevada, save for the heavy pistol and gun belt hanging from his waist and the repeating rifle he held. Those weapons marked him for a claim jumper.

For the thousandth time he scanned the surrounding hills before turning his gaze back to his four companions by the stream. He moved over to a rock to sit while he watched the others busily pulling claim stakes from the ground. Those markers belonged to the previous owner, one who the law might say was the legal owner. But here possession was the law, and now these five occupied the claim. Any complaints would be settled with bullets before any chance of reaching a court. If the former owner was foolish enough to show up, the issue would be settled quickly and abruptly.

The guard yawned. He was hot and dry. Spending last night drinking in the saloon while they plotted to jump this claim had left him with a splitting hangover. Worse still, his bowels were rebelling over the tacos and beans still inside him.

A rolling cramp hit him, and he grunted in discomfort. Squatting beside a mesquite bush and backing his bare behind into a scorpion left little appeal to him. An anecdotal story of someone crapping on the head of an angry rattlesnake ran through his mind, so he tried to ignore this urgent call of nature.

Another cramp struck him. Below, where his friends were wrecking another man's camp with undisguised gusto, was a pole shack and a board-covered outhouse. He needed to use that facility, the guard realized. Needed it badly.

"Boys!" He waved his hat to get their attention. "Can you spell me? I got the runs real bad."

Only raucous jeers greeted his plea.

"Well, to hell with you," he mumbled. "I'm heading for that shitter. Ain't nobody around for miles, anyways." Even though no one heard him, he hurried down from his post and vanished into the privy.

No sooner had he closed the door and dropped his pants when a lone figure appeared on the rise he had just vacated. Wearing a wide, straight-brimmed Stetson and dressed in black trousers and black vest, the solitary man walked his horse into the camp.

Sliding from the saddle with a fluid move that belied the gray in his hair, the man surveyed the destruction wrought by the others. The four men stopped their labors and turned to face this interloper.

"Who the hell are you, mister?" one of the thieves, a tall, thin man with bad teeth, snarled. "And what do you want?"

"I came to see what you're doing to my claim," the man responded with no show of emotion in his voice.

His equanimity alarmed the four men, and they looked about for others. Only a crazy man would ride alone into the midst of four heavily armed men while they jumped his claim.

"What's your name?" the thin man demanded.

"William Stapp," Wyatt replied, giving the pseudonym he used in writing to his son, Nathan. "I'll thank you, men, to stop pulling up my stakes. If you stop now, you'll save yourself the trouble of having to pound them back into the ground. This ground is damned hard to drive stakes into; I can vouch for that."

The leader studied this lone man. He wore only a single revolver, but the long barrel and the worn holster hinted darkly
that the man knew how to use his handgun. Still, they out-
numbered him four to one, five to one if his brother, Cadge,
finished his business. Without another word, the four men
spread out into a half-circle, fanning out around this stranger.

"This here is our claim, now, Stapp," he said. "We jus' took
it. Best you find yerself another."

When this interloper turned to leave the thin man planned
on shooting him down. Then his fool brother could drag the
corpse over that rise and plant him in a shallow grave. That
would be a fitting punishment for Cadge for leaving his post.
No one would find the body if Cadge piled enough boulders
on top of it to discourage the buzzards and the foxes from
picking at the bones. The desert was full of similar shallow sep-
ulchers, hiding lost men whose deaths few mourned. This fool
would simply vanish, one more like the rest that the desert had
swallowed up and digested into oblivion. The leader licked his
lips as he coveted the long Colt. It was a handsome piece. His
other colleague might even fit into the man's knee-length
boots.

Wyatt shook his head. "Sorry you feel that way, friend. My
claim hasn't paid out much in the way of color, so I don't
reckon it's worth a man's life."

"Good thinking, Stapp. This mine ain't worth yer life for
certain. Move on, and we'll call it even. And you're lucky that
I'm feeling generous. I'm too hot today to kill you."

"I meant my claim wasn't worth *your* life," Wyatt corrected
the man's misconception.

"Mighty bold talk for a lone man facing four of us, bub. Do
you know who I am?" the leader growled. He was losing patience with this nuisance.

"Can't say as I do. Just who are you?"

"Port Lampert."

"Port Lampert?"

"Yup. You know the name?"

Wyatt shrugged his shoulders but kept his eyes fixed on

this fellow. Lampert stood four paces directly facing him while the other claim jumpers waited a good twelve feet to both sides with rifles in their hands. No one had a shotgun, Wyatt noted thankfully.

"No. Can't say that I do."

Lampert bristled. "I'm a gunman, that's who I am. I'm wanted for murder in Arizona and Texas. I'm famous."

A wry grin flickered across Wyatt's lips. "Really. Well, what is a famous *pistolero* doing stealing my gold mine? You ought to be robbing trains or banks. That's where the money is."

Lampert growled. This dude wasn't showing the proper respect, nor the amount of fear Lampert expected. He looked around. No sign of anyone else, and his three companions held their rifles at the ready.

"Your jawing is getting tiresome, Stapp," he said. "I was thinking about running you off, but now I think I'll just kill you. What do you say to that, old man?"

Wyatt stiffened. His eyes hardened and the muscles of his jaw knotted. "What did you call me?" he asked.

"I called you an old man, Stapp. That's what you are. Killing you won't be nothing at all, you old graybeard—"

Lampert went for his gun, but the stranger did the unexpected. Instead of backing away to get a clear shot or running for safety, as Lampert expected, this old man rushed him. And with lightning speed. Before Lampert's gun cleared his holster, the man was on top of him, his left arm ensnaring Lampert's gun arm in a hold the gunman thought would snap his forearm.

Lampert had one quick look into the iron gray eyes. Suddenly he realized his arms were pinioned and helpless while this old man spun him about like nothing at all to use as a shield. To his horror, Port Lampert saw his friends raise their rifles to fire.

"Don't shoot!" he cried desperately.

Two slugs struck Lampert in the chest. The third passed harmlessly through Wyatt's shirtsleeve to whine off into the distance. Wyatt's long-barreled Colt fired at the man closest to his exposed right flank. His bullet hit the man's shoulder, knocking his rifle into the air. The wounded felon staggered for safety behind a boulder.

Wyatt squeezed off two more shots that scattered the remaining men. They scrambled for cover while keeping up a barrage of fire.

While more bullets snapped through the air around him, Wyatt backed away with the limp body held in front of him. The clouds of gunsmoke and confusion from the rapid firing of the two riflemen helped him reach the safety of a pile of rocks to one side of the outhouse.

Wyatt released Port Lampert and watched his body roll onto his back. Lampert stared upward with unseeing eyes and a look of perpetual surprise fixed on his face.

"Guess you're no longer famous, whatever your name is," Wyatt mused. "Called me an old man, did you? See what it got you." He ducked as a bullet hit the rock by his head and sent splinters sailing through the air. With his back to the rock, Wyatt ejected the spent shells from his revolver and reloaded. The bullet hole in his shirt caught his eye, and he poked his finger through the rent. Josie would be mad as hell, he realized. She had just bought him that shirt. He could see her standing with arms folded across her chest ready to give him a scolding.

The whine of a bullet ricocheting past drew him back from his thoughts. Despite the loss of their leader, the gang still held the upper hand. He was pinned down behind this rock with nothing but open space for fifty yards in all directions. All the robbers needed to do was wait. From the safety of their cover they could pick him off if he made a break. The closest other protection was the rickety board outhouse that he had hammered together at Josie's insistence for privacy. But its thin planks offered more in the way of concealment than cover, and even that was too far. Wyatt decided against running for the privy. Maybe they would listen to reason. It was worth a try.

"Listen up!" he shouted. "Lampert here is dead. You boys drilled him with your rifles. I'm willing to let the rest of you go if you leave now. What do you say?"

Wyatt could hear them arguing, but he couldn't make out the exact words. His ears still rang from the close gunfire. One man sounded ready to cut his losses and run. He sounded in pain, too—that must be the one he'd winged, Wyatt decided. The other one wanted revenge, or at least some reward for his pains. The third sounded undecided.

"What do you say?" he pressed his point.

"Go to hell, you son of a bitch," came their reply. "You're going to pay for Port's death." Another bullet smacked the rock that shielded his back.

Wyatt squinted up at the sun. The cloudless sky did nothing to block the painfully yellow orb that burned a whole quarter of the blue sky into molten gold. The angle of the sun spared none of the red dust and rock around him from hammering blows. Simmering waves of heated air danced before his eyes, but he saw precious little hope for shade.

In another five hours it would be dark. Maybe under cover of darkness he might slip away. Until then, it would only get hotter. He thought about his water canteen tied to the saddle of his horse in the next *arroyo*. It was foolish not to ride in, he knew, but these clowns would have shot his horse. It was best what he did, approaching the camp on foot. But he wished now he'd carried his canteen.

Cadge Lampert squeezed his eye to the crack in the outhouse wall and struggled to focus on the man whose back faced him barely fifteen feet away. The abrupt gunfire had caught him unprepared. By the time he got his pants up, the fight had shifted. Now he struggled with a flood of mixed emotions. His brother, Port, was obviously dead, but Cadge was uncertain who had shot him. He guessed it was the stranger whose back now faced him.

In some ways, Cadge welcomed the death of his older brother. Port was a bully who never missed the opportunity to cuff and kick Cadge. More than once Cadge had considered plugging Port himself. But his brother had raised him after poisoned water took the rest of the family, and Cadge reckoned Port did the best he knew how, for all his cruelty. Shooting unarmed Mexicans and Indians along the Rio Grande seemed to delight him almost as much as belittling his younger brother.

Still, Port had been his brother. So Cadge finally decided he ought to avenge him. Moving as quietly as he could, he raised his rifle to the crack and sighted on the black vest of the stranger. It was an easy shot from here. He squinted along the barrel. He rested the sights on the brass buckle joining the straps on the back of the stranger's vest.

A rustle diverted his attention for a split second. His gaze flicked to the floor of the outhouse. A bright-eyed pack rat was estimating the value of the shredded roll of toilet paper inside a battered tin coffee can beside Cadge's foot. At length the rat decided to keep the horn button it held in its front paws and scurried out through another crack near the floor.

Unaware that his life hung in the balance of a rodent's whim, Wyatt wiped the sweat from his forehead and probed his defenses for weak points. The cluster of rocks behind the outhouse worried him. With a sigh, he wrestled the body of the late Port Lampert into a hunched-over sitting position to the right of him and propped it up. The corpse provided no shade, but it might help if one of the riflemen circled around behind the privy.

Cadge turned back to find his rifle sights lined up on the back of his dead brother instead of the man he wished to shoot. "Damn," he cursed quietly. Now he could do nothing but wait for a clear shot.

Wyatt stretched out his right leg to relieve a cramp. Ever since the dislocation of that joint in San Francisco years ago, that leg was fickle. More than anything he knew, it could always foretell a change of weather.

A bullet kicked up a plume of dust not more than a finger's width from the heel of his boot. Instantly Wyatt withdrew his leg. Those claim jumpers were not sleeping, that was for sure, he realized. He chewed the corner of his mustache. This would be a long day.

. . .

Josephine Earp stood before the saloon doors, straightened her shoulders, and pulled down on the bodice of her dress. Despite her trim figure, these new fashions tended to ride up on her, and her hurried dressing had not helped.

Waiting for Wyatt that afternoon, she had fallen asleep only to awaken to darkness and an empty house. Not that her husband never forgot the time if he held a winning hand, but today he had promised to take her for an afternoon stroll after the day cooled. When he still didn't come after two more hours, Josie decided to beard the lion in his den and confront her husband.

It wouldn't do to embarrass him in front of his friends, so she planned to dress as if she were out shopping and just happened to be in the vicinity. Now, with a wrapped beefsteak tucked under her arm, she parted the doors of the Northern Saloon and stepped inside.

Josie acknowledged the greeting from the bartender with a smile as she marched toward the back of the saloon. Wyatt's favorite table was occupied with men engrossed in losing their money. Josie thought little of gambling herself, wondering why men didn't simply throw their money away instead of preferring to lose it through the lengthy process of playing poker. But Wyatt loved gambling, almost as much as his brother loved digging in the dirt for gold. Sometimes Josie wondered what shortcoming in the Earps's upbringing led them to these foolish pastimes. With a gentle sigh, she reminded herself that when she fell in love with Wyatt she took him with his pluses and minuses.

She arrived at the back table to a shock. Wyatt was not there. His brother Virgil and Wyatt's friends Frank Leslie and Frank Canton were. But the fourth man was Henry Jamison, a mining engineer.

All four men scrambled to their feet in a rush of scuffling chairs and scattered poker chips. Virgil doffed his hat, and Buckskin Frank Leslie swept his Stetson off in a gallant gesture. Josie smiled and curtsied in return. Leslie's gentlemanly act warmed her cheeks, but she remembered all too well his

Richard Parry

fatal weakness for womanizing. Before he turned to the law, Leslie had shot a woman's husband and married her before the man's body was cold. He also was said to have killed another woman. Josie wondered if only his loyalty to Wyatt prevented Frank Leslie from sparking her.

"Why, Mrs. Earp," Leslie said, "what brings you to grace our day with your presence?"

Josie's smile widened. She often wished Wyatt could utter such flattery, but she might better expect the sun to rise in the West. Wyatt was kind and gentle but straight-talking and direct as those telegraph poles that dotted the land.

"Ah, I was just passing by—shopping, you know—and I thought I might induce my husband to take me out for dinner," she fabricated. "I completely forgot the time, and I'm afraid I have not prepared anything for Mr. Earp's supper."

"Why, Wyatt's not here, Josie," Virgil responded.

"Not here?" She frowned. "I thought he was playing cards with you-all."

"He was, ma'am," the heavy voice of Frank Canton interceded. The retired Alaskan marshal was due to return to Oklahoma in the morning. He made no bones about how bored he was in retirement, and Josie felt sorry for the man. "But he left about noon to check on his claims. There's been word of more claim jumping recently."

"Claim jumping?" Josie's voice sounded alarmed.

Virgil shot Canton a warning glance. "We thought Wyatt had gone home, Josie. Don't worry. You know Wyatt. He probably lost track of time. Gold fever can do that to you." He uttered a strained chuckle. "Just look at me. I'm sure he'll show up."

"I just came from our house, Virgil," she admitted. "Wyatt's not there."

Wyatt stopped his shivering to listen to the cry of a hoot owl somewhere in the distance. In the inky blackness of the star-filled night, the owl's call only added to his discomfort and feeling of isolation. Wyatt longed for a cigar. He had three in his vest pocket, but, smoking one was out of the question. He dared not light even a single match. That might illuminate him to the men who surrounded him and held him like a trapped animal. Instead, he thrust the unlit smoke into his mouth and chewed sourly on its cold end.

A hundred doubts and fears waited at the edge of his mind like the sounds emanating from the blackness that engulfed him. Easy does it. Push those thoughts clean out of your mind, he ordered himself. Don't let your imagination take over and run wild. That leads to foolish mistakes. And that leads to getting killed.

Wyatt knew a dozen men whose minds had aided in their demise far more than what their adversaries had done. Just getting better, he repeated. Getting better. He stopped his mantra and looked around. With no moon, the night was as black as the inside of his hat.

What I'm really doing is *just getting colder,* he corrected himself. Freezing my ancient ass off out here in the desert with these two-bit crooks. Wyatt snorted in disgust. *If I let these jokers take me, I deserve it.* They've even built a fire! That shows they're either the most stupid outlaws in the territory or the most overconfident. Still, he conceded, they're warm.

Rubbing his arms together, he peered cautiously at the shadows dancing against the backdrop of boulders that screened the fire from view. The flickering lights painted the red rock a lurid crimson as if the stones themselves dripped blood. Well, not my blood, Wyatt thought. Not if I can help it.

"Hey, boys!" he yelled. He didn't want them sleeping if he couldn't. "Got any hot coffee over there?"

"Yeah, Stapp," came the reply. "Come on over and git yerself a cup. Be sociable."

Wyatt stretched to combat the stiffness in his shoulders and gritted his teeth. "Best you boys just leave the pot and ride out. Keeping me from my beauty sleep is starting to try my patience. If I do come over there I'm liable to be anything but sociable."

A string of invectives poured from the location of the fire along with another rifle shot. Wyatt ducked back into a tight crouch. He tried to read the face of his pocket watch, but the light was too dim to see the watch's hands.

Cadge Lampert squeezed his arms tightly against his chest in the cramped space of the privy. He'd never known an outhouse could be so cold. The only blessing was the chill took the edge off the smell. Unable to get a clean shot at this Stapp fellow, Cadge could only wait. If he tipped his hand or made a break for the gang's lines, he might get shot—either by the man who now hid behind his brother's body or by his own friends as he rushed toward them. And while he did, he kept quiet as that pack rat that scurried about. The thin slats of the privy would never stop a bullet, he realized. That notion made him nervous. The idea that he was a fish in a barrel haunted him. No, he realized, he would only have one chance to even the score for his brother. One shot, and he'd better make it good.

Wyatt sensed the coming of dawn before his vision could note any brightening of the sky to the east. Something in the way the world acted always augured a new day long before dawn. It was the newness that filled the air, he thought. So when the sunrise traced the edges of the mountains into colors of burning copper wire Wyatt was long prepared.

With just enough light to see, the attack would come. He checked his Colt for the hundredth time while his fingers counted the cartridges in his pistol belt. Too many empty bullet loops, he noted begrudgingly. He should have filled his belt with bullets back in town.

All that talk of retirement had put him off his stride, Wyatt admitted. What with Canton griping about boredom and Buckskin talking about hanging up his badge, Wyatt realized he'd been sloppy. A man in my line of work only retires one way, he calculated—suddenly and involuntarily.

Lem Bailey eased his left arm back into the sling he had fashioned from his shirt. With his bullet-shattered shoulder, any movement sent a spasm of pain through him like the twisting of a knife blade, but tucking his forearm inside his flannel shirt, between the buttons, was the best he could do.

This outlawing and claim jumping was not what Port Lampert advertised. So far, all Lem had to show for riding the outlaw trail was his busted shoulder. Port was dead, and Bailey had no idea where Cadge was. For all he knew Cadge could be just as dead. Bailey wanted to go home. His pa would fix his shoulder and probably give him a licking, but that was better than this. The other two were hard cases like Port. Lem feared they would shoot him in the back if he tried to split; besides, that man in the black behind the rock gave him a bad feeling. He didn't act like any miner Lem had even met. And he shot too damned straight for someone who spent most of his time with his hands wrapped around a shovel.

Best to do what the others said, Lem sighed. It was light enough to begin the attack. They'd all creep from rock to rock until the hard cases had outflanked Stapp while Lem kept him pinned down with his rifle. In a few minutes it would all be over.

Lem levered another round into his Marlin .45-70 and eased himself into a sitting position with his rifle against his good shoulder. He could just see part of their quarry moving behind his own boulder. He squeezed the trigger and winced as the rifle bucked. Through the smoke he saw Stapp press himself against the rock as the bullet whacked off a chunk of his protecting stone.

Lem heard the metallic click that came from cocking. The trouble was he had not worked the lever action of his Marlin yet. He had less than a split second to consider this puzzle.

A cold barrel poked him hard behind his right ear.

"Just ease off on that rifle, youngster," Frank Canton commanded. His words, while barely whispered, sounded harder and colder than the gunmetal itself. Canton emphasized his order by pressing his pistol smartly against Lem's skull.

Lem raised his good arm and sat back from his rifle.

"Good boy. I can see you've some good sense," Canton said. "Get your other hand up, too."

"I can't. It's broke."

Canton peered around at the bloodstained hole in Bailey's shoulder. His appearance startled the youth almost as much as the pistol. This wraith had sprung out of the shadows of the rock itself where minutes before Lem had neither seen nor heard anything. The way he searched Lem for weapons and his bearing screamed of professional competence. And the way he moved reminded Bailey of that Stapp fellow behind the rocks. *My Lord.* Lem shuddered at the thought. *We done robbed some gunfighters instead of a dumb gold miner.*

Canton inspected the wound. "You're lucky Wyatt didn't plug you between your fool eyes, boy."

"Wyatt? Who's Wyatt? That fellow Bill Stapp shot me."

Canton smiled crookedly. "Oh? Yeah. My mistake. He *is* Stapp."

A flurry of shots shattered the morning air. Both Canton and his prisoner craned their heads in time to see one of the claim jumpers staggering to a halt halfway across the clearing. The man stopped, then tumbled onto his face in the sand. A wreath of smoke covered the boulder the outlaw had tried to rush.

More smoke hung above the rock far to the right. A man stood slowly from behind that outcropping and waved his rifle over his head.

"Is that the last of them?" Canton bellowed to the man signaling with his rifle. His voice caused Lem Bailey to flinch.

"Yup!" Frank Leslie hollered back. "This one's dead. He ran into my bullet by accident!"

The flurry of shots woke Cadge Lampert with a start. He had fallen asleep with his head resting against the wall of the outhouse. His rifle almost slipped from his stiff fingers when his body jerked awake. The attack had started, he realized. Hastily he pressed his eye to the crack. From his vantage point he could see little of his attacking partners except for a cloud of gunsmoke at the far corner of his vision. But Stapp and his rock were clearly in view. Men were shouting, but Cadge couldn't make out what they were saying.

To Cadge's amazement, his target rose slowly from his protection and stood with his pistol still smoking. Cadge had a clear shot. He eased his rifle barrel through the crack.

A massive jolt shook the outhouse, one so great that Cadge imagined an earthquake had struck. His world turned upside down as the privy tilted at a precarious angle before slamming down with the door underneath.

Cadge's ears rang and his head spun from the concussion. His rifle clattered against the door, and Cadge tumbled onto his back. Red dust filled the narrow confines. A shaft of daylight poured through the business hole of the structure.

A wicked-looking double-barreled shotgun poked through the hole.

"Toss out your irons before I ventilate this crapper!" Virgil commanded.

Hastily Cadge obeyed. First his Winchester, then his Schofield revolver flew through the oval opening.

"Good. Now wriggle your sorry ass out here where I can see you," Virgil ordered. "Come out with your hands first."

The shock of tipping over in the outhouse was nothing to what greeted Cadge after he'd crawled out. Four armed men were standing around watching him. That fellow Stapp was with them, and sitting on the ground was his friend Lem Bailey, looking lost and frightened.

Cadge blinked. The rest of the gang were laid out in a neat row close to the rocks. The youth swallowed hard when he realized he and Lem were the only survivors.

But what really startled Cadge was the similarity of these four men. The man who had captured him was heavier than the others, but their dress and movements and mannerisms looked identical.

"Who are you guys?" Cadge stammered. Lem seemed unable to talk. The man named Stapp looked at Cadge, but the one they called Buckskin shot him a fearful grin.

"Why, boy? Don't you know us?" he asked.

"No, sir." Cadge shook his head.

"We're the Smith Brothers," Frank Canton said with a chuckle.

"The meanest sons of bitches this side of the Canadian River," Leslie added. "You boys picked the wrong claim to jump."

Cadge looked at the row of corpses. Lem started to cry, sniffling quietly by his side. "I guess we did," Cadge said slowly. "This is the first such affair for Lem and me, and I guess it'll be our last. I'm sorry we bothered you, Mr. Stapp."

Wyatt studied the two boys. He was remembering his own youth—when he stole a horse. None of his friends were pure as the driven snow, either. He saw the others watching him, and he knew they were reading his mind. "Stapp's not really my name, son," he said. "I'm a Smith like the others."

Cadge wondered why all four men grinned at that remark but decided against asking. He wondered whether they would hang the two of them or just shoot them like they'd done to the others. Hanging it was, he decided, when he saw the big walruslike Smith brother lead their horses over.

"Mount up, son," Virgil instructed him, "and help your friend onto his horse."

"You're . . . you're going to hang us?"

"We're letting you two go," Wyatt said. "Make the best of this second chance. Those three over there didn't get that opportunity."

Cadge gripped his saddle horn to keep from fainting. "I don't know how to thank you," he stuttered.

"Split off the outlaw trail," Virgil advised with his gruff voice. "It'll be for your own good."

Buckskin Frank Leslie nodded his head. "Don't never do nothing like this again!" He raised his hand and smacked a pony hard on the rump. The animals bolted away, glad to escape this place where gunsmoke and the smell of death assailed their nostrils.

As Cadge Lampert clung to the back of his galloping horse, he heard the four men cheer, "To the Smith Brothers! The meanest sons of bitches in the valley!"

★ ★ EIGHTEEN ★ ★

Fairbanks. Ezra Hayes looked glumly at the crumpled front page of his newspaper on his typesetting table. A thousand copies lay stacked beside his front door, ready to sell. So deep was the editor's shock that he failed to swat the spring mosquito that landed on his forehead and drove her sucker into a pulsing vein near his temple. His eyes kept darting from the papers to Nathan Blaylock to the stern face of Judge Wickersham, then back to the papers. Finally, his shoulders sagged, and he removed his wire-rimmed spectacles to wipe the lenses with his ink-stained thumb. His action only smeared the printer's ink more widely across his glasses. As if unaware of the sorry state of his glasses, Hayes replaced them and returned to staring.

After a few minutes, Ezra lapsed into a catatonic state from indecision. His inaction dropped the tiny office of the *Fairbanks Daily Times* into a heavy stillness that oppressed all present.

Wickersham broke the silence. Stepping up to the table, he snatched the edition up and crushed it into a tight ball with his hand. A look of stern reproach and righteous indignation flowed from his face like light from a watchtower.

"You cannot print this scurrilous trash, Hayes," he fumed. "It amounts to out-and-out libel, and I will order the deputy marshal to confiscate and burn all copies if you do."

"What about freedom of the press, Judge?" Nathan protested.

Wickersham turned on him with the quickness of a hawk. "There is no freedom to libel, young man. You're lucky the mayor does not sue you for this attempted libel. Only my appealing to his generosity and both our desires not to involve this growing city in a scandal have stopped him from doing so. And I certainly believe he has a case. If this case comes before me, I will rule against you and Ezra Hayes."

"But it's the truth, Judge," Nathan argued. "I did see a newspaper clipping last year, and it did say E. T. Barnette was convicted of stealing. I didn't make that up."

The judge adjusted his own glasses, mindful of the dysfunctional pair riding on Hayes's nose. Carefully he uncurled the crumpled newsprint and smoothed it out across the trays of type. His finger jabbed at the blaring headlines: E.T. BARNETTE CONVICTED IN WASHINGTON!

"Listen to me, Blaylock. Everyone in the whole valley is aware of the bad blood between you and Mayor Barnette. Do you deny that?"

Nathan shook his head. "No."

"And," Wickersham shifted to point at the apoplectic editor, "there is no doubt that Hayes's paper is decidedly hostile to the mayor. Am I correct?"

Nathan nodded. "What other choice does he have?" Nathan wanted to scream. He had the distinct feeling that Wickersham was enjoying this more than he let on.

"It stands to reason, then, anything *this paper* prints about E. T. Barnette is suspect."

Wickersham pronounced "this paper" as if they were dirty words. Nathan wondered if he spoke in such low terms of his own newspaper, which was very pro-Barnette. The young man wished Ezra would help in this argument, but the loss of a whole edition of the *Daily* so shocked the editor that he could barely stand, let alone defend this edition.

"I *did* see that clipping."

"But you don't know what happened to it. You don't have it now."

"No. But—"

Wickersham played his trump card. He leaned over the type desk, setting his elbows on the remains of the printed paper and taking care not to soil his coat with ink. A handful of loose type fell to the floor, displaced by the judge's arm, to clatter across the floor. In the silence of the room, the effect was like grapeshot fired from a broadside. The rattle jangled the nerves of Hayes and caused Nathan to shift his weight from one foot to another. The sound also served to herald what Wickersham planned to say far better than a fanfare of trumpets could.

Judge Wickersham's eyes narrowed while he assumed his best judicial face. He spoke slowly. "When I first got word of your allegations and found out editor Hayes planned on printing them, I made inquiries to Seattle about the serious accusations you've made." Wickersham paused for dramatic effect. Somewhere in the back of his mind he could see himself using this tone to campaign. Perhaps for territorial governor or even senator if Alaska ever became a state.

"And?" Nathan's impatience proved the perfect foible for Wickersham's dramatic trap.

"And . . . nothing! My contacts in Seattle notified me that E. T. Barnette has no record of arrest nor jail sentence in the state of Washington. The mayor has no record of wrongdoing in Washington at all."

"That can't be!" Nathan protested.

Wickersham straightened his back as if Nathan's denial affronted him personally. Two more pieces of type rattled to the floor. He withdrew an envelope from his inside coat pocket and dropped it carelessly among the scattered type pieces where he had just been leaning.

"Here is the report. Maybe you'll believe what you read."

With that, Wickersham spun on his heel and strode to the door. But the man's innate instinct for survival caused him to pause at the entrance. From bitter experience the judge knew to provide himself with a loophole.

Right now fate had linked him to E. T. Barnette, but the man was indeed a dangerously loose cannon. Wickersham harbored no doubt that Barnette was capable of what Nathan accused him of. In fact, the judge suspected the captain of dozens of underhanded deals, and his heavy-handed treatment of the miners who needed supplies bordered on usery. Worse was the animosity Barnette had managed to pull down on his head in so short a time. Half the town already hated him.

Wickersham realized that animus might spread to infect him. Barnette's generosity was benefiting the judge no end. But that largesse might also taint him. He must do everything possible to appear impartial. His judgeship and his future depended upon it. Wickersham smiled inwardly. Walking a narrow tightrope was something he'd done before. . . .

Judge Wickersham stopped at the door and turned to face the crestfallen Blaylock. "I am always open to further information. Justice is my prime concern. But I must have facts. Supposition and speculation have no place in my court."

The door slammed shut. Neither man moved until the door reopened and that broke the evil spell engulfing them. Jim Riley looked at them with a bemused expression on his face.

"What did you two do to make old Wickersham so happy?" he snickered. "The little windbag nearly bowled me over. He's prancing back to the capt'n's digs on his tiptoes. He looked pleased as a pig that got tickled pink."

Hayes came to life. "He just sunk our exclusive, that's what he did." His foot played with the stack of newspapers. "I guess we can use them to wrap fish or start fires." His voice trailed off as he looked out the window at the receding figure of the judge. "There he goes now to report directly to his lord and master how he sunk a stake into our hearts."

Nathan unfolded the sheet of paper that the judge had left and bit his lip while he read the paper. "Well," he sighed, "this report confirms what Wickersham told us. Barnette has no criminal record in Washington State. Damn it! I know that newspaper clipping said he was convicted of stealing. You saw it, Jim!"

"Sure." Riley shifted his hat to the back of his head. He snatched the coffeepot from the potbellied stove and filled a tin cup for himself. Swallowing a slug of the steaming brew, he dropped to his haunches and squatted beside the stove. The chill of the last winter still hung within his bones where it had burrowed over that long, dark period.

But the cold and gloom of the arctic winter failed to halt the continued explosion of Fairbanks. With each day, Barnette's place in the oxbow of the rocky river grew and expanded in an ever-growing circle, pushing back the stands of black spruce to the south and the fields of willow and silver birch across the river to the north. A new bridge to replace the disastrous one at Cushman now spanned the river at Turner Street, and barges and shallow-draft sternwheelers darted about the river like June water bugs.

Roads from the mining camps converged on Fairbanks like spokes on a wheel, hacked in haste from the forest during the winter until a traveler could drive in any direction he desired as long as he wished to go to town. Now the three feet of snow that blanketed the ground had melted, and stumps cut level during the winter poked up like broken ribs. Driving a team from the mines required carrying a cross-cut saw to make it to town.

But no one complained—or even bothered to look back. Snared in the raptures of gold fever, who worried about civic planning where a fortune awaited? Who was foolish enough to waste time on anything but the pursuit of that yellow metal? Except sources of recreation. While streets suffered, whorehouses and saloons flourished.

Now spring brought the breakup of the ice that choked streams and rivers in the valley. And running water reawakened the sluice boxes and the steam drivers that thawed the frozen ground. Thawing and turning that shield into flowing muck released the bedrock that hid the gold.

So, once again, the valley rang to the sounds of axes chopping wood and the chug of wood-fired boilers, and a thousand tendrils of smoke sprouted from the ground like prairie grasses. Men emerged from their cabins where they had spent the days of darkness chopping frozen loaves of bread with an ax and panning their piles of pay dirt with water thawed on their woodstoves. The winter's work left their cramped log cabins filled with piles of dirt.

The more adventurous used mercury to leach tiny flecks of gold from the soil's stubborn grip. Heating the mix burned off the mercury and left the precious metal. But the poisonous mercury vapors killed dozens and crippled the survivors with damaged brains. The miners learned all over again what English haberdashers had discovered the hard way. Using mercury vapors to shape and block beaver hats, the clothiers had suffered tremors and palsies from mercury poisoning to their nervous systems. Shaking and twitching from this injury, the afflicted earned the bitter appellation "mad as a hatter."

More than one miner in town went "mad" from using mercury to get rich. But they were hardly noticed. What was one less life? Nothing but one less body to share the valley's riches with.

Worse still, Fairbanks and E. T. Barnette led a charmed life. While his town grew and wealth poured into the captain's pockets, their only rival, Chena, withered on the vine like a place saddled under an evil curse. Whatever Barnette tried prospered, and whatever Belt and Hendricks and their mayor, Martin Harrais, did failed—even if they did the same things. The railroad into Fairbanks succeeded where the Chena spur faltered. Men had no explanation for Barnette's good fortune—except to call it luck. And every miner knew luck could be contagious. What better way to find gold but around a man with the Midas touch? So they dug close to wherever the captain's shadow fell.

Riley found all this disturbing. Nathan loathed the growth just as much, if not more. Both men preferred the vast emptiness of the Interior, where they could roam to their hearts' content in the spruce forests or high above the tree line where the silver-tipped grizzly reigned.

But gold changed all this. More and more their favorite haunts vanished beneath the unending assault of the double-bladed ax and the sluice box. Like the wild animals, the two

men could only find freedom at the far fringes of the land—
where living was harder and mostly precarious.

Why hadn't they left, Riley asked himself, when they had
the chance? Now they were ensnared in this place that grew by
the minute and sucked them deeper into its workings like some
monstrous tar pit. He looked out the window and answered
his own question. Susie, his mule, raised her head from the
hitching rail and angled her great ears at him as if she could
read his thoughts. She couldn't survive a winter in the bush, he
realized. This last winter he'd learned that the hard way. On a
trip to Circle, over a hundred miles away, the mule nearly froze
to death. Summer was bad enough, with the no-see-ums and
the mosquitoes plastered to her eyes and her lips, but winter
proved impossible. Susie needed grain and oats to keep warm.
None of that grew here naturally. The gunfighter was forced to
limit his travel from one stable to another where Susie could be
fed and work at odd jobs. So Riley hung around the place and
hated every minute that he did.

Now I know why your previous owner sold you so readily,
Susie, Riley thought. A flash of cloth caught the corner of his
eye and provided him with the reason Nathan remained. Molly
Hayes flounced down the boardwalk with a basket under her
arm. She stopped to scratch Susie behind the ear. Riley
watched the two. The mule returned the favor by giving Molly
the closest thing to a smile he'd ever seen.

"Females," he snorted out loud. "Damned if they don't understand each other even when they don't speak the same lan-
guage!" He dropped his head and rubbed the back of his neck.
"They're in cahoots. Nat and I don't stand a chance."

Nathan was too preoccupied to notice. His hands kept fid-
dling with the judge's report while his mind sought a solution
to his dilemma. Both he and Riley distinctly remembered the
scrap of newsprint that had condemned the captain, pried
from the frozen hand of a dead man who'd used it as his last
will and testament. Nathan could still picture the blue-gray
corpse propped against a tree on the trail as if it were yesterday.

The note, scribbled with the last ounce of the man's strength, flared in his thoughts along with the black holes in the man's face where the ravens had pecked away the writer's eyes. Why, then, did Wickersham find no report of Barnette's wrongdoing?

Molly's arrival interrupted his thoughts. She stepped inside and frowned at the glum threesome. Nathan automatically rose to his feet while her uncle hunted around inside one drawer of his desk for something to drink. Faced with defeat, he sought companionship with his old friend John Barleycorn.

"What a bunch of long faces!" Molly exclaimed. "And on such a fine spring day." She kept her vision fixed on her uncle, but she stopped directly in front of Nathan. Unseen by the others, her free hand reached behind her to stroke the inside of Nathan's leg. "You'd think *someone* would be glad to see me," she purred.

"What? What's that you say?" Ezra looked up at his niece. His finger snared a bottle at the back of the drawer, which he withdrew triumphantly. He held it up to his ink-stained glasses to study.

Molly used his distraction to back against Nathan and wriggle expertly. All the while she remained the picture of insouciance while Nathan's thoughts of everything but her evaporated.

But Ezra Hayes broke the spell. "Look at this!" he proclaimed. "A bottle of Doc's elixir. The back of the drawer has four bottles. He must have stashed them there before . . . before . . ." The editor's voice trailed off.

"Before he was murdered," Nathan completed the sentence. He placed his hands on both of Molly's shoulders and gently moved her aside. Now it was her face that lost its smile.

"Well, here's to Doc Hennison," Hayes toasted. The cork popped abruptly, the newspaperman tilted his head back and poured a third of the bottle down his throat. He gasped, and his face turned scarlet. "Good God," he wheezed. "Has this got a kick. Poor Doc should have let all his hooch age this long. It does nothing but improve with age." He guardedly took another, smaller sip and passed the bottle to Riley.

By the time the bottle had circulated among the men for the fourth time, the three were toasting whatever good they could dream up about the late Doc Hennison, one-winged surgeon and snake oil salesman, and debating the need to crack open the reserves. Glumly Molly watched her chance to seduce Nathan evaporate. One more, she figured, and he'd be useless in bed for anything but sleep. With the fifth circuit of the elixir, she acted. Her hand darted out and caught the bottle before her lover could take another drink. Deftly she handed the flask to her uncle, bypassing Nathan. He started to protest until the few drops spilled by her action landed on the woodstove.

The elixir exploded. For its size and amount, the snap and flame of those few drops illuminated the entire room. Hayes and Riley stared at the smoke in amazement.

"This must be the batch Doc added too much gunpowder to," Riley slurred.

Hayes continued to look at the scorched spots on his stove. "Gosh," he said. His hands fumbled at Riley's shirt as he pulled him back from the firebox. "Best we not drink too close to open flame," he advised.

Nathan stared at the dissipating cloud. Before he could speak, Molly was pushing him out the door. When she saw the other men gaping at her brazen action, she curtsied and smiled sweetly.

"I'm taking Nathan for a picnic," she explained. "That's the reason I came here in the first place. Good afternoon to both of you."

The two men stared at the door after it closed.

"I'll bet Nathan don't know it, but he's the main course," Riley managed to blurt out.

While Molly decamped with Nathan and the two older men sampled a second bottle, Judge Wickersham arrived at the back door of Barnette's bank. Contrary to the image he had left with those at the *Fairbanks Daily Times,* Wickersham was far from smug. Fate dictated that his fortune be spliced to that of the town's mayor up to this point. Doing so benefited both of them. Wickersham now had wealth, power, and property thanks to the largesse of E. T. Barnette. Wickersham preferred the word *generosity.* After all, Fairbanks was the best choice for the judge's court. Look what a mess Chena had become. The captain's generosity only made Wickersham's decision easier to implement.

But Barnette knew no bounds, none, at least, of common sense, Wickersham realized. The captain's appetite for power and wealth rivaled that of a Roman emperor. His questionable deal-making drew the man into Wickersham's court with increasing frequency—always as a defendant. Finding for him took stretching the law further than Wickersham felt comfortable doing.

Wickersham rubbed his chin as he pondered this. Time to separate himself from Captain Barnette, he decided. The vexing issue was how to do so gracefully. Both men stood balanced on an empire that really was a house of cards. If Barnette toppled, Wickersham didn't want to fall with him. The judge paused to correct himself—when, not if. What he had learned from his investigation made Barnette's ruin highly likely.

"Hello, Judge. Sneaking up the back stairs like the rest of us?" a voice snickered.

Wickersham didn't have to look around to know the voice belonged to Billy Wilson. One more reason to back away from Barnette, he thought. This blatant killer, Billy Wilson, resembled a mad dog more than a human. Or a weasel loose in a hen house with nothing but murder on his mind. Wickersham had warned the mayor about Wilson, but Barnette refused to fire him.

"I am not 'sneaking,' as you so crudely put it, Wilson."

"Then why'd you use the back way? My guess is you don't want to be seen getting your payoff in broad daylight, Judge."

Wickersham pushed past the gunman and climbed the stairs to the upper level where Barnette kept his offices, opened the door, and entered. To the judge's discomfort, Wilson followed him.

The office of E. T. Barnette reminded the judge more of a high-class San Francisco brothel than an office for a bank president and mayor, not to mention postmaster of the town. Flocked red wallpaper patterned after paper used in Versailles covered the walls in contrast to the deep blue paint of the wood trim. The new electric lights hung from gilt fixtures, splaying pools of yellow light over the swirling motif and onto the thick Persian rug. The odor of cigar smoke hung heavily in the air, and Wickersham half-expected scantily clad dancing girls to prance into view.

The marked contrast between his austere office down the street and this den convinced the judge of the correctness of his decision. The judge constantly harped on their public image. Appearance counted for much, especially when one faced the rampant paranoia that gold mining bred. Until they could be smelted into ingots stamped with identity marks, raw nuggets and gold dust knew no loyalty—and had no memory. The hand that held them at the moment owned them. As expected, men whose whole life suffered in search of this yellow metal grew more closed-lipped and secretive with every ounce of gold they mucked from the earth.

So Wickersham constantly urged the captain to be discreet—with no success. Barnette owned the best bank in town, and he knew it. For the time being, the miners had no other choice if they wanted their gold locked securely away. They *had* to use his bank.

"Afternoon, James," Barnette greeted his visitor from behind his heavy desk, exhaling a cloud of cigar smoke that masked the upper half of his body.

"Elbridge." Wickersham shook the hand that extended from the smoke screen. He grimaced at the wide expanse of polished mahogany. Not a single scrap of paper or ledger marred the near-perfect surface. Wickersham recalled his own desk, piled so high with books and court documents that the judge vanished whenever he sat down to work. This isn't the desk of a careful banker, Wickersham noted, just another example of Barnette's facade.

"Sit down, James. Cigar? Brandy?"

"No, thank you. I've just come from the *Daily*. You needn't worry about that special edition. Ezra has canceled that issue."

Barnette leaned forward, rising out of his leather-upholstered chair. His head and chest emerged from the smoke. "Capital, James, just capital."

Wickersham looked over his shoulder at Billy Wilson. Standing behind him, the gunman made the judge nervous. With men like Wilson around, you found yourself waiting for the sound of gunfire. Wilson's presence was like letting a rattlesnake into your parlor: you knew it was only a matter of time before he struck.

"Ah, I have another matter to discuss, Elbridge." Wickersham paused to look over his shoulder meaningfully at Wilson. "One best discussed in private."

"Wait outside, Billy." Barnette stopped smoking.

Wilson backed out of the room with a fixed smirk on his face. All the while his little coal black eyes watched them without blinking. The door closed silently, shuttering across his evil face like a guillotine. Both men released their breath.

"A necessary evil," Barnette apologized. But he noted the concern on the judge's face and secretly relished it. As long as he had Wilson around, Barnette knew he had one more lever over this pompous old prig whose memory and gratitude only extended the length of his short arm. Without my help, Barnette fumed silently, Wickersham would still be sleeping in roadhouses.

"A damned dangerous one, too! Get rid of him, Elbridge. The sooner the better."

"All in due time. What about this other matter?"

Wickersham leaned over the desk, moving his face as close as he cared to. Even this early in the day, the captain reeked of whiskey and stale cigar smoke. "Just this!" He withdrew a folded sheet of paper from an inner pocket.

"And?"

"I thought it wise to confirm your account of that robbery accusation—"

Barnette widened his eyes in false alarm. "You didn't trust me, Your Honor? I'm terribly hurt by your lack of faith in my credibility." All the while his thoughts fixed on the paper in Wickersham's hand.

"You were right," Wickersham said simply. "My agent found no evidence of wrongdoing in Washington State."

The captain relaxed and sank back into his chair. "Good."

"Washington," Wickersham repeated. "But my agent searched further—"

"What!" Barnette bolted from his chair in alarm. His hand snatched the paper from the judge's hand, and he quickly scanned it.

"But not Oregon. Blaylock and Riley mistakenly believed the newspaper came from Seattle. So they told Ezra Hayes your crime was in that state. But they were mistaken."

Elbridge Barnette watched the judge speak. His face drained of color, turning a chalky white, and the hand holding the report shook noticeably. His mind snapped back to that courtroom years ago: the jury foreman reading his verdict, the judge pronouncing sentence, the prison walls looming before him as the gate clanged shut, and iron bars and stone walls sealing him away for over a year. His stomach cinched itself into a knot.

Wickersham continued. "You swindled a man named De-Wolf out of twenty-three hundred dollars back in 1887, and . . . you spent over a year in prison in Oregon for it."

"I was young then," Barnette replied defensively. "The governor pardoned me."

"Yes, but can you imagine the effect if this becomes generally known? It wouldn't matter one whit if you lived the life of a saint now and had just taken holy orders. Why, there'd be a run on your bank. You'd be ruined."

Barnette stared at his polished desk. A run on his bank would come up short for sure.

And this was Fairbanks, not San Francisco or even Seattle.

For all its newfangled electric lights and steam-generated power, the town was an anomaly in the center of the wildest land left on the face of this earth. The men here reflected that fact, hard, brutal, and apt to swiftly redress their wrongs with a rope or a gun.

Where the expert presence of the Mounties kept the lid on the Klondike gold rush in Canada, Alaska had nothing remotely similar—only a scattering of U.S. marshals to cover millions of acres. Their task was impossible.

Gold rushes in the Territory of Alaska bred lawlessness—and that drove men to their own violent solutions. Skagway with its notorious Soapy Smith gang and Nome with its Spoilers proved that. As a last resort, the army could declare martial law, usually one day too late and one hanging too short.

A run on the bank was one thing, a lynching something else entirely. The captain carried no delusions about an invitation to a necktie party should the miners rush his vault. Escape would be next to impossible. The river and the railroad all visited towns connected by Billy Mitchell's telegraph lines. Barnette could picture the grim-faced delegation waiting on the docks or train station for his arrival. And fleeing by the primitive roads would be no better. Where could he go but south to Valdez or northeast to Circle? Once again, the telegraph line linked those routes.

He looked up at the judge. "What do you suggest?"

"For God's sake, be careful! Hayes searched in the wrong state, but it was a damned close thing. I put the fear of a libel suit in his head, so I don't think he'll try that again. No one else seems the least bit interested in digging up your past except those two, Riley and Blaylock. By the way, how did you manage to find out that Hayes was planning to expose you?"

"Oh, just made a lucky guess. Hayes has been threatening something like that."

"Well, it certainly was fortuitous. He had the whole shop filled with his special edition. I'm not sure I scared his two friends off. Blaylock and Riley don't frighten that easily, and they've got no assets to worry about losing in a court battle. All the older man has is a broken-down mule. Nathan has even less."

Barnette nodded slowly. That made three nuts for Billy Wilson to crack. Four, if he counted the judge. He toyed with that idea. Only those four could tie him to a criminal past. Four out of ten thousand. Good odds, he calculated. He decided to wait on Wickersham. As long as the judge still proved useful, removing him would be wasteful. After all, James Wickersham couldn't open his mouth without incriminating himself.

"And most of all . . . be discreet," Wickersham continued. "You've got to look as honest as George Washington. None of these gaudy trappings." He waved his arm at the decorations. "They look irregular. The last thing a banker with a black past wants to do is look irregular!"

He had mistaken the faraway look in the captain's eyes for confusion and indecision when just the opposite was taking place. Had the judge known he had just been judged himself and narrowly missed receiving a death sentence, he might have toned down his sermon. But nothing in Elbridge Barnette's manner or actions exposed the deadly thoughts he pondered.

Instead, the captain rose and vigorously pumped the judge's hand. "Thank you for what you've done, James," he gushed. "You're right. I'll change my ways. I confess, I've been too . . . too exuberant for someone in my position. You've given me a second chance, a new lease on life, and I won't forget it. I'm eternally grateful."

Still shaking hands, Barnette guided Wickersham to the door and ushered him out. Wickersham locked eyes with Billy Wilson as the man stepped from the shadows. The judge blinked first, then hurried down the back steps. If Barnette planned some dark deed with this pathological killer, Wickersham wanted no knowledge of it. He could feel Wilson's stare boring into his back until he reached the street.

"You wanted me, boss?" Wilson grunted as he watched the officer of the court scurry away.

"Step inside, William. We have some irregularities to resolve."

Wilson kicked the door shut with the heel of his boot and flopped into the chair that was still warm. Strange that such a cold fish as the judge should generate this much body heat, Wilson mused. Bet he'd bleed like a stuck pig, too, he concluded. One bullet in his gut is all it would take.

When Barnette offered him a cigar, Wilson knew his unique talents were needed. The captain's treatment of Wilson varied from open contempt when a public show of propriety was needed to this show of congeniality when nothing but dirty work would suffice. When the captain got friendly, he wanted Wilson to kill someone.

Wilson waited while Barnette lit his cigar. He drew in a mouthful of smoke and blew out a series of smoke rings. "Who . . . ?"

A soft knock on the door prompted Barnette to raise his hand to silence Wilson.

"Come in." The captain watched the doorknob turn.

Isabelle Barnette tentatively peered into the office. Her caution came from bad experience. Not long ago, she had barged in on her husband while he was occupied. She did not know the woman by name, but what she was doing to Isabelle's husband and her state of undress clearly marked her as a person who plied her trade behind the high board fence that masked activities of the Row from decent folks. The quarrel that followed left scars still unhealed.

"I'm sorry, Elbridge. I thought you were alone," Mrs. Barnette said.

"Come in, my dear. William and I were just discussing business. But this involves you as well."

"It does?" She sounded uncertain, but she entered the room. Isabelle was quick to note that neither man rose.

"Yes, my dear. I want to thank you for your information about Ezra Hayes and his plan to print those scurrilous lies about me. We—I mean the judge—dissuaded Hayes from publishing them." All the while he talked to his wife, the captain kept his eyes locked on Billy Wilson.

Isabelle twisted her handkerchief into a tight coil as she

listened. "I'm so glad. Mr. Hayes's niece, Molly, let slip their intentions. She was most unpleasant, and the things she said—"

"All lies, Isabelle. I assure you. Judge Wickersham will vouch for it. He ordered them not to distribute the paper, or I would sue them."

"I'm greatly relieved, Elbridge. I was so worried." The more she learned of her husband, the more Isabelle Barnette feared what Molly had told her was true. Were it not for their baby daughter, she would leave him.

"But she was right about one thing, Isabelle."

"What?"

"Your friend Nathan Blaylock and Jim Riley are in on it." Barnette swiveled in his chair to watch the effect of his words on his wife. Her response did not disappoint him. Before she could reply, he sprang from his chair and pushed her through the open door. Slamming the door, he braced his back against the wood as if the sheer weight of his body could prevent what had happened between his wife and that young man from seeping into the present.

"I want them dead! All three. Hayes, Riley, and especially Nathan Blaylock!" he bellowed. "Do you understand, Wilson? All three!"

Billy Wilson smiled. Without even turning his head to acknowledge the death warrants, he nodded slowly.

NINETEEN

Tonopah, Nevada. Josie Earp backed away from the telephone mounted to the post office wall as if it were a venomous snake. Her eyes dropped to the earpiece in her hand. Its black wire cord hung loosely in the still air, connecting her hand to the box on the wall. But the weight of the cord seemed to pull her toward the machine, dragging her entire being into this machine that looked so inanimate, so clement, yet carried such foreboding. Her fingers released their hold, and the hand piece plummeted the length of cord to dangle above the dusty floor in a lazy arc. The scraping noise it made against the wall was the only sound in the room other than the ticking of the clock on the opposite wall. Josie turned away to face her husband. Her face was as pale as the white lace collar she wore at her neck.

"Virgil's dead, Wyatt."

Wyatt said nothing, but his lips pressed themselves into an even thinner line beneath his graying mustache. His gaze remained fixed on her face, and he watched her eyes grow to enormous pools of gentle light that longed to enfold him and shield him from this sorrow. But others were watching him, curious how the great Wyatt Earp, marshal of Tombstone, showed his grief. Would he laugh at this misfortune, as some thought, or break into tears like other mere mortals? Would he drown his anguish in whiskey like his old friend Doc Holliday?

Like ghouls, these good citizens flocked in droves to gasp at the dead bodies lying in the street, to dip their handkerchiefs in the still-warm blood, and to whisper as they viewed the corpses of the men Earp had killed as they lay showcased in store windows, but these townsfolk crossed the street when they saw him coming. One thing he would not do, he vowed, was give them the satisfaction of witnessing even his slightest emotion.

Gently he took Josie's arm while replacing the receiver on its cradle and led her out into the blazing sunlight. Such a fine day, he noted. How could the day be so warm and beautiful while he felt so cold and empty? His wife sniffed, and her hand dug inside her purse for a handkerchief.

"Steady, Sadie, girl," he cautioned. "Don't give them the satisfaction." His grip on her arm tightened to emphasize his point.

Josie gave the barest nod. The two of them strode, backs straight as arrows, to their buggy. Wyatt helped her in, tipped his hat to the minister who wavered in the wings, and cracked his whip.

They rode without speaking for twenty minutes with Josie clinging to Wyatt's arm, until they came to that rise with its clump of silver aspen that Wyatt loved so much. From there one could view the mountain range, shimmering in the heat, and the parallel tracks of the wagon trails crisscrossing the plains. The land went on forever—unlike a person, Wyatt thought.

With deliberate care Wyatt set down the reins. Instantly Josie was in his arms, holding him, patting his back as she would a little child.

A drawn-out sigh escaped from him, but no tears came. Here in the privacy of this special place, he thought he might cry for his brother, but he could not. His loss went deeper than mere tears. Something, a part of his being, like a limb, was now gone. Nothing could bring it back. Not tears, not anger . . .

A great tiredness blanketed his shoulders. Virgil, the old bear, who was always there when he needed him, was gone. Virgil with the wound in his leg from the shoot-out at the corral and the shattered right arm from Clanton's ambush was gone. It didn't seem possible. Wyatt had always considered Virgil made of granite. His square-shouldered brother, who so loved to dig for gold that Wyatt thought him more gopher than man, would joke with him no more. His great shade would no more cast itself to the right of Wyatt's shadow, solid, dependable, and unwavering in its loyalty. Wyatt found it hard to believe.

"I'm running out of family, Sadie," he said at length. "Not many left, now—with Virge gone."

"You have me, Wyatt," she said. "And there's still James. . . ." Her voice died off, and she looked away, unable to face his steady gaze. Her fingers resumed their restless twisting of her handkerchief.

Wyatt removed his hat and slid from the carriage seat to the ground. His boots kicked up a swirl of alkali dust that coated the toes of the black leather and spoiled their shine. The sun beat directly on his gray head without bringing him any of its warmth.

Wyatt studied his boots. She still can't bring herself to mention Nathan, he noted. Even now, with our family numbering less than a handful, she won't bring herself to accept the boy as my son. It was like a wall between them. Always there.

He changed the subject. The telegraph delivery boy had brought a message early that morning to call Allie. Instinctively he knew it was bad news. Allie never spoke to them unless Virgil was present. She and Josie were not the closest of friends. Each woman loved her husband fiercely, and maybe that's where the trouble lay. In times of trouble they closed ranks, the Earps against the world, but in times of peace petty rivalries surfaced as each woman sought to advance her man. Funny, the girls could never see the men had none of that, Wyatt thought.

"What did Allie say happened?"

Josie played with the corner of her handkerchief; her nails plucked at the lace border. "It was the influenza, Wyatt. She said Virgil came down with it the end of last week. Over thirty people in Goldfield have died from the flux so far. Allie believed she could nurse Virgil back to health. But he got worse.

She said he asked her to light his cigar and place little Hickie's letter under his pillow. Then, he died."

Hickie's letter, Wyatt thought. Virgil's grandniece from his long-lost first marriage. He never knew his daughter existed until '98. Why could Allie accept that so readily while Josie firmly refused to recognize his son, Nathan?

"Well, she always could," he noted. "She did so many times before. Remember when the Grizzly Mine collapsed on him and crushed his feet and his chest?"

"Yes." Josie smiled. "We all thought he was a goner that time. Allie, bless her heart, pulled him through."

"Not this time, I guess. My dream of raising horses in California is looking less promising. A one-man ranch—well, it's not what I pictured. . . ." His words trailed off into nothing as he turned and walked to the rim of the rise.

"There's still James," she added hopefully.

"James is too crippled from the war. He could never build a ranch, much less break horses."

Wyatt thought about the Civil War. Over forty years ago, and it still cast its pall over the West. Arizona, Nevada, and even California were hardly touched by the war, being too young, like Wyatt himself was to be drawn into the fight. But men that lived here still carried the scars of that fight—both externally and internally. That bloody conflict had spawned a host of lawless years. And those years had shaped his life and the lives of his brothers.

Strange, he thought, how the war's violence nurtured his talent with a gun. From shooting buffalo for hides he and Bat Masterson had learned to squeeze a trigger so gently that you never knew exactly when the rifle fired. Only the neck-snapping buck of the heavy Sharps announced the event. It took all one's concentration to keep the front sight aligned with the notched rear blade while those great shaggy beasts shimmered in the distance. You developed a kind of detachment in that line of work. It was a business. For each cartridge you expected a hide—as simple as that. A matter of economics. While you blinked away the eye-watering cordite, your hands automatically jacked another round into the rifle. You only stopped long enough to sponge down the red-hot barrel. Or when the herd was reduced to shaggy piles that moved no more.

It was that cold detachment while killing that ensured Wyatt's success as a lawman. Transferring it to killing humans was something else entirely. Many men could shoot buffalo all day long without a qualm yet would blaze away in panic when faced by a person with a gun. Wyatt had seen a man empty both six-shooters at another who was so close you could spit in his face—and miss with all twelve shots.

To most men, a gunfight meant a heart jackhammering away in their chest so hard it felt as if it would burst through the ribs, ears pounding, and hands so sweaty the pistol grip slipped around like greased pork. Half the time they never saw their target, let alone the front sight of their revolver. Those men died young, or retired early if they were lucky enough to live through their first fight.

The successful gunmen dominated those feelings or had none at all. The cold-blooded killers like Clay Allison or Wes Hardin looked on human life as little more than something to be squashed like an insect. Wyatt was sure those murderers felt next to nothing when they put a bullet through a man. It stood to reason that they cared nothing for those they killed.

Bat and Wyatt were different. They had honor, respect, and values. That forced them to follow the law rather than break it. For them, the problem was much harder. But they learned to keep cool and concentrate on the business at hand. Like the front sight that touched the silhouette of the buffalo, they forced their pistol's front sight to always find those that opposed them.

You had to disconnect your thoughts from all else but the business at hand, for even this was a business, no matter how deadly. Front sight, press the trigger—ever so gently so as not to jerk the muzzle off target. Forget about all else. Life, death, pain, everything must be pushed out of all thought. Just front sight, press. So simple, yet so hard to master.

He and Bat could do it. Sometimes he wondered if they simply lacked a normal imagination, so they couldn't visualize the effect a red-hot ounce of lead had on human flesh. But it was more than that. Men called it nerves of steel, or guts. But Wyatt couldn't put a name to it.

Wyatt and Bat had it, and their brothers did not. Maybe that was why Wyatt and Masterson were still alive. That or luck. For Virgil it was mostly luck. Wyatt knew his brother never mastered the deadly ability to disconnect his feelings as he could. That was one reason Wyatt loved Virgil all the more, knowing his brother always backed him in spite of his fears. It was a rare bond that not all brothers had.

But now Virgil's luck had run dry.

Wyatt saw Josie watching him, waiting hesitantly, uncertain what to do. He dropped his hat and held out his arms to her. Instantly she was in his arms.

"I'm really going to miss Virgil," he said as he finally put words to his grief. His eyes filled with tears.

"I know, Wyatt," she whispered. "We all are."

The two sat under the shade of the aspen for most of the day. As the sun set, they mounted their buggy and rode slowly back to town, knowing there would be no more sunsets for Virgil Earp.

★ ★ TWENTY ★ ★

Fairbanks. The spring morning heralded another day of cloud-less skies. With little snow from the previous winter and even less rain, the land swallowed what few ounces of water came from the snowmelt and shriveled into patches of parched and fissured soil. Distant funnels of smoke from forest fires in the flats across the Tanana muddied the air and caused the sun to hang in a smudgy sky like a sullen copper ball. The smell of fires filled everyone's nostrils.

People simply shrugged and went back to digging. Gold cared nothing for events on the surface. Hidden away from the light for millions of years, the yellow metal waited indiffer-ently within its frozen walls for those lucky enough and persis-tent enough to find it. Whether or not smoke filled the air mattered little in the hunt for the saffron-colored element.

Not everything about a dry spring was bad. Without water, mosquito eggs could not hatch. Everyone counted this May's singular lack of the buzzing and biting insects as a blessing—certainly a boon worth a lungful of smoke. Besides, the myriad of fires thawing the frozen overburden and fueling the steam points contributed their fair share to spoiling the air.

So, few of the bustling citizens paused for a instant to con-sider the risk of fire to the town. Exactly a year ago, floodwaters had threatened the town when the Cushman bridge and logs from the sawmill diverted the river into First Avenue. This was Fairbanks, the near-mythical site that sprung from the wilder-ness almost overnight like Minerva from the head of Jove. This was the Second Coming of the god Mammon. Those who missed their fortune in Nome or the Yukon now miraculously received another chance.

And to many a sourdough Fairbanks seemed a spitting image of Dawson during its heyday. The saloons, the sawmills, the streets looked identical. Even the occupants were the same, having trekked north from the worn-out Dawson.

If water and freezing cold could not stunt the place's growth, what else was there to worry about as long as the gold held out?

No one thought of fire.

No one in their right mind, that is. But if fortune favors the prepared mind, misfortune aids the twisted brain, and Billy Wilson's mind was prepared to use whatever was available to his advantage.

As Wilson slouched down Cushman Street amusing himself by kicking stray dogs and stirring up plumes of dust from the bone-dry street with each step he took, a dentist in his office lit the wick of his alcohol lamp. The lamp's flame would sterilize his dental instruments. Then he left his instrument room to tend to a patient.

An ill-fated wind wafted window curtains into the open flame. In seconds the muslin drapes burst into flames. Quickly spreading to the sash, then to the ceiling, the fire engulfed the whole office. The dentist and his patient fled.

With the dry winter and spring, the wooden structures of the entire town represented nothing more than dried tinder. The liberal use of sawdust—a cheap and readily available material—as insulation in the walls and ceilings compounded the risk.

Wilson paused as the panicky dentist rushed out into the street, shouting and gesturing to his office window on the second floor.

"Fire! Fire! My God, my office is burning!" the man cried.

Wilson followed the man's gesturing arms in time to see smoke and flames streaming from the open window. As he watched, the flames leapt along the wood siding to the third floor. Wilson's eyes lighted. He had always loved fires, even as a child. Before he could grin, the roof erupted into a dozen tongues of yellow flame.

The sawdust insulation exploded. Within five minutes, the largest building in Fairbanks, situated in the very center, sported flames from every window. A low roar like that of an onrushing locomotive filled the air, punctuated by sharp pops and snaps as dried wood splintered and split in the flames. A dozen fire alarms sounded; the sharp metallic clanging of barrel hoops being hit with a hammer added to the confusion of sounds. Soon shrieks and other sounds of frightened men grew to rival the thunder of the burning building. Men and women rushed into the street like frantic ants with arms full of their possessions. Overhead, an ominous pillar of dirty gray smoke billowed into the cerulean sky.

Billy Wilson slapped his knee and laughed out loud as people tumbled and fell in their haste. Crates, boxes, and bolts of cloth cluttered the street while the endless string of salvagers worked. Finally, the intense heat drove them back. All they could do was watch helplessly as fire consumed the building.

But the fire wanted more. Released from its bondage to humans, its appetite grew. One building, even Fairbanks' finest, was not enough. Especially when so many other suitably dry structures stood so close.

A dry wind arose, fanning the flames. More crackles and snapping sounded. Men dragged hoses and hand pumps designed for mining rather than fighting fires into position and snaked lines down to the Chena River. By the time the building was burning beyond all help, a dozen puny streams of water laced into the shimmering wreck. The water merely vanished on contact, changed to steam. Clouds of sparks rose into the sky to blow in the wind.

Those who fought the fire were storekeepers, miners, and stevedores, untrained in firefighting. Mesmerized by the blaze, they continued to direct their hoses at a building far beyond any help. They should have played their streams of water onto the roofs of the nearest buildings; instead they battled to save an already-dead edifice.

Crashing into the second floor, the roof flung blazing boards and showers of sparks to ignite the rooftops of all the buildings surrounding the fire. Splintering and shattering logs screamed like dying horses as they toppled to the street. The firefighters retreated before this bombardment. The skin-blistering heat drove them back to the river's edge.

Panic spread. Men dropped their hoses to bat at themselves as their clothing ignited. Others fled as they saw their own houses threatened. Everywhere lines of people hurrying to salvage their goods choked the narrow streets and blocked any relief.

Wilson broke away from the throngs. The fire's rapid spread fueled an idea of his. Ezra Hayes's newspaper and the two rival banking offices lay close by the center of the inferno. Why not help the fire in their direction? With all the confusion, who would notice? The paper and banks could easily be added to the list before the end of this day. The Butte Cafe and the Senate saloon sported dancing flames across half of their flat roofs. Tar and sun-dried sod used in the building materials proved ready fuel for the fires.

Racing down Lacey, Wilson found one bank already ablaze. Quickly he ran on to the next, just half a block away. Even now, windblown sparks filled the air and showered down on the entire section of town. A five-gallon can of coal oil, lying beside a bale of china crockery, blocked his way. Scattered there with a hundred other things, the materials provided Wilson with the makings of a torch. He rolled the cotton packing from the bale around a stick and soaked it with oil.

With a quick look over his shoulder, Wilson ducked into a narrow cleft separating the second bank's wall from the Sargent and Pinskas Hardware store. Splashing the rest of the oil on the wall, he lit his torch and touched it to the siding. The dried wood exploded in fire, almost trapping the arsonist in a blaze of his own making and singeing the hair around his ears. Wilson fell back, shielding his face from the scorching rush of air. He flung his torch onto the low roof. By the time he'd retreated to the main street, the second bank was burning out of control. That left only Hayes's paper to deal with. Riley and Blaylock might be there. The thought chilled Wilson in the midst of the scorching heat. He'd better get some help.

This is easier than I hoped, Wilson thought to himself. Smoke, fire, shouts, and confusion filled the streets as Wilson doubled back in the direction of the newspaper. Forty-five minutes had passed since the initial fire began. But now the entire center of town burned from Turner Street to Lacey and from First Avenue to Third Avenue.

Looking up from the docks at the first cry from the captain of the riverboat, Nathan Blaylock turned to follow the line of the man's outstretched arm, but the side of the Northern Commercial Company's warehouse blocked his view. All he saw was an ominous pall of smoke rising beyond the sheet metal roof. The muffled cries and shouts carried to the riverbank by the wind reached his ears and sent shivers down his spine.

Taking the steps of the boarding plank two at a time, Nathan rushed aboard the ship. The crew lined the rails and stared fixedly at the burning town. Nathan pushed past them and headed for the ladder to the pilothouse. His fingers gripped the polished brass rails while he raced to the highest deck. There the captain stood watching the fire with morbid interest. The man turned briefly to acknowledge Nathan's arrival.

"Here now. What the devil are you doing on the bridge?"

"What's happening?" Nathan demanded while he struggled for his breath.

"Whole damned town is ablaze," the skipper answered. "Looks like what happened to Frisco earlier last month. After the quake, the place burned up."

Nathan's mouth gaped at the inferno. Where this morning a row of saloons, stores, and houses stood, packed shoulder to shoulder on the banks of the river, now a blazing pyre stretched for the entire length. Smoke, steam, and shimmering heat waves made identifying the individual places impossible. All now blended into a terrible sight of flames, punctuated here and there by the burning skeletal remains of one building or another. Fire leered from ruined window frames like the lighted eyes of some giant grotesque jack-o'-lantern. Green, blue, and whitewashed structures lay reduced to ash and drifts of glowing coals and blackened rubble. The young man could hardly believe his eyes. An hour before, the place had been alive with frantic bustle as people pursued their dreams of riches. Now people streamed to the river for safety. The business center of Fairbanks smoldered, destroyed by fire.

And the fire still spread.

Nathan reclaimed his senses and looked about. A strong wind was driving the flames toward the river and west in the direction of the Northern Commercial Company's warehouse and generating plant. With First Avenue already finished, the water's edge would stop the fire. But a good many log homes spread along the bow of the Chena behind the power plant. A gap in the buildings just before the warehouse severed the unbroken string of combustible fuel for the flames. If they could stop the fire before it reached the warehouse and generating plant, all those homes would be saved.

"Good thing I've got a head of steam," the captain interrupted Nathan's thoughts.

"What?"

"Got my boilers fired up. I aim to loose my mooring lines and back away downstream before my ship catches fire with the rest of this burg. That's what the others are doing. Damned sensible thing to do." He gestured to five or six boats of various sizes drifting away from the disaster ashore.

Nathan looked at the powerful pumps lining the afterdeck of the sternwheeler. Used to blast silt from the paddlewheels and in case of flooding, the steam-fired pumps would make excellent pumps to fill fire hoses. "You've got to use your pumps to fight the fire before it crosses that gap!" He jabbed his fingers at the low building sitting within the space. "It's the only chance to stop the spread!"

"The hell you say? My ship's no goddamned fireboat! She might burn along with this damned town! Look at all the sparks in the air!"

"You've got to!"

"Well, I won't." The skipper looked around for his first mate. "Jonas! Throw this fool off the ship. Then prepare to cast off."

Jonas's hand grasped the knife stuck in his belt as he started up the stairs to the pilothouse. His right foot reached the decking only to find the unexpected waiting for him. The hard barrel of Nathan's Colt caught him squarely across the part in the center of his hair. Steel struck greasy hair with a subdued thud. Nathan's other hand snatched hold of the mate's shirt just as he went limp. Without another sound, Nathan lowered the senseless man as far as his arm allowed before letting him slide the rest of the way down the ladder. The first mate crumpled softly into an untidy pile at the bottom of the rungs.

Nathan turned back to the skipper in time to find him furiously searching the inner pocket of his coat for his derringer. The man ceased his quest when Nathan poked his pistol under the man's nose.

"This is piracy!" the skipper blurted. "Piracy, plain and straight!"

"I don't want your ship, Captain. I only want to borrow the use of your water pumps to fight the fire."

"You have no authority—"

"I'm the deputy fire marshal," Nathan lied, "and this Colt gives me all the authorization I need. Don't you agree?"

The captain's beefy face drained of color. He licked his lips while his eyes darted to the inert form of his mate. The rest of his crew stood with their backs to them, entranced by the blazing waterfront and oblivious to the events on the upper deck. Slowly his head moved up and down in a series of spasmodic jerks. He carefully kept his hands raised and far from his pocket with the derringer.

"I agree under protest."

"Good. You'll have to move your ship closer to the fire."

"What!"

"Just do it. Order your deckhands to haul in the bow ropes.

That will move us upriver and within range of the water hoses. Call the men aft to start the steam pumps and play their hoses on that flat house in front of the Northern's warehouse. We'll stop the fire there if we can."

The skipper eyed him suspiciously. "You've sailed before, or I'd miss my guess."

"A while back. Now, give the orders, Captain, and I'll make you a hero."

Nathan slipped behind the man, keeping his barrel pressed firmly into the man's spine, while the skipper picked up his trumpet and shouted orders to his men. In minutes, the deck crew was slacking the stern lines and hauling on the bowlines with the help of the deck winches. Inch by inch the stern-wheeler moved ahead against the river's current to within range of the fire.

The skipper paced nervously back and forth, shouting orders and cursing his men for their slowness with Nathan following him closely, like a Siamese twin. The blistering heat of the fire seared their faces and filled their eyes with tears. Shimmering before them, the picture appeared straight from Dante's Inferno.

Too late, the skipper realized that his only chance to save his own ship was to stop the fire at the spot Nathan identified. Were it to leap this gap and spread behind them, his boat would be encircled and would catch fire before he could drift away from shore.

With this realization, the man threw all his energies into preventing its sweep behind them. Steam pumps creaked and groaned, pushed to their limits to siphon water from the river and spew it onto the blaze. Streams of water arced onto the roofs of the warehouse and the flat house that filled the space between the fire's devastation and the remaining town. Belowdecks the stokers worked frantically to keep the boilers fed with cordwood. Should the pressure drop, the hoses would sputter into impotent dribbles.

A small crowd gathered on the opposite side of the river to

cheer the vessel's valiant efforts on behalf of their town. The captain paused to acknowledge them with a brief wave of his hand.

"Hero, perhaps!" He cursed the crowd and Nathan. "More than likely I'm to be skipper of a charred wreck not worth the effort to salvage, that is, if the ship's owners don't flay my hide—what's not burned of it!"

"Just keep on pumping and pray the wind doesn't strengthen," Nathan advised coolly. His voice sounded more confident than he felt. To his eye it was a standoff. The fire continued its assault but lacked the strength to jump the breach as long as the ship placed a wall of water into the slot. It would be touch and go for another hour. One minute of faltering would see the other side victorious.

Nathan's spirits soared when he saw a familiar figure ambling along the burning river's edge as if he were on his way to a picnic. Despite the confusion, the old gunfighter shuffled along, unflappable as ever, pausing from time to time to scratch the back of his neck while he viewed the mounting disaster that swirled about him. Studying the fire with scientific detachment, Riley poked at burning lumber and peered through the haze when something particular caught his interest.

Jim Riley stopped to watch two people struggle past with a grandfather clock on their shoulders. He removed his hat and brushed away a handful of smoldering cinders caught in the felt nap of the worn Stetson.

"Jim! Jim! Up here!" Nathan waved his own hat in the smoke-filled air.

Riley scanned about with his eyes squinted against the heat. When he caught sight of his friend on the upper level of the sternwheeler, he grinned and waved back. "What're you doing up there, Nat? Ain't no need to take to an ark," he joked. "This here's fire and pestilence, not no flood."

Nathan smiled. "Have you been reading the Bible again?" he shouted down to his friend. Indeed, Riley seemed blessed because of his detachment from the catastrophic happenings.

"I have. And it's marvelous reading at that. It sure pegged

this damned Sodom and Gomorrah right. But I skipped over to the New Testament. You know, the part where it says blessed be the poor. I figure I'm sitting pretty in the midst of this here glorified prairie fire 'cause I ain't got nothing valuable enough to burn 'cept my hide, and that ain't worth an honest cord of wood."

"What about Susie?"

"Oh, she's safe out of town. I led her upriver to the black-smith's. Didn't even have to blindfold her like you'd expect. That mule's got it over horses that way. She's smarter than Lot's wife, too. Never once looked back." He donned his hat and looked down the length of the steamboat. "So just what are you doing?"

"The captain and I are fighting the fire," Nathan replied rather grandly.

"Under protest," the skipper corrected him. "Under protest."

"All by yourself?" Riley looked around, again. "Appears like you're losing," he drawled. "Lordy, there's nothing left back of me but hot cinders. And me without a wiener to roast."

"Well, I didn't work on that part, Jim," Nathan confessed. "I just got started right here. I think we got a slight edge, but it's too close to call."

"Well, then. Guess I better lend a hand. That's what pards are for." Riley snagged the collar of the first man who ran within reach and stopped him in his tracks with a jerk that nearly sent the frightened fellow falling onto his back.

"Let go," the man protested.

"Shut yer yap, and take hold of that hose over there," Riley commanded. He pointed to a coil of water hose on the bank. With no more hands to man the pumps, the crew had heaved the hose ashore in hopes someone would lend a hand.

"What do I do with it?" the man stammered.

Riley pointed to the generating plant of the Northern Commercial Company. An isolated band of workers was un-rolling hoses from the plant under frenzied direction of their foreman. Either Nathan's efforts had inspired them to help or

they had suddenly realized the only hope to save their building
lay in holding the gap. "Git over there and hook it up with
them," Riley ordered. "And don't give no thought to sneaking
off. I got my eye on you, and if I see you crawfishing for the
woods, I'll come git you and throw yer worthless butt into the
fire. Understand?"

The stunned man nodded mutely. He knew Riley's reputation with a gun all too well.

"Good. Now, off you go. You'll be able to tell yer grand-
children in years to come how you single-handedly saved Fairbanks. Now, git."

Within ten minutes, Riley had eleven men working fire
lines from the shore. Like a drill sergeant on the firing line, the
gunfighter strode up and down his command barking orders
and giving encouragement to his men.

Tense minutes stretched into what felt like hours as the
battle seesawed back and forth over possession of the gap. A
foot here and there fell to the fire only to be regained a minute
later. The fire attacked like a wild beast, probing for weak spots
and springing with full force whenever it found one. Other
times it crept silently along the open ground, slithering with all
the stealth of a snake where brute force could not prevail.

Back and forth the battle surged. The wind supported the
blaze, but now men caught a glimpse of hope, and so they
threw themselves into the fray with fevered abandonment. To
each man in the fire pit, the blaze became something personal,
a private demon, a lost cause that fate had given them a second
chance to make right. As line handlers dropped from heat or
exhaustion, others stepped forward to take their place. Fighting the fire had become a battle, paramount. The battle was
now a total war.

The ship's captain screwed his fists into the hollows of his
eye sockets to clear his vision of smoke. His actions left two
chalky canyons in a face painted dark with ash. Looking more
like a death's-head than a man, the skipper showed his white
teeth between blackened lips as he pounded the ship's rail

with both fists. "By God, I think we're holding the bastard!" he crowed. "I never would have believed it!"

As he spoke, the water from the ship's hoses faltered, drooped, then turned to a mere dribble.

"What the hell . . . ?" he swore.

"Captain!" someone called up the voice pipe from the engine rooms. The speaking tube gave the words an eerie tinny sound that sounded all the more frightening against the roar of the fire and the hoarse shouts of the men fighting the inferno.

"What! What?"

"We're out of firewood for the boilers," came the reply. "We've burned what's in the storage bins and the wood stored on the aft deck. We can't keep the pressure up in the boilers."

"Goddamn it!" the skipper cried. He spun about, searching for the cords of wood usually stacked on the riverbank. At a dollar a cord, trappers and Athabascans cut spruce and birch and piled it along the river routes for the hungry paddlewheelers. "I need something to burn!" he shouted.

His gaze met glowing pyres on the fire's side. Cords and cords of wood burned less than a hundred yards away. Ignited by the burning town, the fuel was useless. And the fire, taking advantage of this weakness, roared even stronger.

"Find something to burn!" he ranted.

"What?" came the plaintive cry from below.

Nathan grabbed the skipper's arm. "Weren't you just unloading bacon before the fire broke out?"

"Bacon? Yes, hundreds of slabs of salt pork and bacon for the N.C. Company. For the mines." He looked at Nathan without understanding. "So?"

"All that grease will burn, Capt'n. It ought to give a mighty hot fire."

The light of comprehension flared in the man's eyes. "Blast my eyes, boy, but you're a quick one! Yes, bacon will burn like the fires of Hell."

A string of orders flew from the skipper so rapidly that his end of the voice pipe foamed with spittle before he'd finished.

Richard Parry

Men raced into the storehouse, and soon slabs of bacon danced down a line of sweating men, relayed back into the belly of the beast that had delivered it hours before.

The wonderous aroma of sizzling bacon rose from the ship's funnels to mix with the stench of the burning town. Pressure in the oilers soared, and the streams of water once more blasted back the advancing fire.

Then, the wind turned light. Without its aid the fire failed to bridge the gap and retreated, turning its wrath back along its smoldering path. Little was left to feed the blaze. Begrudgingly, the flames lowered, the smoke thinned, and the active fires crashed into coals with the collapse of the last of the blazing framework still standing. That part of the town survived.

Spontaneous cheers rose with the smoke. Men flung their hats into the air until a few sailed into the coals and burst into flames before anyone could retrieve them. Everywhere tired, happy survivors dropped where they stood. Some said prayers of thanks; others gathered their strength before embarking on a search for the nearest surviving saloon. Ironically, the best had perished, but the walled fence, erected to shield the tender eyes of the proper townsfolk from the fancy ladies who worked the Row, was saved along with the shacks of the soiled doves—and E. T. Barnette's Fairbanks Banking and Safe Depositing Company. If the captain was grateful, he never showed it, but the whores displayed their appreciation with cold beer and free service.

The skipper slapped Nathan on the back and chortled. "Heroes, eh? I guess we are, boy." He pointed to the line of waving women standing before their intact fence. "Would you like to receive your reward?"

Nathan shook his head. "No thank you, sir. I have a lady of my own and . . ." He stopped in midsentence, and his heart jumped into his throat. The wind's shift now enabled him to see east to where Ezra Hayes's newspaper office ought to be and where Molly lived behind the press.

Nothing but smoldering ruins remained of that block.

252

Nathan vaulted over the last smoldering cross-beam, arriving out of breath and anxious at the ruins of the *Fairbanks Daily* with Riley hard on his heels. The two men had sprinted the entire distance from the riverboat to the site, skirting still-blazing patches and leaping glowing coals. With each stride that drew him nearer, Nathan's fear doubled.

It was worse than he feared. The entire building lay burnt to the ground. Charred beams and smoking slats angled inward, scattered like jackstraws across the cooked remains of the printing press, where they had fallen with the collapse of the roof. Trays of type, burned to cinders, had allowed their once carefully sorted letters to fall to the ash-strewn floor. Nothing recognizable remained of the living quarters in the back save for a heat-slivered and warped mirror lying on its side.

Nathan could do nothing but stand and stare at the smoldering ruins. Riley poked about halfheartedly, head bent as if at a funeral, while his foot stirred the ash and shifted the charred scraps of wood.

"Don't see no remains," he volunteered tentatively. "Molly and Ezra must have got out in time."

A groan came from a pile of lightly charred wood outside the foundation of the house. The jumbled scrap covered part of what once was the narrow alley between Hayes's paper and a saloon next door. The wreckage must have fallen away when the walls collapsed along with the roof. This part fell into the space and so was spared by the flames as they leapt from one tinder-dry building to the next.

The two men rushed to the sound and dug frantically beneath the debris. Under half a foot of boards, Nathan found a boot. Ignoring the coals that singed his fingers, he scattered the cover to expose a leg . . . one covered with a pant leg—a man's leg.

A mix of relief and concern flooded his mind while he and Riley uncovered the body. It looked like Ezra Hayes, lying facedown. His clothing smoked and showed signs of charring where the fire reached past his protecting boards, but burning did not appear to be his main injury.

An eight-inch spruce log lay across his left leg where it had fallen from the ceiling. The leg projected from beneath the log at an unnatural angle. When they pried the pole off, they saw why. White bone protruded from a tear in the flesh of his thigh. The ivory bone shone unnaturally through a rent in the trouser and contrasted grimly with the surrounding blackened wood and gray ash.

Gently they rolled the man onto his back while protecting his shattered limb. Even so, he groaned in pain. Nathan used his sleeve to wipe dust and grit away from the clenched lips and tightly squeezed eyes. He cradled the old man's head in his hands, but blood covered his right hand when he withdrew it.

"Ezra," Nathan called softly. "What happened?" He steeled himself for the question he dared not ask but had to know the answer to. "Where's Molly?"

Hayes's lips moved, but no sound issued from them. The man made an extreme effort. "The skunks took her. . . ."

"What skunks?" Riley asked, kneeling beside the two.

"Wilson and his friends. All three of them. They broke into the shop when the fire started. They poured coal oil on the walls and lit a torch. Molly came out from the back when she heard the shouting, so they grabbed her. I . . . I tried to stop them, but Wilson hit me." Hayes rolled his eyes about in panic. His hand sought Nathan's arm, and his fingers clamped around the young man's wrist. "They've got her, Nat!" he rasped painfully. "You've got to save her! She saw what they did! They'll kill her to keep her from talking."

"Which way did they go, Ezra?" Nathan asked.

"Don't know. They set the shop afire and went out back. Wilson hit me from behind. He kept hitting me. That was the last thing I remember. When I came to, fire was everywhere. I managed to drag myself into the alley, but the wall fell on me. Go after her, lad. Save her!"

"I will, Ezra. But first we'll get you to a doctor."

Hayes's grip tightened fiercely. His nails dug into Nathan's wrist until they broke the skin. He fixed Nathan with a dreadful gaze. "Leave me. I'm finished. Go after Molly."

Riley examined the printer's head wound. Nathan saw him grimace, and the look Riley gave Nathan made his heart sink. Slowly, Riley shook his head.

"They can fix you up, Ezra. You'll see. . . ."

But Hayes's jaw opened as if he planned to scream, his back arched, and a terrible sigh escaped from his lips. Then his body went slack and his head lolled to one side. The fierce light that always filled his eyes faded until nothing was left. Where a moment before the flame of life burned now were unseeing eyes, lifeless and spent as the surrounding cinders.

"He's gone under," Riley said. "Old Ezra was right to the end. Weren't nothing could be done for him. Wilson squashed in the back of his head like a ripe melon."

Nathan looked up at his friend. No words to express his grief came to him. So Riley spoke for both of them.

"First Doc and now Ezra. Billy Wilson's got a lot to answer for. The time has come for us to get serious and track Sweet William down and ventilate his sorry ass."

Riley rose to his feet and drew his pistol. He blew ash from the Colt and checked the cylinder. It spun softly with the oiled clicks of a finely tuned watch. Nathan did likewise. He withdrew a cartridge from his belt and inserted it into the sixth chamber he normally kept empty beneath the revolver's hammer.

Riley watched him, nodding his head in approval. "Good idea, son. Odds are we'll need that sixth round for the fight.

We're more likely to be shooting the whole wad at Wilson and his bunch rather than worrying about accidentally shooting ourselves by carrying a round under the hammer."

Nathan removed his coat and draped it over the body of Hayes. Both men cinched their gun belts before heading out onto the burned-out street. People stopped their salvage efforts to look at them as they passed. From the rigid hunch of their shoulders and the grim set of their jaws no one doubted the two men carried rapid retribution on their hips.

Halfway down what once was Second Avenue, Riley stopped. Approaching them on horseback was the blacksmith, leading Susie along with a string of three horses. White ash and soot covered the man and all his animals. Only the white coat of Susie appeared a shade darker than usual. The procession looked ghostly amid the ruins. The weary man reined to a halt alongside them. He studied them carefully while he drank from his canteen. Normally, he might offer them a drink as well, but today their hardened faces dissuaded him.

"Like to wore myself plumb out chasing after these fool mounts," he volunteered the reason for this parade. "They took off for the foothills when the fire broke out. Every damned one of them except Susie. I just brought her along to help quiet the others down. She's better than a bell mare."

Susie snorted and ambled forward to nuzzle Riley's gun arm. His face softened, and his hand stroked her velvet-soft muzzle.

"How are you, girl? Miss me? Has this cheapskate been shorting you on yer oats?"

"I never did nothing of the kind," the blacksmith protested. "In fact, she's getting an extra bucket of grain today for helping me round up these nags." He looked around as if seeing the devastation for the first time. "Jesus. What a mess. I'm lucky my barn is on the edge of town. What are you fellows up to?"

"Going to kill Billy Wilson," Nathan answered darkly.

The blacksmith nodded while his horse shied and tossed her head at the smell of fire. "Good riddance, I say. I saw him down by the back of Capt'n Barnette's bank as I passed. He's got five of his men with him."

"We figured the rat would head for that rat hole."

Riley rubbed the stubble on his chin as he thought. "Ken, could you see yerself clear to loan Nat one of your horses? We might have need of a rapid means of departure after our discussion with Wilson and his boys. You know what I mean?"

The blacksmith leaned forward in his saddle. Without another thought, he dismounted and handed the reins of his horse to Nathan. "I sure do, Jim. Take Bob here. He's the best of the string, excepting for Susie, of course. The others are so spooked by the fire they're just liable to go all spavined on you at the first sound of gunplay. I'll walk them back to the barn. Bring Bob back when the smoke clears." He patted the young man on the shoulder before leading the rest of his string down the street.

Riley and Nathan mounted. "What do you say to my going in while you hold our rides?" Riley asked.

"No."

The old gunfighter sighed. "I figured as much. Okay, we'll tie them up in the alley. I never thought I'd be happy that the captain's bank didn't burn, but it'll help our getaway."

Nathan stood in his stirrups to look ahead. His right hand felt for the rifle scabbard only to find it empty. Of course, he couldn't expect the blacksmith to anticipate a shoot-out when he saddled the horse, but it also meant their two six-guns would be all they had for the fight.

"Funny thing, Jim. Did you notice only Barnette's bank didn't burn? His competition went up in smoke. I'll bet Billy Wilson had a hand in helping them just like he did with the paper."

Riley spit onto a glowing pile of coals. He smacked his gums appreciatively as the spittle turned to steam with a loud hiss. "Time to set things right," he said.

Without another word, the two men turned their mounts away from the river and rode in a wide circle, heading away from the bank until they struck the unburned section of town. Then they worked their way past crowds and piles of salvaged goods until they stopped in a narrow alley one block south of the Fairbanks Banking and Safe Depositing Company building.

Preoccupied with salvaging what remained of their property, few of the citizens gave them a second glance. Outside of the burned center of town, there was much to do, unlike where the fire had struck. There stunned people simply stood and gazed at the damage. Here a frenzy of activity flowed around the intact buildings.

Reaching the alley, both men dismounted and tied their animals to a hitching post at the mouth of the lane. Hidden by shadows, they worked their way to where the back of the bank was just across the road. The street narrowed into nothing more than a crack that separated the walls, and the men were forced to move in single file. Riley held up his hand. Nathan slid silently beside him and looked over his shoulder.

Two men lounged against the back wall of the bank. A third sat on the raised plank porch built in front of the back entrance, rolling a cigarette while a Winchester lay across his knees. The other two also carried rifles, one Marlin lever action and a Winchester 1895 Model. All three men wore side arms.

"My, my, there's our reception committee," Riley whispered. "You'd think the capt'n expected a gold shipment with all them arms."

"Or us. . . ."

"Yup. Don't see no scattergun. That's encouraging." Always the teacher where Nathan was concerned, Riley asked, "How would you handle this, son?"

Nathan grinned fiercely. "The smartest thing would be to run."

"Well, I know that! But I also know we ain't gonna do that. We ain't known for always doing the smartest thing, are we? Otherwise we'd have left this burg a long time ago."

"Right. Since they've got rifles and we don't, the best thing would be to close with them as fast as possible so they can't use their long guns to their advantage."

"Smart boy. Yer daddy's breeding and my training is paying off." Riley pointed his chin at the patch of sunlit street that separated them. He judged the distance to be fifteen to twenty yards—too far for a mad dash. The guards would see them before they got close enough. "But how do we do that?"

As if the gods of good fortune heard him, the solution presented itself that very instant. Two boys struggled into the alley with their arms piled high with hatboxes. With six boxes apiece they swayed into the narrow path, balancing their load like jugglers. The first boy crashed into the back of Nathan, and his parcels rained down upon him and Nathan with a muted crash.

"Sorry, sir," the lad stuttered while he struggled to replace the lids and spilled hats. "I didn't see you."

"What have you got there?" Riley asked. "You look like you robbed Isaacs Brothers of all their sombreros."

"Oh, no, sir. Their shop burned up, but we helped them save most of their goods. Now they're paying us to move their stores out of the street."

"How much are they paying you?" Nathan asked.

"A dollar apiece," the boy answered suspiciously. "But it's hard work. We still have to carry all their pants."

Nathan looked at the boxes piled around his feet. He dug into his pants and produced two shiny silver dollars. "I'll pay you two dollars extra if you let us borrow a few of those hatboxes."

"Borrow?"

"Yes. All my partner and I want to do is carry them across the street. You can pick them up after that, but I'd wait half an hour before I did. There might be some gunplay. Here's what we plan."

Both boys' eyes grew big as saucers as Nathan whispered in their ears.

Tom Green swore as he spilled half the tobacco he was rolling into a cigarette onto the boardwalk. So far three attempts had failed to produce a decent smoke for him. The blister on his left thumb made success impossible. In disgust he crumpled the cigarette paper and its remaining leaf into a ball and threw it into the street.

"Damn!" he swore. "This here blister is the size of a watermelon. It's hindering my efforts. I can't make a smoke to save my life. Roll one for me, Zack, would you?"

"Hell, no," the man with the Marlin retorted. "Serves you right for being clumsy. If you'd cold-cocked that girl like Billy told you to instead of playing touchy-feely with her in the coals, you'd never have burnt your paw. I hope a good grope of her was worth it."

Tom leered at that, exposing a wide cleft between two rotten front teeth. "Yeah, it was at that. She's a mighty trim filly. I might have had fun if she didn't scratch and fight so. And we had the time." He ran his fingers over the deep scratch on his neck. "She's some wildcat."

Zack hawked a gob of phlegm from the back of his throat and spit it into the cinder-strewn street. All this smoke and ash made his throat dry as a bone. "I still don't see why Wilson wanted to take her along. She saw what we done to the newspaper office. She can finger us. We should have bashed her head in like her uncle's."

" 'Cause she's bait."

"Bait? What the hell for?"

"Wilson figures Nat Blaylock and that old coot Riley will come for her." Tom Green paused in his discussion to watch two boys burdened with parcels emerge from the alley diagonally to his right. The boys crossed the street and headed briskly away. Two others followed them with similar loads.

The last two carried a tall stack of hatboxes that defied gravity. Green wondered how these two could see where they were going, for their bundles obscured the upper halves of their bodies and blocked their vision. One had five hats balanced on his head like some street vendor. As they approached, swaying and sidestepping to balance their stacks, Green considered sticking his foot out just to see the man fall and drop his load. He decided to do it. A good laugh might take his mind off his throbbing thumb.

But before he could trip the carrier, the fool stumbled. In his effort to keep from falling, the bumbling worker brought the heel of his boot down sharply on Green's toe. The bone cracked with a loud snap.

"Ow! Damnation! Watch where you're stepping!" Green howled. He sprang to his feet, bringing his rifle up to club this fool who'd injured him.

"Sorry," Riley said as he let his boxes fall. The five hats balanced on his head tumbled to the street with the containers. "My fault."

Suddenly Green realized why this man carried his parcels so awkwardly. His right hand also held a cocked Colt .45. The heavy barrel caught Green across the side of his neck, just above the fresh scratches and precisely at the angle of his jaw. Another crack sounded, this one louder than the one from Green's toe. The guard crumpled to the porch like a sack of potatoes.

Nathan released his hatboxes at the same time. The two other gunmen, without warning, faced a grim Nathan Blaylock instead of some peripatetic laborer. They struggled to their feet with their rifles still held at the ready although Nathan stood too close for comfort. And certainly the long-range advantage of their rifles no longer existed.

"Drop your rifles!" Nathan commanded.

Zack noticed that Nathan's pistol still remained in his holster. He'd heard the boy was fast, but then, every gunman boasted of speed. It was their best card for bluffing. The bigger the bluster, the more one was able to avoid actually shooting. Besides, there were two of them. And he'd never seen Blaylock draw.

"Don't do it!" Nathan warned, but his words were barely out before Zack swung the rifle at him. The other guard did the same, lurching to one side so as to widen the gap between the guards and make it harder for Nathan to aim at both riflemen.

Nathan drew his pistol with a blur of blued gunmetal that could only come from hours of practice.

Zack fired first. His rifle barrel aligned with the second button of Nathan's flannel shirt when he jerked the trigger. He blinked involuntarily with the explosion. In that fraction of a second when his eyelid twitched, his target vanished. To Zack's astonishment, the gun fired into empty air.

Nathan dropped to one knee, dropping almost as fast to meet his Colt as it flew into his hands. The rifle blast deafened his right ear, and the powder burned his forehead, knocking his hat off and into the street like a stone skipping across a pond. But the rifle bullet missed by a mile.

Nathan's shot didn't.

The solid smack of his heavy bullet striking Zack squarely had little time to register before Nathan's front sight swung to capture the image of the third man cocking his rifle. Nathan squeezed the trigger. Take your time and shoot as fast as you can, the paradoxical words of his father, Wyatt, echoed in his mind. Nathan knew the message by heart, learned the hard way from Jim Riley's hard tutelage. Hard lessons for a hard work. *Draw fast and shoot carefully.*

Oddly, his pistol bucked in his hand, but the sound appeared doubled. A detached part of his mind puzzled over this until he realized both he and Riley had shot at the same instant. The last guard lay facedown when the smoke cleared. His rifle stuck, muzzle first, into the churned dirt, presenting a strange picture with the owner sprawled beside it.

Nathan glanced wildly around. Riley stood over the man he'd buffaloed with his gun barrel, and the man called Zack slouched against the bank wall with both hands locked over a smoking hole in the center of his shirt.

"Git going!" Riley shouted. "I'll cover yer back."

Nathan's shoulder crashed into the back door, shattering the frame and wrenching the door off its hinges. Before the door swung crookedly against the wall, Nathan bolted inside with his pistol ready. In three strides he was down the darkened corridor. A startled man with gun in hand burst from a side door to collide with Nathan's gun barrel. Another sickening crack, and this man reeled back into his office while his revolver dropped from nerveless fingers.

Nathan heard shouts and screams coming from ahead. He raced in the direction of the commotion. Crashing through another door, he skidded to a halt in the front room of the bank. Panic-stricken women clutched each other while the men present threw up their hands, expecting a bank robbery. Through the front door, beyond the room, Nathan heard Molly's voice, then the sound of horses galloping away.

His heart sank when he realized the crowd jammed inside blocked his path to the front door. Already two women had fainted near the entrance.

Behind him Riley raced up. He grimaced at the wide-eyed men and women standing with their fingers reaching for the ceiling.

"Put yer hands down," the gunfighter snapped to the gathering. "This ain't no damned holdup! It's a rescue. Where's Molly?"

"They're getting away!" Nathan cried in desperation. "Back up! I've got to get to my horse."

A comedy of errors ensued while the two men hastily retreated. Another woman collapsed while a third screamed at the men present to stop the robbery. A half-dozen men along with one of the tellers produced pocket weapons. Brandishing their guns, the men charged down the narrow passageway, hard on the heels of the two would-be rescuers. A dozen shots, fired at random by the pursuers, choked the corridor with acrid smoke and blew chips and chunks of wood and plaster from the walls.

"Sweet Jesus," Riley cursed as he dodged the wild shots, "preserve us from well-minded citizens. Don't they know we're the good guys! We're trying to prevent a kidnapping."

"Amen," Nathan added. "But I'm not stopping to debate the point." He winced as a wood splinter struck the side of his face. "How about you, Jim?"

"Hell, no! That's the way to git yerself hung."

Given the added incentive of a maddened mob, the two men retraced their route in record time. Passing the dislodged door, they reached the street. Fortunately, the ruckus out front simply added to the confusion in the back.

Of Wilson's guards, only Tom Green moved. Dazed and with blood pouring from his split scalp, he crawled about on his hands and knees with his head dragging in the dirt. Nathan and Riley raced past, heading for the alley where Susie and Nathan's horse waited. From the corner of his eye Nathan caught a fleeting glimpse of Wilson galloping off at the head of his gang. The smoke and swirling dust parted enough to give him a tormenting image of Molly in the grasp of one of the gang.

"Jim! They're heading south towards the Tanana." Nathan pointed to the escaping group. "We've got to get them before they disappear in the bush."

Reaching their animals, both men mounted and spun their mounts around to gallop into the street behind the bank. There was no other way, Nathan realized, even though that route led them back toward the rear door of the bank and the oncoming mob. Turning the opposite way, around the block, would force them to thread their way past the confusion of the salvage with all its obstructions. Too much precious time would be lost.

Riley and Susie took the lead, bolting into the street. His unexpected rush caught the foot posse by surprise, just as they boiled out the back door and onto the bank's porch. To aid the confusion, Riley fired a shot into the air. The citizens scattered. Digging his heels into Susie's flanks, the old gunman dropped low in his saddle, hugging his mule's neck while shouting words of encouragement to her. The big mule responded with a series of powerful bounds.

Next came Nathan on the hostler's animal. Keeping low, he used his knees to guide the horse. But Bob was a docile horse, used to hauling supplies rather than bursting through a hail of gunfire. He shied away from the bodies on the street, almost tossing Nathan from the saddle. The young man held on desperately while he fought to control his skittish animal.

Regrettably, in the time he lost Nathan's pursuers regained their senses. A fusillade of shots clipped the air around him. Bob panicked and started to buck.

Something struck Nathan in the side of his neck. His right hand lost feeling, dropping the reins, and he reeled in the saddle. The world spun around as pain exploded from his neck in a cascade of a thousand fiery needles that poured down his entire right side. He tumbled from his horse into the ash and dust.

Dazed, Nathan struggled to his knees in time to see Jim Riley rein in Susie and start to gallop to his rescue. But Nathan knew it was futile. Already he sensed men racing to his side. He waved his left arm feebly.

"Go back, Jim!" he shouted with the last of his strength. "Save Molly!"

A blow to the back of his head drove him to the ground. All around him feet were rushing to surround him. Nathan raised his head in time to see Riley wheel about and gallop away. He let his head drop into the dirt. Somehow, it felt warm and comforting. Rough hands were shaking him, dragging him away from the amenity of the ground, but he no longer cared.

Behind him a voice shouted, "Get a rope! Let's hang the murdering son of a bitch!" A chorus of cheers followed. Then Nathan slipped down an ever-darkening tunnel into total blackness.

TWENTY-TWO

Tonopah, Nevada. A cold shiver ran through Wyatt, making him shudder involuntarily. Like someone walking on my grave, he remembered the old saying. Yet the sun was still high in the sky, still baking the alkali dust and red rock to the point where its shimmering heat waves turned the horizon into dancing light. As far as he could see, the land cooked silently. Not a cloud was in sight.

What caused this feeling? Wyatt wondered. The thought distracted him from his task, and a dull thump at his feet followed by another thud rewarded his loss of concentration. He looked down at the two apples lying beside his boots. Even now a brownish bruise spread across the skin of the nearest fruit. He looked disgustedly at the remaining apple in his left hand.

"Wyatt, what on earth are you doing?"

He stiffened and tried to hide the apple in his hand. "Er, nothing, Sadie. Nothing at all."

"Yes, you are." Josie approached him. "Skulking out here behind the house like a little boy eating a stolen watermelon. You have that same guilty look, too." She reached his side and stopped with a graceful swish of her dress. Her eyes transfixed the apple he held before settling on the two others by his boots.

"What on earth . . . ?"

Wyatt scratched behind his ear awkwardly. "Ah, well. Well, I was trying to juggle—"

"Juggle?"

"Yes, juggle." A trace of exasperation crept into his voice. It was ridiculous having to account to her. He was taller than his wife by over a foot, older than she was, and he was the one wearing a gun belt. Yet at times she made him feel like he'd been caught with his hand in a cookie jar and was about to have his knuckles rapped with a spoon.

Josie sensed his displeasure and softened her tone. She lowered her eyes and purred. "I didn't mean to intrude, and I certainly hope I didn't sound like a shrew. I . . . I was just worried about you."

"Worried?"

"Yes. You've been awfully quiet these last weeks. You seem out of sorts. I hope it's nothing I've done."

Wyatt looked at the apple in his hand and let it drop. It plopped next to the other two. "No."

"Good." Her smile rivaled the brightness of the sun as she slipped her arm inside his. "Then what is it? It can't be the saloon. It's doing well. Certainly we have no need of money. We have enough."

"No, it's none of those things."

"Well, what is it?"

Wyatt squinted at the hills in the distance. He shrugged. "Just a bit edgy, I guess." He couldn't tell her his fears concerning Nathan.

Josie realized it would be best not to press further. She'd lived with Wyatt long enough to know he was a private man with many locked doors that would never open to her. Her intuition sensed this involved Nathan. Her heart cried out to accept the boy, to heal this breach that separated their present life and Wyatt's past, but her pride stubbornly refused.

Since Virgil's death, Wyatt's concern for his family—all his family—had grown with each passing day. On more than one occasion Josie had heard Wyatt mutter that his family was dangerously close to extinction, that he could not afford to lose any more with Morgan, Warren, and now Virgil gone. Although he never mentioned it to her, she knew he included Nathan Blaylock in his assessment.

Josie bit her lip as she turned away so Wyatt could not see her face. She hated herself for being unable to acknowledge his bastard son, but try as she might, she could not. She wished she could.

Her eyes fell upon the three apples. "Why would you want to juggle, Wyatt?" she asked, seeking a desperately needed diversion.

His faraway thoughts vanished, and he was in control again, the steely-nerved man with ice water in his veins she knew and everyone expected. A crooked smile creased his lips, but he looked self-conscious. "You won't laugh if I tell you, will you?"

"Cross my heart. I won't laugh."

"I read in the *Police Gazette* that a man ought to try new things to keep his wits sharp and stay young. They recommended cold baths, brisk walks, and . . . juggling. Juggling is especially good for the hand-to-eye coordination, they said."

It took all of Josie's past experience on the stage to keep a straight face. "Really?" she said. She hoped she didn't sound too sincere. "And is it?"

Wyatt stopped and retrieved the apples. "I don't know," he said slowly. He turned the pieces of fruit over in his hands. "I can't get the damned things to work. I keep dropping one."

"Well, dear," she said with practiced solemnity. "It takes practice. If you can't juggle, it doesn't mean you're old. Or losing your faculties."

"Blast, I know that, woman. I can still shoot the eyes out of the deuce of spades at twenty paces. But I can't keep three stupid apples in the air at one time. And I mean to!"

"Wyatt—"

Unexpectedly he handed her the apples. "You can juggle, Sadie."

"No, I—"

"Yes, you can. The first time I saw you in Tombstone you were practicing juggling with that other actor when I went backstage to meet you."

"Anthony?"

"Yes, Anthony, or whatever his name was. He was teaching you to juggle."

"My Lord, Wyatt, you remember that? There's certainly nothing wrong with your memory. That was years ago."

"How could I forget? You were the prettiest thing I'd ever seen."

She curtsied. "Why, thank you, kind sir."

He pointed his finger straight at her. "Juggle," he commanded.

"You won't be upset if I can do it while you can't? Promise? It takes lots of practice."

"I won't be upset. I give you my word. I want to watch how you do it. The illustration in the gazette makes no sense whatsoever."

"All right," she said reluctantly. "But you can't be angry."

Shifting two of the apples to her right hand, Josie squared her shoulders and started to juggle. Her first two tries failed, but on the third attempt, she kept all three apples circling in the air. Wyatt watched this intently until she grew tired and let the apples fall.

She studied his face. "You're not angry? You promised."

Wyatt kissed her cheek. "No, dear, I'm humbled but not angry. Thank you for the lesson. I think I get the idea." He drew her into his arms and squeezed her tightly. "No man ever had a more beautiful teacher."

Josie whispered in his ear, "Maybe tonight I'll juggle for you in my altogether."

He held her at arm's length. "Why, Mrs. Earp, what a delicious idea. I'll definitely look forward to that. Now run along and leave me to fumble my way clear."

Wyatt waited until Josie closed the back door before picking up the apples. Remembering the way she had held her hands, he tried again.

Twenty minutes later his back ached from the constant bending to retrieve the dropped apples. The fruit also showed signs of fatigue, with tears in their skin and chunks of missing pulp. Only once did he succeed in keeping two apples in the air at the same time. The rest of his efforts were dismal failures.

"Damn," he muttered. "Pretty bad when a man's wife can juggle and he can't."

With three deft snaps of his arm, he threw the apples over the back fence.

Wyatt tipped back in his chair and wiped his mustache with his napkin. Josie had outdone herself with this evening's meal. Potatoes, a thick beefsteak, and apple cobbler for dessert. He felt like he might explode.

"Lord, I made a pig of myself, didn't I?" he confessed.

"It was good to see you eat, Wyatt. You have hardly eaten ever since . . ." She stopped herself, furious at the way she had let her thoughts slip. But the damage was done.

"Since Virge passed away?" he completed her sentence.

"Yes. You've got me worried, Wyatt. I don't mind telling you that. For months all you did was pick at your food."

He chuckled at her, reaching out to pat her hand. "Sadie, too many more meals like this and I'll end up heavier than Virge ever was."

"You could use a little more meat on your bones," she said with a pout. "I swear, people will think I don't feed you properly."

"And since when do we care what people think?"

She pursed her lips and looked away from him so he would not see the tears welling in her eyes. She should have saved the effort. His hawklike sight never missed a thing.

"I haven't been too easy to live with since Virge's death. I realize that, and I'm sorry. But don't you worry your pretty head. I'm pulling out of my funk. I've felt more like myself today."

She wiped her eyes on her apron. Giving him a sideways glance, she said, "Even though you haven't yet learned to juggle?"

His response surprised her.

"I'm not finished yet," he said.

Most men would attempt to dismiss their failure or reduce

its significance with a shrug or a sneer, but he did not. He folded his hands on the edge of the table, interlocking his long, slim fingers carefully, and looked at her levelly. His hands always amazed her. Thin and aristocratic, they belonged to a doctor or an artist, not a man who once broke horses and shot buffalo for a living.

Josie knew there were those who called her husband a cold-blooded killer—always behind his back. None of them had the courage to call him that to his face. But she knew he was not. In private, during quiet talks like this, she saw a gentle man. And his hands always reminded her of that.

"What are you looking at?" He followed her stare to his interlaced fingers.

"Just your hands, Wyatt. For all these years I've never seen you come to the table or touch me with dirty hands."

Wyatt turned his hands over, inspecting them. "Well, they weren't always this clean, Sadie. There were times when Bat Masterson and his brother, Ed, and I looked like red Indians, we had so much buffalo blood on us. It took me a week of sanding myself with a chunk of sandstone just to see my true color. And getting rid of the stench was an even worse battle."

"Ed Masterson? You never talked much about him, Wyatt."

Wyatt poured himself another cup of coffee. "Do you mind if I smoke?" he asked her. Normally he smoked outside or in the parlor.

"Please do. I enjoy the smell of your cigars. Tell me about Ed."

"Ed was a good man—too trusting to be a lawman. It got him killed in the end."

"How so?"

"One night in Dodge City—I believe it was in 1877 or '78— Ed was city marshal, and Bat and I were deputies along with another man named Nat Haywood. Two cowpokes named Wagner and Walker got to whooping it up. Wagner had a pistol, which was against the city ordinance, and a mean streak a mile long when he'd been drinking. Ed took Wagner's pistol away from him. And then he did a foolish and fatal thing." He stopped to pare the end from his cigar and light it with a match.

"What?" Josie leaned forward. Wyatt was talking so softly she found herself straining to hear his words. Rarely did he talk about gunfights. When he did it was only to minimize the event with the most sketchy details. She realized tonight was special, so she moved carefully so as not to break the spell.

Wyatt puffed thoughtfully before he blew a perfect smoke ring. "His trust did him in. He gave Wagner's pistol to Walker, the man's trail boss—something I'd never do. Ed believed Walker, as Jack Wagner's boss and a man of responsibility, could be *trusted* to do the right thing. But Walker was no better than Jack Wagner and just as drunk."

"So what did he do?"

"He gave Wagner his gun back, and both men followed Ed out into the street only to draw down on him. Jack Wagner's gun went off in the struggle and shot Ed clean through the stomach and out his back. It was at point-blank range—so close the powder set Ed's vest on fire. Ed got off four shots of his own. He hit both Wagner and Walker. Wagner died the next day, but Walker survived. Ed Masterson walked into George Hoover's saloon and collapsed. I can still see him lying there with his shirtfront smoldering. He lasted until Bat and I got there. Then he died about half an hour later." Wyatt blew a cloud of smoke. "Ed depended on the wrong people to do the right things, and it cost him his life. He was a good man, well liked by everyone. I think he believed the best of everyone he met. That's a fatal error where gunplay is involved. When a man has a gun in his hand and he's facing you, expect the worst out of him, and nine times out of ten you'll be right."

"You can trust me, Wyatt," Josie replied. How terrible, she thought, to know your life hung in the balance of worthy expectations. Even more terrible that a good man should die for believing better of his fellowman.

Wyatt smiled at her. He wished he could tell her of his inner feelings, his deepest concerns. But that would require mentioning his son. From Nathan's letters Wyatt sensed that same optimism Ed Masterson had. Nothing specific, but reading between the lines, Wyatt felt that goodness with every pen stroke the lad put down on paper to him.

Where did he get that? Wyatt wondered. Certainly not from his mother, Mattie. Her legacy would be bitterness and self-pity. He hoped not from him. Maybe it came from all those years in the orphanage. Whatever the origin, Wyatt worried it would get the boy into bad trouble.

Belief in the goodness of your fellowman was an admirable and noble trait, Wyatt had no doubt. But one best suited for men of the cloth or optimistic philosophers, not a shootist. It reminded Wyatt of a bear hunter believing all the great animals he tracked were nothing more than timid beasts. Sooner or later, that nimrod would learn the errors of his beliefs—most likely the hard way.

Well, Wyatt thought, the boy is young. Youth carries with it an exuberant optimism. Silently Wyatt thanked the stars above that Nathan had Jim Riley by his side. That old gunman knew the score; otherwise he'd never have lived long enough to grow all those gray hairs. Wyatt counted on Riley to watch over his son since he could not.

This self-imposed exile hurt Wyatt the most. Knowing it was for the best did little to ease his pain. Without thinking, he let a great sigh escape.

In a flash, Josie read his mind. Her face flushed, and she sprang to her feet. Wyatt's lowering of his shield was so uncharacteristic that it caught her off guard, and she reacted without thinking.

"It's *him* you're really thinking about, isn't it!" she shrilled. "Not Ed Masterson, *not me*, not anyone but that . . . that . . . bastard!"

"Sadie—"

"No! No!" She beat her fists on the tabletop, spilling the coffee cups and rattling the silverware across the crocheted tablecloth. The dam had opened, and all her fears, rational and irrational, justified and not, poured forth. "That's why you've been moping about all this time. And here I thought it was over poor Virgil. But no, it's that boy that you *think* is your son! You've only seen him for a few short days, and yet he occupies all of your thoughts—day after day after day! What about me, Wyatt? Don't I count for something? What about me!"

With that, she rushed upstairs to their bedroom. The door slammed shut so hard the walls shook. The minute her body hit the bed, Josie hated herself for what she had said. She didn't mean it, not most of it, but the words were out. Josie wished she could take them back, but the damage was done. Her foolish pride—how could she have let it run wild? Now she had hurt Wyatt for doing something admirable—worrying about his son.

In her heart Josie knew Nathan was Wyatt's flesh and blood as sure as she knew how dearly she loved her husband. Only her fierce pride blocked her from saying so. She would have to admit, then, that Mattie Blaylock was better than she was, that that wretched woman could produce a fine and handsome son where Josie could not. A thousand times a day, the youth reminded her of that painful fact.

Moreover, nothing she did could change that reality. The harder she dug in her heels, the worse she made things. Most perplexing of all, she realized that, yet she was powerless to change her feelings. Her emotions always took control like a panicked horse racing back into a burning barn and wrecked any rational action on her part. Her outburst tonight piled another stone in the wall she unwittingly had built between herself and the man she loved more than anything else in the universe. Miserable for hurting her husband when she wanted to be a pillar of strength and support for him, Josie cried herself empty.

Even through the closed door, Wyatt could hear her sobbing. He stared at the glowing tip of his cigar. His life seemed to be disintegrating into ash just like the white refuse on the end of his cigar. Depressingly, he was powerless to stop it.

For what felt like a year Wyatt sat there in the darkness of his dining room watching his cigar burn to a stub in his hand. Josie's crying stopped at last, the stars appeared, and the moon rose while he watched.

TWENTY-THREE

Nathan awoke with a jerk. The right side of his neck seared as if red-hot coals lay against his skin. Something pulled at him and raised his injury to another magnitude of discomfort. Lancinating pangs followed this movement. Instinctively he pulled away.

"Hold still, son," a voice urged. "I'm trying to get this bullet out."

Nathan sat upright while his hands fended off this source of agony. His head exploded in a shower of lights, throbbing from the sudden movement. He blinked furiously until his vision cleared. Struggling to focus on his surroundings, Nathan fought back a wave of nausea. Unsteadily he grasped the edge of the cot on which he lay and gingerly moved his head to look around.

Robert Whyman, one of the town's physicians, loomed over him, hands tinted red with blood while he held an evil-looking probe in his right hand. Nathan blinked at the bloodstains on the man's white butcher's apron. From the various smears on the garment the lad realized his blood was not the first to blemish that piece of clothing. Prescience told him his blood would not be the last, either.

Nathan forced himself to look further. A packed dirt floor and rough peeled log walls greeted him. But the iron bars blocking one side of his cell and covering the tiny window told him everything.

"I'm in jail?" he asked. "What happened?"

Whyman stepped back. He laid his surgical probe in a basin

half-filled with bloody water and handed Nathan a square of cloth. "Best hold that against your neck to stop the bleeding, son," he said. "If you want to talk first, the bullet will have to wait. I already stitched up your head while you were unconscious."

"My head?" Nathan's hand reflexively touched his head. He winced when his fingers met a row of stiff silk sutures sprouting from his blood-caked scalp.

Whyman studied Nathan over his wire-framed glasses. He'd always liked the easy grace of this young man. Perhaps he envied and admired the lad's loose freedom. While his association with the late Doc Hennison, whom Whyman considered a pariah of the worst sort, left a lot to be desired, Whyman considered himself a man of tolerance. A man should not be judged solely by his fallen friends. Still—

"You're lucky to be alive, young Blaylock. Why that blow to your head didn't mash your brains to porridge is a mystery to me. You must have a skull like granite. That and the fact that this bullet in your neck is a hair's width from your jugular vein tell me either you're a very lucky man or the angels up above are watching out for you. Any other man would be dead by now."

"Maybe Doc Hennison is acting as my guardian angel," Nathan answered without emotion.

Whyman flinched. "I seriously doubt that. That miscreant is dancing on hot coals right now, or I miss my bet." He started to say more, but the look from Nathan silenced him. One never knew what harm this man was capable of doing—after all, he'd just shot two men—and Whyman was acutely aware of the fact that he was locked inside a barred cell with Nathan.

Nathan studied the bars. The memories of the gunfight, the confusion in the bank boiling out into the street, and his capture returned.

"Why'd they lock me up?" he demanded. "I didn't do anything wrong."

"Not if you don't believe shooting down two men and attempting to rob the bank is worth mentioning," Whyman replied offhandedly. "One man's stone cold dead, and the other isn't expected to live, either."

"We weren't robbing the bank! We were trying to rescue Molly Hayes. Billy Wilson and his gang kidnapped her. They burned down Ezra's newspaper during the fire and Molly saw them. And they killed Ezra."

The doctor sat down on a corner of the cot and began to wipe his instruments on his apron. "Well, that's your side of the story. The mayor and two dozen witnesses say you and your partner, Riley, killed editor Hayes and tried to do the same for his niece, Molly. Barnette's men say they rescued her and took her to the bank to protect her. That you two rushed in after her and shot up Barnette's bank guards in the process."

"Bank guards!? That's bullshit. Those men were in on it."

"Well, we might never hear their testimony since one is already dead and the other can't talk. You might have thought of that before you shot them."

"They were shooting at me. And they fired first."

"Well, do you want me to remove that bullet in your neck, or don't you?"

Nathan avoided answering. "You can ask Molly. She'll confirm my story."

Whyman sighed. "The poor girl is not available for questioning at this time. Capt'n Barnette is keeping her safely hidden until the trial. Since your friend Riley escaped, the capt'n fears for her safety. He said his man, Wilson, will be providing her protection."

Glumly Nathan slumped back down onto the pole cot. Barnette had it all figured out. With Molly in the captain's grasp and Riley labeled a fugitive, only Barnette's version would prevail. Worse, Barnette had Molly, and Nathan feared for her safety. She was the one witness that could link Wilson's crimes to Barnette. Nathan realized his only hope was that Riley had remained uncaptured. Now he needed time to think. The not-so-gentle probing of Dr. Whyman would help him focus his scattered thinking.

"Go ahead; dig the bullet out." Nathan uttered the words with no show of feeling. His mind already raced through an escape plan.

The first touch of Whyman's metal tool caused a shock of pain to run up into the back of Nathan's skull. The doctor paused, expecting Nathan to jerk away, but all the lad did was utter a muffled grunt. With eyes compressed to narrowed slits and his lips so tightly pressed together that they vanished into little more than a razor's slash, Nathan suffered in silence. Save for the rare catch in his breathing, only the flicker of his clenched jaw muscles betrayed the agony he felt.

Once when the probe grated incessantly against the raw edge of his neck bone, Nathan's mind rebelled and reeled in terror. But the young man drew his brain back under control by sheer power of his will. Like a wild bronco, resisting efforts to break to the saddle, his thoughts panfished and bucked only to eventually submit.

Whyman paused to wipe the sweat from his eyes even though the dirt-floored cell felt cold as the grave. The surgeon knew his probe flitted with vessels capable of bleeding the young man to death in five minutes. One slip was all it took.

"The slug's lodged next to your cervical vertebra. The sixth one, I think. It clipped off the transverse process and stopped against the body of the vertebra." Whyman waited, half-hoping Nathan would call off this task.

"Dig it out," Nathan ordered.

Whyman blew out his cheeks in an aborted pant and hunkered closer. If the lad was pigheaded enough to kill himself, well, so be it.

It took Dr. Whyman a full hour before Nathan heard the metallic clank as the lead slug rattled into the basin. Whyman stood up and groaned. His back ached from bending over the low bunk. He also marveled that Nathan had not moved so much as an inch or issued a single sound while the doctor's probe bounced off raw nerves and grated against exposed bone in its relentless hunt for the bullet. Whyman knew it hurt, more than he cared to ponder. The physician had gained new respect for the boy's hidden strength.

Secretly Whyman had begun to believe Nathan's story. Everyone in town knew young Blaylock and Molly Hayes were lovers and that old Ezra valued the young man. It made no sense that Nathan would murder his own friends. And there was the captain himself to consider. Half the town would be happy to see Barnette lynched for all his nefarious deals, and the other half would shed crocodile tears if that happened— if they shed any tears at all.

"My God, you're a tough bird," Whyman issued his praise begrudgingly. "Anyone as stubborn as you must be telling the truth. You'd be too proud to lie, whatever the outcome." He applied a bandage to Nathan's bleeding neck and tied it in place with a roll of gauze. "If it doesn't fester, you should be all right. But you've lost considerable blood. You'll be weak for days to come."

Nathan grinned fiercely, gaining small consolation from the fact that his wolfish leer caused the doctor to start. He pointed his finger at the doctor's bag. "I couldn't convince you to, say, let one of your scalpels accidentally fall out of your bag, could I?"

Whyman hurriedly retrieved his tools. He paused to weigh the request before shaking his head while he clutched the black patent-leather satchel to his chest. "Ah, no. . . . Believe me, I'd like to, but . . . you understand."

"Just fooling, Dr. Whyman," Nathan responded. But he wasn't fooling. Still, he appreciated the fact that Whyman had considered helping. Before Nathan could say more, the heavy door separating the front offices of the jail from the cells opened. The reek of stale tobacco and sweat poured into the dank prison to overwhelm the musty odor of the place.

Two men stood in the doorway, backlit by a single lamp in the front office. Nathan realized it was the protracted alpine twilight that suffused the late spring days with slanting rays of ethereal light. He also recognized the two men. The one acting as jailer was named McGinnis, a drunk well-fixed in the pocket of E. T. Barnette. Beside him stood the squat figure of none other than Judge James Wickersham, supreme arbiter of law in the Interior.

Wickersham motioned to the jailer and waited as the man drew his revolver and advanced toward the cell. Nathan stiffened, and Dr. Whyman sucked in a lungful of breath in alarm. Surely, the doctor thought, they wouldn't kill them both?

"Keep clear of the bars, Blaylock," McGinnis warned, "while I let the doc out—unless you want me to finish the job we started this afternoon."

"That's enough of that, McGinnis," Wickersham snapped. He stood to one side with both hands thrust into his coat pockets while the jailer unlocked the door. The frightened physician bolted past the grate and out the door.

To Nathan's surprise, the judge walked into the cramped cell and sat calmly down on the stool, but not before giving the dusty chair a perfunctory swipe with his gloved hand. The man's manner gave Nathan the impression the High Court had deigned to visit the condemned man.

"Now, leave us, McGinnis. I wish to talk to the prisoner *alone.*"

The jailer jangled his keys nervously. "I . . . I got my orders, Judge."

"And those orders come from the marshal, and his orders come from me," Wickersham retorted tiredly. "Now, leave us. You can lock me in if it makes you feel any better."

McGinnis moved forward only to stop as Wickersham raised his hand. The judge studied Nathan's pale face closely. "But Mr. Blaylock will give me his word he won't try anything rash while I'm here. Won't you, Mr. Blaylock?"

Nathan nodded carefully. Any movement rekindled the fire in his neck, and his head still threatened to split.

"Good."

Wickersham waited until McGinnis closed the door behind him. Without first turning directly to face his prisoner, the judge began. "You've got yourself into a pretty pickle this time,

Blaylock—murdering two bank guards and attempting a bank holdup in broad daylight. Especially doing so on the heels of the most disastrous fire this territory has ever seen. Why, the entire business district of my . . . er, this city has been leveled by fire. Only a truly callous man would add such a grievous insult to the town's fresh injury."

"We didn't rob the damned bank. Like I told Dr. Whyman, we were trying to rescue Molly Hayes. The captain's man Wilson kidnapped her."

Wickersham glanced at the closed door. So Whyman knew, too. The judge cursed his lapse of good sense in letting the physician in to treat Nathan. But, McGinnis had assured him the youth was unconscious and incapable of talking. So much for taking the word of idiots, Wickersham reprimanded himself. Disturbingly, Nathan's rescue alibi even now was spreading through town, finding ready believers by the minute.

Maybe this alarming spread grew from its believability. Wickersham found himself finding merit in the boy's story. Wilson and his ruffians were all too capable of using the fire to their benefit. The fact that *both* Barnette's rival banks and the paper most critical of the mayor had perished in the flames while Barnette's bank had survived strained coincidence beyond reason. Wilson could do it all right, but he wouldn't without Barnette's order.

The judge rankled inwardly at the crude excuse the captain gave for holding Molly Hayes a virtual prisoner. The idea that people would believe this young man or his friend Riley would harm the girl was drivel. Clearly, Barnette had crossed the line on this one. To support him would be fraught with peril. Especially since the judge fully expected Molly to meet with a fatal accident before she could ever testify.

Wickersham decided to disengage himself from the captain as quickly as possible. His confirmation as judge was still stuck in the U.S. Senate, thanks to enemies of Barnette who continually shed light on his dealings with the judge. Anything more would scuttle his judgeship for good.

"What about the two men who were shot? What can you say about their murders?" he asked.

"I heard only one was killed?" Nathan questioned.

"The other man died an hour ago. You're facing two counts of murder." Wickersham paused as he considered a ploy. "Unless it was Riley who shot them," he said slowly.

"He did his share, Judge, but my bullets got there first—on both of them," Nathan lied. If he was going to swing, he'd clear his friend. "But they shot first. It's the gospel truth."

"You're saying it was self-defense?"

"They shot first. We ordered them to drop their guns, but they didn't. All Jim and I wanted to do was get to Molly. Those three out back of the bank stood in our way."

Suddenly Wickersham saw a way: he would use this young man to bring down the high-and-mighty Barnette. The courtroom would provide an excellent forum. Wickersham could protest in private to Barnette, pretending to be helpless in the face of unfolding facts, while the trial of Nathan exposed the black side of their mayor for all the good citizens to see. Then no one could accuse the judge of being in Barnette's back pocket. With enough luck, Barnette's downfall would leave him unscathed. It would take care, the judge realized, and finesse to separate himself from the captain without him realizing. It would be like loosening the grip of a drowning man from your own wrist—finger by finger—and doing it so skillfully and adroitly that the doomed person never realized his grasp was being broken. But it could be done!

Wickersham stood up. "I can't say as I believe you, Blaylock. But you deserve a fair trial, and I aim to see you get just that. Say no more. My advice is to seek legal counsel and to divide your defense into two parts. First, plead self-defense in the shooting of those guards. Secondly, press your arguments that you entered the bank to rescue Miss Molly Hayes."

Nathan blinked at this sudden change. Wickersham had always regarded him as lower than dirt. Too weakened by his wounds to question the judge's motives, Nathan could only stare as James Wickersham swept back out the cell and exited the back block of cells.

Four days passed with no other visitors. McGinnis brought Nathan two meals a day, mainly water and stale bread with an occasional bowl of cold gruel. Other amenities included a fresh pitchforkful of straw.

Nathan used the time to mend. Although Dr. Whyman never returned, his handiwork prevailed, and both the scalp and neck wound healed. Nathan healed as furtively as possible. Whenever McGinnis entered the back room, he found a pale, listless Nathan bundled in the threadbare blanket and looking a half-step from eternity. No sooner did the door close than the young man resumed rebuilding his injured muscles and regaining his strength. With youth on his side, he recovered quickly.

Nathan pressed his mind along with his body. To stifle his growing fears for Molly and his worry over the whereabouts of Riley required constant effort. Dark thoughts crept into any gap they could. So, the young man schemed and hatched a hundred plans to escape.

One of his last resorts proved the riskiest.

On the fifth day, he begged McGinnis for pencil and paper. As expected, the man refused.

"I'll trade you my boots if you let me write a letter," Nathan pleaded. "Just one letter."

His jailer eyed him distrustfully. But Nathan could see the man coveted his footwear. "You can write?" McGinnis grunted.

"Yes."

"Well, who do you want to write a letter to?"

"An old friend. I aim to ask him for money to hire a lawyer. I know he'll send me enough. He has plenty, and he would be saddened to see me in jail." Nathan had carefully planned his response, and his heart soared as he saw the impact on McGinnis. The glint in the man's eye proved the jailer took his bait. Who was there to stop McGinnis from diverting some or all of the funds when they arrived? From his look Nathan knew the jailer planned on doing just that.

"What's this friend's name?" McGinnis asked suspiciously.

"Bill Stapp. William Stapp. Have you heard of him?"

The jailer shook his head while he scratched his beard. "No. Can't say as I have."

Good, thought Nathan. So far, so good. "He lives in Nevada. Will you let me write to him?"

"Okay. But poke your boots between the bars first. How do I know this Stapp fellow mightn't refuse to cough up your funds? I'll have them boots on account."

"Get the writing materials first."

"Damn you. I can just come in there and snatch your boots if I've a mind to."

"Come on, then," Nathan taunted. He knew the jailer wouldn't.

An awkward period of silence passed before McGinnis reached the solution that Nathan had expected. "Slip off your boots while I get pen and paper. We'll pass them through the bars simultaneously."

When the man returned with a soiled scrap of paper and envelope, the transaction took place smoothly, although McGinnis acted as though he were parting with the family jewels. Nathan retreated to the farthest corner to compose his letter.

Half an hour passed before Nathan's plea to his father for help lay signed, sealed, and safely in the pocket of the guard. And not a minute too soon.

The jail door opened to admit E. T. Barnette. The mayor gave McGinnis a harsh look, prompting the man to scurry past him in a rush to the outer room. McGinnis hastily shut the door behind him. The reaction of the guard informed Nathan far better than any salute that McGinnis worked for Barnette, even though the man was supposed to be under the town marshal.

Barnette watched the back of his minion vanish before turning to face the prisoner. He came directly to the point. "I hear the good judge paid you a visit. What did he say to you?"

Nathan gave his interrogator a look of insouciance. "Actually, he came to inquire on my health," he drawled.

Barnette's face flushed and the muscles of his jaw twitched. Nathan watched a vein creep up past the man's celluloid collar. Clearly, the mayor was unused to insolence—something Nathan expected and counted on. With each encounter, Nathan had found Barnette's ego inflated as his power and wealth grew. While that made him more dangerous with each passing triumph, it also made him more vulnerable—or so the young man hoped.

"I won't bandy words with you, Blaylock. You're in a tight fix, but I might be able to help you."

Barnette's offer stunned Nathan. The man obviously wanted something from him. But what?

Nathan's silence encouraged the captain. He continued. "We've had our differences in the past, Blaylock—and not without good cause. Your taking advantage of my wife, when she was vulnerable, comes immediately to my mind. Any decent man would agree I have been injured by your actions enough to have you shot."

"You forget you tried to lynch me," Nathan corrected him sullenly. He opened his mouth to add: "Your wife was the one who started it, not me. She couldn't keep from jumping all over me." But he thought better of it.

Barnette waved his hand, dismissing the rebuttal. "Water over the dam," he snapped. "If you can put the past behind you—like I can—I'm willing to make you a deal."

"What sort of a deal?"

"I can . . . er, arrange for you to conveniently escape. But you must promise not to shoot anyone during your escape."

"And what do you expect in return?"

Barnette drew in a long breath. "I want you to leave town. Permanently. Never come back. Take that murderous sidekick, Riley, with you."

"That still leaves Molly Hayes. What about her?"

"Take that girl as well. I know she'll follow you."

"Dr. Whyman told me you're holding her for safekeeping. To protect her from me," he added sarcastically.

Barnette nodded rapidly. "I know. That was a big mistake. Billy Wilson has her, and I'm afraid of what he might do. He told me you were trying to kill her, as she had witnessed you fighting with her uncle."

"And you believed him?" Nathan snorted incredulously.

"I-I didn't know what to believe," Barnette stammered.

I'll bet, Nathan thought to himself. I'll just bet you're covering your own ass.

The captain picked up on Nathan's disbelief. "Believe me," he pleaded, "I never expected Wilson to go this far. If he suspects his side of the story will not prevail, I have no doubt he'll do Miss Hayes great harm."

"My fear exactly," Nathan echoed.

"Then you must rescue her. I don't know exactly where he's holding her, but it must be across the Tanana at one of the fish camps. You've got to find her and take her away from him."

Nathan's frame sagged. He was powerless to do anything in jail.

"What do you say?" The captain paused to smile wryly. "After all, the whole territory of Alaska, except Fairbanks, ought to be enough breathing room for the three of you."

Nathan studied the captain's face, but the man averted his eyes to avoid direct contact. "Why are you offering me this? What's in it for you, Capt'n?"

Barnette commenced pacing before the iron bars. Perhaps the sight of the grating reminded him of the time he spent in the Oregon State Prison. But he kept those clues to himself. "It's no secret I aspire to becoming governor of this territory. I have the money and power and the connections to do it. But my political enemies in Washington will use anything to stop me."

Nathan nodded slowly. Your high-handed dealings give them plenty of fodder, he thought.

Barnette continued. "Your presence in Fairbanks is an . . .

an embarrassment. I admit I was heavy-handed when I first built my trading post, but I needed to be! This spot on the river was a wilderness then, and harsh methods were called for. Now things have changed. Look what has come of my efforts. Fairbanks is being called 'The Paris of the North.' Surely what I've built justifies my actions?"

"Your Paris just got burned to the ground, Mayor," Nathan added dryly.

"We're rebuilding already. That's the other reason for letting you escape. The town needs to focus every last ounce of effort on rebuilding before winter comes. The last thing we need is a divisive trial at this time. Trying you would divide the community when the reconstruction can least afford it. We need to pull together, don't you see?"

Nathan found himself believing the captain. His youthful optimism looked for the best in everyone, and Barnette's genuine love for a town he believed he had built obviously shone in the man's face.

"How do I know I can trust you?"

"Why would I make this offer otherwise? I can just sit back and do nothing and let you go to trial."

Nathan pondered his dilemma. An escape managed by Barnette worried him no end. If Jim Riley were in charge, he would jump at the chance. But where was Jim? Nathan had hoped his friend would have sent him some word by now. With every day that passed not knowing how Riley fared, Nathan grew more worried about Molly and more edgy. Barnette's plan was all he had.

"All right. I accept your offer. What are the details?"

Barnette made sure the door to the office remained closed before he spoke. "Tonight McGinnis will bring your supper before he heads over to the Model Café for his own meal. But he'll be careless. He'll leave the keys to your cell on that chair over there. After he leaves, you can reach them through the bars, unlock your cell, and escape."

"And then what?"

Barnette continued. "Slip out the back door into the alley.

288

Stay in the shadows. There's still enough light until midnight for someone to see you, so I'd wait until then. If you head through the alley to Fourth, a horse will be waiting there for you. I'll see to it the saddlebag has food for three days and one hundred dollars in gold. Get on the damned horse and ride. I don't ever want to see your face again. Is that clear?"

"What about my gun?" Nathan pressed. Wyatt's pistol was his son's most prized possession.

"No. I don't want you shooting anyone. A pistol is not part of the bargain."

Nathan fretted over the possibility of escaping into the wilderness unarmed, but the set of the captain's jaw showed him that the matter was closed. On the other hand, the lad couldn't leave that long-barreled Colt behind. He would find a way.

"All right," he agreed. "I don't have much to say in the matter, do I?"

"You're lucky to get this," Barnette said sternly. "Midnight, then. No sooner and no later. That's very important. I don't want anyone seeing you and raising a ruckus. The quicker and quieter you vacate my town, the better for all concerned."

The deal done, Barnette spun on his heel and left. Once outside and beyond earshot of Nathan's cell, the captain began to whistle.

TWENTY-FOUR

The remainder of the day dragged painfully for the young man, torturing him with each tick of the Seth Thomas clock mounted on the far wall. With the clock hung directly across from his cell, he could do little to avoid staring at the swinging pendulum. With each arc of the gilded counterweight, Nathan's mind soared in fanciful flights of imagination. He would slip away, collect Jim, and rescue Molly. From that point his dream splayed out into several scenarios: One saw him riding back into town to the cheers of the townsfolk to clear his name and drive Barnette out of town. Another found him discovering the mother lode with the help of his two friends in some remote part of the valley. With limitless wealth and power he would undo the captain's stranglehold on Fairbanks, returning at the head of his own army like an Alaskan version of the Count of Monte Cristo.

The rattle of his bars awakened Nathan. His heart sank as he realized he was still in jail. All his grand schemes amounted only to dreams. The clock showed ten o'clock.

"Here's your grub," McGinnis greeted his awakening. "It ain't hot, but it ain't got no bugs in it, neither." He waggled a tin pot, complete with wire bail and lid at his prisoner. "I got it at the café. It was hot when I started, but I stopped for a quick drink, and—damned if it didn't cool off."

From the raucous cackle and the cloud of whiskey-laced breath that came from the jailer's mouth, Nathan doubted the "quick drink" story. "What's to eat?" he asked, finding himself ravenously hungry. Wisely he realized this might be his last meal for some time, lukewarm as it was.

"Stand back from the bars," McGinnis ordered. He unlocked the cell and slung the pot inside. Before Nathan could turn around, the man slammed the grate and snapped the lock closed with surprising quickness.

Nathan followed the ooze of grayish-brown slop that seeped from the overturned pot. It flowed onto the dirt floor and then, as if reluctant to add any more dirt, came to an abrupt halt in an irregular congealed mass at Nathan's feet. He winced at his meal. "What is it?" he asked.

McGinnis shrugged. "Dunno. Best I could do for ten cents." He slumped uncermoniously into the chair while he spun the key ring around his finger and kept an eye on his prisoner. A shadow crossed his flat face. "Ain't you going to eat it?" he growled.

Nathan stooped over and raised the container. It felt stone cold. He understood now why the stew had scarcely leaked out. Most was already hardened. He dipped his finger into the mess and sampled what clung to it. The strong taste of rancid tallow and turnips assailed his tongue. Unwittingly he grimaced.

McGinnis howled in amusement. "Ain't no Delmonico steak and potatoes, is it?"

To spite his jailer, Nathan forced himself to smile. He jammed a handful of the paste into his mouth and ate it with great smacks of appreciation. "No, it's real good," he lied. It took all his will to keep from gagging on the foul glop, but he gained a perverse satisfaction in denying McGinnis even the smallest satisfaction.

Disappointment showed on the jailer's face. He grumbled a few unintelligible curses before shambling out. Nathan listened as the man's footsteps faded and he heard the outer door slam shut. The youth's eyes darted to the chair. The keys to the cells hung from the back of the chair!

The next two hours took forever to pass.

Nathan watched the pendulum until forced to stop. When

the minute hand slipped over the number twelve, he was ready. The door between the cell block and the outer office remained open a crack, but no sounds had emanated from the front since McGinnis left over two hours ago. Still, Nathan held his breath and cocked one ear. All that he heard was the ringing in his ears from the deathly silence and the pounding of his heart. The jail was empty save for him.

Taking a deep breath, Nathan eased himself along his cot until he pressed against the bars. If someone should come in, he could drop back on his cot and feign sleep. Swiftly his arm darted between the bars to the wooden chair and its precious cargo of the keys. His fingers touched the wood, and an electric feeling surged through him. Freedom was within his grasp.

"Oh, no!" he gasped out loud.

McGinnis, in his drunken state, had left the keys hanging from their stout key ring and looped over the back of the chair. The youth's fingertips could just touch the cold brass keys, causing them to shift and clank. But the heavy metal ring that held the keys rested securely over the raised limb of the chair's back—beyond his reach! All he could do was slide the keys back and forth with his fingertips. The chair was just far enough away to prevent him from obtaining a grasp.

Nathan withdrew his arm to gaze at the tantalizing keys to his freedom. So near, yet beyond his grasp, he grunted at the key ring in frustration. He drew his knees to his chest and tried to ignore the pain in his neck while he thought. Already fresh blood was seeping from his wound where he had opened it in his efforts to stretch through the bars.

What would my teachers do? he wondered. All three, Wyatt, Jim Riley, and the late Doc Hennison, sprang to mind. Suddenly his cell was filled with their presence. Not surprisingly, each offered wildly different advice.

Riley simply stood there, suspicious of the whole escape plan, shaking his head in warning. In Nathan's mind he could see the late Doc Hennison ranting and railing at that imbecile of a jailer for messing up his part in the escape plan. Doc would even throw the stew pot against the bars in a wild fit. And Nathan saw his father, Wyatt, cool and coiled as a diamondback rattler, studying the problem. To Nathan's astonishment, Wyatt pointed to the pot that Doc was now busy bashing against the bars.

Nathan blinked and the three vanished. He looked down at the glue pot that had been his supper. That was it! The pot had a wire bail.

With as much speed as his trembling fingers allowed, Nathan snatched the pot and detached the wire handle. Bending the wire until it was straight, with a hook on one end, he returned to the bars and extended his arm, now holding his wire hook, toward the keys.

The front door banged open. Someone was coming!

Nathan dropped onto his bunk with the wire hidden beneath him just as the inner door swung wide. A rumpled man wove into the back and sat unceremoniously on the floor in a pile of disheveled clothing. It was Felix Pedro, discoverer of the first great gold strike in the valley.

"Felix! What are you doing here?" Nathan blurted in wonder.

"I'm a little bit too drunk," Pedro slurred.

Since his strike, life had unraveled for the little prospector. Devoting all his life and efforts to finding gold, the poor man found himself unprepared for success. As he was preyed upon by swindlers and plagued by bad investments, his fortune had vanished. Worse still, his health was gone as well. Now the founding father of the Interior Stampede was reduced to a wandering drunk, kept inebriated by drinks bought by well-wishers.

"Too damned drunk to go home," Pedro elaborated. "I come to sleep here. Turn myself in for being drunk and disorderly." With that simple statement, the little man toppled to one side and began to snore.

Nathan held his breath, half-expecting to see McGinnis. The clock now showed half past midnight. Surely the deputy could not be expected to stay away much longer. Nathan decided to gamble that Felix's arrival had not attracted attention. Silently he arose and returned to the task of retrieving the key set.

His makeshift hook snared the ring easily. With great care, Nathan lifted the ring from off the chair and withdrew the wire holding it. But the greasy wire spun in his hand, and the keys clattered to the floor—right next to the sleeping miner.

Felix sat upright and looked around with bleary eyes. Nathan froze. It took all his will not to look at the keys on the ground beside Pedro. Pedro blinked uncertainly, then lay back down.

Nathan's heart restarted only to skip another beat at what he saw. Felix was lying on the keys.

Slipping onto his knees, Nathan wriggled his wire under the prospector's body until it touched the key ring. But the man's weight kept snagging the hook and preventing retrieval of the keys. Sweat dripped into Nathan's eyes as he struggled to free them. Finally, he hit upon a plan.

Carefully he snaked the wire out until it hovered over the sleeping man's face. With infinite skill, Nathan brushed the loop across Pedro's nose, ever so gently, time and again until the drunk wrinkled his nose, snorted, and did what Nathan had hoped. He rolled onto his side.

With the keys exposed, Nathan snared them with a lightning catch and jerked the precious cargo into his cell. Instantly he fitted the key to the lock and opened his cell. The wall clock showed ten past one.

Easing past the sleeping Pedro, Nathan crawled on all fours to the office door. The outer room stood empty. Nathan cursed as he eyed the gun rack. A heavy hasp and stout lock held a pair of Winchester 1895 Model lever actions. The thick iron strap dashed all his hopes of borrowing one of the rifles. A careful search of the desk drawers turned up nothing he could use to defend himself. From what he could see through the barred window, the street facing the jail looked clear. Neither beast nor man ventured down that road. The far side, leveled by the fire, did nothing to block the light of the rising moon from adding its pale light to the eerie twilight of the nascent summer solstice.

Hairs prickled on the back of Nathan's neck, even under his bandage. Something was wrong. Leaving by the front door left him too exposed. He decided to try the back.

Pedro had turned on his side and tucked his knees to his chest like a sleeping child. His snores provided the only sound save for the ticking of the clock that had so tormented Nathan. As a afterthought, he checked Pedro for any usable weapon, but he found nothing.

Out the back door, the shaded alley held more promise. Narrowed to twice a man's width, the alley ran straight as an arrow for twenty paces before widening behind a dry-goods store. There a pile of barrels and crates lined the route, providing additional cover besides the shadows. Beyond that the alley jogged to the right just before it transected Fourth Avenue.

From where he crouched Nathan could see a horse, saddled and carrying saddlebags, tied to a hitching post. The narrowness of his view precluded seeing much more. So far, so good, Nathan told himself. Just as Barnette had said, the horse was waiting. The youth took a deep breath and eased into the alley. Keeping as low as he could, he pressed himself tightly against the rough boards of the building and moved forward. Cloaked in the thin shadows, Nathan still felt the uneasy sixth sense that a rifle barrel was pointed at the small of his back. He paused to listen like a vole worried about a great horned owl.

A muffled sound reached his ears, more of a soft thump as if something yielding had met an uncompromising object. Nathan froze. He waited while his eyes probed the dark shadows and his ears struggled to hear over his thundering pulse.

Nothing more alarming caught his ear, but his uneasiness only grew. He moved on. The pile of crates was only yards away.

Emitting a sigh of relief, Nathan reached the relative safety of the boxes in two lighting bounds. He pressed his back against the barrel staves and blew out his cheeks. He half-chuckled to himself. His last leap had been a blur of blinding speed. Bet I would have outrun a bullet on my last jump, he mused. Now only a dozen yards stood between him and the horse.

Gingerly Nathan edged out from the shadows and crouched for the last run. He stretched his arms out in the dirt like a sprinter ready for the starting gun.

His fingers touched a body. A warm body.

Nathan's hand recoiled like he had encountered a scorpion. Any minute he expected the numbing shock of a bullet to strike him. Again, nothing happened. With infinite care, he inched around the barrel while his fingers searched for the body. His eyes followed his fingers onto the prone figure.

It was his jailer, McGinnis.

The man lay facedown, breathing heavily. Had he passed out? Nathan's fingers quickly discovered the cause of the man's condition. A giant goose egg sprouted from the back of the man's scalp.

"Sweet Jesus!" Nathan gasped.

"Ain't nothin' of the kind," a voice out of the gloom whispered.

"Jim! Jim, am I glad to see you."

"You ain't seen me, yet," Riley answered sanguinely. "And if you don't lower yer voice, you ain't gonna."

"Where are you?"

"Right here." The faintest flicker of movement betrayed a hand moving ever so slightly, so Nathan wondered if his imagination was playing tricks on him. The hand appeared to materialize straight out of the building itself. He blinked again. There was a crack in the building barely wide enough to admit an arm. Nathan suddenly realized a cold storage shed must have been constructed onto the wall of the structure that formed this side of the alley. To the casual observer the wall appeared solid.

"I never saw that opening," Nathan admitted.

"Neither did this porker, McGinnis," Riley grunted. "Appears he ain't never hunted no Apaches, or he'd have fed an anthill long ago. From the size of him, he'd have kept them ants busy for some time. But he got off lucky with me. All he's gonna have in the morning is a powerful mean headache where I cold-cocked him."

Nathan realized McGinnis had been lying in ambush for him, only to be knocked senseless when Jim reached his pistol through the unseen opening behind the crates and belted the man unconscious.

"I can forgive yer ignorance, son, 'cause I ain't taught you about hunting Apaches, yet. Seeing as how there ain't none in Alaska, I figured it could wait. You had so much else to learn. But I may have been mistaken."

Nathan almost cried with relief. "Well, let's get out of here, Jim."

"Not so fast, boy. There's four other men waiting to ambush you when you reach that horse. It's a trap."

"Four?"

"Yup. They ain't taking no chances should you get past the fat boy here."

"But Capt'n Barnette—"

Riley swore softly. "Jesus. You believed that weasel?"

"He offered me a chance to escape if we took Molly with us and left Fairbanks."

"Not a bad idea, but the capt'n had other ideas up his sleeve. Appears like you was about to get shot escaping."

Nathan edged over to the opening. Clearly, he could not squeeze through into the storage shed. "Thanks," he said with a smile. "I guess I hoped Barnette was telling the truth this time."

Riley's hand reached through the crack to pat Nathan's head. The boy winced when the calloused hand struck his injured scalp, but he said nothing. Riley could not see his head was cut.

"Hell, I can't fault you for believing the best in folks, but it's a decent attribute you ought to shed real quick. Not doing so will get you killed." Riley squinted into the shadows at the horse tethered beyond reach. "Got any ideas, Nat? I can work back to

Fourth and come out a-whooping and a-blazing. Hopefully you can use my ruckus to reach the horse and make a getaway."

Nathan realized his friend was offering his life for him. Four men, hidden with rifles, were more than even the vaunted Jim Riley could take. "No. You'd never stand a chance. We've got to think of something else. Something the captain wouldn't expect."

"I'm listening. . . ."

"Rushing out into the street won't work, I'm too big to fit through these boards," Nathan reasoned out loud, "and there's nothing behind me except the jailhouse." He stopped as a more important concern entered his mind. "Did you find Molly yet?"

"Nope. But I got a pretty good idea where she is now. Fatty here was talking to the others about their hideout shack near the mouth of McDonald Creek. I reckon Miz Molly is tucked away over there on the Tanana Flats. From the sound of them, she's still safe, but I wouldn't count on that for long. Wilson's got his blood lust up. When he's done for you, my guess is your gal is next on his list."

"Is Billy Wilson out there with the four?" Nathan asked. "It might even be worth getting shot just to put a bullet into Wilson."

"That's crazy thinking, boy," Riley scolded. "Ain't no shine on that idea—trading yerself off just to plug a polecat. Anyway, he ain't with them. So think of something bright and make yer daddy and me proud of you."

Nathan smiled grimly. "Jim, you've got to slip away and rescue Molly. I'm going back to my cell."

"Yer cell? That don't make no sense. What's to keep Barnette and his gang from shooting you inside the jail and claiming you was making a break for it?"

Nathan touched the jail keys still inside his pocket. "Because Felix Pedro is passed out drunk in the back of the jail. I'll drag him into the cell with me and lock the door. Barnette might want to shoot me, but he'd have to shoot old Felix for his story to hold water. He'd never be able to explain why it was necessary to shoot both me and the town's most famous miner when we're both inside a locked jail. You see, I plan on keeping the keys with me until morning."

Riley shook his head. "Still sounds a mite risky to me."

"It's our only option. I'm hoping they think you're still in hiding, Jim, and drop their guard when you rescue Molly."

"Are you sure I can't slip you a hogleg before I go? Leaving you defenseless like this don't sit right in my craw. It kinda sticks."

"Thanks, but I'm safer this time unarmed."

"Okay, but I don't like skipping out on you. What about lard ass here? If I could squeeze him through this here gap in the wall I could slit his throat and dump him in the Chena. He'd be halfway to Nenana by sunup."

Nathan snickered. "Getting bloodthirsty in your old age, Jim?"

"These folks are a-pissing me off, Nat, messing like they are with my family. I'm stirred up enough to shoot every goddamned one and all their dogs and all their chickens—if they got any. Anyway, you ain't gonna reform the lot of them, even if you read the Good Book to them until the cows come home. They ain't no better than varmints. And there's only one known way to handle varmints, and it ain't by inviting them to tea."

"First, you rescue Molly and get her to safety. Leave McGinnis be. They'll figure he hit his head on something in the dark. He certainly was drunk enough to do so." Nathan fished a pint whiskey bottle out of McGinnis's pants and emptied the flask over the man. He also lifted a small crate of canned bread from atop a barrel and placed it strategically by the unconscious man's head.

Riley reached both hands through the opening and clasped his friend's hand. "Be careful, now. When next you see me, Molly will be safe. I give you my word."

Nathan blinked, and in that instant Riley was gone.

Retracing his steps to the back door of the jail took Nathan less than a minute. He found Felix Pedro had not moved from the floor. Nathan lifted the little man onto his shoulder and carried him into the cell. Placing the prospector on his own cot, Nathan covered him with the only blanket before he curled up on the floor. As an afterthought, Nathan rose and locked the cell before placing the key ring on top of Pedro.

Struggling with sinking hopes, Nathan willed himself to sleep. His throbbing neck and head conspired to keep him awake, but he focused on Molly's rescue.

The wall clock showed four in the morning when Nathan awoke to see E. T. Barnette glaring at him through the bars. Four heavily armed men stood behind Barnette. Two supported a shaky but frightened Deputy McGinnis. Before either man could speak, Judge Wickersham shouldered his way to the front of the cell.

"I heard there was an attempted breakout!" the judge bellowed. "What happened?" He stopped and a look of puzzlement crossed his face when he saw the two men inside the cell.

Nathan sat up and smiled sleepily. "Must be some mistake, Your Honor. Felix and I have been here all night. He decided to join me to sleep off his liquor." Nathan jangled the keys before he tossed them to the startled judge. "The deputy left his keys. I wouldn't want them lost."

Wickersham spun on his heel. "Clearly, there was no attempt at escape," he said tersely. The judge stared knowingly at Barnette. "The *absolute safety* of these two men is therefore *assured* while they are in custody." Then Wickersham stomped off.

Nathan did little to conceal his glee while the men filed out after Wickersham. As the last man left, a tiny snicker escaped Nathan's lips. That was a mistake, he realized, but he could not help it. However, it brought Captain Barnette up short. His back stiffened just before he whirled around to face Nathan.

"Don't think you're so smart!" Barnette snarled at the lad. "You may have slipped out of this one, but I'll finish you yet!

And don't think you'll get help!" He shook his fist before the startled youth's face.

Nathan gulped. Clutched in Barnette's fist was the crumpled letter he had written to his father. . . .

TWENTY-FIVE

For the tenth time in a row Sid Weaver paced across the floor and peeked out the tiny chink in the log cabin that served as a window. In his travels, the cramped room forced him to step over the legs of the five men sprawled about the dirt floor. It was a task that would try the skills of the finest ballroom dancer, which Weaver was not. His boot heel crunched down on the side of an outstretched hand.

"Goddamn it, Sid! Watch where you're walking. You just mashed my hand," a man named Fields complained. "I'm going to need that hand if we gets to fighting."

"Yeah, sit down, Sid. You're making us all jumpy," Billy Wilson ordered. "So jumpy," he added, "that I'm liable to shoot you myself."

Weaver retreated to the farthest corner from Wilson, which gave him little assurance of safety since it was less than ten feet away from his leader's hairspring temper and deadly pistol. "Sorry, Billy," he mumbled an apology. "Just this waiting is getting on my nerves. I wish that fool McGinnis hadn't fallen down and sprung our trap. We'd have both Riley's and Blaylock's hides tacked on the wall and be drinking in the Senate saloon by now. Instead, we're still stuck out in the flats hiding out with this girl." He cast a baleful glance at Molly Hayes, tied to the only chair in cabin. The look she gave him in return would have withered a spider.

Wilson stopped cleaning his nails with the point of his bowie knife to use the same point to pick his teeth. He picked out a brownish chunk with his finger and studied it, trying to decide whether it came from beneath his fingernails or was a residue from dinner.

"Just shows how stupid you are, Sid," Wilson snapped. "The Senate burned down, and I don't think McGinnis knocked himself out. I think our old friend Riley helped him. And . . . unless I miss my guess, Old Jim will be paying us a visit real soon."

The four other men stiffened at that remark. Both Weaver and Fields jumped to the window to look out. Wilson, on the other hand, strolled over to the bound Molly and stood before her with hands on both hips. He studied her like a buyer appraising a side of beef, and his gaze made Molly blush.

"I don't know, Billy," Fields added cautiously. "That was three days ago. I don't think Riley can find us."

Wilson ignored the comment. He smirked at his bound captive. "Did you miss me, darling?" he teased. "I'd have been back sooner, but I had business in town. I was planning to kill your boyfriend, but he got away."

Relief flooded Molly's face, but this only aggravated Wilson. He ran the back of his hand along the side of her face. She jerked her head away. The hand continued down her neck to slip inside the front of her dress.

Molly issued a muffled curse and her teeth ground into the dirty gag stuffed into her mouth. Unexpectedly, Wilson snatched the cloth from her mouth. "How about a kiss, darling? I know you like me. All the girls like Billy Wilson."

Molly gasped her first lungful of fresh air since early that morning when they had fed her. She watched Wilson's lips move closer, willing herself to hold steady until he came in range. The stale cigar smoke and rotten smell of his breath churned her stomach.

Quick as a flash, her teeth fastened onto his lower lip. She bit down with all her strength.

"You dirty bitch!" Wilson yelped in pain as this she-wolf fastened onto his lip.

His hand flew up and cracked against the side of Molly's face, causing her ear to go deaf and stars to fill her spinning vi-

sion. The blow broke free her hold, but she noticed with satisfaction that a wide flap of tissue dangled from Wilson's lip and
blood spurted from the jagged wound. She spit out a chunk of
his lip in disgust. "They won't like you as much now, Billy,"
Molly snarled.

"Goddamn you!" Wilson blubbered through the blood filling his mouth. He held his ruined mouth together while his
other hand seized a coil of rope. Using it like a whip, he beat
the girl until she fell unconscious.

The other men stood about apprehensively. Finally, Fields
called out, "Don't kill her, Billy, please! The capt'n said not to."

Wilson spun on him. Madness spilled from his wild eyes,
causing his men to shrink back. "Look what she did to me!" he
cried. "I'm going to beat her to death."

Weaver held up both hands imploringly. "You can beat her
cold dead later, boss. We got to fix your lip before you bleed to
death."

Wilson felt the raw edges of his wound. His fingers came
away soaked with blood. "How bad is it?" he asked anxiously.

"Not so bad, Billy," a third man named Spense replied.
While he'd done many things in his sordid career, even Spense
balked at whipping a tied woman to death. "We can fix you up
good as new."

That seemed to mollify Wilson. "Think the girls will still
like me?" he asked.

The fourth man, a half-breed called Indian Pete, grinned
and bobbed his head. "Sure thing, boss. Your lip is going to
give them fancy ladies something interesting to run their
tongues over when you kiss them." He looked over at the unconscious Molly. "Don't kill her until we can all have a go at
her. She won't be no fun dead."

Wilson approved of that idea. "Okay," he slobbered, "who
can fix my lip?"

Exchanging worried glances, the men finally settled on Indian Pete, who was known to have sewn up his dogs when they
got into fights. Pouring whiskey into Wilson's mouth with great

care to keep the alcohol from the wound, the men prepared their patient. Pete produced a horse needle, trailing a string of lynx gut sinew, and wiped it on his trousers.

"Don't make no mistakes." Wilson grinned horribly as he drew his pistol and poked it into Indian Pete's belly. His action make the man's hand shake like a threshing machine gone wild during harvest.

Fields poured a generous slug of liquor into Pete to fortify the would-be surgeon. The Native eagerly gulped the offering and begged for more. If he were to die, he reasoned, why not die drunk?

Weaver pulled back Fields's hand. "Don't give him too much. He gets crazy when he's drunk. No telling what kind of a job he might do, then."

With both patient and surgeon comfortably anesthetized, the work began only to stop immediately until Indian Pete got over an attack of hiccups. Compounding matters, Billy Wilson, the killer, turned out to be a big baby. Whenever Pete stuck the horse-sized needle into his lip, Wilson jerked his head away. The result was much swearing, more blood spattered about, extra holes in Wilson's wounded lip, and several false starts.

"Hold still, Billy," Fields pleaded. "Pete can't get a good shot with you moving like you are."

"Damn it, he's poking me with that spear, and it hurts," Wilson retorted.

Resorting to one desperate swipe, Pete skewered the flopping portion of lip and nailed it down. The one stitch held the lip together too tightly, producing a permanent pout in the patient's lower lip and adding to the surly snarl of Billy Wilson's face. Pete jumped back, wiping the sweat from his face, and declared. "All done!"

With that the Indian, now sober as a church deacon from fright, ran out the door.

"How does it look?" Wilson asked while he turned his head from one man to the other.

"Looks great," they replied in unison. Behind Wilson's

Richard Parry

back both Fields and Spense exchanged grimaces. Weaver issued a silent prayer of thanks that the tiny cabin had no mirrors.

From his vantage point in the willow thicket Jim Riley studied the cabin with an expert eye. Despite his having a good idea of its location, the cleverly concealed hut had eluded Riley's search for two days. Built into the backside of a rise along the north bank of the Tanana below the mouth of the Chena rather than McDonald Creek in the flats as Riley had surmised, the cabin sat against the bluff, hidden from view by a dense stand of birch and alder. Downriver from the stony outcropping called Becker Ridge, the Tanana had carved a small island off from its north bank where the ridge shaded a flat parcel of land. The wide but shallow braid of the silty river could be crossed by foot in several places where the water had piled thousands of stones into riffles that acted like an enormous sluice box.

It was a perfect hideout, Riley realized. Hidden from view on all sides except from the river, the half-cabin, half-dugout hid among the island's timber. Nothing about the tiny hideout gave away its location.

Cleverly, the outlaws burned only seasoned spruce, which gave no smoke. Riley had only found the cabin by following his nose and seeing the heat rising from the stove as a shimmering column against the evening sky as he lay atop Becker Ridge. Riding Susie in a wide arc down the steep side of the ridge, he tethered his faithful mount downriver on the sloping hill where she could graze among the early clumps of blueberries.

Neither Wilson nor his men lost much sleep for fear their hideaway would be found. No one had ever discovered it before. But find it Riley did, and all day long he waited for the short spell of darkness to settle in over the swamp.

Now he was ready. He pressed against the cold silt and watched when a man he knew as Indian Pete emerged from the cabin and hid in the willows. With mud and glacial silt smeared over his face as protection from the hordes of biting mosquitoes and silt caked over his clothing, Riley blended in perfectly with his cover. Over him lay a blanket painstakingly coated with pitch from nearby spruce trees, which he had covered with silt and bits of twigs, leaves, and grass until it all but vanished to the eye when placed on the ground. Beneath this camouflaged cover he waited and watched while the man cautiously returned to the cabin.

Silence settled over the island save for the raucous warbling of a pair of ravens fighting over the rotting body of a Chinook salmon on the riverbank. In the distance the black smoke of a paddlewheeler laced the cream-and-orange twilight that settled over the endless Tanana Flats, producing the only flaw in an indefectible work of Nature's artistry.

Inch by inch, Riley's piece of the hillside moved toward the highest side of the cabin, creeping so stealthily that the fighting ravens never noticed when it passed them. He slipped into the stream, ignoring the icy water that stung him like an electric charge, and drifted across without a sound. In the blink of an eye Riley slithered onto the island's bank and vanished into the brush. Silence returned to the island once more.

Billy Wilson tossed back another slug of whiskey to deaden the throb in his swollen lip. He contemplated the bullwhip hanging on the wall. When he got the okay from Barnette, he planned to flay Molly Hayes in return for what she had done. A grim smile twitched across his damaged lip, only to vanish with the onset of a stab of pain.

The other men avoided looking at Wilson while stealing swigs of whiskey whenever he neglected the bottle. With the heat of the cast-iron stove inside the cramped quarters, the liquor rapidly took effect. Everyone save Molly was drunk.

Sid Weaver scratched at the scab of a day-old bite and coughed. He watched the cabin blur before his eyes with little comprehension of the smoke slowly filling the room. Five minutes passed and the coughing of all inside increased before they realized that smoke poured from the stove.

"What the hell?" Sid staggered to his feet.

Spense lurched to his feet. "Fire! We're on fire!" he shouted.

"It's the stove," Weaver coughed. "It's not drawing!" He made the mistake of opening the door to the firebox.

A great cloud of sooty smoke billowed into the cabin. Instantly the room vanished in the pall. Men collided in the confusion, swearing and kicking at the door. The sound of the small window breaking followed closely on the thump of feet rushing outside for air.

Wilson wobbled into the fresh air and looked at the stovepipe jutting from the sod roof. A clod of sod was wedged into the sheet metal cylinder.

"Goddamn it! It's a trick!" Wilson screamed in spite of the pain in his lip. "Get the girl, now!"

The men rushed back into the shack, fanning their arms to clear the smoke. Molly Hayes was gone! The chair lay tipped on its side with the ropes that had bound her neatly cut and scattered on the dirt floor.

"Outside!" Wilson howled. He snatched up a twelve-gauge shotgun that rested beside the door and raced around the side of the cabin.

His men followed, but nothing caught their eye. Then a woman's groan reached their ears. It came from the west end of the island. Like a pack of howling wolves, the gang charged into the brush toward the sound.

Wilson led the charge, driven to madness with pain and drunkenness. The corner of his eye caught his prey just as he broke out of the thicket and reached the bank of the stream.

Jim Riley struggled to lift Molly over a fallen sweeper that had snagged the corner of her dress. In doing so the limb had pulled the girl off balance, and she had fallen heavily on her battered side. Her groan had exposed their escape route.

With both arms around Molly, Riley turned when he heard the gang. In a flash he ripped away the restraining fabric and dragged Molly over the tree trunk. He could not let go of her to draw his pistol, or she would slip into the icy water to founder. As he hurried the injured girl along, he looked over his shoulder in time to see Billy Wilson drop to his knee and raise the double-barreled shotgun.

Riley leapt behind Molly, shielding her with his body, just as the shotgun's blast roared through the stillness of the night.

Molly never knew that Riley saved her life or even that the buckshot hit him. The old gunman only emitted a soft grunt and straightened his back when the pellets struck. He never slowed his efforts to rush her to safety.

A dozen shots followed. Bullets clipped the air around the fleeing pair, but the smoke from Wilson's twelve-gauge aided the escaping couple with a smoke screen. By the time the four men splashed across this shallow ford, an empty riverbank and a silent forest greeted them.

Wilson bellowed in rage. His cry echoed off the steep sides of Becker Ridge to add to his fury. "Spread out!" he shrilled. "Beat the brush. They can't get far. The girl's hurt too badly to run fast, and I think I winged them. Look for blood."

Thrashing away like beaters, the men spread out into a wide arc and worked their way inland from the river's edge. The dense undergrowth impeded their search, along with the clouds of mosquitoes that rose to attack them with each footfall.

Wilson stopped in waist-high willows to bellow at his men, two of whom were no longer visible, "Keep searching! I know they're here somewhere!"

Less than six feet from where Wilson stood, Jim Riley gritted his teeth against the fire that smoldered across his back and choked back the frothy blood that threatened to bubble into his throat and force him to cough. Concealed and unmoving beneath his camouflaged blanket, he stared at the feet of Wilson while his right hand aimed his Colt at his enemy. His left hand clamped firmly over the mouth of the terrified Molly while he willed her breathing to slow.

Riley's eyes narrowed at what he saw. Lying beside Wilson's boot a patch of blueberry leaves sported a drop of blood. Blood from Riley's wounds had left a trail straight to where they hid.

If Wilson looked down at his feet he could not miss the sign.

With fatalistic resolve, Riley planned to kill Wilson as soon as he discovered the blood. The rest was up to fate. The wounded gunman knew he was too weak to run farther, even if Molly could make it, which he doubted. With abundant brush for concealment but little actual safe cover, Riley realized the other four men stood an excellent chance of killing him. But he meant to keep his word to his friend Nathan. Whatever it took, he would see Molly to safety.

Wilson edged closer to where the two hid. Riley prepared himself. Billy Wilson's deliberate movements made it impossible for Riley to know whether or not the blood trail had been spotted. Riley's thumb caressed the hammer of his pistol in readiness.

"Over here!" Indian Pete shouted. "Look what I found!"

Wilson spun on his heel and raced away. Jim Riley blew out through his lips, licking away the bloody foam that spewed out. He eased his hand to allow Molly to breathe.

"They're moving away," he whispered to the shivering girl. "Maybe we've got a chance after all." He raised his head cautiously to follow the sounds of the men thrashing through the brush. Riley's hopes dashed to splinters when he saw what led Wilson away from their trail, and his heart seized.

Standing clear on the banks of the slough so that Riley could see him clearly beyond the willows stood Billy Wilson with an evil grin further distorting his horrible face. In his right hand he held a gleaming bowie knife. His left hand held Susie by her bridle!

"Come out, come out, wherever you are," Wilson cooed. "I know you can see me, Riley. I know you're out there. Let's make a trade: your mule for the other filly. What do you say? You hand over Molly, and I let Susie here go. Otherwise . . ."

To illustrate his point, he lashed the mule's reins to a stout birch. With the frightened animal securely bound, Wilson slashed her along the side of her neck with a vicious swipe of his blade. Susie's scream pierced the night air while her frantic struggle to escape shook the leaves in the tree.

"Oh, God," Riley moaned. But he never moved. Instead he gritted his teeth and tried to block out the cries of his pet.

Molly struggled to her hands and knees only to have Riley drag her down. "Let me go," she protested. "I'll . . . I'll give myself up. I can't let him torture Susie. I know how much she means to you, Jim."

"Git down and stay down," he ordered. "Going down there ain't gonna do nothing but get yourself killed. You can't make a deal with the likes of Billy Wilson. He'd shoot his own mother out of spite. He'll just kill you and Susie both."

Another piteous cry filled the air. "Come on, Riley," Wilson taunted. "Your mule is hurting real bad. She needs you. Don't let her down."

"I wish I had my Sharps," Riley sobbed. "Wilson's too far for a pistol shot. I'd only give our hiding place away with the smoke without doing any good. But with my Sharps, I'd separate Wilson's rotten head from his shoulders before he could take another foul breath."

Susie screamed again. "I'm cutting myself a strip for a new belt, Riley!" Wilson crowed. "You'd better come quick, or there won't be enough left of your mule to ride."

"Please, let me go down there," Molly begged. "I can't bear to hear Susie's cries. Please, let me go." She implored Riley's face with tear-filled eyes, but he shook his head. Their eyes locked, and she stopped. The pain and anguish she saw in Riley's face dwarfed her own feelings. The man appeared to be suffering more than the tortured animal.

"I can't let you do that," Riley said. "I gave my word to Nat that I'd protect you at all costs."

"But . . . surely not this . . . ?"

"All costs. Nathan means more to me than life itself. He's the only family I've got. He and Susie are my whole family." He stopped to wipe away the blood in his mouth. "He loves you, and he trusted me to protect you. That's what I'm going to do. I'd be down there in a minute if I thought it would save Susie, but it won't. Best I can do now is keep my word to what's left of my family and save you."

Slowly, Molly nodded. She curled into a ball and clapped her hands over her ears to shut out the screams. But the shrieks bored past her hands and into her very soul. In the end she was reduced to sobbing silently to herself.

Riley's anguish burned past all bounds. Like a piece of metal thrust into a forge and fired until it showered white-hot sparks, his pain transformed itself into an immutable will. Like that passive metal changing to an active, dangerous state, his suffering turned to anger. He would survive this, he told himself. He would return and find Billy Wilson, even if it meant hunting him down to the edges of the earth, and avenge Susie. Thus resolved, Jim Riley hunkered down to endure the longest night of his life.

Just before the birth of a new day, when the rising sun to the east cast its rays to ignite the Alaska Mountain Range into peaks of blazing orange, Susie's cries stopped. Wilson stepped back from the mutilated body of the mule with no sign of remorse. The other four men shifted about nervously, embarrassed and sickened at their part in this senseless deed. Quietly they filed back to the cabin.

Two hundred yards away, the beaten Molly and the gravely wounded Jim Riley crawled along the bottom of Becker Ridge.

TWENTY-SIX

Nathan lost track of the days while he waited for news. But none came. Jailed, isolated from events involving Molly and Jim Riley, and, worst of all, being helpless nearly drove him mad. He was used to action, and imprisonment weighed heavily on him. To maintain his sanity, he formulated an escape plan. He stole a spoon from his meager food tray and filled his spare hours in the dead of night by scraping away at the iron rods barring his window. Hour after hour, he carved into the wood framework, saving the wood chips on his blanket. Just before morning came he would pack the chips back in place to disguise his efforts.

As he was busily at work scraping one night, movement in the outer office alerted him. He scarcely had time to hide his handiwork and flop onto his cot when the door burst open and four men entered with a frightened McGinnis at their head. Nathan's stomach tightened when he recognized Billy Wilson pushing McGinnis along. He noted the other three, Weaver, Spense, and Fields, were part of Wilson's crew. A strong smell of whiskey accompanied the men.

"I sure hope we woke you up," Wilson grunted. "You don't need no beauty sleep."

Nathan started at what he saw. A filthy string had repaired an ugly wound in Wilson's lower lip. But the repair left much to be desired. Instead of apposing the edges with some degree of accuracy, the suture gathered the swollen tissue into a purse string. The result was horrible to view.

Nathan sprang to his feet and faced the bars of his cell.

"What happened to you, Billy? Did you kiss a buzz saw?" he asked.

Wilson clapped his hand over his ruined lip to support it while he talked. "Your bitch, Molly Hayes, gave me this. She bit me, but she won't get away with it. When I find her, I'm going to let the boys have their way with her before I beat her to death. That goes for your pard, Riley, too."

Nathan's heart soared. *Molly had escaped!* Jim must have found her, and the two got away. But he kept his feelings hidden. Holding his voice as level as he could, he quipped, "I hope she didn't get rabies from biting you."

Wilson sneered. "Think you're so smart, do you? We'll see what tune you sing after I finish with you. You'll be only too happy to tell me where Riley and the girl are hiding out."

Nathan backed away from the bars and into a corner of his cell. "Even if I knew where they were, I'd never tell you, Wilson," he replied truthfully. He doubled his fists and prepared to defend himself.

"Now, you promised not to kill him, Billy," McGinnis piped up. "Only get him to talk."

"Shut up," Wilson snarled. "Give me the damned keys! Now, get him, boys!"

With the snap of the opening lock, Wilson's three henchmen rushed Nathan. The first ran afoul of the blanket Nathan threw in his face. The young man used his attacker's inertia to drive his head into the wall. His right hand chopped the second man at the angle of his neck, and that man dropped to his knees with a choking gasp. But the confines of the jail cell prevented Nathan from escaping the onrush, and his feet tangled with the thrashing man enmeshed in the blanket. Instantly the men were on top of him, punching and kicking.

Nathan struggled on his back as the others pinned his arms and legs. He glared up at Billy Wilson. "You aren't man enough to try by yourself, Wilson," he panted. "Or with a gun. . . ."

Wilson considered the challenge for an instant. "You always were tricky, Blaylock," he said. "You might even get out of this with a whole skin, and I wouldn't want that. Knowing you,

you'd come after me to settle the score. I got better things to do than be looking over my shoulder for you. So, I'm going to fix it so you can't ever hold a gun again, my friend."

Nathan swore. "You dirty, stinking coward!"

"Hold his right hand out so I can stomp on it, boys," Wilson commanded. "I'm going to mash the bones into all sorts of pieces."

As Nathan struggled, the men stretched his right hand out on the dirt floor. Wilson strode over and stood poised above him with the heel of his boot raised above the wriggling hand. Wilson raised the boot and lurched forward to deliver all of his weight with the blow.

But, at the last moment, Nathan drove his own foot into the one that supported Wilson's entire weight. With everyone concentrating on holding the young man's hand as still as possible, they had neglected his legs. His blow knocked Wilson off balance enough to spoil his aim.

The heavy boot crashed down on Nathan's forearm instead of his hand. Even so, the force was considerable. Nathan felt one of the bones in his forearm snap, and a stabbing pain lanced up his arm. "Damn you, Wilson!" he cried.

Frustrated, Wilson kicked at whatever he could. The blows rained on the spread-eagled lad, striking him while he could not protect himself. Grimly he knew Wilson would kick him to death in another five minutes.

"Hold it!" a voice commanded. "Kick him again and I'll blow your goddamned heads off!"

The men in the cell froze, moving their heads only enough to see who had issued those orders. Facing them was Ed Wickersham, the judge's brother and deputy U.S. marshal, with a ten-gauge shotgun firmly gripped in his hands. Behind him stood Jesse Noble, the miner, and a livid-faced Judge Wickersham.

"What in the hell is going on here?" the judge questioned.

Wilson straightened slowly but kept his hand in the air. "The prisoner was trying to escape, Judge. He was choking McGinnis. My boys and me were passing by and heard the guard call for help. So . . . being civic-minded citizens, we rushed to help."

Judge Wickersham gave McGinnis a piercing stare. "Is that what happened, McGinnis?"

"Yes sir, Your Honor," the man stuttered. "That's exactly what happened. Blaylock lured me into his cell and then jumped me. He would have killed me but for Billy and the others." McGinnis looked back at Wilson for approval. He relaxed when Wilson nodded.

Jesse Noble made a disgusted noise. "It's a lie. I saw them kicking Nat—all four of them—as I walked by the window. That's when I ran and got the marshal. They would have kicked him to death if you hadn't stopped them."

"Back out of the cell, slowly," Ed Wickersham ordered. He waved the barrels of his scattergun for emphasis. The double-barreled ten-gauge would easily make mincemeat of everyone in the cell.

The judge looked down at the battered prisoner. "Jesse, go fetch Dr. Whyman. By God, this whole thing stinks to high heaven. This man is under my jurisdiction, and I won't have him beaten to a pulp." He turned on Billy Wilson. "You had better hope he recovers, or—"

"Or what?" Wilson spit. "You ain't gonna do nothing. You're as much in the pay of the capt'n as I am, Judge. The only difference is I do his dirty work in the open and I call it as such. I don't go around all high-and-mighty and puffed up, pretending to be righteous. I know I'm a sinner, and I don't give a damn."

"Out of the mouths of babes," Nathan added trenchantly.

"Shut up!" Judge Wickersham commanded. "And get out, Wilson! Take your mob with you."

"You go with them, McGinnis," Marshal Wickersham added. "You're fired as jailer. I don't want to see you in here again or I'll throw you in a cell myself."

Wilson and his men strolled past the marshal. The thug paused at the door to stab his finger at Nathan. "We ain't done with you yet," he threatened. "Not by a long shot."

Nathan eased his back against the far wall and splinted his forearm against his chest. While his body throbbed in a hundred places, he sensed his ribs were intact and no vital organs were damaged.

Marshal Wickersham turned away from staring at his brother to kneel beside Nathan. "Looks like they broke your arm," he said. "Anything else broke?"

"I don't think so."

The judge meanwhile paced around the room like a feverish squirrel. He stopped for a minute when Dr. Whyman arrived, then resumed his treading while the physician examined Nathan.

"When can he be moved, Doctor?" Wickersham asked.

Whyman finished tying the last bandage over the splint covering Nathan's forearm. He caught the warning look in Nathan's eyes and grasped its meaning. *Give me time to heal,* the look said. *I'll stand a better chance if you can buy me some time.*

Whyman straightened his back but kept his eyes fixed on Nathan's face. What was happening to this young man was beyond all reason. It only made Whyman believe Nathan's story all the more. The doctor found himself taking Nathan's side. He would do what he could.

"He's suffered a broken radius. That's one of the bones in his forearm. I've set it, and it should heal properly—*given the correct care.* He needs to keep it splinted for at least four weeks. Besides, he's had the living Jesus beat out of him. His ribs are bruised at best, maybe one or two are cracked, but his lungs are not punctured. He's a mass of bruises and bloody welts. And this licking broke two of my stitches in his scalp and reopened the wound in his neck. How can you expect the boy to mend when he suffers a beating like this? I couldn't possibly expect him to be strong enough to be moved before two weeks, maybe three weeks."

Whyman's heart warmed when he saw the look of gratitude that crossed Nathan's face. The doctor made up his mind to stall for more time if possible. He would also visit the youth every day to ensure his continued safety. He decided to an-

nounce those intentions so there would be no mistakes or mis-
understandings.

"I'll need to check on him every day," he said knowingly.

Wickersham nodded. "You do that. When he's fit enough
to travel, I'm moving him to Valdez. If he were tried here in
Fairbanks, it would split the town in half. That's the last thing
I want to see happen. We need all our efforts to rebuild."

Wickersham took his brother aside. "Ed, I'm counting on
you to see Blaylock is well protected while he's recuperating."

"I'll need to hire extra deputies, James. Men with no ax to
grind and no attachments to E. T. Barnette. Wilson will try
again, I have no doubt of it, if the boy's left unprotected." The
marshal looked mindfully at his brother. "If he's killed while
in jail—without a trial—there will be grave repercussions . . .
for all of us."

"Hire whatever men you need. If word of this ever reaches
those senators in Washington, any hope I might have of my
judgeship being confirmed will vanish. It's best I distance myself from this whole unfortunate affair. I wash my hands of him
after that."

Nathan overheard the conversation. He looked at the
judge and shook his head in disgust. "Wash your hands of the
whole affair, Judge? Just like Pilate, don't you think?"

While Nathan struggled to survive within his jail cell, Molly en-
deavored to see the next day as well. Beaten and cold, the girl
nevertheless marshaled all her strength to half-drag, half-carry
the wounded Riley downriver, away from the hidden cabin and
the hateful Wilson gang.

Always staying within the protection of the willows and
alders that grew near shore, Molly screened her escape by hiding whenever she heard or saw anything and always keeping to
the wide arc of the riverbank. Using Riley's blanket, with its
dappled colors and stippled as it was with leaves and grass,
aided her movement. The flimsy blanket did little to keep them
warm, but its cover fended off the clouds of mosquitoes and biting gnats they encountered.

Time and time again, sheer exhaustion forced the girl to stop. Then she and Riley would chew on horsetail grass to lighten their hunger and sip water from the silty pools to slake their parched mouths. Molly never remembered being this cold, even in the dead of winter. The icy water of the Tanana River cooled the riverbank and cast its profound chill over the silt upon which they crawled. There was no relief from it. The cold seeped into their injured bones and threatened to sap what little vigor they could muster. She and Riley would huddle together, quivering and with teeth chattering, until they pressed onward.

Once, Molly's heart leapt into her throat when a black bear sow and her two cubs ambled within arm's reach while the two rested. Being upwind, the bears never caught their scent and vanished in search of berries as quietly as they had appeared.

Riley helped as much as he could, but the wounds in his back took a fearsome toll. He never complained, but Molly saw the tightness of his lips and knew he suffered. A great guilt overwhelmed her whenever the injured man carried her along.

More than once men passed within hailing distance as they poled their birch bark craft down the mighty Tanana to trade in Nenana. But Molly in her feverish mind feared these men might be part of Wilson's men, so she always hid until they passed. The sternwheelers *Isabelle* and the *Columbian* churned past in midchannel too far away for anyone to hear Molly's weak cries.

'Long about the second day, Molly and Riley knew they could go no farther. The willows that once offered so welcome a mantle now impeded their progress by entangling their limbs in a dense mat of twisted shoots that wove around a stand of stunted and gnarled cottonwood.

Riley set the girl down with infinite care before he slid facedown beside her. The heart of the old war horse urged him on, but his legs refused.

"Can you go on without me?" he asked weakly. "I'm done for."

The anguish in his words hurt Molly worse than her bruises

from Wilson's coil of rope. She knew how much it pained Riley that he could not keep his word to protect her.

"It's all right, Jim," she said soothingly. Her hand smoothed his matted hair. "I can't go any farther, either. We'll just rest here until we regain our strength." But the dark spreading around the torn holes in Riley's shirt told her otherwise. Neither of them would grow stronger no matter how long they rested.

Riley bowed his head. Molly dropped onto her side and gazed up at the sky. It must be midmorning, she thought. Funny how the sun would never reach them to share its warmth as the ridge held them in shadow. She marveled at the intensity of its color. Without a single cloud to flaw its azure perfection, the sky beckoned to her, offering solace. Molly started to close her eyes.

Suddenly a face filled her view—a savage-looking face. An Indian stood over her! Molly's mouth opened to cry out in alarm, but no sound came. She was too weak for even that.

The face vanished only to return in minutes with others. Gentle arms lifted her and Riley and carried them to birch bark pirogues. Molly almost giggled in relief. These savages she once had feared were obviously rescuing her from the savagery of her own kind. It was too fantastic to believe.

But it was true. Guiding their fragile craft past sweepers and rocks that could easily rip the flimsy bark skin, the Natives paddled downriver to their fish camp miles below Goose Island.

Nestled on a side slough of the Tanana that the salmon had chosen to follow since the first day these fish returned from the sea, the Gwitchin camp sprung from the riverbanks whenever the salmon returned. For salmon were the meat and potatoes of these people. Smoked or split and hung to dry, the rich, fatty meat sustained them throughout the long winter. A good run of salmon meant a comfortable winter. A bad run meant starvation.

It was no wonder, then, that an entire village arose on this barren stretch the minute the first salmon arrived. Tents dotted the hillside. Dogs barked and fought over salmon heads, and laughing children played in the water. But all around these diversions the serious work of snaring the hearty fish progressed day and night.

Fish traps and weirs poked above the pewter waters like tiny bones protruding from the river's skin. Finely woven nets stretched from trees along the bank into midstream to trap the fish, and everywhere the smell of smoking fish and alder coals billowed from drying racks bending beneath the weight of hundreds of pounds of bright, copper salmon.

The canoes ground ashore, and more hands carried Molly and Riley to a tent where the women washed and dressed their wounds. A white-haired elder oversaw the operation, adding her skills and secret herbs to the poultices applied to the injuries. More than one woman clapped her hand to her mouth when viewing the cruelty these people had suffered. Truly, the Natives thought, the white men who did this were uncivilized beings, worse than the wildest beasts.

For two more days Riley flirted with death, burning with fever and dropping into unconsciousness only to reemerge weaker than before. The wound that punctured his lung festered from the patch of cloth driven into the tissue by the buckshot.

While Molly rapidly recovered under the watchful eye of the shaman, Riley showed no improvement. When the girl asked about Riley's chances, the old woman only shook her head and mentioned in broken English about sending for help from the next village.

That evening Riley opened his eyes to see Molly sleeping beside his bed. Beads of sweat covered his face and dripped into his eyes while his whole frame shook with fever. He raised his head with great effort and looked about. The flap of the tent opened, and the alpenglow outlined a figure standing in the doorway. Riley felt the hair rise on the back of his neck. Even in his fevered state, he realized he was looking at a ghost. A one-armed ghost.

"Have you come to fetch me to the promised land, Doc?"

he coughed, his voice reduced to a hoarse whisper. "I was hoping I'd see my ma instead of you."

The figure neither moved nor spoke.

"I must be going straight to Hell," Riley continued, "if you're my guide, Doc, unless the Good Lord is far more forgiving than anyone could even hope."

Drained by his effort, Riley's head fell back onto his caribou pillow. His eyes followed the apparition of his dead associate. To his amazement, the specter clumped over to him, kicking over a woven basket in the process. Somehow, Riley always had assumed ghosts hovered silently rather than stumbled about.

Then the ghost of Doc Hennison raised Riley's dressing and poked his fetid wound with his one arm.

"Ow," Riley complained. "That hurt. Ain't no need to jab me like that! If you're here to carry me off, git on with it. But don't be punching my wounds. They's real sore."

"I'm trying to determine the extent of the infection, you crazy coot!" the ghost answered uncharitably.

Riley's hand shot up to grasp Doc's left arm. His fingers fastened on solid flesh and bone. "Doc? It that really you? You ain't dead?"

"If I were dead, do you think I'd waste my time on you?" Doc complained. "It's bad enough they dragged me out of my warm bed and stuck me in a leaky canoe just to treat the likes of you, Jim Riley. If I'd have known it was you the Indians wanted me to see, I'd have refused to go."

In truth, each rejoiced at the sight of the other. Other than the fact that he was standing, Doc Hennison looked as bad as Riley. Both men appeared sallow, with gaunt faces and sunken eyes. Yet Doc's eyes shone clearly where Riley's burned with fever.

Molly rose sleepily, awakened by the verbal abuse of the two. Upon seeing Doc, she sprang to her feet while her hands clutched her caribou robe in consternation. She moved close to scrutinize the doctor's features. With a cry of joy, Molly hugged him.

"Doc! You're alive! This is wonderful!"

Hennison flushed with embarrassment. "Yes, it's me."

"How can this be? We thought you had drowned. You must explain."

Doc recoiled from the staccato questioning. He held up his hand to stop Molly. "Whoa. One thing at a time. I've got to drain Riley's wound and clean it out. I suspect there's some debris driven into the wound tract and that's raising holy hell. Get me some hot water and some clean rags for bandages. And build up the fire. I need to sterilize a knife."

Molly returned moments later with a handful of cloths torn from an old checkered shirt and a steaming kettle. Doc borrowed a long-bladed knife used for boning fish, squatted by the fire outside the tent, and plunged the blade into the fire. Riley struggled onto one elbow to watch.

"If you ain't dead, Doc, why didn't you send us word? Nat's been grieving for you for weeks. We even had a real fine funeral for you."

Hennison stopped what he was doing to look up at the gunfighter. "What? A funeral? How could you bury me when I'm standing here in front of you? Who did you get to substitute for me?"

"It was a symbolic gesture, Doc. We buried an empty pine box since you didn't have the common decency to float to the surface."

Hennison acted offended. "Decency? Don't talk to me about decency. It appears to me you ought to check whether a man is dead or not before you hold his funeral."

"Well, why the hell didn't you let us know you was still kicking? We could have saved the expense of the funeral."

"How the hell was I to know you were planning to bury me? Besides, I've been under the weather myself." Hennison stood up and paced around the tent in agitation. "Truth of the matter is, I didn't know who I was until three days ago. When the explosion went off, all I remember was being tossed into the air. Then I hit the water. I don't recall any more. Must have hit my head or something. The Gwitchin tell me they pulled

me out of the Tanana near Charlie's Slough. I was clinging to
a log and ran right into one of their salmon nets. The Indians
in the fish camp below this one dragged me out and cared
for me."

The white-haired medicine woman, who had followed
Molly into the tent, cackled and pointed a bony finger at Doc.
"Big salmon in net," she chuckled.

"My Lord," Molly gasped. "You floated six miles down the
Chena and then another ten miles down the Tanana, Doc, and
lived to tell of it?"

"I guess."

Riley screwed up his eyes as he forced his brain to calculate.
"So where you been the rest of this time?"

Hennison looked embarrassed. "From what I can gather, I
had the D.T.'s."

"The what?" Riley asked.

The old woman spun her fingers around her head in aim-
less fashion. "Whiskey crazy," she explained.

Hennison raised his eyebrows apologetically. "The D.T.'s,
delirium tremens . . . the shakes. I was used to drinking a few
bottles of my elixir a day, and my unexpected river junket left
me high and dry—so to speak. Well, no one in the village had
a drop. Drinking during fish camp is a serious taboo, I gather."

"As is selling whiskey to the Indians," Molly added. "No
wonder there was none around."

Hennison nodded. "I've been out of my head until a few
days ago." He held up his trembling fingers. "I'm still out of
sorts."

"And you're going to operate on me?" Riley asked.

"Don't worry. There's no skill to digging out a bullet. If
I'm shaking too badly to ease it out, I'll just get the tip of the
knife underneath the bullet and let my shaking screw it out,"
Doc answered with grim finality.

"What if you screw it in deeper, instead?"

Hennison rubbed his nose. "I guess that could happen."

Riley sighed. "Go ahead, then. I ain't doing so good as it is.

I reckon you can't do no worse." With a stifled groan, he rolled onto his side.

Molly squeezed Riley's hand. "You'll be just fine, Jim. Doc will fix you up."

"Sorry I've got none of my elixir to ease the pain," Hennison said. He added lamely, "I could use some myself right now."

Riley winked feebly at Molly. "You just keep holding my hand, Miss Molly, and I won't need anything else. An old goat like myself don't get much chance to have that honor."

"Well, it's not worth it," Doc interjected. He watched his shaking hands with growing apprehension.

Molly ignored Hennison's derisive remarks and kept her face turned toward Riley. She smiled while she used every ounce of her will to keep the tears from filling her eyes. She remembered how this man had endured the torture of his beloved mule to save her life.

Doc peeled off the poultice covering his friend's back and studied the swollen mass of flesh surrounding the entry site. Angry red blisters covered the mound. The doctor's fingers tapped the rise. Doc's face twitched at what he felt. The boggy sensation was unmistakable.

"Abscessed," he said to no one in particular. No wonder Riley was faring poorly. The pus trapped inside the wound was extending along plains of little resistance—into the man's lung. He would have to work fast.

"Hold him," Doc ordered.

Riley tensed his muscles and clamped a mouthful of his hide blanket between his teeth.

No sooner had the white-hot tip of Doc's knife pierced the wound when a rush of blood and pus spurted out. The force spattered the gore in all directions, even splashing into Hennison's face. "Lovely," he grumbled, but he continued to operate.

More blood and fragments of darkened clot poured from the wound. Riley held his breath with each twist of the knife yet never moved. Molly watched her fingers turn white as the injured man's grip tightened.

Doc fished out a patch of Riley's shirt, so coated with pus and blackened clot as to be scarcely recognizable. Still he worked his blade deeper, well aware that the tip was a hair breadth away from hitting the lung. All the while the old Indian woman watched and waited with a bowl held in both hands.

"Christ, the bullet's got to be close by!" Doc exclaimed. The deadly duel between his blade and Riley's lung was wearing him down. Failure to remove the lead with whatever cloth surrounded it would mean the operation had failed. The wound would simply continue to spread into Riley's lung until he died of sepsis. But one slip would allow air to rush into the opened chest cavity and collapse the wounded man's lung. That, too, could be fatal.

In the silence of the tent, everyone heard the clink as the knife tip encountered the bullet.

"Got you!" Doc crowed. He twisted the blade and withdrew it.

Lying atop the steel blade was a flattened lead pellet partly wrapped in a small swatch of cloth.

A sigh of relief escaped from all within the tent.

Suddenly Hennison tensed. Frothy blood, bright red in nature, bubbled out of the opening. A disturbing sucking sound emitted from the entrance with the foam.

"Damn it! I'm in the lung!" Doc wailed. He staggered back in dismay.

Quick as a flash, the old woman sprang forward and jabbed one elbow into Riley's side. He grunted in pain and gasped, sucking in a deep breath. With her other hand, the squaw slapped a black glob from her bowl into the open wound.

The bubbling and air leak stopped.

Doc choked in amazement, his eyes threatening to pop from their sockets. "Pitch! By God, pitch! She stopped the air leak with spruce tar." He turned to pound the grinning Indian on her back. "Who would have thought of it? But it worked."

. . .

With the source of sepsis removed, Riley turned the corner. Backtracking from death's door, the gunman steadily improved under the watchful eye and tender care of Doc and his new Native associate. Molly helped as much as she could, but her beating had left her as weak as Riley.

The Gwitchin for their part hid the three while they healed. Barnette's dealings with the Natives had made him no friends here. Realizing they faced a common enemy, the Indians did what they could to protect their guests. While Billy Wilson and his gang mounted forays in all directions for his escaped prey, no one ever stopped to look in the bustling fish camp.

Day by day the three, including Doc, struggled to recuperate, knowing that every minute that passed left Nathan still in the clutches of E. T. Barnette and his cutthroat, Wilson. Yet none of them were strong enough to help him. This maddening thought tormented their every waking hour. While Molly recovered enough to walk around the fish camp, Riley and Doc could scarcely stand—let alone hold a gun.

Then, one day word came from a half-breed who beached his canoe at the encampment on his way downriver to Nenana. He had heard that Nathan was to be moved under armed guard to Valdez in three weeks. Disturbingly, rumor had it that Barnette would be supplying the deputies. Odds were running high in the gambling houses that Nathan Blaylock would never reach Valdez alive.

TWENTY-SEVEN

Tonopah, Nevada. Wyatt looked at the rubber juggling balls in his hands with all the mistrust one would have for sticks of dynamite. He hefted the two in his right hand only to have one evade his grasp and fall to the floor. Disgustedly he dropped the other two bedside their fallen comrade and turned back to the opened valise on his bed. He jammed another shirt inside, following it with a handful of celluloid collars.

Then, he recanted. He stooped to retrieve the rubber balls and stuffed them in beside the shirts. One day, he vowed, he would get it right. He would juggle. But not today. Today, he was packing.

A footfall behind him caused him to stiffen, but he continued to pack.

"Wyatt, what are you doing?" Josie asked. In spite of her best efforts, concern edged into her voice.

"I'm packing, Josie," he answered flatly.

"What on earth for? Where are you going?"

"Fishing. I'm going fishing. I've been feeling the urge, so I thought I'd . . . go fishing."

"Oh. You're packing an awful lot of things. How long do you plan to be gone?"

"Um. Three to four weeks, if I'm lucky."

"I see."

Wyatt turned to face his wife. She stood in the doorway with both hands clasped tightly behind her back. "Maybe . . . longer."

"I don't see your fishing pole," Josie said. She bit her lower lip.

"I know. I can't find the damned thing. It was just here yesterday, but now it's nowhere to be seen. It simply can't have grown legs and walked off," he added in exasperation. "Well, I'll just have to get me another one. Still, I'd prefer to have my old one."

"Do you want to tell me what this is about, Wyatt?" she asked.

"Well, it's kind of personal, Sadie. I just have to do it." He walked over to her and wrapped his arms around her quivering body. She tried hard to hide her emotions. He looked down at her and smiled. "Don't worry. It doesn't involve another woman."

Her response startled him. She broke away. "Don't worry, you say! You just might get yourself killed, and you tell me not to worry. I almost wish it were another woman, Wyatt. Someone I could deal with! I know it's not another woman!" she cried. From her apron pocket she withdrew a battered letter and waved it in his face. "It's this!"

Reflexively Wyatt reached for the inner pocket of his coat. It was empty. "You took my letter out of my pocket?"

"Don't act so surprised, Wyatt," she laughed scornfully. "We women have been checking little boys' pockets since time began—and we've never stopped."

"And you read it?"

In response, she opened the folded paper and read aloud. Although she knew the text by heart, the childlike scrawl still demanded her full attention, and she frowned as she read.

"To William Stapp,

"This here is from Jim Riley, the pard of your son. I ain't never asked no favers of you, and I ain't now. But I thought you oughta know your son needs your help real bad. Capt'n Barnette and his gang plan on murdering him on the road to Valdez in three weeks' time. He's held in the Fairbanks jail until then, and will be safe until the move. You know all about crooked judges, so you know Nat ain't gonna get no help from the law. I'm nursing a load of buckshot in my back from the same fellows as got yer boy, or I'd have shot my way into town before now.

"Your son is the most decent man I ever met, and you ought to be real proud of him. I couldn't write this letter if he had not taught me to read and write. He don't deserve to be shot with his hands tied. He never done the things he is accused of. His only crime is standing up against tyrants, which I figure he gets from his pa. When they ride out with Nat, I'm gonna be standing in the road to meet them.

"Jim Riley

"P.S. Any help you can throw my way would be greatly appreciated."

Josie stopped and looked at Wyatt. There were tears in his eyes now.

"I . . . I know how you feel about Nathan, Sadie, and I didn't want to hurt you. But I have to go. I couldn't do anything about Morgan, or Warren, or even Virgil, but I've got a chance with Nathan. Besides, James, you, and the boy are the only family I've got left." He turned his back on her to hide his tears.

"You were just going to slip away and leave me to worry?"

"I was going to write you a note."

"It's that important to you that you'd risk your life?"

"I'd risk my life if I didn't go, Sadie. I couldn't be the man you love and turn my back on my family's needs. I just couldn't. . . ."

He hung his head and waited in the deafening silence.

"I love you, Wyatt Berry Stapp Earp," she whispered. "But I

don't think I'll ever understand you. You best go rescue your son. And you certainly better take your old fishing pole."

Josie held out her hand. Wyatt turned back to see her holding his gun belt, the leather worn smooth as satin with use, and his Colt Peacemaker.

"Yes," he said slowly, "that's just the fishing pole I was looking for."

TWENTY-EIGHT

Wyatt stopped his pacing and stooped to retrieve the rubber ball he'd just dropped. His back ached from bending to pick up the balls he'd fumbled over a hundred times. Maybe I should try juggling on my knees, he thought. That way I won't have so far to reach when I drop them.

He got onto his knees and started again. The rocking of the ship made his task all the more difficult, but he pressed on. Bending his mind to the task of mastering this silly skill kept his imagination from running rampant. Time was running out on him, and he felt it clearly as if the sands in an hourglass trickled through his own fingers. He had so far to go and so little time.

From Nevada he had raced day and night by horse, motorcar, and train to Seattle in record time. There he caught the fastest packet available for the North. Now the spring storms and arctic winds conspired to block his run with gale winds and high-standing seas.

Seasick from the minute he stepped on board, Wyatt struggled to settle his fears along with his stomach. While trying to juggle made his mal-de-mer worse, it occupied his thoughts.

A knock on the cabin door caused him to drop one of the two balls he was practicing with. Without delay the door flew open. An astonished third mate, wearing a spray-soaked blue jacket with gold lace on the sleeves, nearly stumbled over the kneeling Earp. The seaman's mouth dropped open, and a bewildered look filled his face.

Wyatt scrambled hastily to his feet. "Don't you wait for your passengers to answer the door before entering?" he snapped. He brushed off his knees and placed the rubber balls behind his pillow, using the time to compose himself.

But the mate's eagle eyes had caught Wyatt's action. "What are you doing?" he asked.

"Juggling, if you must know."

"On your knees?"

"Yes," Wyatt answered irritably. "It's harder that way. What can I do for you?" The sooner this subject changed, the better it suited him.

"Well, Mr. Earp—"

"Stapp! The name is Stapp, remember?"

"Of course, sir." The officer winked conspiratorially. "Mr. Stapp. I just dropped by to inform you of our progress. We're one day out of Wrangell. We've made up the day we lost in that last storm, and the captain ordered me to present his compliments and say we will arrive on time. Then, on to Valdez at breakneck speed."

Breakneck was the right word for the bone-rattling drive of this ship, Wyatt thought. But he smiled instead. "Thank you. That's good news indeed. Please tell the captain I am indebted to him. Time is so very important."

The young officer swelled with pride over meeting so famous a person. "No need to mention it, Mr. Stapp, and I must apologize for the lack of amenities. The *Aurora* is, after all, a fast steam packet used for delivering the U.S. mails. Its main purpose is speed and not comfort. It's not often we carry passengers, except for important government missions. I assume this is one of those, hence the need for such alacrity."

"It is highly confidential," Wyatt answered gravely.

"Say no more, Mr. . . . . Stapp."

"And there is no record of my passage . . . other than under the name of William Stapp."

"None. When your friend John Clum, the postmaster for the Alaskan Territories, requested we offer you all assistance, both the captain and I knew it must be important."

"Good. I shall mention your efforts to Mr. Clum."

"Thank you, sir. Oh, I should warn you there is another passenger aboard." Schemes and plots danced in the mate's vivid imagination. Already he had fashioned foreign agents and villains poised to block this famous lawman's secret mission. "You might wish to stay in your cabin until we make Wrangell."

"Another passenger?"

"Yes. He slipped aboard at the last minute. You were—well, so indisposed that I decided not to bother you with that information."

"You mean seasick," Wyatt spoke plainly. Even now his stomach churned in open rebellion to his will.

"Ah, quite so." The thought of his hero, the great Wyatt Earp, green as a pickle with seasickness struck the mate as incongruous, but he pressed on. With a knowing squint in his eyes, he explained. "This other passenger has the look of a gunman about him. I sensed that about him when first I laid eyes on him. He looks quite dangerous."

"Oh? And did he say what his name was?" Wyatt raised his eyebrows.

"Smith," came the reply from the passageway. "Frank Smith."

The third mate visibly jumped off the deck plates at the reply. He whirled in midair, half-expecting a hail of bullets to catch him in a cross fire.

"Hello, Frank. What are you doing here?" Wyatt struggled for words at the sight of his old friend Frank Canton. He extended his hand to Canton while he collected his wits. "What a coincidence."

The former U.S. marshal and recently pardoned bank robber stepped into the cabin and shook Wyatt's hand warmly. "No coincidence at all, Wyatt. Your wonderful wife, Josie, wired me and asked me as a personal favor to her would I look out for you."

Now it was Wyatt's turn to gape. "She did?" he stammered.

"Yup. Damned glad she asked me, too. I got her telegraph and caught the next train out of Oklahoma City. Damned near missed the boat, though."

"It was good of you to come, Frank," was all Wyatt could say. Sadie had telegraphed Canton? He looked at the mate, whose eyes darted from man to man and from gun belt to gun belt. "But call me William Stapp."

"Stapp? Oh, yeah. Anyway, I owe you a favor for keeping my secret when I was marshal in Alaska. It gave me a second chance." Canton slumped onto Wyatt's bunk and crossed his legs. "Hell, I was so damned bored in retirement, I would have gone over Niagara Falls in a barrel if someone paid me a dollar. What she suggested fit the bill just perfectly."

Both men stopped to look at the wide-eyed ship's officer. But the silence that followed failed to clue the man in. He lingered hoping to learn more about this great adventure.

Finally, Canton addressed the man. "Why don't you run along, sonny," he said directly. "The skipper might need your help."

His words deflated the officer, and the man's face dropped.

Wyatt smiled and ushered the mate to the door. "Thank you again, Mr. Hobbs. Mr. Smith and I might call on you in the future for your excellent assistance."

Wind returned to the man's sails, and he left with a spring in his step. Both men watched his back as he vanished down the corridor, then climbed the rungs of the ladder to the upper deck. Wyatt shut the door.

"So what's this all about, Wyatt? All the cable said was: 'Wyatt needs help. Come quick and bring your irons.' Of course, I knew exactly what she wanted, so I packed my firearms and came a-running. I hope it isn't illegal."

Wyatt opened the drawer to his bulkhead dresser and withdrew two cigars. He hoped the smoke might settle his stomach, but he doubted it would. Still, it was his way of offering his friend a drink. "It's a long story, Frank. Before I tell you, I want your word to keep it a secret."

"Sure, Wyatt. You have my word." With that Frank Canton settled back as Wyatt began his tale. The story of Nathan, Mattie Blaylock, Judge Wickersham, and E. T. Barnette rolled out in a flood.

An hour later, Wyatt finished. Canton blinked at the tip of his cigar. It had grown cold in the interim. Canton returned to chewing on the smoke in astonishment. Still looking at the soggy roll of tobacco, he struggled for the right words. "Holy Jesus!" was all he could say.

Wyatt chewed on the corner of his mustache. "You can back out, and I won't think the worse of you, Frank. I feel I'm doing the right thing, but others might not see it that way."

Canton put his fingertips together and studied them. He pursed his lips, causing his cigar to jut from his face like the bowsprit of a sailing schooner. "We've both seen how the law gets bent in Alaska. I've seen men I knew were innocent hanged while the worst of the lot went free. That's one of the reasons I retired. It wore me down. My snow blindness simply gave me an excuse. If Nathan's all you say he is, he deserves to be helped. Besides, he's your son. So, count me in. One word of advice, though. When the smoke clears, we'd better make damned sure our side has the only living witnesses."

"My thoughts exactly, Frank. I just hope we make it in time."

Late the following evening, the *Aurora* docked in Wrangell. A gray drizzle, typical of southeastern Alaska's peerless weather, greeted the ship. Wyatt and Frank stayed below, where the heat from the ship's boilers kept them sweating but more comfortable than ashore. Little time would be wasted in port except to take on fuel and exchange the cargo.

Wyatt used this brief respite from the incessant rolling of the packet to sleep. Canton ran ashore only to return with a bottle of whiskey. While his friend slept, the ex-marshal sipped his drink and studied the peeling paint on the bulkhead above him.

The frantic knocking of Mr. Hobbs destroyed their respite. Once again, he burst into the cabin, but this time he was breathless.

"There's a U.S. marshal come on board," he gasped. He

paused to accept a drink from Canton and to steady his nerves. "Thank you, Mr. Smith," he said.

"A marshal?" Wyatt frowned.

"Yes, sir. I saw his badge while he talked to the captain. He just strode on bold as you please, without asking permission or anything. And he *knows* you two are on the ship! Asked for you both by name: Mr. Smith and Mr. Stapp. He knew your secret names," Hobbs blurted.

"Did he give his name?" Wyatt asked. The presence of a marshal asking about them disturbed him. Had Judge Wickersham or Barnette discovered his plan?

"Smith," the marshal answered. "Same as your name, Frank."

The third mate choked on his drink. The marshal must have followed him down to the cabins. "I'm sorry, Mr. Stapp," Hobbs started to apologize.

"That's okay, Mr. Hobbs," Wyatt replied. A broad grin spread across his face. He rose to shake the hand of Buckskin Frank Leslie. Dapper as always, Leslie wore his trademark fringed leather shirt, now dripping with rain. "What the heck are you doing here, Frank?"

Leslie pointed his finger at Frank Canton. "Hello, Frank. I suspect you're here because Josie sent you a telegraph, same as me. She asked me to look after her husband. She knew he was too dense to ask for help himself, so she asked for him. Man, that's my kind of woman. If she weren't married to you, Wyatt, I'd make a play for her myself. Besides, it sounds like there's action brewing, and I don't want to miss all the fun."

Hobbs looked from one to the other. "Frank? Smith? You're both named Frank Smith?"

Leslie looked down at the mate. "Yup. We're the Smith Brothers."

"We're the Smith Brothers, all right. But we have different parents," Canton added. Before Hobbs could ask another question, Canton ushered him into the corridor and closed the door in his face.

Leslie accepted the bottle from Canton and took a long drink. "So, what's this all about?" he asked.

Wyatt shook his head in amazement. This was more help than he had ever imagined.

Canton stepped up. He raised the bottle. "We're short one member. But I know Virgil is with us in spirit. *It's time for the Smith Brothers to ride again in the cause of justice. . . .*"

TWENTY-NINE

Fairbanks. Nathan watched with a stormy face as Ed Wicker-sham snapped the handcuffs closed on his wrists. Seated on a horse, he scowled down at the marshal.

"Don't be glaring at me, son," the marshal retorted. "I'm just following orders." Avoiding Nathan's eye, he tightened the cinch of Nathan's saddle and led the reins to his own horse. He also looped a rope around the forefoot of Nathan's pony and carried that back to his own mount as well. If his prisoner got any fool ideas of making a break for it, that trip line would bring his horse up short and dump the young man on his head.

"Just following the wrong orders doesn't make what you're doing right."

"Look, Nathan. My job is to see you safely out of town and as far as the crossing at the Salcha River. That's as far as I go. That's the end of my jurisdiction. I guarantee no harm will come to you while I'm guarding you." Marshal Wickersham stopped there, unwilling or unable to elucidate the matter further.

"And who do you hand me off to, Marshal? Who's going to take me the rest of the way to Valdez? Answer me that."

"The mayor has assured me a legal posse of deputies will be waiting there." The words somehow stuck in the lawman's throat.

Nathan gave an ugly laugh. "Care to place a bet on just who those men will be?"

"They're fully deputized officers of the court, and they should act accordingly."

Nathan spit in the dust beside his horse. "My God, Marshal! You don't really believe that, do you?" He twisted his hands within the bracelets so as to count with his fingers. "Let me see? Will it be five or six of them? Want me to name them, Ed?"

"No."

Nathan ignored him, flicking open his fingers for emphasis as he spoke. "Fields, Weaver, Spense, Indian Pete, maybe McGinnis—he's certainly had experience as a deputy. And let's not forget my friend Billy Wilson. I'm sure he'll show up."

"Look, Nat—"

"I'm not asking you to let me go, Ed. I'm just asking for a chance. You know I'll never reach Valdez alive. I'll be shot trying to escape. That or some other cock-and-bull excuse. Pumped full of lead with my hands still shackled in these cuffs. Then they'll remove them. Please, take them off before I meet Wilson and his men and give me a gun. At least that way I stand a chance." In reality, Nathan held no hopes of besting six heavily armed men, but he dearly wished to take as many with him as he could.

Ed Wickersham swung into his saddle. Just as he was about to answer Nathan, he caught sight of his brother, the judge, striding toward them on tiptoes with Mayor Barnette alongside. The marshal winced at the way his brother always sought to appear taller whenever he was with Barnette. The sight of those two banished whatever thoughts the marshal had of considering Nathan's plea. "Sorry, Nat. I can't do that," he said.

"Morning, Ed." The judge ground to a halt beside Nathan's horse. He was within range of Nathan's boot, but the young man decided kicking the judge or Barnette would accomplish nothing.

"Judge. Mr. Mayor." Ed Wickersham tipped his hat.

"Everything all ready, I see," Barnette gloated. "This town will rest easier with the likes of him gone. Rebuilding should occupy all our energies, not dealing with his kind."

"My kind, Mayor? Do you mean honest men?"

Barnette ignored the remark. He turned his back on

Nathan while jamming both hands in his vest pockets. "What about breakfast, James? I hear the Model Café has a fresh supply of strawberries and cream. Fresh eggs as well. This clear morning air has whet my appetite. Shall we go?"

Judge Wickersham did not answer at first. He was remembering how Nathan had likened him to Pilate. The comparison kept returning to his mind in spite of all efforts to erase it. He turned to say something, but Nathan dug his heels into his animal's flanks and the marshal's horse followed. The judge found himself staring at the backsides of both animals as they left.

The ride to the Salcha crossing took most of the day. Nathan rode in silence, refusing to give his guard the satisfaction of conversation. He stopped when Ed Wickersham made him, but he ate nothing and drank only sips of water. All the while he did what he could to impede his mount's progress without appearing to do so. Every minute he could stall was more opportunity to hatch an escape plan. His mind worked feverishly for a solution. But Ed Wickersham knew his job well. Unlike McGinnis, he drank only water or cold coffee while keeping ever alert to any tricks his prisoner might play.

Nathan watched the clouds race overhead and the land around him teem with activity. He'd never seen so beautiful a day. Perhaps so wonderous, he reminded himself, because it might be his last. Clouds of winged ants and damselflies scattered before the track of their horses, and hares darted ahead. Beside the trail a cow moose with her spindly-legged newborn paused to study the procession. Satisfied that these horses were neither related nor any threat, the moose coaxed her shaky calf into the brush and vanished without a sound. Even the creeks they forded and the brooks they crossed bubbled along merrily in keeping with the glorious day. All the Arctic seemed bent on making the most of their precious respite from the oppressive white hand of winter.

All this depressed Nathan. He realized that tomorrow the birds would fly and the wind would flip the aspen leaves—

whether he was alive or not. The universe did not revolve around him, as he often imagined. He was simply nothing more to this land than another salmon lying bleached on a gravel bar or a clump of silt cut from the bank by the relentless race of the river. That realization disheartened him all the more.

The two men rocked in the saddle, dusty and weary as their horses plodded along. The sun dipped behind the rising hills that surrounded the Salcha River, and for a moment Nathan's skin crawled with a chill that followed when the shadows set upon his sweaty skin. Along his right the braided streams of the Tanana swung close to the trail. He watched the water flowing past like molten lead, and his heart sank. Another mile would see the mouth of the tea-colored Salcha where it fed its waters in the silty Tanana. The Salcha's clear contribution kept its identity for less than a mile before being lost in the silt-laden flow. Nathan sighed. He was destined to vanish without a trace just like that clear water, swallowed up in the enormity of this wilderness.

He straightened his back. At least Jim and Molly had slipped free of Barnette's grasp. He only wished his letter to Wyatt had reached his father. It was hard finding your father only to have your own time cut too short to enjoy it. His horse stopped as Ed Wickersham reined in his animal.

"The crossing," the marshal murmured.

Nathan counted the men waiting for him. Six. They were all there. He made a last plea. "Ed, this is my last chance. . . ."

Wickersham shook his head and dug his spurs into the flanks of his animal. Both horses jerked forward.

"Thankee kindly, Marshal." Billy Wilson sported a Cheshire grin as he and his men surrounded Wickersham and his prisoner. "You're right on time, Ed. We want to cross the river before it's too dark. Wouldn't want to have no accidents with a night crossing. Men have been known to drown crossing this stream in the dark, and we wouldn't want that."

A chorus of guffaws rose from his men. Nathan studied each man. All were armed to the teeth. Taking no chances,

Nathan surmised. "I must be one dangerous hombre to warrant an army this size. You afraid to face me one-on-one, eh, Billy? Even with my arm broken?"

Wilson's grin grew wider. "You can't goad me into a fight, Blaylock. I'm a deputized officer of the court, and I have my civic responsibility."

More laughter filled the silence.

Wickersham leaned forward in his saddle and handed the reins of Nathan's horse to Wilson. He felt as though he'd just sprung the trapdoor on an innocent man. "I want your word, Billy, that you'll see Nat safely to Valdez for trial." No sooner had he spoken those words than he knew his order was futile. The look on Wilson's face told him that.

"You have my word, Marshal," Wilson giggled. He yanked the reins viciously and spurred his own horse down the bank toward the swirling waters of the mouth. "Hang on tight, Mister Prisoner. You wouldn't want to fall off and get wet," he joked.

Both animals plunged into the icy water. The mouth of the Salcha changed from month to month with the whim of water. Scattered islands appeared only to vanish overnight. Shallow fords turned to deep pools.

Wilson gave his horse its head, and the animal churned across the water, making for the closest island in midstream. Nathan's animal followed, arching its neck and lurching across whenever its footing vanished in deeper water. Nathan barely had time to kick his boots from the stirrups and loop his manacled hands over the pommel before his mount dropped into a hole. Water swept over Nathan, and he held his breath. The animal surfaced blowing and wheezing while its flanks heaved as it swam.

Wilson forced his horse onward, risking danger in hopes Nathan's animal might founder and roll on him. But the youth hung on. Each jerk and twist of his horse pulled his arms and sent shocks of pain along his limbs. Nathan felt the ends of his broken bones grating against each other with each plunge.

To the surprise of all, Nathan reached the opposite bank. Wilson stood in his stirrups and waved his hat at Ed Wickersham, who watched them from the bluff. Wickersham refused to return the salute, merely wheeling his horse around and riding back to Fairbanks. The rest of the gang charged across to regroup around their leader.

"Shall we drill him right now, Billy?" McGinnis asked.

"Not yet, stupid. I don't want Ed hearing any gunshots. Let's ride a ways first to give that old fart a good chance to be long gone. Besides, I might not want to shoot Mr. Blaylock. That might be too quick."

"We could hang him. Real slow-like so his neck don't snap," Weaver suggested. "I seen that done. They gets all purple in the face with their tongue hanging out and their legs kicking up a storm. It's bad."

"Hmm. Something to think about," Wilson wriggled his eyebrows at Nathan. "Does that sound tempting, Blaylock?"

"Or we could roast him," Indian Pete volunteered.

An animated discussion followed while the party rode along. Nathan shut out what they were saying, forcing his mind to remember the good times he'd had with Riley and Molly and Doc. Whatever these bastards did to him, he would disappoint them and die with dignity.

The trail wound around clumps of silver birch and somber spruce as it left the Salcha behind. The ground dropped slowly, and the road widened where it crossed a field of waving horse-tail grass.

Billy Wilson reined in his horse. "By God," he crowed. "Will you look at that? This is my lucky day, boys." He jerked his thumb at the clearing.

Standing alone in the center of the sea of waist-high grass stood Jim Riley.

The twin ruts of the wagon tracks led straight to where the old gunfighter stood. His widespread legs straddled the wagon ruts, and he held a sawed-off shotgun in his right hand. His left hand clutched a pole cut from diamond willow upon which he rested heavily. Even from this far distance, Nathan could see his friend was using the crutch for much-needed support.

Wilson turned to his closest gang member. "See, Fields. I

told you we winged the old buzzard." Wilson looked at the wide expanse of grass surrounding Riley. "The old fool didn't give himself no cover. No trees nor rocks."

"Nor room to escape," Fields grunted. "He's in the damned middle of the field as pretty as you please. Sort of reminds me of the way them Indians used to stake themselves out before a battle so they couldn't run."

Weaver squinted at the man before them. "He ain't gonna run," he said flatly.

"All's the better," Wilson chuckled. "We'll know for sure we got him this time. He's got nowhere to hide."

Weaver shifted in his saddle. "Riley's still damned fast with a gun," he warned.

Wilson thought for a minute. "But he's short on brains. Look, he's only got his side arm and that scattergun. And we're still outside his range."

"Yeah, he ain't got no rifle, neither," McGinnis noted. "We could just shoot him from here with one of our rifles."

"Run, Jim!" Nathan shouted. "They're going to bushwhack you! They're too yellow to face you up close."

"Shut up!" Wilson lashed Nathan savagely across the face with his quirt.

"Don't be hitting my pard when he's got his hands tied!" Riley called out across the open space. "Don't worry, Nat. I figured these sidewinders wouldn't have the sand to face me. You just get ready to duck when I start slinging lead," he added meaningfully.

The six men shifted nervously on their mounts and craned their necks in search of a possible ambush. For a trapped man, this Riley was acting not the least bit fearful. But Riley was alone in the center of the open field, and the tree line was a good hundred yards away.

"He's bluffing," Weaver said.

"McGinnis, shoot the old fool," Wilson commanded. "And let's get on with it."

"Be my pleasure." The ex-deputy withdrew his Winchester 1895 and jacked a shell into the chamber. Rising in his stirrups, he brought the rifle to his shoulder and squinted down the barrel to the front sight. Above the bead, he could see Jim Riley leaning on his staff amid the shimmering horsetail grass.

"Run, Jim!" Nathan cried, again. "Run for it!"

Time stopped as the specter of his friend casting his lengthy shadow over the moving field drew Nathan's gaze and held it like a snake fixes a rodent. He could not look away. His heart stopped in anticipation of the rifle crack.

When it came, the shot roared louder than he could ever imagine. Instead of a sharp crack, the explosion struck his ears like a clap of thunder. Nathan flinched and his eyes blinked, but his mind still held the image of his friend standing in the field.

Nathan forced his eyes to reopen, dreading what he would see. He gasped. Riley was still standing!

The horses shied at the gunshot, and the lad's animal lurched to one side, ripping its reins free of Wilson's grasp. As his mount spun around, Nathan caught sight of McGinnis sitting fixedly in his saddle. A puzzled look crossed his face as his rifle slowly slid from his hands.

But McGinnis's attention was not on his rifle. He stared instead at the fist-sized hole in the center of his chest and the dark stain his blood spread over what was left of the front of his shirt. Then, McGinnis toppled from his horse like a bag of meal.

Nathan spotted a cloud of smoke rising from a gnarled spruce, well beyond normal range. The others saw it, too. Stepping into the open, a man Nathan had never seen before raised his rifle and fired another shot.

The bullet tore past Billy Wilson's head close enough to cut a scrap of felt from his hat. That second shot had the desired effect of sending the riders into a panic. Men swayed in their saddles as their horses spun and sunfished.

Now, Nathan realized why the rifle shot sounded so different. This man, whoever he was, had a long-barreled Sharps. The .50-caliber buffalo rifle made its own thunder.

Frank Canton smiled grimly. He'd done his part. He reloaded his Sharps and strode toward the men. The rest was up to the others.

Instantly Nathan kicked his heels into his horse and dashed toward Jim Riley. Nat laid his head alongside the animal's neck, praying it would not stumble or be shot before he reached his friend.

His escape galvanized his tormentors. A hail of bullets snapped through the air on either side of him. With no reins, Nathan could not make his horse dodge. Instead, he spurred it on and flattened himself against the pounding back, hoping speed would save him.

"After him!" Wilson shouted. "Ride him down! Ride them both down!"

The five men galloped after Nathan with pistols drawn and blazing away. The young man had a twenty-yard lead, but their fresher mounts closed the gap. Nathan dared not look over his shoulder. Instead, he concentrated on the growing image of Riley—still standing immobile across the track. If he could get to Riley and use one of his weapons, they might stand a chance. Nathan realized he could not stop his terrified animal, so he planned on rolling from the saddle when he reached Riley's side. Another thirty yards would do it. He tensed, ready to spring.

Without warning, two figures rose from the tall grass on either side of Jim Riley. One man wore a black vest and pants with a white shirt and tie. A fancy fringed buckskin shirt covered the other man. Like night and day, the dress of the two was so contrasting. But there was no mistaking the similarity of the Colt six-guns in their hands.

Nathan cried out in astonishment. The taller man in black was his father, Wyatt Earp! Nathan tumbled from his saddle, hit the packed dirt, and bounced onto his back. He scrambled to his feet in time to see Wilson's gang close with his three protectors.

A cloud of smoke erupted as Wyatt, Frank Leslie, and Jim Riley loosed a deadly fusillade into the faces of the riders. At point-blank range the fire took a fearsome toll.

Indian Pete flew over the back of his saddle under the full impact of Riley's buckshot. Sid Weaver snapped off a shot at the buckskin jacket he saw through the smoke. But the leather coat vanished just as he jerked his trigger, and his horse thundered past his target. Frank Leslie calmly dodged to one side and fired both of his revolvers into Weaver. Killed instantly, Weaver fell from the saddle. His foot caught in the stirrup, and his panic-stricken horse dragged him, bouncing down the road.

Wyatt calmly aimed his front sight at Spense while the man charged him. Spense emptied his revolver at Wyatt, but the bullets missed. Wyatt fired once. Spense reined his horse in at the impact. Both horse and rider crashed to the ground beside Wyatt. Spense scrambled to his knees, But Wyatt fired again. His second bullet struck an inch from the first. The gunman fell, face forward, into the dusty road with two bullets through his heart.

Billy Wilson frantically jerked the reins of his animal. His men were down, and his own shots had missed. He would escape, run for the trees. As his mount spun around, Wilson swiveled for a parting shot.

Jim Riley swung his shotgun with all his might just as Wilson passed. The heavy barrels caught Wilson across the chest. The force knocked him from his saddle, and he flew into the air to land with a thud. His pistol spilled from his fingers.

Wilson jumped to his feet with both hands high in the air. "Don't shoot! Don't shoot!" he screamed. "I'm unarmed."

Nathan scrambled to Riley's side. "Give me a gun, and let him face me," he demanded.

Riley looked from Wilson to his friend. His gaze dropped to the handcuffs enclosing Nathan's wrists. "Not this time," he said. "We don't have the keys to yer bracelets."

Wilson's eyes darted from one man to the other, then to his pistol lying in the dirt at his feet. He watched Frank Canton saunter over to the scene of battle. "I'm not drawing, not against any of you. I'm unarmed. I surrender. You've got to take me in."

"Same as you were going to do with Nat?" Riley snapped. "We ought to just shoot you and be done with it."

"We can't do that," Wyatt spoke. "We'd be just like him, then. No better."

"What do you suggest we do with him, Wyatt?" Frank Leslie asked.

"Wyatt?" Wilson's eyes grew round as saucers. "Wyatt Earp?"

"Yup. And you were planning to murder my son. Why don't we let *him* decide your fate?"

Nathan's chest swelled with pride so that he felt he would burst. He looked from face to face. Leslie and Canton only smiled. "Let him go. I'll get my chance later," Nat said.

"Good choice, Son," Wyatt murmured approvingly. "His kind will always hang themselves if you give them enough rope. Anyway, he's not worth giving yourself a guilty conscience."

The men crowded around Nathan, patting his shoulder and slapping him on the back, Wilson forgotten for the moment. He would slink away to be dealt with on a later date.

But Billy Wilson had different ideas. Seeing their backs turned, he dove for his pistol. His fingers snatched the grip while he thumbed the hammer. Dropping back on his knees, he raised his pistol.

Nathan saw the blur of movement from the corner of his eye. "Look out!" he cried.

Four shots rang out, each so close to the other that they sounded like one. Billy Wilson gaped at the four bullet holes piercing the front of his vest. Not more than a hand's breadth separated the shots. His unfired pistol dropped from nerveless fingers, and he flopped onto his back. He emitted a long, gurgling sigh before his eyes fixed forever on some unseen point.

"Once a weasel, always a weasel," Riley commented.

"Like Wyatt said, give him enough rope," Frank Canton grunted. He looked at his smoking pistol. The other three looked at the smoke from theirs.

"That was mighty fast," Leslie noted. "Who do you think hit him first?"

"Me," Wyatt said with a smile. "It was obvious."

THIRTY

Molly Hayes hugged Nathan's arm and pressed closer to his side. Although the sun shone across the snow-covered mountains and set fire to the turquoise waters of Valdez Harbor, the cold wind from the water chilled her to the bone. Still, she stood on the dock with him and watched the last of the passengers board the steamer. Three men, looking curiously alike, were the last to climb the gangplank.

Molly gazed into Nathan's face, trying to gauge his mood. Was it happy or sad? Perhaps a mixture of both, she judged. Her topaz-colored eyes sparkled as she spoke. "I'll miss them, too. Without their help, who knows what might have transpired? We'd both be dead. Instead, you're a free man, and I'm free of fear."

Nathan smiled. "Well, with you as the only witness, the judge had to throw out those charges against Jim and me."

"Do you think they'll ever come back?" she asked.

"I hope so."

"What was that Wyatt said about the captain?" she pressed.

Nathan squeezed her arm. "He gave me a bit of fatherly advice. He said Barnette was like a big tree he once tried to cut down with an ax. But the trunk was too thick and too tough to make much progress. So, Wyatt used his head and attacked the roots and waited. When the next windstorm came around, the weight of the tree helped bring it down."

"I don't think I fully understand. Did you tell him about Barnette's jail sentence that we couldn't verify?"

"Yes, I did, Molly. The two Smith Brothers seemed very interested in that. They told me I wasn't looking in the right places. They said they'd check their contacts."

"What did Wyatt say to that?"

"He said that if Barnette had been fined for even spitting on a street west of the Rockies, the Smith Brothers would discover it."

"And?"

"And then, he'd start cutting some roots."

"Wyatt? Wyatt Earp?" a short man next to them started. "Is that Wyatt Earp at the railing? I thought I recognized him. I met him once in Frisco, but that was years ago. He should look much older now."

"No." Nathan shook his head. "That's William Stapp, my father. He came for a visit with those other two, the Smith Brothers. People say he looks a lot like Wyatt Earp."

"I see," came the disappointed response. "My, all three have the look of gunfighters." The man stopped to watch the three figures as the ship cast off its lines and moved away from the dock. "He sure looks like Wyatt Earp. But what the devil is he doing with his hands?"

Nathan laughed out loud. "Why, I think he's juggling. . . ."

Soon after Wyatt and the Smith Brothers returned home, news of E. T. Barnette's investment of bank funds in the Gold Bar Lumber Company of Seattle reached Fairbanks. Realization that Barnette's brother-in-law, A. T. Armstrong, owned the troubled company caused a run on the captain's bank. No sooner had Barnette reorganized his bank when he was hit with a lawsuit from a former partner, James H. Causten. Wisely, Causten brought his case in Superior Court in Seattle, well beyond the reaches of Judge Wickersham.

During the trial, Causten's attorney used material supplied to him from a source he later refused to identify. He asked E. T. Barnette, banker, mayor, postmaster, and would-be governor of Alaska, one question: had he ever been convicted of robbery and sentenced to four years in the Oregon Penitentiary? The captain was forced to answer under oath.

The answer was—yes.

Admission of his criminal past struck Fairbanks like a second fire. Another run forced the closure of Barnette's newly organized bank. Many investors lost their life savings.

Now the most hated man in Fairbanks, E. T. Barnette fled town with his family in the dark of night in a double-ender sled drawn by a white horse. He never returned to Alaska. Without roots, the tree had fallen.

Association with a known criminal doomed forever James Wickersham's chances of being confirmed as a federal judge.